Topaz Fire

TOPAZ FIRE

Brian Rayfield

LEGEND

LONDON SYDNEY AUCKLAND JOHANNESBURG

To Maureen, Alan and Briony who joined with me to complete the seasons, the flowers, the dragons and the four winds of heaven.

First published in Great Britain in 1992 by Legend Books
Random House Group
20 Vauxhall Bridge Rd, London SW1V 2SA

Random House Australia (Pty) Ltd
20 Alfred Street, Milsons Point, Sydney, NSW 2061
Australia

Random House New Zealand Ltd
PO Box 40–086, Glenfield, Auckland 10
New Zealand

Random House South Africa (Pty) Ltd
PO Box 337, Bergvlei 2012, South Africa

The catalogue data record for this book is available from the British Library

Printed in Great Britain by Clays Ltd, St. Ives PLC

Phototypeset by Intype, London

ISBN 0 09 926321 1

1

Zachaw Ca'lin Curos, K'tan of the Topaz Wind of the Great Army of Chaw, carefully stroked his horse's head as he changed the damp cloth over the animal's nose and mouth. Hidden in the shallow depression excavated in the enormous, rolling cornfield of Corninstan, he felt strangely alone, despite the closeness of a hundred other Topaz Wind mounted archers.

Just eight hundred paces from the main road into the province's capital, the elite Topaz Wind were a key part in the cunning ambush which Curos' father, High General Commander Zachaw Pa'lin, had planned for the advancing barbarians. He had hidden the highly trained Winds of mounted bowmen close to the main road. If they could disrupt and harry the Western Barbarians before they achieved formation it would give the main mounted bow T'sands, or regiments, the time they needed to launch a devastating mobile attack. This would be followed up by the heavy lance and scimitar cavalry.

Curos' mind strove to control the building fear and anticipation. Weeks of training and scrupulous selection of the men for this honoured task made Curos almost completely confident in his own force, but one horse in any of the five Wind attack groups could ruin the whole plan.

The advance guard of mail-clad barbarian lancers was on the road. Curos whispered soothing words to his restless animal. Now he could plainly hear the impact of hooves on the dry earth. Any sounds of his own men or their equipment were lost in the whispering of the tall, ripening corn.

His throat was dry and his breathing tight. The fate of the war, the grain supply to the starving lands of Chaw rested on five hundred men concealed under thin cotton camouflage sheets behind a wall of yard-high corn. The horse sensed his tension and shook its head anxiously. Again the young commander reassured him, dampened the nose-cloth and stroked the well-groomed mane.

The Westerners' horsemen had passed. Now came the lighter tread of the footmen. Pikemen and bowmen. It was the dreadful power of the foot-bowmen that concerned the High General Commander. These, and the mighty war engines which could hurl sheaves of arrows and stones over two hundred paces, gave the barbarians formidable fire power.

Curos heard men talking and even a hearty laugh. With the horsemen probing ahead and the cornfields seemingly empty for several miles in either direction, what would they have to fear? Even if each valley and orchard were swarming with the ant soldiers of Chaw, the men of the West had plenty of time to take up formation. Pikemen would protect the bowmen and behind would be the devastating mangonels and ballistas.

Curos permitted himself a smile and kissed Thunder-Arrow. The over-confidence of the barbarians would be as crucial as the training of the Wind attack groups. His short, highly recurved bow was strung and ready. Each arrow had been checked for straightness and sound fletching. The curved cavalry scimitar was polished to a brilliant sharpness. Particular to the Topaz Wind were the tallow-soaked torches and sulphur matches.

At last he heard the rumble of wheeled carts and war engines, the target for Topaz Wind. The tension was at its peak; surely it was time to attack.

Far away at the edge of the apple orchards the signal horn sounded. Immediately Curos leapt up, threw off the thin cotton sheet and guided Thunder-Arrow to his feet. He forced himself to take time with the horse. There were still several minutes in which to form up his men – it would take the enemy that long to start to react.

Behind and on either side of Curos, men in light padded armour were appearing with their small, swift-footed horses. Curos had sufficient time to take in the whole sweep of the barbarian army. Directly to his front were the lumbering carts and wagons of the supply train and the rear-guard of protecting pikemen. Ahead of the carts moved an untidy array of catapults and their operators which Curos was to attack.

Stretching further away to the left, along the wide Corninstan Road, marched the main barbarian army. Alternate groups of archers and pikemen were mixed in with the swordsmen, who could be identified only by their large rectangular shields. The whole impression was of a disorganised mix of infantry.

Curos mounted, then turned in the saddle to confirm that his men were ready. Topaz Wind had no need for heroic shouts or strident trumpets. As soon as he urged Thunder-Arrow forward his men followed.

Their speed built up steadily from a walk to a trot – just as they had practised in training. It was necessary to give the horses time to recover from their prolonged inactivity.

The enemy troops had only just now realised their danger and were breaking their marching formations to prepare for battle. Few soldiers had been marching in mail armour or with strung bows and full quivers. Curos could see their panic as swordsmen sought to pull on mail coats, pikemen tried to take up defensive positions and archers grabbed bundles of arrows from the small trek carts.

Curos' heart sang with exhilaration. Guiding Thunder-Arrow with his knees, he gripped his bow and nocked his first arrow. Behind him came the Topaz Wind. The horse-tail standard dyed topaz yellow streamed above them as they swept down on the confusion surrounding the carts and the strange war machines.

Zachaw Curos yelled the war scream with the full power of his lungs and laughed with joy as it was echoed by the heroes who followed him to glory. To his left the other Four Winds were flying into battle, Silk, Ruby, Emerald and Jet – winds of death whose volleys of arrows would flatten this barbarian army like fragile stalks.

Now at full gallop, Curos drew back his bowstring. Suddenly in an instant of disaster, the dry yellow corn burst into a livid flash of crimson and a barrier of heat, flame and smoke streamed up before the charging horsemen. Horses reared and turned in panic; terror-stricken men dropped their bows and attempted to control the crazed animals. Only the superb training and the ultimate trust between man and horse saved the company from destruction.

Curos' bow dangled on its wrist-strap, the arrow discarded. 'Demon Sorcery,' he cursed as he fought Thunder-Arrow's terror, his own fear submerged in the need for action.

The flash of devil-fire was over and now the corn burned with real smoke and flame. The barbarian sorcerers were buying their army time by this evil display of power.

It was impossible for Curos and the Topaz Wind to force their horses through the flaming barrier which stretched the whole length of the barbarian army. To his left the Emerald Wind was driven back by a sulphurous flare as it attempted to crash through the flame wall. The Silk and Jet Winds wheeled in time-wasting confusion.

Around Curos, flat impassive faces waited stoically for instruction and leadership. He could almost feel the pressure of dark slanting eyes as his men stared at him from under their fur-rimmed war helmets. U'tan Khol Dalgan half smiled to show his lack of fear and the words of the training lessons flooded unbidden into Curos' mind: 'A Wind not in motion is powerless still air, a leader who does not lead permits panic . . .'

With a sudden clarity of vision Curos saw that less than three hundred paces to the right the fire-wall ended. Emerald Wind's commander had shown recklessly that it was impossible to break through – could Topaz from its position ride around the flames? He turned Thunder-Arrow to face his waiting men and half bowed in the saddle. The deliberate salute would show respect and his own absence of fear before he led them around the barrier which baulked their direct advance.

Trusting his men to follow, Curos skirted around the unnatural sea of heat to a place where he could see the rear-guard of barbarian pikemen formed up in a line to protect the supply wagons. Topaz, moving as one, outflanked the pikemen and ignoring the carts closed in on the war engines. At less than thirty paces' range they loosed their first volley of arrows into the knots of men struggling to arm the strange catapults.

Guiding Thunder-Arrow with the lightest of knee pressure, the K'tan shot three arrows as he galloped along the line of the enemy's machines. Without watching to see the effect, Curos turned the horse away in a wide circle. Screaming venomously he came round to attack again. On this second pass Curos' spirit soared with elation at the devastating power of the attack, a circle of mounted bowmen eroding the enemy's valuable catapultmen.

It was time to stop being a Wind-Rider and to become a

disciplined commander. On the left a phalanx of pikemen advanced on him in a steady, purposeful trot. To the right his view of the battle was masked by more carts and the massed barbarian infantrymen. The rest of the Wind regiment had been held back too long. They had lost their advantage of surprise and must now be fighting on hopeless terms.

Curos' previous excitement evaporated as in the distance he heard the horns and trumpets which the main Chaw bow and lance regiments used to guide their forces into the attack formation. The High General had committed his main force to the battle.

Curos' own duty was clear. He could only help his brother officers by firing the war engines as planned. He shouted to Khol Dalgan, his Lieutenant, indicating the pikemen. Then, turning in his saddle, he called, 'Torch, men, light your torches.'

While Khol Dalgan led half the force off to harass the pikemen, twenty warriors remained with Curos to light the large tallow and tar-soaked lance torches, following Curos' own actions exactly.

'Go!' he shouted unnecessarily as he raced Thunder-Arrow at the nearest ballista, scimitar and reins in one hand, flaming lance in the other. This attack should have been supported by the bowmen that Khol Dalgan was now leading toward the enemy pikes but the catapultmen still cowered behind their machines, fearful of another deadly arrow attack.

Curos cast his lance into the framework of the timber construction where the melting tar could drip down onto the beams. Overcoming the temptation to close in and use his sword, he swung away to give the next man a clear run.

Again the bow. A tall, bearded barbarian with pale hair ran out to seize the flaming lance which Curos had placed so accurately. Curos' first arrow hurtled into his leather jerkin. He turned, cursing, and fell as a second arrow punctured his stomach.

Khol Dalgan was inflicting heavy casualties on the pikemen but they were now almost too close to hold off. Away to the right, dust told of the approach of mounted enemy troops. Just a few more minutes were needed for the fires to destroy the dry, blazing war machines.

Curos bit his lip, taking in the scene once more before calling an order to Khol Dalgan. Just two harsh syllables, and Khol Dalgan led his section of the Topaz Wind in a fanatical charge on the pikemen.

The frenzy of their onslaught gave them some initial success but then their charge was stopped. Held off by a hedge of long weapons, they paid a high penalty in men and horses in that one hideous charge. Khol Dalgan and over twenty other men of the Topaz Wind were left impaled on the long, murderous blades of the foot-soldiers. Curos called his men away before they could charge again. The pikemen cheered and moved forward.

Less than two hundred paces away a detachment of enemy archers was also advancing on Curos. He sent one more volley of arrows sweeping around the now blazing war engines. Even if they were not totally destroyed they would not be used in this battle. As he gave the order to withdraw, arrows curved up from the enemy archers and sped towards his men. Incredibly, at over one hundred and fifty paces, a man and two horses were hit.

Biting back anger and shame, Curos led his depleted force away. They picked up speed and easily outdistanced the enemy's heavy cavalry who were now supporting the fiendish long-range bowmen. The enemy did not follow but wasted futile effort in fire-fighting.

The K'tan half considered attempting to destroy the virtually unguarded supply carts but he had too few men to do significant damage and the Wind's supply of arrows was almost exhausted. Then a trumpet sounded, and he gasped in sudden amazement as he recognised the notes of full retreat. The Great Army of Chaw had been defeated!

On the main battlefield the sight which greeted Curos was worse than a thousand nightmares. Wounded and riderless horses milled in desperate, mindless panic. On the burned stubble lay the piled bodies of men and horses – some terminally still, others writhing and screaming. A small wall of Chaw bodies lay along the ranks of barbarian pikemen, but more still had died from the deadly ruin of the long arrows with their heavy, needle-sharp piles.

This scene with its stench of blood and burning would be etched in Curos' memory for ever.

Even in triumph the barbarian foot-soldiers showed their discipline. Steadily, in an even line, they advanced over the field killing the wounded, looting the dead.

As Curos obeyed the call to retreat he heard the jeers from the victorious enemy. He reined in Thunder-Arrow and sat indecisively. His men shared out their small stock of arrows and tried to bind wounds with the decorative long silk scarves worn to distinguish individual detachments.

What should he do, how could he live with the shame of this defeat? Then the shock of Dalgan's death hit Curos and tears flooded his eyes. He turned angrily as someone touched his shoulder.

'Pardon, honoured captain.' The Ataman, or under-officer, inclined his head in an attempted salute and drops of blood dripped from a pike slash across his cheek. He pointed to where, some distance off, a detachment of barbarian cavalry were hacking into the remains of a T'sand, who were trying to disengage. The stronger Western horses and better armour were being used to good effect in the close fighting.

Here was honour. Curos rapidly assessed the state of his force. The many wounded men were ordered to give up their remaining arrows and make their way off the field. It was Curos' first duty to save his own men, then to help the embattled T'sand. An Ataman who had an arrow head embedded in his thigh was given the topaz-coloured horse-hair standard and explicit instructions to hold back from the fighting.

'You have fought well and with great honour,' Curos shouted to the men who had survived the battle. 'We have been defeated only by sorcery. Let no man throw his life away in shame at our defeat. I will lead you to kill again but this time only with the bow. As K'tan of the Topaz Wind I order this. If in any charge you get within sword distance of the mounted devils, you will turn and fall back to the standard. There will be no personal glory. We only fight to try to save our brothers.'

As they moved forward a wounded Chaw soldier rose up from the half-flattened corn. A long arrow projected from his side and his face contorted in a death mask of agony. Desperately he raised the red horse plumes of the Ruby Wind. Even before Curos' men could reach him he fell back into his death, leaving

7

them to stretch down and retrieve the standard, all that was left of the proud war band.

Curos led his men in a raking charge which swept along the flank of the barbarian heavy cavalry. Men and horses fell to the sharp, venomous Chaw arrows but all too often a well-aimed shot would be deflected by the enemy's heavy mail armour. As the barbarians turned to meet this attack the Topaz Wind broke away, using the speed of their lighter, faster horses to carry them out of reach of the heavy swords and lances.

In this brief respite the Noyan of the Chaw Scimitar Cavalry mounted a counter-attack before again allowing his men to fall back in good order. Curos watched with admiration. The banner proclaimed the 41st T'sand, Uzan Province. Although beaten, reduced by a third of their number and with many wounded, they did not break and flee. Their commander must be a worthy man to hold them together and inspire their disciplined resistance.

Curos ordered his men to continue their retreat off the field, link up with their wounded and move back to the campsite of the previous night. He himself wanted to speak with the general's staff and learn if any plans or orders had been issued.

The solid barbarian infantry had resumed their line of march to the Corninstan capital and most of the cavalry units had been recalled. The rising heat haze obscured the view of the baggage train, making it impossible to detect the extent of damage to the catapults and ballistas. The destruction of those fearsome engines of war which had once seemed so important had been irrelevant to the final outcome of the battle.

Some distance away another small drama was unfolding as a knot of Chaw horsemen fled from an equally small group of barbarian cavalry. Only an hour ago Curos would never have believed that Chaw soldiers would retreat in such an undisciplined manner. It was too much for him to bear. He urged Thunder-Arrow forward once more and drew his scimitar.

'Dishonourable cowards,' Curos roared to the fleeing Chaw horsemen as he rode his own exhausted and sweating horse past them, scimitar outstretched like a spear as he closed on the leading barbarian. At the last instant he pulled Thunder-Arrow up short and sent the poor animal staggering sideways with a vicious heave on the reins. The barbarian lancer hurled past, spear locked under his armpit, his face a ferocious mask under the conical steel cap and nasal protector.

Almost past his adversary, Curos struck backhanded with a long cut which connected fiercely with his opponent's arm. With that accuracy and power it should have given a maiming wound; instead it merely glanced off the hard steel rings of the barbarian's hauberk. Without thought, Curos pulled Thunder-Arrow outward, away from his foes and moved in for another attack.

He realised with a grimace of recognition that the barbarian had completed a similar manoeuvre, hauling his heavier mount around in an equally tight turn. *An expert horseman who would care more for his steed than for his own life?* This time Curos attacked first with a feint cut to the magnificent black stallion's head. The shock showed visibly on the barbarian's face as with desperate speed he tried to parry the slash with his heavy lance. Curos swung his weapon round and changed his aim to a precision cut under the barbarian's jawbone, beneath the helmet's side-plates. The barbarian stiffened in the saddle and fell in a shower of his own blood.

Now Curos came under attack from two barbarian horsemen. He barely had time to deflect a lance point before he was ducking away from a downward sword slash. His vain attempt to parry the blow was beaten down and the long, straight broadsword smashed into the thin steel of his war helmet. It cut through the metal down to the leather skullcap and padded helmet rim. At the same time the barbarian's huge war-horse crashed into the slighter form of Thunder-Arrow, throwing the exhausted animal down onto his haunches. Dazed with the impact of the sword blow, Curos frantically kicked his feet clear of the stirrups as he rolled off his mount's back.

Thunder-Arrow struggled to his feet between Curos and his attacker. In the valuable seconds this gained him, Curos scrambled upright. The barbarian horseman swerved his mount away and joined another lancer whom Curos had avoided. The two men laughed together – the battle was won, this mad Chaw could be used for sport.

As Curos backed away from the danger he felt sickeningly

vulnerable. All his battle training had been based on being mounted on a fast, agile, well-trained horse. His heel touched an inert body – the barbarian he had so recently killed. Vainly he stumbled backwards over the dead man. Yet even this small barrier might slow the attackers.

The two men were starting their charging run about five yards apart. There would be no chance of avoiding both weapons; either the lance or the sword would strike home.

Thunder-Arrow nudged Curos from behind but there was no time to remount. He pushed backwards with his free hand, trying to get the animal to move away. No time, no space and no hope. In sheer frenzy he roared out the single word of his Wind's battle cry, 'Topaz! Help me, Topaz!' Inexplicably the air before him exploded with glowing yellow light as the topaz stone in his pendant blazed with incandescence. Curos staggered backwards in surprise. His whole body was recharged with vital energy, a sheer life-force that flooded through his whole being. The energy flowed outwards towards Thunder-Arrow and beyond.

Shock and disbelief momentarily robbed Curos of the ability to move. His eyes fastened blankly on the two half-blinded barbarians in front of him who were frantically trying to control their terrified horses.

Curos sensed the vitality which reflected back to him from Thunder-Arrow and the stupor seemed to clear from his mind. He seized the willing horse's bridle and vaulted into the sheepskin padded saddle. Swinging up the scimitar on its wrist-strap, he grabbed the hilt in one fluid movement.

A gift of help should not be spurned and Curos launched a furious attack on his foes, slashing and cutting as they tried to clear their vision. He thrust at one of the barbarians, driving the scimitar's needle-point deep between the iron rings of the hauberk. As the wounded man slumped in agony Curos again made the precision killing cut to the throat.

Heartened by Curos' charge and the Topaz energy, several of the fleeing Chaw cavalrymen returned to the fight. A blinded barbarian was hacked mercilessly, another was contemptuously shot through the back at less than four yards' range. The remaining barbarian cavalryman gave one last demonstration of the power of the Western war-horse as he rode down a Chaw who blocked his way and galloped off to rejoin the main army.

Brisk trumpets were now recalling the last of the barbarian cavalry from their harrying of the defeated Chaw.

Curos was anxious for the men to secure as many of the barbarian weapons as possible. He himself took the reins of the magnificent black stallion but as he led the small group of men and horses away rage and disbelief clouded his reason. The Great Army of Chaw had suffered its first strategic defeat for three hundred years, overwhelmed by the advance force of the main barbarian army. It would now be powerless to stop the occupation of its ally, Corninstan. The Chaw commanders could only hope to fall back across the great Janix river and attempt to hold the eastern part of the province. How could such a thing have happened?

He absent-mindedly fingered the heavy silver and topaz medallion which hung at his neck. In a sudden reaction he let the ancient piece of jewellery fall against the thin steel plates which covered his quilted armour. The stone felt somehow angry and exhausted.

Curos recalled with striking vividness how it had saved him and he convulsed with cold fear. The logical, well-ordered Hinto philosophy by which he lived had twice been shattered by sorcery. Two instances of inexplicable power: one had destroyed the Chaw army, the other had saved the insignificant and unworthy Zachaw Curos.

2

Curos woke suddenly at a slight, unnatural sound close to his face. It took a few seconds for him to surface from the depths of sleep and the nightmare in which he relived the battles in Corninstan, now some two months past. He and his small force were camped on the edge of the Sibrea Forest, weeks of marching beyond the northern border of Chaw. Silently his hand moved under the pillow to locate the handle of his tantos dagger which gave instant reassurance. With that deadly knife Curos felt the equal of any man, even in the thick, dead darkness. Slowly he sat up.

There was no noise, no sound of breathing or movement. Still Curos felt a threatening presence in the confined space of the tent. Desperately he strained to hear any warning sounds from the nearby nocturnal forest. For an eternity he waited in the silent blackness until he heard the sentry pass on his round of the camp. He relaxed and breathed deeply to dispel the built-up tension. There was no danger, just his vivid imagination and fear of the nearby immense, alien woodlands to which his father had sent him to seek the aid of the mystic Dryadin.

One small part of his mind was unconvinced and continued to scream danger signals. Sleep was impossible. Curos felt uneasily for the brass box with its sulphur igniters. The long match sprang into flame, a flame which was quickly transferred to the stubby camp candle where it flowed effortlessly into a brilliant, comforting light. Only as the interior of the small pavilion become visible did his eyes come around and stop in startled shock. Less than six feet away sat a threatening figure: cross-legged, head veiled except for the eyes, clad in robes of the deepest black. The gloved hands held a short, recurved bow, arrow nocked and pointing at Curos.

Curos' stomach tightened in fear but even as his leg muscles contracted for a desperate, life-preserving leap the figure's voice carried huskily to him. 'Do not try to move, Zachaw. You are still half full of sleep and fear. My arrow would strike you down before you could gain your feet.'

Deep in his soul Curos knew this was true and again he strove to control the rising terror which would rob him of any chance of effective action.

'Before you start to plan any counter-attack, look at your bedding.' One brief glance away from the menacing, dark figure was enough to register the long-bladed bronze knife thrust down into his pillow. 'You begin to understand,' continued the voice. 'If I had wished your death that thrust would have been deep into your neck. By now your blood and your life would have flowed into the soil to join the spirit of S'lan, the Eternal Forest.'

Silence enveloped the tent as Curos' eyes flicked over his unwelcome visitor, first taking in an impression of size – slightly taller and thinner than a true Chaw. The eyes which were just visible through the veil were however slanted and brown – not the hard blue eyes of the invading barbarians from the West.

Curos had recovered from the first surge of fear and when he spoke his voice sounded confident and firm. 'Although I welcome you to my pavilion, Dark One, I would have preferred that your coming had been by the entrance.' Curos indicated the slash in the back wall of his tent with a slow, unthreatening gesture. 'Now that you are in my presence, I, K'tan Zachaw, bid you explain your business.'

'Very good, Zachaw,' said the stranger in a voice muffled by his face covering, 'but I believe the protocol is incorrect. I am a Dryad of the Eternal Forest S'lan. It is I who ask your reasons for invading with three hundred armed soldiers. This violates the ancient treaty between the Dryads and the Chaw and cannot be allowed. Know also that each cut tree, each killed animal and each fire can be charged against you in blood.'

Curos considered the long speech with an impassive silence which concealed his racing thoughts. He was sure that his father and any other generals of the High Army Command had long ceased to pay any regard to the ancient stories of the Emperor Xan II and his battles and treaties with the Dryadin. 'The Emperors of the Xan dynasty are no more,' he started to say.

'We know this,' said the Dryad, 'but the treaty of words was

13

made with Xan II on behalf of the people of Chaw to the people of the Dryadin.'

'This is not known to me,' Curos replied, 'but I do know that the Chaw are starving and that the barbarians threaten our very existence. The Chaw are desperate; soon famine and revolt will sweep our land. It is for that reason that my honoured father, High General Commander Zachaw, Noyan of the Army of Chaw, has sent me to the great forest to seek your aid.'

'I did not come here out of concern for your problems,' explained the Dryad thoughtfully. 'We feared that you came as the leader of an invasion, and as a full Council member, I was chosen to invite you to meet with our leader.'

The Dryad moved slightly but his relaxed grip on the bow never faltered. Curos had considered several means of attack but with his legs snared by the camp sleeping sack he would be quite unable to reach the Dryad before the narrow, barbed arrow committed his soul to the void.

'I do not mean to be uncivil,' said the Dryad, 'but I feel our conversation could be most useful if conducted without the raised bow and the drawn dagger.'

Curos considered the Chaw military code and its many tenets of honour. In such a situation a personal truce was permitted with an adversary of equal grade, provided there was no treachery to Chaw.

Almost as if reading his mind the Dryad spoke, with a hint of amusement in his voice. 'I can assure you, honoured K'tan, I am quite equal to you in what you would term grade. There will be no loss of face for you in our truce.'

'I agree,' said Curos. 'I, Zachaw Ca'lin agree to a personal truce with . . . '

'Aalani-Galni,' said the Dryad.

'With Aalani-Galni,' continued Curos, 'provided Aalani-Galni does not threaten the people of Chaw.'

'Good,' said Aalani, lowering his bow and flexing tired arm muscles. 'I have some authority but I do not understand the full implications of what you say. Our leader Caflin-Bans, the Ze Dryadi, is the spokesman for the Dyrad people and is guided by the spirit of Eternal S'lan. As he is nearby I would suggest that you enter the forest tomorrow and speak with him.'

14

A lone meeting was far from what Curos had intended. As an ambassador from the High Army Command he had planned to enter the forest with all due ceremony. 'It is difficult and unseemly for a commander of three hundred men to depart without being noticed,' he stated.

'Difficult, but not impossible for a man who has the fate of the Chaw in his hands,' replied the Dryad, standing up slowly. 'I would be grateful if you would return my knife before I depart,' he added.

'How shall I find you tomorrow?' asked Curos, handing the Dryad the long, slim leaf-bladed dagger, noting that it was fashioned of bronze rather than steel.

'Take a line due north from the camp until you reach the forest. Do not enter the trees but wait for us to find you.'

The next morning a strangely apprehensive Curos called an early meeting of his officers to discuss their plan for the day. His subordinates were the two combat officers Chalak Konn and Bhal Morag, who also commanded the supply train and its fifteen men. The formalities of greeting over, Curos announced that he had decided to give the men some recreation by organising a sweeping hunt for any game in the area. The waste of one day was not important and would give him some time to make informal contact with the Dryadin.

As Curos arranged the details for the day he was fully aware of the difference in the two officers. Chalak Konn commanded the Ulus of twenty guardsmen and the five Foot Ulus which made up the first Hund of the 22nd T'sand. Officious and self-important, he was also hard-working and efficient in an unimaginative way. The other K'tan, Bhal Morag, commanded the 22nd Tsand's 3rd Hund and two Ulus of horsemen. Diffident and uninterested, he did a bare minimum to the extent that even thought and speech appeared an effort.

Bhal's lack of interest was not shared by the men and by mid-morning long lines of excited beaters were driving the scant game across the scrub-plain of the dry-wasteland which separated Chaw from the huge northern forests of Sibrea, called S'lan by the Dryadin. It was during the inevitable confusion and disorgan-

15

isation that Curos turned the placid camp hack towards the north as directed by the Dryad.

An hour's hard ride and he was approaching the start of the true forest. The trees rose up like an ominous wall in total contrast to the stunted bushes and coarse grass of the plain. Curos realised his vulnerability only too well. The scrub and bush could hide a dozen or more bowmen without any visible sign. There was, however, something about his conversation with the Dryad assassin which drew Curos to the meeting place. The methods which had served Chaw in the past had failed; the army had been defeated in battle and his father was in disgrace. To counter the all-powerful sorcery, something new was needed. Something which must be found outside the lands of Chaw.

3

A single Dryad was sitting partially concealed beside the barely discernible track. As Curos approached, the tall dark-clad figure stood up and raised an open palm in a gesture of friendship. Despite this sign of greeting Curos' neck twitched coldly. The need to look around and search for treachery was intense but must be resisted. To show any fear, any lack of confidence, would cause great loss of prestige.

Without speaking, the figure beckoned and led Curos through a grove of trees and shorter bushes to where two other Dryads waited with patient aloofness. Curos felt instinctively that the hooded Dryad must be Aalani-Galni. The other Dryad was bare-headed, his ancient and stern face displaying the unmistakable authority of a ruler. Some distance from the Dryadin Curos stepped down from his horse and walked forward before making a deep bow as to a high ranking superior. He was aware of his Dryad guide making a similar obeisance before retreating from the clearing.

In silent stillness Curos stood waiting for the ruler to speak first. When the Dryad finally did so, it was with a deep, slightly haughty voice. 'Welcome, Zachaw Ca'lin, to the domain of the Forest of Eternal S'lan. Here the Dryad serve as mere stewards, protectors of the trees and animals as the vast spirit S'lan desires.' The elder Dryad indicated that Curos should be seated and then continued, 'I am the Ze Dryadi, the speaker for the Council of the Dryadin. We have considered your words of last night, K'tan Zachaw. We hear of the famine in Chaw and understand your fear of the black plague.' The Dryad's voice had a quiet, husky quality, similar to that of Aalani-Galni. 'The famine you fear so much could be the solution to your problem, Zachaw. There are too many souls of men in Chaw and the balance of your land is sorely disturbed.'

In his heart Curos knew this was true. Only the Green Plan of the High Agriculturalist Galtar would have had any hope of long-term success. In four years it had barely started to produce results before the disaster in Corninstan had struck at the lifeline of Chaw's food supply.

It was evident that this older man, the Dryad leader, was going to conduct the discussion and Curos replied accordingly. 'So the honoured Galtar now teaches us,' said Curos respectfully, 'but just as we seek to revert to the ancient harmony the barbarians push in upon us, threatening to enslave the whole Land of Chaw.'

'We know Galtar Paft well,' said the Ze Dryadi, interrupting Curos. 'He is strong in the understanding of H'tao and reveres all life, as do the Dryadin.'

'So Galtar is a H'tao,' said Curos.

'Yes, a High H'tao,' commented the Dryad. 'We would willingly have allowed him to stay in Eternal S'lan but he feared for Chaw, as you now say you do.'

'There are some Hinto, even War-Hinto, who care more for the land of Chaw than the Dryad may think,' said Curos bitterly.

Again silence descended until the Ze Dryadi said, 'The High H'tao stayed with us for nearly two cycles of seasons. He explained to us the problems of Chaw, the pressure of too many men on the land, the draining of spirit from the soil and the reliance on food from other lands. To us his words sounded as blasphemy against the True Order but we listened and advised as he conceived of his Green Plan. Our understanding, taught to us by Eternal S'lan, is much deeper than any Chaw could achieve by prayer and meditation. The plan of Galtar required a lessening of the people of Chaw; plague and famine could well work to speed his gentle purpose.'

The callous words of the Dryad stung Curos. It was easy to talk of plague when you sat in the cool, green northern forests. If Ze Dryadi had been in the heat of the city with friends or family bloated and black with plague, screaming their last hours of life away, he might well have felt differently.

'I feel your anger at my words,' said Ze Dryadi, 'but I speak true as a H'tao. A balance must be achieved and it matters little to the Dryadin if the Chaw are ruled by the white-skinned, blue-eyed barbarians. In time the Chaw might rise up and throw out

18

the invaders or they may find barbarian rule more enlightened than their own.'

Curos sat outwardly impassive, his face immobile, but he was finding it difficult to achieve his apparent self-control. One part of him roared that such words threatened the very people of Chaw, while deep inside the icy voice of reason replied that Chaw needed the wisdom of the evil Dryad, needed it as much as when Galtar had sought their aid eleven years before.

'I hear the words of the Dryad High H'tao,' he said with formal gravity, trying hard to disguise the anger which crept into his voice. 'It would be disrespectful of an unworthy soldier, a Hinto of poor understanding, to dispute the wisdom and logic they contain.'

'But you do,' said Ze Dryadi. 'You do and you can hardly keep your hand off the hilt of your weapon. You are far from being a simple commander of mounted archers, Zachaw. You must have knowledge that I do not. I have spoken freely – do me the honour of sharing your wisdom with me.' Again there was just a hint of humour in the voice as he continued, 'To cool our thoughts and our throats from long talking I can extend my hospitality to a drink of honeyed water.'

They drank in silence and Curos chose his next words carefully. 'I have listened to your words,' he said, 'but your deep wisdom has no knowledge of the Western Barbarians. My honoured father has studied and spied on them for many years. A Noyan and General Commander of the High Army Council, he even joined with merchants travelling through Corninstan to see for himself the lands of these people. At that time the barbarians permitted trade and their armies were yet far off. Truly, Ze Dryadi, as my father saw at once, they are an evil people. Physically they are tall and strong, their faces long and cruelly ugly with hard, blue eyes. As a people they have even less feel for order and piety than the city slum-dwellers.'

'You are perhaps a little biased,' murmured Ze Dryadi.

'No' said Curos vehemently. 'In their own lands they have cleared whole forests for fuel and to build ships. The people they conquer are butchered almost to extinction; only those needed for slaves are spared. Whole provinces of farmland and cities are cleared to leave great open plains. Do not believe that

19

the forest of Sibrea, your S'lan, would be inviolable from these tenacious people. They are mighty indeed, but worst of all, their rulers are served by hideous, unnatural sorcerers of immense power.'

'You now go too far, Curos,' said Aalani, joining the conversation. 'There are, as I have seen, sorcerers and magicians in every town in Chaw. You also have many high H'tao. Surely the barbarian magicians are not so . . . so hideous as you say?'

'I have seen the power of the sorcerers. Without them the barbarian would be as nothing.' Curos snapped his fingers contemptuously. 'The army of Chaw, like soldier ants, would swarm over them.'

'There are some advantages to over-population then,' said Aalani.

Curos ignored this and continued. 'If necessary a hundred Chaw would die to kill each barbarian until their army was gone, picked clean like the bones of a carrion animal.'

'You are too illogical,' said the Dryad leader. 'You show displeasure when I speak freely of plague, and then boast of killing thousands of young men to win a battle. It would be more useful for you to tell us of the sorcerer you fear so much.'

Again Curos sought to control his anger at the hard irony in the Dryad's voice. 'I will tell you briefly of the campaign in Corninstan,' he said, 'where my father, honoured Zachaw Pa'lin, commanded the mounted Bow Regiments, and his unworthy eldest son, myself, had the command of the Topaz Wind of a hundred bowmen.'

'I am sure the unworthy son did this with distinction,' said Ze Dryadi. 'I have been reading your face and your manner. You have been born and trained to command. But continue.'

Curos ignored the interruption and continued quickly. 'The barbarians had advanced through the half-barren lands of North Imranstan and were poised on the border of the fertile valley of the great Janix river which makes up most of Corninstan. Some of the Corninstan War Lords claimed that their land was paying tribute to Chaw and getting little in return. They quickly forgot times when Chaw food and Chaw soldiers had been sent to their aid. Soon one faction of the nobility were seeing advantage to themselves in an alliance with the scum of the West. When the

20

Khan died early last year, probably by poison, the traitors invited the barbarian army to move in and prevent a possible civil war. We had been warned of this by friends in Corninstan, particularly far-sighted merchants, and by my father's spies. A great army was therefore made to camp in the O'san desert. As soon as the barbarians started their ponderous march into the western provinces our mounted army swept into the eastern regions and joined up with those Corninstani loyal to the Khan's son.'

Without hesitation or any sign of the pain it cost him, Curos related the events surrounding the defeat of the Chaw army in Corninstan. He dwelt particularly on the effects of the devastating blasts of sorcery. 'And so,' he continued, 'with our trade routes blocked, our leaders now turn to other sources of aid.' He looked directly at the Dryad. 'But do not underestimate the Chaw, most honoured Ze Dryadi. Our power to wear down all things is relentless. Even the Dark Forest and the evilness of the Western sorcerer could yet succumb to the Ants of Chaw.'

The discussion proceeded at a slow pace. Often the Ze Dryadi would stop speaking and withdraw into blank silence as if listening to outside voices. Suddenly he would return his attention to Curos with a series of pointed, sometimes belligerent questions which made it quite evident that the Dryadin cared little for Chaw or its people. Their only concern was for the forest, S'lan the Eternal. There was one long final silence which stretched on and on. Even Curos, with his hard training and stoical outlook, found the wait close to unbearable.

'It is unfitting for you and I to bargain,' the Ze Dryadi said eventually, as if returning from deep meditation. 'I feel you are, or will become, the true representative of Chaw despite your present low rank.' He stopped speaking to stare fixedly at Curos as if searching for some sign or emotion before continuing. 'The Dryadin will support the people of Chaw as our ancient treaty promises, but the extent of our aid cannot quickly be defined. In return you, K'tan Zachaw Ca'lin Curos, must give an assurance that the forest of Eternal S'lan will be safe from any ravages of the Chaw.'

'My part of the bargain is easily defined, although perhaps difficult to deliver,' suggested Curos. 'But what form of aid will the Dryads give in return?'

21

'That has not yet been decided and will be discussed at length but I would propose to give you what you need most desperately.' Ze Dryadi smiled. 'The services and advice of a Dryad sorcerer.'

'One man in return for the safety of a whole land of forests?' asked Curos. 'I feel the Dryadin drive a hard bargain.'

'We do not bargain, we offer freely. It is not one man that you get but one sorcerer. One powerful sorcerer to elevate you to power in Chaw and then to defeat your nation's enemy. There is nothing you could take from S'lan by force which would serve you as well. You may leave our presence now, Zachaw. Your sorcerer is waiting for you on the main path beyond this grove and will accompany you for several days until the full Dryad Council can debate this issue.'

'If the sorcerer is ready to leave I humbly presume that you had chosen to help the Chaw before I made my poor arguments,' suggested Curos.

'That choice is not mine.' Ze Dryadi smiled again. 'Rather say that we wished to be prepared in order to act swiftly and to gain more information.' He rose from his sitting position with a finality which suggested that the audience was truly at an end.

'There is still much to discuss, honoured Ze Dryadi,' said Curos in some confusion. 'I have little knowledge of sorcery or sorcerers.'

'We have had discussion enough to last for many days,' said the Dryad leader. 'The Dryadin people will need time to consider and assess the disturbing news that you bring. During that time one of our sorcerers will accompany you back to your camp so that our understanding of each other can continue to grow.'

Playing the role of ambassador, Curos bowed and retreated from the leader's presence, waiting until the Ze Dryadi had departed before mounting his horse. Curos' mind was in a turmoil and he allowed his mount to pick its own route along the narrow path.

He reined in his horse harshly as a black clad figure appeared, walking swiftly down the narrow path towards him. Three long, fluid strides, then an outstretched hand reached up to touch the mouth of his nervous horse. Almost at once its uncontrolled movement ceased and its head dropped.

'That's much better,' said a husky female voice. 'Now we can talk. I am called Xante, or Topaz in your language.' She laughed at his surprise. 'Either by chance or by the wisdom of Eternal S'lan I was called Topaz at birth. Since I was chosen to help you, only in the last day have I realised the significance of my name.'

This was impossible for Curos. With two unwanted wives the thought of a female Dryad as his companion was unacceptable. 'What is this?' he shouted. 'Ze Dryadi swore to give me a most powerful and wise sorcerer. I will not be fooled . . . '

'Fooled with a mere female!' replied the dark voice. 'I am chosen as the one most able to provide the aid that Chaw needs. Also, since I am female there will be less suspicion that I am guiding you against your will. Such a thing would seem impossible to the Chaw.'

'Stop!' growled Curos. 'I need a dread sorcerer, not a quick-tongued girl.'

'It's too late to bargain with Ze Dryadi,' said the sorceress, a hint of ice coming into her voice. 'He has already departed. Your bargain is made; I am the Dryad's part of it. It is important for us to establish a proper relationship, K'tan Zachaw,' she continued, ignoring Curos' anger. 'We have much work to complete in the few days I will be staying in your camp.'

'It is first necessary to transport you to my camp,' barked Curos. 'As you have no mount you will share mine until it is possible for me to achieve a better arrangement.'

The girl started to speak but Curos cut her short with an angry, impatient gesture. 'I do not have time for unfruitful discussion, nor do I wish to wait while you walk leisurely. Climb up in front of my saddle – you are not so heavy.'

He barely noticed her gesture of defiant rejection, for in the distance a party of Chaw horsemen appeared, hopelessly lost, and Curos raced up to them, commanding one of their mounts for Xante. Seated unsteadily on an unfamiliar saddle, she was enclosed in a haze of anger which more than matched Curos' own.

Curos did not introduce Xante to his officers but took her directly to his own quarters. Leaving her somewhat brusquely in the tent, he stopped in mid-stride and called the under-officer

23

of the Commander's Guard Ulus to him. The Ataman seemed smart and capable but Curos considered his grip and authority over his guardsmen less than confident. To ensure that the sorceress was treated with all due respect Curos pointedly defined her status, and ordered food and drink to be prepared.

He then sought out Bhal Morag who was even more surprised than Curos by the developments with the Dryadin. It had been planned to enter the Forest by the Old Road with a full ceremonial guard, banners of peace and the music of gongs and trumpets. That the Dryadin leader preferred a rather demeaning personal audience with a single Chaw K'tan was unthinkable.

There were however more pressing problems to be dealt with before Curos could start his discussions with the Dryad woman. Chalak Konn and a good number of the Chaw soldiers had not returned from the disorganised hunting expedition. There were only a few hours of daylight remaining and many of his troops would be ill-equipped to spend a cold night in the open plains. With his mind full of the day's events Curos was pleased when Bhal Morag showed unexpected initiative in organising cavalry sweeps of the bush land and the lighting of signal fires.

Wary of the expected confrontation with the Dryad woman Curos allowed himself the unaccustomed luxury of a moment's inactivity. Leaning against the wheel of a forage cart, he watched the dark smoke rise up in vertical columns and considered the quality of his soldiers. The men were basically good material but poorly trained; set free from direct control for a few hours they dissolved into almost total confusion. How would such poor organisation stand up to the shock of the Warchaw army?

4

When Curos entered the tent Xante stood up from the folding camp stool. She was still swathed in the dark Dryad tunic and trousers and through the narrow slit of the veiled head-covering her eyes regarded him warily. For once Curos was unsure of himself. How should he proceed after his initial animosity to the sorceress? He allowed the tent flap to close behind him and faced the dark figure.

The woman broke the silence with her husky voice. 'This night, perhaps the next hour, will be the most important in your life, Zachaw. More important than your marriage day, or even the day of your death. We must work together, work on whatever terms are best for our peoples.'

'Then let us start by leaving talk of marriage days and dying days out of our conversation, Madam. Soldiers do not talk openly of death and I have two totally unwanted wives already.' He paused to indicate that she should sit and opened up a second stool for himself.

'If we are to help each other we can have no secrets, no reserve and no barriers,' she said quietly. 'We do not trust each other enough yet by far.'

'Trust will not be easy for me,' said Curos. 'I have no friends and no colleagues. Even at my minor level in the army I am almost isolated by duty and command.' Again he stopped speaking and sought to read her half-hidden eyes before continuing. 'I trust no-one and rely on no-one; in our society such things are not necessary.'

'There are other problems,' Xante replied. 'You do not respect any woman as an equal. And in turn I feel your people are too hard and insensitive to be helped. These prejudices are all part of the barrier we have to break down.'

'It is difficult for me to be frank and open with you, madam,' he ventured. 'It is unusual among my people to have the face covered except when, as with the nomadic tribes, we ride in the sand-stinging desert.'

'Please excuse me. It is customary for my people to cover their face when outside S'lan,' she said as she began to remove her outer tunic and head cover. The wide sash and then the frogwork fastenings were undone and the tunic coat removed. Xante was slightly taller and slimmer than a Chaw woman but the fine flax shirt and loose-fitting trousers suited her well. Gracefully she unwound the turban-like head cloth, the final turn of which formed the veil over the lower face. Her eyes held his as he studied her face with mounting excitement.

She was beautiful, Curos' ideal of perfection. Her almond face with its high cheekbones and her glossy black hair formed the perfect setting for the dark eyes with their exaggerated upward slant. The fixed, immobile face was galvanised with dynamic life by those eyes, pools of mystery and passion which generations of Chaw painters had striven to portray. Her mouth was small and exquisite but the words she spoke were not registered by Curos whose mind was lost in remembered poetic phrases used to decribe the perfect mistress.

'Zachaw Curos.' Her voice at last penetrated his thoughts. The once husky voice now seemed to possess a new and desirable quality. 'Your perception of me is entirely wrong. I am not here to share your bed. I am no plaything for an arrogant junior army officer.' His attention snapped back into focus at the angry outburst but he felt only humour at the aura of rage which surrounded the beautiful girl. Women were women whatever their background.

'Your confidence in your strength and your intellect needs to be shaken,' she continued in a voice cold with menace. 'For us to proceed we must be equals. Defend yourself, Zachaw. Defend yourself and show you are worthy of being the leader of Chaw.' Automatically Curos' hand moved to the chisel-pointed dagger but an arrogant smile crossed his face as he changed his mind. There were better ways of dealing with an unarmed girl.

The anger which surrounded Xante was almost tangible while the dark eyes focused intently on Curos. The first shimmer of fear entered his mind. Imperceptibly a tightening band was being drawn around his skull. Unthinkingly he rubbed his brow and forced the smile back to his lips: it was a mere conjurer's deception. Inexorably the pressure increased. He saw images of tangled ivy growing into strangling, constricting coils and felt the needle-pointed anchor roots probing into his consciousness. The pain increased and his vision seemed filled with the two black, malicious pools which were Xante's unblinking eyes. His near paralysed hands moved ineffectually, now quite incapable of action.

Sheer dread and revulsion rose up in Curos like a destroying wave. The Dryad tendrils were killing him. He was betrayed and would be assassinated; the word of Ze Dryadi was worthless. Curos fought to overcome his fear but momentary loss of mental control had further reduced his power to resist. Even as his consciousness began to fade he sought some new means of combating the unnatural assault.

'The Pendant of Topaz will not assist you against the Dryadin, but you do well to call it to your defence.' The voice of Xante seemed to speak deep in his mind even as that possibility occurred to him. Instantly the crushing coils disappeared and Curos swayed drunkenly as near terror was replaced by the humiliation of defeat.

His body trembled as sensation returned and gradually his blurred vision began to recover. Slowly he became aware of Xante, her face now beaded with perspiration and drawn with strain. Only enormous will power kept the exhausted girl upright and her voice was weak with fatigue. 'You have a very strong mind, Zachaw Curos. Very, very strong.' She gripped the tent pole for support and lowered herself onto the stool.

'Sorceress,' Curos snarled. 'I should cut out your heart and burn your body. You tricked me into defeat.'

'I doubt you could cut the heart from a fly at the moment,' the woman said wearily, 'and my Jitsu is the equal of your dagger. You bargained for a sorcerer and you have one. If you want a whore, go to the slave market.'

Curos drew a deep breath and slowly forced his anger to subside. He performed a bow of respect and said in a formal tone, 'Sorceress, welcome to my tent. Please accept my apologies for the discourteous behaviour I have shown towards you since our first meeting.' He slumped back onto the other camp stool, nearly upending it. Leaning sideways, he pulled a handtowel from a rack and handed it to Xante.

'Have you ever apologised to a woman before?' she asked, wiping her face.

'No, and to no man other than my father.'

'And no man has ever made me angry enough to kill. We make a good start, you and I.'

'Yes, allies who deliberately draw back from killing each other must have a future. Let us start anew,' said Curos seriously. 'My family name is Zachaw, my given name Ca'lin Curos.'

'I have only one name, given at birth,' said the woman. 'All call me Xante, or Xante, daughter of Yani. There is one who calls me beloved but the strain of this task threatens to come between us.'

'You are his mistress?'

'That degrading term has no meaning to us,' she said. 'Our customs are very different from yours. We choose who we pair with, one man, one woman. Dromo is not happy that I have accepted this task, to leave him and go to a strange people. If he is not strong enough to face my duty then I fear the bond between us may be broken.'

Curos had no intention of explaining the details of the marriages that his father had arranged for him, the first in his eighteenth year and the second two years later when no heir had been born. Such matters would surely be as unimportant to Xante as they were to Curos himself. The Zachaw family line was, after all, already assured by his younger brother's two sons.

The exertion of the encounter had drained both Xante and Curos of energy but to his surprise Curos found that the wary tension between them seemed to have been dispersed. Conversation flowed freely as if between old acquaintances. Only in the presence of Khol Dalgan had Curos ever felt so relaxed and at ease. The sudden memory of Khol Dalgan stabbed Curos like a knife of sadness. Dalgan, from the nomadic people of the Sand-Dragon Clan, was Curos' only friend. With one word of command he had condemned him to death on the points of the barbarian pike shafts in the hopeless Corninstan war.

Xante looked questioningly at Curos and hesitated before speaking. 'I feel I am already able to read something of your mind,' she said quietly. 'Dark despair can often be dispelled a little, if only briefly, by the light of conversation.'

'I don't need H'tao axioms to help me, woman,' he snapped in annoyance and then added apologetically, 'I fear remorse makes me uncivil; please excuse my rudeness.'

'You fear the conquest of Chaw by the barbarians?'

'The possibility of conquest and the destruction of the Chaw seldom leaves my thoughts,' he murmured.

'But that was not the blackest part of the shadow which passed over you?'

'No, that was caused by the death of one man. A friend who sacrificed himself out of duty because I ordered it. That was part of the first battle in Corninstan.'

'Ze Dryadi spoke to me of that happening. The battle when the Western sorcerers first showed the power that led to your defeat.' Curos sat silent and Xante continued. 'You take death too importantly, men die, lives are used up. Your peasants sacrifice themselves in a lifetime of toil and misery. Was your soldiers' sacrifice any worse than that?'

'I have heard such talk before,' said Curos. 'But it does not make grief any easier to bear.'

He stood up briskly in an attempt to shake off the dark thoughts and moved to the entrance of the tent. 'I will have food brought and we can continue our talk. It is coarse camp food, rice with dried peas and beans. There will be some meat from our hunting. Please excuse my absence for a short while,' he added as if speaking to an equal. 'I have some small duties to attend to. One of the servants will bring you water for washing.'

Having given orders to the guardsman who acted as the officers' orderly he conducted brief rounds of the camp and collected a large map of Chaw and the surrounding countries from the cache of documents kept by the officer, Chalak Konn.

By the time he arrived back at his personal tent the Ataman and a surly guardsman stood waiting impatiently with food, wine and a leather jug of drinking water. 'Good,' said Curos curtly. 'The rice and dried food has been well cooked?'

'Yes, Lord,' replied the under-officer but he looked slightly apprehensive as Curos lifted the woven lids to the baskets. The food was acceptable but on tasting the water Curos spat a long stream of it out directly into the Ataman's face.

'This is fresh stream water, Ataman Wan,' he hissed in a voice full of anger and menace. 'What do my camp orders say on the subject of drinking water?'

'All drinking water is to be purified by the addition of one tenth part wine or by boiling, Lord.' The Ataman bowed his head.

'And this water for your commander has not been boiled. Are you trying to assassinate me with filth-laden water?'

'No, Lord.'

'I will not tolerate this breach of discipline. The order was given to prevent sickness. You will ensure that the man responsible for this receives five lashes as punishment,'

'Lord,' the Ataman remonstrated, 'it may be difficult to identify the cook who filled the water container . . .'

'Ataman Wan,' said Curos in a tone of cold fury, 'if you cannot attend to such details without ignoring my command you are unsuitable to be an under-officer. Who is ultimately responsible for the protection of the officers and for procuring their food?'

'I am, Lord.'

'Then you have identified the man to be flogged. Increase the punishment to ten lashes for stupidity.'

Inside the tent Curos was still fuming when he spoke to Xante. 'They are ill-disciplined barrack soldiers with no idea of living in the field . . . or the forest. They'll all have dysentry within the week.'

'The man will flog himself?' asked Xante, smiling at Curos' anger.

'No doubt one of his men will help him!' Curos growled. 'I would demote him if any of the other idiots were any better. How will we ever defeat the barbarians if our army can't even obey simple orders?'

'You all obeyed orders at Corninstan Road,' said Xante quietly. 'Let us sit and eat together. Quieten your anger and think of the food which Eternal S'lan has provided.'

'It's nothing to thank S'lan for,' snapped Curos as he sat down irritably. 'This is food from the Land of Chaw.'

'Then thank the land of Chaw for the food and Eternal S'lan for the water and the air. The food will do little for your needs if you are so ill of humour.'

Curos snorted and offered the basket of rice to Xante. They ate in silence until a soldier arrived with a jug of freshly boiled water. To this Curos added a quantity of rice wine and a squeezed lemon. He handed Xante a heavy china bowl and poured for her, suddenly astounded that he was treating her as an equal. Gradually conversation resumed and inevitably returned to the subject of the Western Barbarians.

The meal over, Curos unrolled the large map, hand-painted on heavy waxed cloth. Carefully he outlined for Xante the strategic and tactical situation of Corninstan.

'I am surprised that both armies were so small,' said Xante, looking questioningly at Curos. 'How could eleven thousand barbarians threaten the teeming millions of the land of Chaw?'

'It's all a matter of timing and food supply,' explained Curos. 'The barbarians wanted to secure a base in Corninstan before they committed their main army to the march. We dared not send too large an army into Corninstan for fear that the whole country would have turned against us. We had only to throw back the Warchaw advance guard and our friends in Corninstan would have remained in power and the barbarians might not have risked a second attack.' Xante sensed his bitterness as he added, 'Now most of the Corninstani have sided with those who collaborated with the barbarians. The young king and the noble families friendly to Chaw are in exile.'

'Surely the people see that those noble families who sided with the invaders only did so to gain power?' asked Xante.

'I suppose some do, but success brings success. Only fools will argue against the victors when they are backed by a large, fearful army. There are already fifty thousand barbarians in Corninstan, gradually annexing all power. Soon even the gullible will realise what has happened but it is already too late.'

Curos' mood of depression filled the small tent. Finally he straightened up and looked full at Xante. 'I am sorry to be so defeatist,' he sighed. 'It is easy to relive the past, but that only reduces the will to succeed in the future. I will continue with the events of the battle, if you wish.'

31

'Please,' answered Xante.

She sat quietly as he ran through the events of that day, saying nothing and asking no questions until he had finished the description of the battle in the Road and the later battle when the Chaw attempted to prevent the barbarians crossing the Janix river into East Corninstan.

'Can you follow all that?' he asked at last as he rose to prepare more drink.

'Not really, only the basic outline. What is most important to me is the effect that the sorcerer had on the first battle, on the Road. He did nothing to support the river crossing?'

'There was no need,' shrugged Curos. 'Our men were already beaten in their hearts. We destroyed the bridges and prepared defensive positions as I said but the barbarian engines used fire barrels to break up our formations and their foot-soldiers stormed ashore. We inflicted heavy losses on them at first but . . .' He shrugged. 'Once they were across, our army broke.'

'I see, so they only seem to use sorcery to prevent defeat. A final weapon when nothing else would work?'

'That is also my conclusion.'

Curos talked through the first phase of the battle again and tried to answer all of Xante's questions on the nature of the fire, any feelings or senses of dread and any sighting of the beings involved.

It was late in the night when Xante finally said, 'We have so little to work with. Their power is of a particular, dramatically physical kind. It is not unlimited, since you were able to lead your men around the fire, and it is not used lightly. Even when losing valuable men against your army at the river they chose to use catapults.'

'I had thought of that,' mused Curos. 'Why didn't the sorcerer just blast our defences away? Why did they not destroy our fleeing army by fire? I am also mystified by the power of this pendant,' he added. 'Its effect on the barbarian knights was, well, very welcome!'

'Could I see?' asked Xante, somewhat reluctantly holding out her hand as Curos slipped the thick silver chain over his head. She flinched back. 'No! It repels me. It is charged with energy like the mind of a person who hates.' Curos held the pendant up for her to see. A large, yellow topaz stone was embedded in an ancient and heavy setting. Despite the wear to the silver Xante could just distinguish a leaf pattern.

'It was handed to me by my grandmother when I took command of the Topaz Wind,' explained Curos. 'Its origin is lost to us but it is very ancient. I, in turn, will pass it on to a member of a new generation of the Zachaw family, not necessarily the eldest but whoever seems most appropriate to receive it.'

'So it is old and has power to protect,' murmured Xante. 'It has saved you twice, Curos. Once in Corninstan Road and once in this tent.'

'When?' asked Curos. 'When you demonstrated your . . .'

'No, not then. Although I felt it might have done if I had pressed my attack further. It was absorbing more and more power from my sorcery. To show we now have no secrets I will tell you this. Ze Dryadi's original plan was to assassinate you in your sleep and Aalani was directed to the task.'

'And this revelation is expected to build trust and confidence?' said Curos wryly. 'We had made no hostile move into your Forest.'

'We have had little cause to love the Chaw in the past, but let me continue. When he entered your tent he used a subtle form of sorcery to dull the senses of your guards and yourself. He felt an angry wariness but you were still deep in induced sleep. Aalani struck here,' she indicated the side of her neck, 'with great force and skill, but his blade was deflected and only plunged into your pillow. Aalani was propelled backwards across the tent and despite his efforts you awoke.' Xante smiled briefly. 'It is interesting to speculate who was most afraid in the first minutes of your conversation.'

'He kept face and lied very well,' commented Curos with bitter respect. 'I truly hope I can trust the word of your leader a little more than I could Aalani-Galni. To think I quite liked the man! I now realise how little I understood.'

'I understand even less of your topaz. I think that in Corninstan it became charged from the violent energy of the barbarian sorcerers. In similar fashion it drew power from the sorcery of Aalani and myself. You seem to be able to trigger that energy in your defence.' She laughed for the first time and added, 'If I attack you again I will need to do it suddenly and directly before the stone can intervene.'

'I might be the first to attack you, Lady Sorceress,' said Curos. 'A sudden dagger thrust may be difficult to counter if I took you by surprise.'

'Can friends and allies talk like this?' said Xante in mock surprise. 'But know that I have already stored your mind pattern from when you thought of that before. Any indication of such an attack would immediately trigger a response, even if I were asleep.'

'Or drunk?'

'Or drunk, or in meditation, or in ecstasy.' She smiled. 'Preservation is a very deep instinct.'

5

The next morning Curos awoke in some surprise at the sound of a second person breathing so closely to him. In the dim light of early morning he looked over at Xante's peaceful form on a separate sleeping mat. The sight of her beauty was unbearable; as lovely but as distant as a rainbow. Hastily he rose and dressed in silence to join the duty officer on early morning rounds of the camp. Bhal Morag was far from vigilant and needed supervision.

Some time later when Curos returned he saw that Ataman Wan had mustered his Ulus in the centre of the command compound. Xante sat under the tent awning, partially hidden in the deep, slanting shadow. She watched in fascination as the twenty foot-soldiers were drilled in full ceremonial scarlet uniform by the under-officer. Skirting the temporary parade-ground, Curos made his way unseen by the guardsman to where Xante sat in the cross-legged 'Siddhasana' position.

'Greetings, Zachaw Curos,' she murmured. 'I was awakened by your leaving the tent.'

Curos apologised but his eyes stayed on the Ataman who was calling his men to attention. The men bowed in salute which Wan formally returned before addressing them.

'I, Wan Abac, Ataman of the Guard Ulus, have been reprimanded by the esteemed commander,' he stated. 'The sentence is to be ten lashes of the chabou.' The surprise of the assembled soldiers was almost tangible as the under-officer threw down the punishment whip, removed his tunic and turned his back to them.

'The punishment is to begin. Will a guardsman pick up the chabou and administer ten lashes?' There was a stunned immobility for a few moments until one soldier became unable to resist the order. Warily he picked up the whip to land ten vicious cuts on the exposed back of Ataman Wan. Red blood-dripping weals opened but no sound escaped from between the Ataman's clenched teeth.

'Surely he has lost face with his men?' whispered Xante to Curos. 'How will he be able to command them now?'

'He will fail and that is a pity,' Curos nodded agreement. 'I misjudged a good man and this will destroy him.'

'Thank you!' shouted the under-officer in a voice hoarse with pain. 'The cuts of the whip are nothing compared to the shame I feel at the contempt the commander has expressed for his Guard Ulus. Your discipline and conduct will be improved until the perfection shown by this unit is beyond reproach.' The Ataman stood glowering at the men. 'Now I stand with no tunic and no badges of rank. If any of you feel the need to challenge my authority to command, let him step forward and meet me open-handed.' The under-officer held up both open palms in the ritualistic Jitsu challenge for unarmed combat.

For several seconds no-one responded but then a weather-beaten guardsman stepped forward, arrogantly throwing off his thick outer tunic. 'I have never accepted your ability to command,' he growled. 'You are too young and too soft. A boy cannot lead twenty men. Your death in Jitsu training will prove my words.'

For the first time Curos really noticed Ataman Wan. Short, even for a city dweller, his shoulders were broad and powerful with knots of hard trained muscle. He stood relaxed, knees flexed with his weight falling forward onto his toes, arms slightly above waist height, a classic jitsu position. The weak, uncertain face of the junior under-officer was now transformed into the hard, expressionless mask of the master, Ze Jitsu. As the hint of a smile crossed Wan's face, Curos knew that there could only be one outcome from this contest which Wan had provoked.

The guardsman's attack on the Ataman was sudden, vicious and unorthodox. He leapt forward as if to deliver a kick but instead feinted to the face before launching a fast, straight-fingered spear-strike to the body. With amazing speed Wan moved aside from the strike, grasped the guardsman's wrist and delivered a cutting blow under the nose. Seizing the front of the stunned guardsman's shirt, he crouched into the high shoulder-throw position of the 'Mountain to Valley Drop'. His opponent hurtled forward and was pulled into a sweeping downward arc with no time to breakfall. The heavy guardsman landed on the side of his head, breaking both neck and collar-bone. Death was instantaneous.

Ataman Wan leapt back into the defensive position and faced his men, but no others wished to challenge his authority and they stood in shocked silence at the sudden and violent death of their comrade.

'We all now understand our positions. I command, you obey,' stated Ataman Wan in a voice strained by the pain of the whip cuts. 'We will start again with basic training and continue until we are worthy of respect. Your lesson for today: discipline is the foundation of success in war. Dismiss.'

As Curos stood up to move inside the tent Xante asked angrily, 'Will you let him escape punishment for that unnecessary and premeditated killing?'

'It depends,' shrugged Curos, holding the tent open for her. 'If he is successful I will accept the "training accident" story when it is reported to me formally. If not, I will use the truth to demote and execute him.'

'I see that in Chaw also, justice can be deformed to meet the leader's wishes,' observed Xante bitterly.

Later in the day Curos invited the two K'tans Bhal Morag and Chalak Konn to his evening meal which was served under the awning of the commander's pavilion. He briefly introduced Xante as 'The Esteemed Dryad Sorceress' who had been sent to the camp by the leader of the Dryadin people. The Chaw respect of authority and natural politeness ensured that neither officer commented on the unusualness of the situation nor on Xante's foreign style of dress. Her face remained veiled and she rarely spoke or joined the conversation.

'The whole T'sand is a rabble,' Bhal Morag remarked pompously at one stage. 'I had intended to improve discipline during this expedition but with the haste of our march to the forest there has been little time. I am surprised to see that Ataman Wan has had his men wash and their uniforms are clean for the first time in weeks.'

Already drastic changes had occurred in the commander's compound, due to under-officer Wan's new regime.

'It is an attitude that is essential,' suggested Curos. 'They are now taking care over their appearance and training. I fear I have

37

been too concerned with my own task to take trouble with the men, but a change which has come from within will be more lasting.'

During the next day Curos started to plan the return route for their march back to Chaw. He was intent on making good speed but also wanted to make the best use of any opportunities for exercising the soldiers' skills and improving their fitness as an example to the rest of the T'sand. Curos gave his two officers every chance to show initiative and suggest their own plans. As before, Chalak Konn was officious almost to the point of obstruction and seemed quite unable to comprehend the strength of the impending danger to the lands of Chaw. Bhal Morag affected an insolent laziness which irritated Curos intensely, particularly when he began to realise the sharpness of the officer's potential ability.

Xante found the noise and the smell and the general activity of the camp exceedingly oppressive. It was difficult for her to concentrate except in the quietness of the night or early morning. Several times she and Curos rode out into the bush away from the camp, followed by a small Guard at a discreet distance.

'I do not understand some of your purpose, Curos,' she said on one such occasion. 'You seem to hate and despise these men, yet you take great trouble in the training. Also you dislike Chalak Konn who works hard and is efficient, while you show more regard for Bhal Morag who seems to have little interest, save one, which is offensive to me and could lead him into grave danger.'

'The general army of Chaw has become lax and ill-disciplined,' replied Curos, 'and the 22nd T'sand is not the worst. In some areas the garrison forces have almost merged into the civil population. That is the price of several hundred years' peace. Where the danger of desert bandits or pirates from the eastern seas is high the T'sands are well-trained. If it becomes believed that the miserable 22nd T'sand could achieve even a small victory due to its new iron-hard discipline, it will aid my cause.'

'But discipline will not defeat the Western sorcerers,' commented Xante. 'You have said as much yourself.'

'No,' said Curos. 'The Dryads must do that, but even without their sorcerers the barbarians would still be formidable. To fight them I need a good army, not a peasant rabble.'

'And your attitude to the officers?' she asked.

'Ah! that is more difficult to explain,' replied Curos. 'Chalak Konn is efficient as you say but he lacks real spark and fire. I need men of vision and initiative who can lead and inspire in their own way – Bhal Morag has that ability, he only needs to learn to use it.'

'Then Chalak Konn may already be a dead man,' Xante said gravely. 'His pride would make him an obstacle to your plans and I have seen how ruthless you can be. But what will you do with your problem officer?'

'His talents will not be wasted,' mused Curos. 'I will find a use for Chalak's meticulous efficiency. If his officiousness doesn't drive me to kill him first!'

'Commander Curos' cunning in these matters is beyond my experience,' said Xante seriously after a pause for thought. 'I am pleased for the sake of Eternal S'lan that you are our ally.'

'And I would fear for the land of Chaw if the Dryadin were to join with the barbarians,' replied Curos.

'Mutual respect and a common enemy make for a good part-nership,' said Xante, 'but what you need is not easy to provide. Few of our people are true sorcerers and our powers are of a different, slower character than that of our enemies. I fear Ze Dryadi has given me a task for which I an unequal, as unequal as Chalak is for the role you set for your officers.'

'These things will be discussed when I next talk again with Ze Dryadi,' said Curos seriously, 'but it may be that fate has a greater destiny for you than even your wise leader can visualise. Already I am sure of this; the old ways will not suffice, only with the Dryads' help will Chaw have any hope.'

6

The Warchaw armies which were now causing Curos so much concern had their origins centuries in the past. The N'gol invasions had burst out of the D'was five hundred years ago to nearly destroy the Chaw culture of the Emperors and also expanded westward across Corninstan and Imranstan into the regions of the west. When the N'gol had been defeated in the East by Xan II's armies, many N'gol tribesmen had followed their brothers westward in successive waves of invasion. Ultimately a slow shockwave of moving displaced people rolled up to the western continent. That was a hundred years after the death of Xan II and the energy of these folk movements had been almost expended but they had traumatic effects on the young western civilisations.

Almost cut off from the East by mountains and an inland sea, several distinct nations of similar Warchaw people had been engaged in minor internal warfare as their barbarian culture developed. When two of the nations were attacked from the East the rulers were quick to react. Centuries of warfare had equipped them with highly developed and specialised armies. Their success was however only partial. The invaders were whole nations of moving peoples and were halted rather than repulsed. The West trembled at their losses of men and the size of the enemy forces.

At that time the Order of Gadel was a respected but unimportant association of sorcerers which although originating in the far western islands now spanned the continent. They alone had means of rapid communication from their telepathic powers and were able to understand the nature of the threat from the East. Many of the Order were of warrior or knightly families and had skill and knowledge of arms and warfare. Although having their first loyalty to the Order they were also well aware of their own individual nations' strengths and weaknesses. The bowmen of the western island, the cavalry of the central plains and the footmen of the south all reigned supreme in their own environment but none could match the numbers and mobility of the encroaching Turkistan peoples.

The Order of Gadel was politically neutral and able to give the cohesion the West needed, and under The All High Wizard Mathon the first combined Warchaw army was formed. The archers outranged and pulverised the Turkoman mounted bowmen, making them vulnerable to the shock attack of the mail-clad knights, who themselves developed movements to turn the disorganised armies onto the killing spears of the foot-soldiers. In the first major battle three sorcerers had panicked and used a flash of fire to halt an enemy charge. Weak and ineffective by the standards of the present Order, its effect was decisive in buying time for the archers and it became part of the basic War Plan.

Within five years the battlefields of the West were heaped with the dead of the invading peoples, whole nations slaughtered by the crusading valour of the West. But still fear persisted in the courts of kings and in the meeting places of the Order. In inns and farmsteads, and city squares the stories of the hordes of the East were passed on. Outnumbered five to one or ten to one, the knights, the soldiers and the freemen, aided by the sorcerers of Gadel, had fought and won and then gone on to slaughter the populations of the campsites as big as towns, where women and old men died protecting the children. The next day or the next week a new army of tribesmen would appear, spearheading another minor Turkoman nation's drive into the West. To match the numbers of its enemy the West committed almost all its might into one defensive army. In the next year or the one after that the hordes would break through and be free to harry and destroy at will. The few western towns which had been overrun had been utterly destroyed.

In the mind of The All High Wizard Mathon, the only answer was to move the killing ground eastward into the land of the Turkoman, to smash the armies before they could form into effective fighting forces and to reduce the population before it could move westward.

Previously the N'gol had swept through lands, pillaging and destroying, but they rarely occupied or settled. Many such lands were still weak and recovering from these raids when the new threat to their people's very existence appeared from the West. The army of the Warchaw ground inexorably eastward, and spectacular battles were followed by periods of such destructive subjugation that some nations would never rise to pose even an imagined threat again.

The success of the invasions came close to fragmenting the Order of Gadel and the Warchaw peoples. Distances were too great and communication and loyalties began to break down. For its own salvation the Order instigated a process of sending young initiates from one land away to another for training and constructed a number of Spiritual Meeting Chambers where at least the projected presence of the member could meet with his peers. The most important and powerful of the chambers had been positioned and constructed for the Conclave of Wizards who ruled the Order.

In the western extremity of the Warchaw lands a volcanic Tor stood out stark and clear from a plain of mist-shrouded wet lands. From the most ancient of times when the early peoples had carried their stone weapons up its steep sides, its mystic nature had been evident and many of the lines of power which crossed the land had their focus here. The Tor had become a natural beacon to sorcerers in far lands and here the High Chamber had been constructed by sorcery alone.

From the outside the massive, smooth dome of black basalt exhibited no features or openings to what lay within. The meeting chamber, with its twelve-sided walls curving over to a vaulted roof, was lined with burnished silver and housed twelve throne-like seats set in a pool of mirror-calm quicksilver. It was a completely hidden place which no living being could ever enter, a focus for wraith-like projections of sorcerous power, a place where they alone could meet and combine free from the encumbrance of physical form. Behind each faceted wall was an antechamber where the High Wizard's form could materialise before proceeding with all dignity to his seat.

The form of Valanus shimmered into an image of existence, illuminating the small, arched antechamber with its archaic engravings. Although the equal of any in the order, Valanus was the junior member of the conclave and arrived first as custom decreed. In this place, above all others, it was essential to observe the rituals and protocols which held the ambitious and dynamic leaders of the Order together. The customs of the Order of Chivalry and the Order of Gadel were important to Valanus and on each arrival in this room he felt the same surge of pride tinged with awe.

None were watching as Valanus projected the image of his form into the main chamber. Phantom feet touched but did not dint the molten metal as he proceeded to his place. Behind him on his section of wall was plated an icon of Valanus as he saw himself – the warrior sorcerer with his sword of honour in the right hand and the lightning flash of magical power in the left – an incarnation of Myrdin of old who defended his homeland with arms and with sorcery before being called to the cave of waiting until he and his King would be needed again.

In turn each wizard of the conclave arrived, spirit forms lighting up the oxygenless atmosphere until all were present and the domed walls and liquid floor reflected pure energy. It was then that, in the very centre of their circle, the Stone rose up from the pool, a low plinth with an expectant, empty cavity. This had not been in the original design but had appeared at the first Conclave three hundred years ago as soon as the most senior of the wizards was seated. Some said it was the throne for an All High Wizard but none had been elected since Mathon; others claimed that stone was the natural resting place for Amathare, a hidden object of power.

In these days the Stone only appeared at times of a significant event, a conquest or battle, as if expecting the Amathare would be restored to it. Its appearance now further accentuated Valanus' pride. He was to give an account of the conquest of Corn Land and his proposed plans for the attack on Chaw. Although he had been assisted by two other sorcerers, Neath and, Runanin, the Lady, at the battle of Corn Land Road, it was his victory, his plan and his report to the council. Even the Stone had attended to hear his words. He rose to his feet, a master among peers who knew his quality, and began in the required humble tone.

7

Curos' second meeting with the Dryadin was to be with a larger number of the Council and would be held in one of the official forest meeting places. The arrangements left Chalak Konn confused and concerned. He could not understand the nature of Curos' purpose; if it were so important why were the negotiations being conducted in such an unseemly and personal manner? Curos' curt attempt at an explanation succeeded in annoying him further. Bhal Morag however showed total uninterest in the matter until Curos was about to leave the security of the camp, when he had voiced a warning about his Commander's personal safety.

Curos and Xante rode away from the camp without speaking for sometime until he commented, 'You ride uneasily.'

'I am not accustomed to saddles and stirrups,' she replied. 'I do not find the stirrup a comfortable seat.'

'Ah! that is the problem,' he said gravely. 'Your feet go in the stirrups and your . . . sits in the saddle. It will feel easier now!'

She glared belligerently before starting to explain. 'In Eternal S'lan there are few clear paths and only when we traverse long distances do we ride the small forest ponies, with just a nose band and halter.'

Curos reflected on this. To him riding was as natural, if not more natural, than walking. The horse went with his rank and his family's association with the great western and northern plains. 'You will have to learn to ride well and with endurance,' he said slowly. 'It would be undignified and impractical for you to walk with the footmen, or ride in a carriage. In many cases I will need to move more rapidly than the marching army.'

'I will endeavour to learn,' she said icily. 'I would not have K'tan Chalak accuse me of being unseemly! Each evening I will sit in a bucket of salt water to rectify my sensitivity to the leather saddle.'

'I feel several hours a day exercising on horseback would be more useful,' Curos remarked. With mock seriousness he added, 'Although Under-Officer Wan would be only too ready to provide a bucket of salt brine if you requested it. He has become obsessed with washing himself and his men in the stuff.'

Xante ignored this and halted the docile pony with a click of her tongue. Her unorthodox methods of controlling the animal were a travesty of horsemanship, but very effective. She breathed deeply before turning in the saddle to look back at the camp. 'I never realised how it would be to live in a termites' nest, Curos. Is it not good to breathe clean, fresh air and hear only the natural sound of the trees and the breeze?'

For Curos, the bustle and clamour of camp or city life were ingrained into his very being. Alone with just one other person, surrounded by open countryside, he felt distinctly uneasy. Even in the wide expanses of the western desert which he loved so well he was usually accompanied by at least a dozen other horsemen. His attempts to explain this to Xante as they rode steadily along were less than fully successful.

Soon they were riding amongst taller, more densely packed trees which slowed the horses' progress. Xante sighed with relief and slid from her mount's back. As Curos also dismounted she exclaimed, 'Oh, Eternal S'lan, I am home again! Curos, cannot you feel the living presence of the forest?'

Curos certainly could and did not like it at all. The trees seemed to press in on him menacingly and the soft, springy soil almost seemed to want to pull his feet downwards. 'I thought it was possible to ride,' he suggested uneasily.

'Not here,' Xante explained. 'The entrances into Eternal S'lan have been turned into Closed Ways to keep out intruders. Further on the Main Ways are open to permit travel of the Dryadin. We will have to lead the horses for several yetang before we can ride.'

Although the path was quite visible where they stood, ahead of them it appeared closed like a dense hedge. As Xante advanced, the tree branches became less entwined and they could pass through. To Curos it appeared that the path was opening in front of them and closing behind as they moved slowly forward.

45

'S'lan recognises you as a friend and honoured guest of Ze Dryadi, Curos.' Xante chattered on as if totally unaware of his fear. He wondered darkly what would happen to an unsuspecting soldier who strayed into this region. When he asked Xante about this she replied, 'Why, it is simple, Curos. His body would be absorbed into Eternal S'lan. His alien soul would of course be free to depart back to the land of Chaw.' Curos shuddered as he remembered the clinging, crushing pressure which Xante's mind-power had exerted on him. That was how it would be pinned by the malevolent branches and held until dead. Crushed and squeezed and then absorbed into this disgusting, soggy soil.

Xante caught some drift of his thoughts and she turned, shocked, to speak to him. 'No, Curos, do not think of Eternal S'lan in that way. It only protects itself. Enter as a friend and observe the splendour of Eternal S'lan and be contented.'

Despite Xante's words, the oppressive, damp atmosphere and earthy smell progressively closed in on Curos as they moved deeper into the forest. The horses' pace began to falter and Curos needed to urge the animal on to keep up with Xante's long stride. It was with some relief that he realised the trees were beginning to open out to allow a view of sky ahead. It was not the end of the forest. The path sloped down in a series of gentle zigzags toward a small stream which flowed briskly under an arch of trees. Curos was again surprised at the abrupt change from the dry scrub-bush plain to the damp, fertile forest where such luxuriant growth and surface water could exist.

Xante stopped short and turned to take a firm grip on her horse's bridle. 'Quickly, Curos, stand still and cover your face,' she ordered in a voice barely louder than a whisper. 'The flying guardians are very agitated. Cover your face with your sash and do not speak.'

Curos hardly took the warning seriously but he responded to the urgency in Xante's voice. He wound his topaz-coloured sash around his head like a turban and drew the final turn over the lower part of his face. He was fastening the sash pin when he became aware of the angry buzzing of insect wings. Before he could ask any questions several large flying creatures were sur-rounding him.

He had a brief impression of a huge, eagle-sized dragonfly as it flew at him, forcing him to duck away. He cried out and dived across the soft earth into a rolling breakfall. As he sprang upright the razor-edged scimitar appeared in one hand, the chisel-pointed tantos in the other.

'Do not move suddenly,' warned Xante. 'Lower your sword, it will provoke attack. Give me time to reassure them.'

Curos did not intend to lower his sword. He was staring directly into the face of a huge, insect-like creature which hovered close to him. No words from Xante would quell the fear and disgust aroused by the hideous flying predator. Large, multi-faceted eyes regarded him malevolently and the extending dragonfly mouth seemed poised to tear away lumps of flesh. Curos was surrounded by three of the mutant creatures. The transparent wings were in constant motion, emitting an ominous buzz and filling the air with their iridescent shimmering. Slowly the creatures backed away and their extendable mouths retracted.

'I am sorry for that, Curos,' said Xante, indicating that they should proceed. 'Walk slowly until we are past the river.'

'Are those monstrosities your creatures?' asked Curos stiffly. 'They are slow to recognize a guest of your leader.'

'They are the F'gar,' she explained, still speaking quietly. 'For generations the original dragonflies have been bred and mutated to increase their size.'

'Your control of them seems to be rather weak,' interrupted Curos but Xante only laughed.

'A tame F'gar would be of little use to us. Generally they live as their ancestors did, as savage hunters around the streams and pools. They are conditioned not to attack the Dryadin and large forest animals. They respond to the feelings of the Dryad. Our concern and uncertainty over your news of the Warchaw has made the F'gar more defensive than usual.' Unthinkingly she stretched out her hand to stroke the brilliant yellow and green head of the dragonfly which kept pace with them. 'I hope I have reassured them. They grow tired quite quickly when they hover or fly slowly.'

Curos shuddered as he forced himself to look at the form and shape of the creatures. They did in many respects resemble dragonflies but were as long as a man's arm and seemed to be

47

more heavily built than their natural cousins. With the extendable mouth retracted, the furry head and antennae gave them an appearance of affectionate friendliness.

The F'gar accompanied Curos and Xante until they had forded the small, deep-flowing stream and were far on the other side.

'Are there many of your flying dragons in S'lan?' asked Curos as the creatures turned back to the river.

'No, their numbers are quite small or they would soon eat all the birds and fish in an area. In a time of real danger their pupae development can be stimulated to increase rapidly the number of adults. They can fly great distances to assist in repelling an attack. And of course,' she added as Curos mounted his nervous horse, 'they are only part of the forest's defence. The trees, the F'gar and the Dryadin can all combine as bid by Eternal S'lan to defeat an invader.'

Unimpressed by the subtle shades of green and brown and the damp, tree-smelling atmosphere, Curos was relieved that the path had opened out to permit riding. On his horse's back Curos looked up at the sky and his spirits rose. 'Could we run the horses?' he asked Xante.

'No, I will run,' she laughed, 'and you can ride your animal at my speed.' Without pause she set off in a loping wolf trot, followed by her horse.

'You will tire yourself, Xante,' he called out after several minutes.

'Never,' she shouted back. 'To run in Eternal S'lan is to gain strength at every stride. Even your puny legs would rejoice to be in contact with the living forest.' Curos snorted in disgust and barely restrained himself from spurring the war pony past Xante.

They ran on in this absurd fashion until they reached a large, clear space ringed with giant trees. Small family groups of Dryadin were to be seen seated or standing in a relaxed manner. Xante bounced to a stop and turned her face to Curos. Her head covering had been thrown back and he could now see her flushed face and sparkling eyes. Her ebony hair glistened like some peasant at toil. But no peasant girl could ever look so beautiful.

'Welcome, Lord Zachaw, to the southern meeting place of the Dryad,' she said with a mocking laugh, imitating the pompous voice of Chalak Konn. She bowed and droplets of perspiration fell onto the mossy soil. 'Curos, suppress those thoughts.' He laughed guiltily. 'My father approaches.'

A middle-age man strode over towards them and to Curos' surprise grabbed Xante in a firm embrace. Such behaviour before strangers would have been unthinkable to Curos' family.

'I believe your companion grows impatient at our lack of manners,' Xante's father said with an open smile.

'It is the Chaw way, Honoured Father,' she replied and then changed her voice to parody Chalak Konn's. 'Honoured Father, may your humble and unworthy daughter present the most Excellent Zachaw Ca'lin, commander of part of the 22nd T'sand of the great Army of Chaw.'

'Daughter, please. You embarrass us both,' the man said with a laugh.

'Curos, this is my father, Xatan,' she said, 'who really is honoured among the Dryadin as being Councillor for the sorcerers.'

'I am honoured to meet you, Zachaw,' bowed Xatan. 'We will have much to discuss in due time but now our leader, the Ze Dryadi, and other Councillors would wish to talk to you.'

As they walked to the Council meeting at the centre of the clearing, Xante talked excitedly with her father, their rapid speech strangely accented and difficult to follow. Curos was surprised that they should ignore a guest in this way but it gave him a brief chance to observe the other groups of people in the meeting place. It reminded him in some ways of meetings between the nomad N'gol clans of the Chaw desert regions: small family groups sitting quietly or welcoming friends, individuals standing or sitting as they exchanged news.

Ze Dryadi and Aalani-Galni welcomed Curos and introduced the other Council members who had been called to attend this meeting. As before, Curos observed no outward signs of rank or status and felt that the four men and one woman who represented the Dryad council lacked the appearance of power which he would have expected. Only Caflin-Bans, the Ze Dryadi, seemed to have the unmistakeable stamp of authority expected in a ruler.

Curos and Xante outlined to the Council their discussion of the previous few days but it was evident that the Dryad were unconvinced as to the power of the barbarian sorcerers and did not believe that such small armies could menace the Chaw people or the huge forest lands.

'I fear you may have been too sympathetic to this persuasive young man,' said one of the Councillors reproachfully. 'Even if your statements are true, what could be the motive of such invasions?'

'That is not known to us,' said Curos, mustering his arguments carefully. 'But my father has seen some of the results of the barbarous Warchaw as they have engulfed nation after nation.'

Curos explained how the Warchaw had occupied conquered lands and ruled them from impregnable castles constructed by sorcery and slave labour. Vast areas had been brutally depopulated; forest and farmland were reduced to plains of rolling grassland over which a few Warchaw rode and hunted.

'In far Iriam we estimate that after a hundred years of occupation only a few thousand persons survived from the original population of two milliion. Those Iriam who remain are enslaved to toil as craftsmen, farmers or herdsmen. Among the Warchaw only the profession of soldier or warrior is honourable and each has the ambition to rule his own fief.'

'I still cannot believe that they have such power,' said the Councillor.

'If you had ridden with me to Corninstan Road or stood with the defenders on the banks of the Janix, you would not disbelieve,' replied Curos.

There was silence for some time until Xante and her father, Xatan exchanged a few brief whispers.

'It would be possible to show our people what really happened,' explained Xatan to Curos, 'but it would mean Xante entering your mind and projecting your memories to the Council.' He paused to look hard at Curos. 'It would normally be regarded as a grave invasion of privacy but if you do not object . . .' His voice trailed off into an expressive gesture.

'I believe, sir, that your daughter has already penetrated deep into my mind and if the Council would believe the results I will accept your proposal.'

'It is impossible to lie during such a probing,' said the Ze Dryadi, 'but the subject must be willing and fully open. There must also be a degree of empathy between the two persons involved.'

Even while the Dryad was speaking Curos gradually felt Xante's mind making contact with his. This time there was no pain or pressure but he could hardly stop a rising tide of fear sweeping over his self-control.

'There is no need to fear me, Curos.' Her voice sounded deep in his consciousness. 'You know that now. Just remember back to the start of your first encounter with the barbarians. No, not just the sorcerer, think back to the start.'

Immediately Curos was in the grip of his own personal nightmare, but this time others shared his memories. The images in his mind were projected into a vivid, life-sized scene. Every detail of every view which had been captured by Curos' eye now formed starkly in mid-air before the assembly. The din and the smells of the battlefield were terrifyingly real. Dryad children shrieked and hid their faces at the flashes of demonic fire which had halted the Wind regiments. Adults covered their ears to block out the screams of the wounded and dying. The air in the forest meeting place was filled with the smell of burning and warm-flowing blood. Ze Dryadi turned away from the horrors of the massacre which followed the Chaw defeat as the barbarian foot-soldiers advanced across the devastation of the battlefield, systematically slaughtering the wounded. No experience in S'lan had prepared the Dryad watchers for this.

Xante's face became ashen and drawn at the strain of projecting the images and the mirage developed a shimmering unsteadiness. As through a blistering heat haze the assembled Dryadin felt the defiant despair of Zachaw Curos as he waited sword in hand for the final charge of the two barbarian cavalrymen. Then as the horsemen gathered momentum there came a savage, blinding flash of yellow light.

This was no vision, no mental projection, but the flash from Curos' Topaz. It released the energy absorbed from Xante's sorcery and threw off her link with Curos. The mind picture was blasted away, leaving the Dryadin stunned and dazed by the power of the reaction. Ze Dryadi himself called out in fear and summoned S'lan to his aid.

The tension diffused into a strained and breathless silence, broken only by the sound of the wind moving the trees. Whispered conversation and reassurance developed as the Dryads realised that Eternal S'lan still protected them. The Dryad Councillors had not escaped from the shock of the images or the violent reaction of the yellow stone. Slowly they realised that Curos' strange Topaz bore them no malice, but that its power was as nothing compared to that of the Western sorcerers.

The forced re-enactment had left Curos shuddering with fatigue but neither he nor Xante had been affected by the Topaz. As they emerged from the trance-like state of the mind probe Xante said wearily, 'There was a second battle at the River Janix.'

'No! We have seen enough of the war of men,' Ze Dryadi exclaimed in disgust.

'How could any people so desire to kill in such numbers?' said Aalani-Galni.

'I believe we all now understand the power which imperils both our lands,' added the female Councillor, 'but I do not believe we should be involved in these wars. Our forest defences are strong and have been proved many times.'

There was a pause as if the Council was uncertain as to how to proceed. Finally Ze Dryadi addressed Curos, 'Would you please leave us, Zachaw, that we may speak together freely in our fashion? Xante will see that you receive food and drink. I fear your ordeal has weakened you,' he added sympathetically as Curos stumbled drunkenly to his feet.

The food was an unusual mix of dried forest nuts, fruit and grain, while the drink was water mixed with wild honey.

'We would normally have a salad mixture of various leaves, shoots and edible fungi in addition to this dried food,' explained Xante. 'But it is not permitted to gather food close to the large meeting places lest so many people harm the forest.'

'This is quite sufficient, Madam Sorceress,' Curos replied as he stirred the unpalatable mixture. 'I have no great desire to go collecting fungi! I fear also that your "flying guardians" might consider me an edible Chaw!'

Xante was called back to the Council, leaving Curos isolated and alone. Wherever he looked he could sense that the groups of Dryads were now avoiding his gaze, and trying to ignore his disturbing presence.

Despite the most graphic representation of the Warchaw's power it became evident to Curos that no rapid decisions would be taken by these people. It was growing on into evening when Aalani-Galni and Xante's father, Xatan approached him. Aalani said, 'I fear that even your most eloquent demonstration of events in Corninstan has failed to convince our elders that it is necessary to assist the Chaw in their struggle.'

'You are not convinced of the power that besets all the peoples of the East?'

'Yes,' answered Xatan, 'but the concern of the Dryadin is for Eternal S'lan only. There may be better ways to protect the forest than to open our power to the Chaw who, since after the time of Xan II, have increasingly diverged from us. It needs much consideration.'

'Then I shall return to my camp and await your decision,' replied Curos with barely suppressed irritation, 'but I doubt there is much more to be considered.'

'It is our elders' belief that it would be better for you to stay in the forest as our guest,' said Aalani. 'Your force of soldiers is quite close and, with such a dynamic leader, could prove a threat to us. You are of course free to depart if you wish, but none of the Dryadin will be permitted to act as your guide.'

Curos was quite aware that without a Dryad to conduct him past the F'gar and through the 'Closed Ways' it would not be possible for him to retreat safely from the forest. 'I would gladly accept the Ze Dryadi's hospitality,' he replied, 'and would truly welcome the opportunity to learn more of the Dryadin. I fear, however, that I discomfit these people and my soldiers will grow anxious if I do not return.'

'I will act as your host,' said Aalani, 'and can provide writing materials for you to send a message to your captains – your seal and signature will verify authenticity.'

8

Curos spent an uncomfortable night in the forest. Although the Dryad people were most courteous and provided him with a sleeping place in one of their long houses, it was clear that he was a virtual prisoner with Aalani-Galni, his personal guard. Xante had departed with her father.

The long house was situated some distance from the meeting place and served several related Dryad families. It was comfortable enough, with the floor constructed well above ground level, the vertical poles beneath giving it the appearance of a house on stilts. During the night Curos was aware of the alien atmosphere: sounds of sleeping Dryadin and the forest noises; smells of close dampness and a people not his own. All the time he was surrounded by a sense of being watched, aware that neither the spirit of the forest nor its people trusted him.

The discussions between the Dryadin people proceeded through the next day and into another, with Curos only seldom called to expand on some point of interest or confusion. It was evident that the high Dryadin, such as Council members, hardly needed to use speech at all as they conversed but vocalised their thoughts more for the benefit of those of lesser ability. They were also capable of exchanging information with elders in the ten principal regions of the forest.

Curos became more and more irritated by the time-wasting progress of the discussions and conferences which were even worse than any in Chaw. The N'gol side of Curos, which he owed to his mother, fretted at such a period of inactivity and stillness with little to do but observe this strange, contradictory people. In personal relationships they seemed open and free. It was not unusual to see friends or relatives embrace or for acquaintances to touch hands or arms as they conversed. Their conversations, however, always proceeded slowly as if speaking were difficult – or possibly in many cases superfluous. It could be, Curos concluded that for the Dryad the achievement of empathy was more important than words, and that once this was achieved a minimum of verbal communication was sufficient. The impression of deep tranquillity and unity of purpose became as oppressive to Curos as the forest environment. Here all the undercurrents of differing opinions or views seemed to be submerged.

The second day passed and another night was spent in the forest long hut, where he was now made more welcome at the communal meal. Twelve people – three couples, their children and a young unmarried woman – shared the long house in a state of dream-like Dryad peacefulness. Evidently the Dryadin were virtual nomads within the forest, extended family groups moving from place to place as the comfortable but temporary dwellings became unsound every two or three years. Most Dryadin practised handcrafts with a varying degree of practicality and decorative value but a few were true craftsmen who devoted their time to pottery, leatherwork, weaving and the like in more permanent areas. Pottery and metal-working which required fire were extremely specialised and their products were reserved for only the most essential uses. The unmarried woman of this group was a skilled worker of wood.

The third day of Curos' semi-captivity dawned to a new air of expectation and tension. At first Curos half believed this was due to a decision being reached but it soon became clear that the change in atmosphere had been generated between the Dryadin themselves. The early morning meal was taken before the men and boys drifted away, then other women began to arrive, and regarded Curos and Aalani with some surprise.

'It is time we departed,' said Aalani to Curos, with no other explanation. As they walked back into the familiar wide clearing of the meeting place Aalani was a little more forthcoming. 'Tonight is our Festival of Ki Fru.'

'The same as our peasants' ritual?'

'Yes, and more. The forest life is civilised in many ways, primitive in others. Three times a year we meet to dispense justice, if needed, and to bring our dispersed people together. Fortunately it is at such a time that Chaw ambassador Curos chose to visit us; rapid discussion would not have been possible if the more isolated groups had not been assembled at the area meeting places.'

Curos was aware of groups of people of the same age and gender forming around particular long houses: young men here, young women there; older children with younger brothers and sisters; a group of elders, men and women, in comfortable conversation. Beneath all the affability Curos could still detect an unusual air of tension and expectation.

Aalani led him towards one of the groups of men who were aged between thirty or forty years.

'My peers, I suppose one could say,' Aalani said with irony. 'At least they are of my generation and accept me up to a point.' He waved aside Curos' questions as they approached the informal bunch of friends. Curos was introduced in an easy manner by Aalani and took a seat with the others, content to observe how the morning would develop. After a little consideration one of the men was elected as the president of what developed into a good-natured competition in a number of martial sports. Curos joined in several jitsu bouts and was surprised by the strength and skill of his opponents. There were no champions here of the calibre of Wan Abbac, but without the spur and freedom to use combat strikes Curos was not surprised to lose several contests.

On one such occasion he picked himself up from a fast, sweeping leg-throw and bowed before leaving the circle. His opponent offered Curos a drink from one of the barrels which stood under the shadow of the trees. The water he sipped from the decorated wooden beaker was ice-cold but tasted slightly earthy, almost musty. His new friend smiled at Curos' surprise. 'The taste grows on one throughout the day, as its effect grows stronger.'

'But not for a Chaw,' interrupted Aalani, taking the beaker from Curos and handing it back. 'You had better keep to pure water.'

The other Dryad looked annoyed for a second but then drained the beaker himself. 'Another abstainer, Aalani,' he commented good-naturedly.

As the Jitsu competitions petered out due to exhaustion, an archery target was set out against the Long House wall and new interest was generated. Although most of the party were willing

56

to compete, it was quite clear to Curos that few of them would match his skill. What little shooting was practised in the forest was usually at short distances with light bows. Only those such as Aalani and Xante who had a special interest in this weapon possessed bows of quality and power.

Most of the morning had gone. A light meal was passed around and Curos realised that nearly all of the company were now drinking freely of the strange-tasting liquid which appeared to have a relaxing and uninhibiting quality. Curos and Aalani retained their clothing but the others stripped and began to decorate their bodies in painted stripes, swirls and dots, patterns of extreme barbarity from an ancient past. Curos realised that throughout the meeting place men and women had discarded almost all clothing to give full freedom to their skin painting. Here and there snatches of wild, rushing music broke out, swirled and died.

'I wish no part in this, Aalani.' stated Curos, 'and it seems that you too remain separate. Or have you been ordered to keep the Chaw outsider from harm?'

'Both,' replied Aalani. 'I am separated from the others and am therefore ideal to attend to Ze Dryadi's guest.'

'And the Sorceress Xante-Yani, is she part of this?'

'Most definitely, as will be her father and Dromo – her lover, you could call him. Xante is a true child of the forest and on days and nights such as these her passion and her pleasures will be completely uninhibited. Would that I could be that free!' Aalani's voice held a hint of bitterness.

A procession of elders was making its way to the centre of the meeting place. They retained their long robes and cowled hoods but their faces were painted into grotesque masks like those of the people. A horn-like note sounded and the Dryadin began to assemble in a large circle.

'First comes judgement and punishment and then celebration and frenzy,' breathed Aalani to Curos. It became clear that a young Dryad couple had produced a child before consent had been given. She had been absent from the forest for several months with others who were attempting to revitalise a barren area of the D'was. On her return their passion had been quite understood, even approved, but her body had forgotten the cycle

57

of fertility in the forest and she had conceived. Above all else the Dryad law required a stable and carefully regulated population and only when one person died was permission given to a couple to have a child. Under such law the child was innocent but a place could only be opened for it by the death of an adult. With both parents equally guilty, both would die.

The father attempted to look defiant and made a lucid and reasoned plea for mitigation. The mother stood with the defeated eyes of a person who had given up hope, the baby clutched to her chest, and said nothing. Her parents offered their lives as forfeit for their daughter, but this too was rejected. The mother of the deadly child opened her dress and began to feed her baby. To the cynical this might have been construed as her last chance to evoke sympathy but even Curos realised that the woman knew she was to die and was seeking the last maternal contact with her child.

With slow force the child was taken from her and given to another woman who, with her partner, would rear it as her own. In despair the man rushed to his lover for one last embrace before they were pulled apart and led to their separate places of execution. Men and women in the crowd separated and Curos found himself following the men summoned to watch the father's death.

Curos had witnessed executions in the Chaw capital city of G'tal and had seen men die in battle but he saw no need to participate in this spectacle. He started to move away but beside his elbow Aalani said, 'My friend, you said you need to know the Dryadin. If we are to be your allies, you need to know our strengths and our weakness. You have seen our placid nature, now you should also see our cruelty and our frenzy.'

Reluctantly Curos followed the naked throng of male bodies to the Place of Men's Death. There a fast-growing tree had been bent over and its main branches cut off. Each shoot from the trunk had been sharpened into a shortened spike less than a finger's-width high from the trunk. Nearby similar trees bore the fruits of previous executions, with vertical branches growing through ribcages and pelvis bones.

The Dryad was bent backwards and pressed onto the living, sharp spikes of the tree. With a large, hardwood club both his

58

thigh-bones and his arms were systematically broken so that the mutilated limbs could be tied downwards over the tree-trunk. At first he had tried to suppress his screams; at the end each new indignity brought a barely audible gasp from the shattered body. Two longer but equally sharp shoots were forced into his neck behind the jawbones so that they would grow into the skull.

'He will die in less than a day,' explained Aalani, 'between the broken limbs and quick-growing shoots.'

'Is it necessary to inflict such injuries?' asked Curos.

'It is dependent upon guilt,' replied Aalani. 'An evil man receives no injuries and can take up to five days to die as the tree's new branches grow through him.'

Already the Dryadin were moving away, leaving the stricken man unheeded in his death agony. Some distance away a sharp woman's scream rang out, followed by a gutteral gasp of pain. The penalty exacted on the mother was no less severe.

In the meeting place wild, barbaric music had started to sound and Dryadin of all ages were beginning a slow but swirling dance. Wooden flutes, hand drums and pipes blended in a wind of sound which beat upon and inflamed the senses. At first the dancing was restrained with rings of Dryadin advancing and circling in shuffling steps which bore little relation to the driving rhythms. As the light began to fade the circles dissolved into sets and then into individual couples, steps became faster and more abandoned. Some would leave the dance to eat, drink the musty, drug-laced water, or produce their own musical instruments to replace a musician who felt a need to dance. There was no fire to provide light as in a Chaw country dance, but a pale green, unnatural light seeped out from the surrounding forest.

Sitting to one side of the main celebrations with Aalani and several other sober individuals, Curos felt an extreme sense of being an outcast, an unwanted stranger. As if reading his thoughts, Aalani stood up and beckoned Curos to follow. They passed the group of children, younger ones sleeping peacefully, older ones gazing at the whirling mass of adults in a drug-induced daze. The green luminescence extended out into the forest trees, away from the clearing where the celebration had already transformed into a rite of uninhibited passion. They passed several couples and groups of slithering, naked men and women. The laughter and gasps of exertion and pleasure were unmistakable. Towards the edge of the luminescent area a young man held a girl under her arms, supporting her weight so that her legs could lock around his companion who thrust viciously into her. The sounds were of the most wanton lust Curos could imagine. A second girl approached hesitantly and then flowed into the group, her hands staking her claim, her mouth kissing.

Outside the area of light the forest was cool and still, only the permeating music or a riot of laughter occasionally cutting through the trees. Again, Curos experienced an intense feeling of being rejected and outside the oneness of these people. It was as if the forest sensed and resented his sobriety on this night of lust. The path ascended slowly and ended at a rocky outcrop of considerable size where no trees grew. Here in the moonlight several other fully clothed Dryads were sitting apart, hooded and cowled against the music and madness which floated up from the forest.

'I know how you must feel, my friend.' Aalani addressed Curos in a subdued voice. 'It is a madness which revolts me too.'

'That girl, the one with the two youths, was barely a woman – the night could end badly for her. Has she no parents?'

'She is as much a woman as the boys were men,' replied Aalani. 'Her parents are with each other or with others in the same grip of passion.' He led Curos to where a small outcrop made convenient seating and produced rolled up mats and a large pitcher from a concealing depression. He handed the pitcher to Curos. 'Wholesome drink if not of clear vintage. I ferment honey and wild fruit to form a substitute for wine and keep it for these nights.'

Curos drank deeply, then asked, 'How is it that a man and a woman were executed, mutilated, for producing a child, when less than half a day later the elders condone and encourage behaviour which will produce scores of children, some in girls too young for childbirth?'

'There will be no children conceived tonight,' stated Aalani. 'In the forest our people are only fertile at one time of the year so that children are born in late spring when the growth flourishes and food is abundant. Tonight will satiate desire and give release

60

from the monotony of our lives. By the next full moon a different drink and different music will dull the frenzy that has been ignited tonight. Young people will be discreetly chaperoned; couples and lovers will sleep apart for thirty days unless they are permitted children.'

'A strange life indeed,' commented Curos, 'but for the rest of the year there is freedom from unwanted children.' He gestured a refusal to an offer of more drink and said, 'I fear my head is weak against wine or beer and tonight I do not want to lose what reason I have. You and these few,' he pointed discreetly, 'do not join the – the celebration?' As so often, Aalani did not respond to the question and they again sat without speaking.

The night wore on and Curos observed to Aalani, 'The music, has it changed? The tempo is less wild, less driving, almost sinister.'

'Yes, it is now the dangerous stage. At first the people are drawn together to dance, to touch and to use up their personal lusts. Now as a group they roam and hunt. Those of us who are not one with them can be in danger.' Curos instinctively adjusted the position of his sword and dagger to be more easily to hand but Aalani continued. 'There are several "safe" places in the forest where we will not be disturbed; this is one of them.'

The moon was now full and below them Curos caught glimpses of couples or groups running amongst the trees as in some game. Laughter and voices rang through the forest, but the music spoke of an implied danger and Curos felt as if he was being sought out. The Topaz hanging at his chest had been quiescent but now began to glow with a smouldering light – giving a warning to an attacker or acting as a beacon?

'There is no need to be restless. Up here we are quite safe,' Aalani said reassuringly. Curos knew he was wrong: someone was seeking him out, he could sense their movement through the forest like a coursing hound. The presence drew nearer. He saw a more purposeful figure running towards the hill with fluid strides, a young female. The movement of muscles driving the long legs and the slight movement of her firm breasts sent the white spiral patterns on her naked skin shimmering in the full moonlight. Despite Aalani's restraining hand, Curos stood up and even before he could recognise her face in the dim light he

61

knew it was Xante. The power of her legs drove her up the slope until she stood less than four paces from Curos. She smiled and his bones turned to water. The predatory lust in her face and the deep blackness of her eyes held no terror for him. He could drown in their passion and be reborn to love her again.

'Nothing is forbidden tonight, nothing is hidden.' The words did not so much sound as flow into his brain.

'Stop! Xante, you are not to do this!,' said Aalani in a voice of authority new to him that night. It was as if Xante had not seen him before: her head turned a fraction and the face changed hard and strained and as dangerous as a wolf. Her hands came up into a Jitsu attacking position, long, claw-like nails extending into talons, her teeth bared in animal fury. There was no recognition of Aalani in her eyes and the malice and threat she directed at him were reflected in the movement of her body and arms.

'You cannot intimidate me, Xante, for all your power. He is not for you, go back to Dromo. You are not permitted here on the night of Ki Fru. Ze Dryadi forbids you this man.'

'He is not like you, uncle,' she snarled, her threat not abating. 'I feel his spirit. He comes with me, he will be one with me in the forest.'

Curos was recovering from the impact of her beauty and her naked passion which had threatened to carry him to her.

At the edge of the trees a naked, patterned man had arrived, fatigued with the exertion of a hard run. 'Xante!' he called. 'Leave this place and come with me. We are together. It is Dromo. Come away now.' She ignored his pleading and turned her face to stare openly and questioningly at Curos. He could smell the earth and trees and feel her sexuality radiating out to him. Her tongue darted just visible between barely parted lips, the Wind of Sh Ren swept over him and he knew that they could ignore Aalani and Dromo. As his resolve faltered a new light of expectation flared across her face. He found new strength and his purpose held. Defiantly she smiled and tossed her head back and thrust her body forward.

'I will leave you this night, horse-rider, but I have put forward only a fraction of my power. These two could not stand in my way.' The black hair flew like the mane of a thoroughbred mare as she looked with disdain at Aalani and then she called to Dromo. 'I am not yours, Dromo. I will not be with you this night. For the rest of this night I run alone In S'lan the Eternal. Out of duty I desist but one day I will have what I seek.'

In a flash of patterned skin she was gone, sprinting down the hill and into the trees, toughened feet skipping over rocks and tree-roots. She was gone and Curos' heart died. With more sadness than he could have imagined, he slumped to the ground and drank very deeply of Aalani's honey wine.

'Am I a man or a gelding?' he cried out loud.

'A man of great resolve and purpose,' spoke Aalani. 'What Xante wanted tonight would have destroyed you both, but you held firm.'

'And if I had gone with her?' asked Curos in a defeated, regretful voice.

'You did waver, but then you rallied,' said Aalani. 'If necessary I would have acted. One day Xante will surpass us all in the extent of her power but as yet I could, with Dromo's help, repel her from this place.'

'And if I had fought on her side?'

'The potential is frightening – but,' he shrugged, 'I do not know.'

After some time Aalani drank the last of his wine and said to Curos, 'I fear I must explain much if you are to be able to trust the Dryadin and trust Xante. I have special skills. I have travelled from the forest many times in my forty years and know the life of the N'gol and a little of the Chaw. The Dryadin are not like the N'gol herdsmen with their riding and their fighting. We are herdsmen of trees, we regulate the animals of the forest, plant and transplant seedlings, check fires and stop over-active spread of fungus and parasites. It is a slow, peaceful task. But if real danger threatens from outside then the Dryadin must fight, as the N'gol would to protect their herds. That is why the Dryadin in S'lan must practise war-like arts and have the ferocity to use them. The population must be kept small to maintain the balance of the forest but if disease or war was to deplete our numbers there must be the vitality to recover quickly.'

'I could drink more than a pitcher of wine,' interrupted Curos, who was still quite shaken and cramped by physical remorse and his own unfulfilled visions.

'There is only water left,' apologised Aalani. 'To solve our problem the Dryadin have all the fire, the passion and the vitality of the N'gol but it is held in check except for the festivals when it is released in a safe way. Passion without children, hunting for outsiders without quarry, as you have seen.'

'You are not one with the forest or the people, as you would say, but you would die for S'lan?' Curos asked.

'Of course. It is my life's purpose.' He looked directly at Curos. 'I do not seek to be alone, my friend, it is not easy. But in me there is a flaw, a flaw not noticed at birth or I should have been returned to the void immediately. I cannot fully surrender to the joint will, the oneness. Even if I drink the mescalin water, there is part of me deep in here which will not surrender. I can love women, I can kill men, but at my will. These others on the hill have a similar problem and because of their worth to S'lan have been granted refuge here in safety. The woman over there and I have been lovers from time to time and have had . . .' He checked himself, then continued, 'I am not allowed to father children but in other ways can be permitted to live.'

'It is difficult to comprehend,' said Curos. 'For the N'gol and for some Chaw, surrender is impossible. Death with honour is always respected above surrender of principle.'

'It is not in surrender of principle but surrender of individuality that I fail.'

'And Xante, she has no difficulty in submitting?' asked Curos with an edge to his voice which was not missed by Aalani.

'Not until now. She truly loves S'lan. I am her uncle – I loved her mother Yani, but I was denied by law and Yani took my brother. Xante is the daughter I might have had, Curos, and I fear for her. Her soul burns with fire and rushes like the wind.'

'As say the N'gol.'

'As say the N'gol,' agreed Aalani. 'But to a N'gol a Dryad would be two people. One is a stoical H'tao who loves all living things; the other fights and ruts like a mad animal. She will remember little of what happened tonight, Curos. Ki Fru rules but for one day and is forgotten. It is not permitted to speak of what you saw. I can see you are jealous of Dromo, as he will be jealous of you, but she is destined for neither of you. Xante has deceived herself that her passion with Dromo has a basis of love; now her duty to S'lan and this night has broken that bond. It may break Dromo's spirit. S'lan alone knows what it will do to Xante.'

9

A new day dawned in the forest to find the people fresh and recovered. The orgy of Ki Fru was forgotten. Where yesterday, glints of anticipation had prompted embarrassed looks or unease between couples or friends all was now swept clean and fresh. Hidden yearning and dark thoughts had been exorcised in the madness of one day and the dazed tranquillity of the next. A new level of tenderness had appeared in the personal relationships between couples in the long house where Curos stayed.

He was reflecting on the events of the previous night when he realised that the leader of the Dryadin, Ze Dryadi himself, had entered the Long House. 'Your words are hard and powerful, Zachaw Ca'lin Curos,' said Ze Dryadi, arousing Curos from his thoughts. 'But we have considered them deeply. Come now and hear our decision.' There was no mention of the events of the previous days, the executions and the debauchery, but Curos felt that Ze Dryadi had intended that he, Curos, should see and understand as much as possible of the Dryadin world.

When they were seated with the others, the Dryadin leader continued, 'What you have said and shown us now rings true and explains many things. The changing of the seasons, less rainfall in the forest and the stress and disorder we have felt in the earth and air. The wise among our people have felt power and fear working far off.'

'And,' said the female Councillor who had expressed the greatest doubts, 'the lack of contact with the dwindling few Dryads of the Iriam forest. I fear that we have not gazed out often enough from the beauty and the safety of Eternal S'lan to see the danger gathering.'

Curos had not seen Xante since the night of Ki Fru but when she joined the Council group her face was set hard and she spoke no words and offered no greeting.

'So, honourable Zachaw,' said the Ze Dryadi, 'We reaffirm our aid to you, but our people are few and widely scattered.

Our magic is slow and diffuse. Only a very few of us have the power which you call sorcery, and they already have tasks in Eternal S'lan.' He held up his hand to silence Curos' exclamation. 'You forget your Chaw manners, young War Lord,' he said with a smile, but there was none of the previous curtness in his voice. 'Let me continue. There was an opinion which held that we of S'lan should stand apart from this war of men and only defend the forest when need calls. But now that view has not prevailed, and it has been decided that Xante will stay with you and we will send whatever additional help we can as it is needed.' Curos felt the tension in Xante. Her face was as if carved of hard, yellow stone as the Dryad leader spoke. 'From within S'lan one of our teachers of sorcery will project his thoughts to improve her skills.'

The next words were partly to the girl. 'Xante and I have already spoken and her task is hard,' Ze Dryadi said. 'Each time the Teacher Dromo stretches out his mind to her in the alien land she will remember what might have been. But remember Xante's bond with Dromo was already broken.'

The discussions continued for some little time but Xante did not speak. Only when they walked away from the Council did she show some emotion. 'Before we depart, honoured K'tan,' she said to Curos, 'I would talk a little with my father.' He stared directly ahead to avoid looking at the tears which he felt must be on her face. 'I would have speech with my honoured mother too, but she is far away.' The voice was near breaking.

'I will leave you,' said Curos in a matter-of-fact tone, feigning ignorance at her distress so as not to cause her loss of face. 'I will see that the horses have been well cared for,' he added as he strode off. His own mind was swept by a wind of confusion contrasting the painted savage of the night with the penitent duty Xante had shown at the meeting. As Aalani had suggested, it appeared that Xante remembered little of their meeting or the excesses of the ritual night. How many times had she and Dromo lusted together, how many other men had she sought when Dromo tired?

When they left the gathering place Xante walked in front, leading the pony, her face at all times turned from him. His own thoughts were locked up with future plans into which lightning flashes of memory and jealousy streaked unheeded. The slight mind aura which he had learned to feel from Xante and which had proved so threatening when restraint disappeared was blank and withdrawn from him. She blamed Curos for her sorrows and he resented her actions; the tension between them was growing dangerous.

The silence continued until they came to the Closed Way and Curos was forced to dismount. Some action, some sympathy was needed but he had no skill. Gently reaching out to Xante, he turned her around and looked into her face. Her tears had dried, leaving her eyelids red and sore, but it was the utter deadness of all expression which struck him most forcibly. The frenzy of the rite was deeply buried. He started to voice consoling words but she silenced him with a gesture.

'Do not talk to me of duty, Zachaw,' she said icily. 'I know my duty. It is my duty to go into your land with its hideous smelling, noisy people. It is my duty to leave Eternal S'lan and have my lover broken away from me. It is my duty to have to allow him to teach me mind communication and to know when he has found another woman. That is my duty, Zachaw Ca'lin, and I do not weep over my duty. I weep to mourn a friend who is now lost to me.'

Curos had seen many weeping women. Each of his wives wept regularly at his lack of interest or concern for them, but in those cases he could face them until they dropped their heads in frustration and self-pity. Xante did not weep like that. She stared fiercely into Curos' eyes as her tears welled up and flowed down her cheeks. Eventually it was Curos who turned away.

'I do not need your help or sympathy, Lord Zachaw,' she said huskily, 'but I would beg your leave to divert some little way from our journey. I would be alone with my grief and would still my mind . . .'

'Then I will wait with the horses,' said Curos.

'It would not be safe for you. These trees are hostile to all outsiders and my misplaced emotion has roused them unnaturally.' Without saying more she began to move off.

Several times Xante stopped as if to check her progress until after some time they approached a dense knot of thorn trees. Her voice was not composed as she broke the silence, 'Turn away, Curos. This is not for you to see.' Even after this warning Curos stared fixedly as by her strange power she induced the wrapped thorn branches to fold back. There, impaled on a sharpened branch, was the naked body of a young woman. The blood-stained stump of wood protruded through her chest and her broken arms were drawn backwards round the trunk.

Curos had seen executions, executions of hideous and prolonged cruelty, but none matched this sickening futility. Even the death of the woman's husband had not seemed so extreme. 'What did she do . . . to deserve this?' His voice was a whisper, hardly louder than the surrounding birdsong. He knew the answer but could not believe that was the totality of the woman's crime.

'Nothing could deserve this,' replied Xante, her voice still flat and dead. 'She had a child before it was permitted, that is all.'

'Is that her only crime?'

'Yes. In Eternal S'lan all things not permitted are a crime and the Dryadin punish this way. But this is unjust, her circumstances pleaded for mercy. Her body is untouched even after three days, protected by the very tree which they used to kill her, a sign that Eternal S'lan is witness to her innocence.'

Xante said no more but knelt in concentration for some time. Curos turned away from the scene and stood looking at the peaceful, many hued trees with new eyes. He started at Xante's touch on his shoulder.

'We can go now. Melini is far away. Her spirit and that of her lover are together. Their child is well cared for by another Dryad family. There is nothing more to do.'

'All in Eternal S'lan is not perfect,' said Curos.

'No, Curos, all in Eternal S'lan is far from perfect. Only Eternal S'lan itself is perfect.'

When they had passed through the last tangled trees of the Closed Way Xante looked hard at Curos and said, 'You have what you want, a sorceress for a slave, a promise of more help. Are you contented?'

'No,' said Curos. 'I have what I need to start a long fight and struggle. There is no contentment in any of that for me.'

'Then learn one thing from me, Curos. When your mind is in

69

grief or turmoil, it needs sleep. To sleep the body needs to be exhausted.'

Without further explanation Xante stripped off her head covering and tunic-coat. She rammed them hastily into the pony's saddle-bags and handed the reins to Curos. Still without speaking, she began to run towards the camp. Curos followed on horseback. He saw the linen shirt grow wet and the iron-yellow face redden and twist with pain as Xante ran on and on for nearly two hours until the camp was in sight.

10

By the time Xante reached the camp the long run from the forest had reduced her to a stumbling, exhausted figure. She was hardly recognisable as the aloof, almost sinister Dryad sorceress who had become known to the Chaw guardsmen or as the tigerish woman Curos had seen in the forest. As she staggered towards Curos' tent one of the soldiers exchanged a barely audible remark to a comrade. Xante stiffened with embarrassment, but before Curos could dismount Ataman Wan stalked up to the guardsman and struck him a vicious blow across the face. The force of the open-handed slap brought the man to his knees, eyes streaming.

'Guardsman, your remark has caused our commander annoyance. I, Wan, have said that the commander would be proud of his guard, the first Ulus of the First Hund. A guardsman does not speak on duty unless to answer a superior; a guardsman does not annoy his officer. Understand and correct your miserable conduct. Stand up.' The man unfolded his knees from the submissive position and stood up only to be struck down by a second blow to the other side of his face. 'And you are a disgrace to my Ulus,' snarled Wan. 'You will improve, repeat!'

'I am a disgrace to the guard Ulus, Ataman,' said the man through bruised and swelling lips, 'but I will improve.'

Curos ignored the incident and hastily organised a meal for the exhausted girl. The stress and fatigue of the day's events worked swiftly with the diluted wine to ensure that Xante was asleep less than half an hour after arriving back at the camp.

Despite Xante's distress and his own personal confusion of feelings, Curos was well satisfied with the main outcome of the meeting with the Dryads. He felt compelled to discuss at least some of this with his officers, particularly Bhal Morag. At Curos' request the officer arrived hurriedly, before Curos had finished washing outside the main tent. Waving formality aside, he continued to pull on his blue silk shirt. 'It is a mild evening, Morag.

71

Please sit out here with me and take some tea while the evening meal is being prepared.'

'It will be an honour, commander,' Bhal Morag replied. 'K'tan Chalak begs to be excused, he is checking our stores with the Ataman of logistics.'

Curos concealed his annoyance at Chalak Konn's lack of civility and began an account of the talks he had held with Ze Dryadi. As he spoke he realised the necessity of making a written record for the Ruling Council. An appropriate task for Chalak, he thought, imagining the elegant calligraphy and phrasing the ambitious officer would use in any document to the Ruling Council.

It was several hours later before Curos had settled down to sleep but almost immediately it seemed to him he was awakened by Xante moving. It was just before daybreak. Their conversation was slow with many pauses as they discussed the events of the previous day and what lay ahead. At one stage Curos said, 'I lead a girl's horse so that she can run herself into the ground and my officers consider me a cruel torturer of women.'

'Life is unjust,' Xante replied from the darkness, 'and tomorrow you will order this woman to ride her horse around the camp for an hour.'

'Why?'

'For me to practise my riding. I will need some hard-soled boots to protect my feet from the stirrups.' Curos agreed as Xante continued, 'After my riding I will run leading your horse to exercise my legs. It will all add to your reputation as a hard man who knows how to rule men and degrade women.'

The next day Xante and Curos visited the camp leather worker. A cobbler journeyman by trade, he had accompanied the expedition in the hope of gaining a better profit than could be obtained working in the shop of a craftsman. He was noted for his skill, able to repair a saddle or harness as quickly as a pair of boots, but it was said that he made as much profit with the gaming dice and the Jongg chips as he did with his awl and needle.

'Greetings,' said Curos as the man bowed respectfully. 'I am

72

well pleased with the riding boots you have made for me and would have you fashion a similar pair for the Lady Dryad.'

'Thank you, Lord,' the man replied. 'The other pair that you required, with full felt lining for winter, are nearly completed.'

He produced bulky leather cushions for Xante and Curos and then begged most civilly to be able to measure Xante's feet. Without hesitation she drew off a soft leather shoe which the cobbler examined with interest. 'Most odd stitching, madam,' he commented, 'a wild pigskin upper and an unusual sole.'

His head was deferentially bowed but his half-lascivious eyes sought to penetrate Xante's veil as she replied, 'It is a material woven from cured strips of Linaria bark. It wears well and is supple to allow movement.'

'It allows the stirrups to bruise a tender foot,' he started to comment but stopped in surprise. Xante's long, narrow foot had only four almost equal-length toes and pointed, claw-like nails. Looking up instinctively, he saw that her gloved hand possessed three fingers and a thumb.

'What is the matter?' Xante asked, a trace of annoyance in her voice.

'The lady has a strangely shaped foot,' muttered the cobbler, 'only four toes.'

'It shocks you?' She laughed. 'It is normal. Remember I am a Dryad, not a Chaw woman. Did you notice my hands before, Curos?' Her fingers did indeed seem long and thin – particularly so when she removed the dark gloves. 'This, too, is different,' she added and stretched out her sharp, claw-like nails. Curos had forgotten the claws and the way they had extended when Xante had faced and threatened Aalani. The darkness and terror of that night would cloud his feelings towards her for a long time.

The cobbler shook his head in disbelief but refused to be flustered. 'Is madam able to do that with her feet?' he asked as if it were a normal question at a shoe fitting.

'Why yes, usually when climbing. The nails can push through the woven sole, look, on the left foot.'

'I see. Then, madam, I will leave extra room for the nails and put slightly more felt padding under madam's toes.'

As the cobbler leapt up to bring his screve board on which to

73

draw around her feet, Xante whispered with some concern, 'He is shocked, Curos, almost revolted.'

'He is only a peasant craftsman.' Curos smiled. 'One who has been in trouble over more than one man's wife. It will be a change for him to be unsettled by a woman.'

'Do I unsettle you as much, Curos?'

'A married nobleman, travelled and experienced, such as I?' Curos remonstrated with mock pomposity. 'I have ceased to be surprised by women, Dryad or Human.'

'Liar,' she purred sweetly, her eyes smiling through the slit of her face covering. At the same time he felt her hand rest on his thigh and tighten, four triangular claws driving through the thin leather trousers deep into his flesh.

Xante had only a little time to practise her riding before the long march back through the dry wasteland began. Curos had decided to give the men a few days' rest before starting along the Great North Road of Chaw towards his family estate of Te Toldin. He now had a carefully planned route and training programme which would also give Xante several weeks to adjust to her new life. Soon enough she would be plunged into the meetings with Curos' father and the other Noyans of the army.

The roles of the two K'tans Bhal and Konn had changed slightly. Bhal Morag increasingly specialised in conducting the training exercises which he and Curos devised for the various Ulus, while Chalak Konn preferred organising supplies, reports and the detailed route of the march. The link between Curos, Xante and Morag strengthened but Chalak Konn became more isolated and resentful.

Each day selected Ulus were dispatched on training objectives either separately, under the command of their Ataman, or in groups led by Bhal Morag. Simple provisioning visits to villages were preceded by mock attacks which surprised and occasionally terrified the occupants of the small, isolated communities. At all times the main column avoided even the smallest population centres and kept moving.

This aspect of keeping a body of men in motion in the wilderness, supplied only by detached foraging parties, seemed to appeal particularly to Chalak Konn. The small, meticulous man carefully recorded food and water consumption and refined the system of rationing the men. His instructions to his supply detachments were precise and detailed in a way which would have delighted a career civil servant.

During the day's marches Xante would detach herself from the main force and, kept in sight by two watchful guards, would ride off and seek the solitude necessary for her mind communication with Dromo. This idiosyncratic behaviour was never commented on openly but it remained a subject of great speculation amongst the soldiers. She would choose a convenient spot of shade and dismount to sit in the 'Padmasana' position while the contact was made. This would be followed by a brisk ride to catch up with the column's progress or, most inexplicably to the guards, by a gruelling run on foot. On other occasions, she would ride at a blistering pace with a style and endurance approaching that of a N'gol nomad. This terrified the accompanying guards who were hard pressed to keep the speeding black figure in sight.

One evening Xante entered the camp dejected and deflated, her emotions bruised beyond the limits of mere fatigue. 'It is over, Curos, all over,' she said with great bitterness. 'Dromo, my everlasting lover, has taken another woman and already they have been granted permission to have a child. So soon. He could have waited, Curos, he could have waited until this part of my training had ended. It's as if he wishes to hurt me and drive me away.'

Curos realised how much Xante had hated to leave S'lan but from her behaviour he had believed that her love for Dromo, if it had ever existed, was now dead. 'Perhaps he is instructed to do just that,' he said, with unusual kindness in his voice. 'Your Ze Dryadi does not want you to abandon your duty and return to the forest. Perhaps he insists that Dromo tells you of his new life.'

Xante looked at Curos in disbelief, for once her mind so open to him that he could clearly see the shock and hurt which his words had caused. 'No. No-one could be so unnecessarily cruel. It had been planned that if Melini died after her trial then Dromo and I should take her child and be given permission to have one of our own. That is not possible. I do my duty to Eternal S'lan but one day I will return to my home.'

'Even if it takes a lifetime?' asked Curos quietly. 'Could you spend each day talking to your lover, knowing you could not fulfil that love? The Chaw justice can be cruel but even we don't impale young girls on tree branches for having children!'

There was a silence for several seconds during which Xante stared at Curos. 'I can now see the similarity,' she said eventually. 'You and the Ze Dryadi are the same type. Heartless, single-minded . . .' Her anger was growing to a point which surpassed normal control and reserve. 'In your plans, what does one couple's happiness matter?' she snarled at him. 'You sacrificed your friend Khol Dalgan in battle without a thought. The Ze Dryadi throws me out from my home and you point out his evilness to me to cut me off from the forest.'

'Xante, please. I was trying to help . . .'

'No! At least I thought Dromo happy. Now I shall never know. Perhaps he is as unhappy as I.'

'Could he deceive you? I just suggest that Ze Dryadi has asked him to be brutally frank.'

Xante turned away from Curos and stared out towards the distant forest. 'Go away from me, Curos. I know your weaknesses better than you do.' She began to walk away from him but then spoke angrily again. 'One day you will rule Chaw, Curos. Rule it more completely than ever our Ze Dryadi rules. But think of this. What is behind the barbarians? What drives them on to conquest after conquest? Is it one man of destiny who has too many wives but no children and no friends? A man who loves open, empty grasslands because he himself is empty?'

The next morning Curos awoke early, still surrounded by an atmosphere of hard animosity which blocked any contact with Xante. Silently he left the tent and, dressed only in his silk under-trousers, began the sequence of 'Poses of the Hand and the Foot'. The slow, strenuous exercises for Jitsu unarmed combat required calm concentration which usually cleared and refreshed the mind as they toned the body. Not today. The inner fires of doubt and turmoil which he experienced prevented any such achievement. He hardly noticed the chill, early morning wind whipping his bare chest and legs.

Watched only by an equally chilled sentry, Curos stepped back into the tent to collect his bow and sheaf of arrows. Xante lay flat and still, her open eyes vacant, her breathing slow, deep and regular.

Outside again but now dressed in his soft leather riding clothes, Curos felt warm and more relaxed. He stepped off forty paces from the straw-packed target which Ataman Wan had erected. Slowly with infinite care he went through the deliberate Hinto stages of shooting an arrow. Gradually his whole consciousness became filled with the sequence of archery and the vision of six arrows embedded in the target circle.

As his sixth arrow was loosed another shaft appeared, flying low and flat. He spun around to see Xante clad only in the black flax shirt, her short, powerful, recurved bow in her hand. His surprise turned to admiration of her long-legged body and her magnificent, dream-like beauty. His tranquillity was shattered.

'Do you wish to continue shooting?' His voice tailed off lamely as he realised the stupidity of that remark when faced by such loveliness.

'No, but I fear I have disturbed you. Would you retrieve my arrow? I do not wish to walk halfway across the compound barelegged.' As he returned with the arrows Xante stepped from the tent, wearing the black trousers and head cloth in addition to the flax shirt. Her transformation back to the sinister, assassin-like figure did not please Curos and still the silence hung between them.

With unspoken agreement they sat side by side watching as the red sun climbed up away from the haze-covered horizon. The camp was still cool and quiet and a brisk morning breeze brought in fresh, clean air with a hint of the smell of the green forests to the north.

'We have much in common, you and I,' he said eventually. 'We are both children of the light, liking to watch the sun set and the sun rise. Sleep is for the dark hours only; the light brings action and movement and must not be wasted.' Curos also believed that under her calm, tranquil manner she was impulsive and driven by her emotions but he had agreed with Aalani that what he had seen at the Ki Fru ceremony would never be spoken of.

He could not see her face fully, only her eyes and part of the nose not covered by the veil.

'In some things we are the same, but not many,' she replied. 'To do my task I must become more like you.' He waited patiently for her to explain.

'This morning for the first time I really studied you at your morning ritual. I now understand the difference between the H'tao of wisdom and the Hinto of the warrior. The H'tao strives to understand and to seek the deep, perfect wisdom. The Hinto seeks knowledge also but his way is to practise and exercise to achieve perfect execution. Would you not agree?' When he did not answer she continued, 'I exercise my body to still my mind, I meditate to achieve understanding. You meditate to refresh your mind so as to better control your actions, as with shooting the bow.'

'There is some truth in that,' he replied slowly, 'but for you also, running or shooting the bow have their practical uses, and even their pleasure. And also for the Dryadin there are the festivals which release emotion and tension.'

'A leader who may one day rule Chaw should not allow his thought to linger on details,' said Xante. 'It is the desires that drive our spirits that are different. Only outwardly do the results appear similar. Uncharacteristic moments, loss of control or weakness do not change the underlying purpose. I wanted to explain that my approach to sorcery has been wrong. I must become a hard Hinto Warrior of Sorcery.'

'You may find, honoured sorceress, that there are certain compensations,' said Curos, now smiling openly. 'See Wan Abac, he has also risen early and now does the Jitsu poses and movements. After meditation and purification, he will rouse his men and take them through the less demanding poses for novices. He has been forced to stop contemplating leadership and practise leading. He has moved from being a figure of contempt to being a hard and respected man. He now has more inner peace and happiness within himself than he did five days ago.'

'When I can take pleasure in striking a subordinate to the ground I will reconsider your predilection,' Xante said icily. 'It is my duty to practise striking by sorcery but I will feel no emotion. There is not room for happiness.'

Xante now spent more of each day riding with Curos as he drilled and trained the men but in the morning and evening she demanded an hour of privacy to practise her sorcery.

During one such evening Curos and Bhal Morag walked out across the plain away from the main camp. Despite the still, hot days, the evenings were becoming more chill with the approach of autumn.

'Is it permitted to speak frankly, in friendship, Curos?' Bhal Morag asked.

'There is no regulation against conversation between brother officers, Morag,' replied Curos absently, his eyes on the brilliant star-field of the heavens.

'I have great respect for your ability,' said Morag, avoiding any form of address. 'You are a great leader and . . .'

'Please, Morag.'

'No, it is true. You led the Topaz Wind to subdue the bandits of the Mid O'san Hills.'

'A minor police action,' murmured Curos, remembering the events with pride in himself and the Topaz Wind.

'But successful, where many other attempts had failed. You alone had success at the battles of Corninstan. Chaw has few leaders of subtlety and none who can also lead a Hund to glory in battle.' He smiled ruefully. 'Who else could or would bother to inspire this pathetic rabble of peasants into soldiers eager to face the enemy from the West?'

'I enjoy flattery, Morag, especially from a temperate disposition like yours, but please get to the crux of your disputation.'

'Curos,' said Bhal Morag earnestly, 'I think you have one weakness, one weakness which could bring you down.'

'Only one weakness!' cut in Curos with some humour.

'It is the Dryad woman, Curos,' blurted out Morag. 'I fear she has some hold on you. She could be a spy for the Dryadin, an assassin, anything. You would be a prime target, Curos, one man we could not afford to lose. At any time that woman could wreak some devastation and then leave unhindered – you give her too much freedom.'

'Morag, you do not understand.' Curos smiled smugly. 'I have wives and falcons. The Dryad woman is a falcon which I have already bent to my will. I can let her go as far as she wishes; she will always come back to me.'

Morag shrugged his shoulders but seemed unconvinced. 'Please be warned, friend Curos. That is all.'

When Curos returned to his tent, Xante seemed particularly elated. 'Curos,' she beamed. 'Today I have made great progress. Look.'

She sat on the sleeping mat, covered only in the black linen shift which showed too much of her figure. Curos' eyes were riveted, but not on the small twig which Xante had pressed into the dry earth. Despite his brash words to Bhal Morag, this woman was giving him problems which he did not believe could afflict a well-disciplined man who had become bored with two wives and many women.

'Curos, your attention wanders,' Xante said in a commanding voice. 'Observe this little stick.'

Wrenching his thoughts back, Curos observed. Xante seemed to stare fixedly at the small sprig of wood and hesitantly it began to smoke and then burst into flame.

'Is that not amazing?' Xante purred in pride. 'Say you are impressed!'

Curos stared at the small flame and then at the beautiful, half-clad woman who was so pleased with her achievement. Slowly he reached into his jerkin pocket and drew out a small brass box. Deliberately he struck one of the long sulphur matches and held the blazing flare up to Xante.

'I, Zachaw Curos, have followed my father's orders so that Chaw should obtain knowledge of sorcery. It has taken most of the summer when I should have been killing Warchaw. And what do I see,' he chided scornfully, 'one stick set afire!'

The black eyes blazed with fire far more deadly than Curos could have imagined. 'My progress on levitation has been more dramatic, War Lord,' she growled. Without warning, Curos found himself flying backwards. Propelled by an immense force he hurtled through the tent opening into the dark night. Even as he attempted the Jitsu breakfall, the Topaz reacted to Xante's sorcery with a glow of yellow light and a slight upward force cushioned his fall. Suppressing a muffled curse, he was barely aware of Bhal Morag running to his aid.

'I am unhurt,' he gasped, forcing himself to sit up against the numbing pain in his shoulders.

Morag laughed. 'Are you still bending the Dryad woman to your will, brother officer?'

At that instant Xante appeared, silhouetted in the opening of the tent. 'Curos, I am sorry. I did not mean . . .' Xante's voice trailed off at Morag's stare before she allowed the tent flap to conceal her from the outside world.

Morag helped Curos to his feet. 'Curos, my friend,' he said in an awed voice. 'The dark spectre I feared has become even more deadly.' He stopped speaking and looked blankly at Curos. 'I, Morag, am lost for words before such a vision of beauty. My brother,' he gripped Curos' arm, 'I now see the extent of your peril. May the Gods of Chaw protect you.'

Curos brushed down his jerkin, sending small clouds of dust flying.

'Stop this nonsense, Morag. You sound like a poet, not a soldier. She is but a woman, too long of arm and leg and too flat of face to be desirable.' Part of his mind and most of his body cringed at these words but he pressed on. 'I was showing the Dryad woman a Jitsu throw. There is no mystery and no change in my attitude.' Although he was deeply angered, Curos attempted to dismiss the event to Morag.

When he and Xante were alone he said in a taut voice, 'I feel I should raise the subject of your accommodation. Your status in the camp has changed and . . .'

'My apparent status, honoured K'tan,' she replied. 'In reality nothing has changed.'

'So,' he agreed. 'But now as a powerful sorceress rather than a dubious visitor you may consider it more appropriate to have your own tent, in the officers' compound, of course.'

They sat in strained silence for some time before Xante replied. 'There is some merit in privacy, but this is still a strange world to me. If it proves no inconvenience I would prefer to continue as before. And,' she added with a hint of a smile, 'I must confess I would feel more secure and comfortable at night.'

11

The capital of Corninstan was now firmly in the grip of Warchaw military rule. Any resistance by the population had been brutally suppressed and chosen areas were cleared and turned into fortified camps for Warchaw soldiers. Palaces or mansions had been annexed by even minor commanders or junior sorcerers.

Valanus, as a High Wizard of the Order of Gadel, had been made joint commander of the expedition into Corninstan. Despite his power and influence, he readily allowed Baron Renult full command of the conquered city's administration. It had been obvious that the Baron should take up residence in the Khan's palace and usurp all the splendour and ceremony of office. Valanus was quite content with the small manor house with its park-like garden. There were rooms enough for his personal companions, his guard of twenty archers, his servants and the temporary accommodation for visiting sorcerers. The architecture was definitely Eastern, but subtle and with refined good taste, the rooms comfortable and well planned, the garden pleasant and shady with just enough open space to permit horse exercise.

A tall, well-built man of thirty years, Valanus possessed the fair hair and steel-blue eyes of his mother's people and from her had probably inherited his sorcerer's power. His father, a knightat-arms who had travelled northward to learn from the teachers of the Order of Gadel, had bequeathed his son a love of chivalry and personal prowess of arms. This morning Valanus had risen early before first light, his senses sharpened and agitated by an unknown influence. It emanated from the East, the hideous land of Chaw with its teeming millions. He sat at his desk, head in hands, concentrating on the disturbance. It was weak, too weak to be any but the most junior of his Order, but very similar to an effect he had detected several weeks ago. The fair, shoulderlength hair fell over his face unheeded as he sought to unravel the mystery.

The sorcery, if it were the work of a sorcerer, was extremely weak but also unusually sustained. It flickered once more and disappeared like a feeble candle flame. The Lore said that no sorcerers existed in Chaw, in the N'gol plains or the Northern Forests but this counter-evidence needed probing. Already the Conclave of the Order's twelve High Wizards had failed to penetrate the wall of secrecy erected around the forest which indicated some powerful, unnatural protection at work. Now there were possible signs of sorcery in Chaw.

The Conclave of the Order of Gadel of which he was the youngest had specifically ordered him not to visit or to invade the dreadful land of Chaw. The position in Corninstan must be consolidated and the population subdued before further advances or provocations were considered.

Valanus could not enter Chaw, his word had been given, but he already had spies posing as merchants on the great north trade route which followed the border of Chaw and the wide, flat grasslands to the D'was. Dawn was breaking and he summoned his assistant sorcerer to bring copies of the Corninstani maps they had collected.

Valanus was pacing the room, dressed in the grey robe of the Order, his handsome face creased with a frown, when Bran entered. Valanus turned, noticed that the boy was shaken by the urgency of the telepathic summons and still clouded with sleep.

'I am sorry to wake you so early, Bran' he said in genuine apology. 'You felt nothing from the East?'

'No, sir.'

'No alien sorcery?' Valanus unrolled the map of central Chaw. 'It appeared weak but distances in these lands are so vast.'

'Chaw sorcerers, sir? There are no reports . . .'

'I know, possibly a trick of my mind.' He calculated distances and compared them with his impression of direction and distance. The Corninstani claimed their maps were accurate.

'John Leaver is about here, sir,' ventured Bran, pointing. 'He mentioned this village, I can't pronounce the name . . .'

'No matter, if there was a sorcerer working magic he was north of the capital and further east.' Valanus studied a map. He believed that the first occurrence would have been further north, possibly in the forest. He moved his finger along the map southward and westward to the new disturbance and frowned, remembering that Sigman claimed he had been dazzled by a yellow light during the battle. 'Bran, you can contact John with the red stone?'

'Yes, sir.'

'Ask him to make his way to this village on the caravan route as fast as he can. Discretion is not important – he can steal horses if necessary. I want his eyes open and his nose sniffing for any hint of sorcery. No need to take undue risks when he gets there – it's probably nothing.'

'Could be a desert storm, like as not sire, energy lightning.'

'Probably, Bran, quite probably, or even a bad dream.' There was no need to start rumours or spark alarm, thought Valanus. 'Still, John and his men are near by and it does no harm to check. The village is almost on their intended route. I think we might also talk with that Chaw nobleman who claims he will help us.'

Valanus was still frowning, trying to recall the echo-like impression; he did not like loose ends. Despite his concern, he asked Bran to send in his page with warm water and to prepare the riding gear. He had arranged to ride with Sir Sigmund while it was still cool and take part in the cavalry exercises.

12

At the end of the first week of the return journey, Curos despatched a short report to his father. This was easily achieved from one of the staging posts of the Arrow Rider messengers who travelled the roads of Chaw. From then on Curos intended to continue marching, training and conditioning his men throughout their journey to the capital city but part way he intended to leave them to seek his father on the Zachaw estate of Te Toldin.

Often on still, warm nights not even tents were erected in the temporary camps. On other days when the last harsh, hot winds of early autumn blew, men huddled in their tents until the lashing dust died down. Curos would then drive the soldiers forward in the cool, dark desert nights to catch up the lost time. During the march Xante, Curos and Morag strengthened and defined their relationship. As far as army matters were concerned, Morag was now established as day-to-day exercise commander under Curos' general guidance. Three Ataman under-officers were promoted to field K'tans and given more responsibility.

While Curos, Morag and Chalak Konn discussed tactics and logistics the new K'tans led their men on individual manoeuvres to gain experience and initiative in command. Xante joined the discussions to improve her knowledge of the army and how it moved and fought. Like Curos she had little idea as yet how her sorcery could be used to defeat the Warchaw. Often, she accompanied Curos when he left the line of march for a day to observe an exercise. She now rode like a nomad N'gol, quite able to keep up with Curos, her speed and endurance only limited by the stamina of the horses available.

On one hot, airless day, which defied the approaching autumn, the leader and the sorceress looked down from a high ridge as Wan Abac drove the three guards Ulus along a rough path toward an isolated well village. Less than half a yetang away the men shimmered indistinctly in the mirage-making heat haze. Xante pulled her hooded cowl well over her face to shield her eyes from the dazzling light which reflected up off the pale rock. 'The men are fatigued beyond endurance,' she commented quietly. 'Is this punishment necessary?'

'Training is not punishment,' replied Curos. 'The exercise was to plan a mock attack on the well village. It was Wan Abac's idea to march his men over the back roads and broken countryside to attack the rear while Bhal Morag brought up the main detachment more slowly with the baggage and supplies. I am trying to emulate the barbarians,' he explained thoughtfully. 'Even their foot-soldiers move fast, often in quite small numbers to gain an objective. See the small carts to carry the arms and water? Wan will reach the village by late evening and conceal the guardsmen for a night attack. They will have time to rest. If it were a real enemy position the inhabitants would be disorganised by an attack on both sides. In this case Wan will just enter in darkness, to practise keeping his men in good order.'

'Honoured commander,' said Xante with a mocking but not unkind smile, 'may the unenlightened Dryad ask a question, due to her own stupidity?'

'Xante,' laughed Curos as he shook his reins to urge his unwilling mount forward, 'if you are unwise, may I never meet a wise Dryad. What do you not comprehend?'

'Your force is now divided, separated by over a day's march. If one part were to falter or be detained by the enemy, how could the other part know and modify its actions?'

'You see the weakness of any such plan,' sighed Curos. 'With an attack involving separate bodies of men there is a risk of confusion. Once battle is joined it is not possible to communicate in time to modify the plan.' He smiled at Xante easily. 'You now see why I want one hundred Dryad sorcerers. Imagine one Dryad with each T'sand, all able to communicate with my sorceress. I could hurl T'sands at the Warchaw with a precision never achieved before. Always hit their flanks, exploit any weakness . . .'

'Huh!' shouted Xante, cutting off Curos' stream of excited speech. 'You need too many sorcerers to achieve that plan. There must be another way.'

'What other way? We have men and organisation but I cannot just throw men at the Warchaw. They will drive us back with their sorcery and bowmen. In such a rout one hundred thousand Chaw would trample each other to death in hours.' Curos shook his head and looked down at the straggling men. 'Our lack of mobility is another problem. Most of our army are footmen, and however hard officers like Wan drive them, they can never move as freely as horsemen. With a hundred thousand Wind Riders, even a Tuman of Cavalry T'sands, I could sweep aside the barbarians and conquer the world.'

'Perhaps it is well you cannot get that many horsemen,' suggested Xante. 'High Commander Zachaw would soon become Emperor Zachaw.' She stared fixedly into his face, her black eyes glittering beneath the shrouding head cloth. 'Remember, Imperial Commander, that behind Zachaw Ca'lin Curos stands Xante-Yani. When one man rules Chaw will one Dryad control that man?'

A cold shiver ran through Curos but he forced his face into a laugh to show no weakness. 'Your warning is understood, Madam Dryad. A single point of power is easily identified and attacked.' His voice became serious again. 'I shall seek power to repel the surge of filth from the West, not to rule. I shall plan, organise and direct. I shall drive the army until it falls on its knees, provided its knees rest on Warchaw throats. But I will not weaken Chaw by becoming a central figure which it cannot do without. The Dryadin have shown me the danger of assassination.'

Curos cut off his flood of words and lapsed into an embarrassed silence, then spoke again. 'Have no fear of Curos leading the "Hordes of N'gol" to conquer the world as they did of old,' he said bitterly. 'We have not enough food in Chaw to feed children, let alone breed the horses for a horse army. The nomadic clans of the N'gol cannot increase their numbers on the dry plains. Only the peasant foot-soldiers can save Chaw. They may be slow but they are strong and tenacious. I must learn how to use them wisely and make the best use of the horsemen I have. The Chaw can fight and die, all I ask is that the Dryadin block the sorcerers' fire and direct my T'sands when I need.' He looked at Xante belligerently but she shook her head.

'Such powerful visions, Curos, but it is not to be so. In the whole of S'lan I doubt there are more than ten Dryads who

87

have power to the level you need.' She paused sadly before continuing. 'We must appear poor sorcerers, Curos, but our ability has not developed just to match your dream.'

'You must achieve what I need,' said Curos in a clipped voice. 'That is what I agreed with Ze Dryadi.'

'Curos,' she said desperately, 'don't you realise I am the best sorceress the Dryadin could give you? I have trained until my brain aches while you play soldiers. Even so I can only talk to a few other Dryads close to me. My father and mother and . . . and friends.'

'Like Dromo,' suggested Curos. 'You have no difficulty speaking to him.'

'It is not easy!' she said viciously. 'I bruise my brain to achieve sorcery and I blister my arse to become the best rider in your camp.' She pressed on angrily, ignoring his shock at her crude language. 'And what do you say in return? Get me a hundred more sorcerers, woman. And with your eyes each day you say, woman of no importance, get into my bed!'

A hostile silence descended, broken only by the muffled, slow thud of the horses' hooves on the dusty ridge. At last Curos spoke. 'I think I sometimes do not fully appreciate the efforts of others, Xante. You make difficult things seem easy. You achieve after five days' training that which would be impossible for me or any other Chaw.'

'For you to learn sorcery would not be impossible.' The icy, strained voice had changed completely, the hard tone giving way to one of girlish mischief. 'First you must learn how to run. Only when you can fully exercise your lungs and those bandy N'gol legs of yours will you be able to master the arts of H'tao sorcery.'

'Run in this heat? The horses can barely walk!'

'Your guardsmen are being driven at a fast walk. Come on, get your feet on the ground and run.'

'No Xante, do not be . . .'

'I am not stupid. Throw off your heavy horseman's clothes and run, let your body run free with me.'

'I cannot do it,' he laughed.

'No, you could not, because your mind is closed to the possibility. One day you will lead the Chaw. With your vision and ability you will make it possible. With the same vision you could train to run with me. With an open mind you could become a sorcerer of ability, great ability.'

'As good a sorcerer as Xante and Yani?' he asked with sudden humour.

'No,' she laughed back. 'but better than many in S'lan and better than any in Chaw.'

The atmosphere of anger seemed to have been dispelled between them as quickly as it had appeared.

'Will you practise sorcery today?' asked Curos. 'Making a dagger spin in mid-air or deflecting arrows?'

Xante looked unenthusiastic. 'My problem is that I train for an unknown purpose. The ability to produce massive fire seems beyond me. It is like lifting a weight, no matter how much you try there is a limit – my limit for creating conflagration is very small.'

'Then you must ignore that and exploit your strengths,' Curos started to say.

'I have a better idea, Curos,' Xante cut in. 'I will defend the well village against your Guard Ulus tonight. It will be a test of my ability and,' she looked directly at Curos with a smile more devastating than any woman's, 'it will test the resolve of your new Man of Iron, Wan Abac.'

Many hours later Curos and Xante stood concealed beside a rocky outcrop some distance from the well village of Dar Tol. Behind them the settlement lay dark and silent, a small cluster of tradesmen's huts and a decrepit inn. To their front loomed the ridge of hills stretching up into a star-lit desert sky.

For some time they had been charting the almost silent, invisible progress of Wan Abac's men as they advanced in three distinct groups toward the village.

'It is time,' whispered Xante with unnecessary caution. 'I will start by building up an image of terror. First it will be the spirits of dead villagers, outraged souls angry at the approach of raiders.'

Curos was only dimly aware of Xante's projections. Subtly she reinforced the superstitious fears which lurked deep in the minds of the soldiers. In the dim moonlight Curos could detect that the purposeful stride of the guardsmen was beginning to falter.

'They carry their own horrors with them, Curos, but Wan Abac is almost like you. His mind is closed so firmly against any magic there is nothing to work on. He does not believe, therefore it cannot be. I will show him something more vivid.'

'You plan no harm to Abac?'

'No and not to any of the others. Look.' Slowly a curtain-wall of fire grew up before the now terrified guardsmen. Each of the Guard Ulus was blocked off from Dar Tol by the raging flames. 'It is an illusion only, a weak illusion which can be passed if tested.'

From the distance they could hear Ataman Wan shouting to his men to stand firm, to ignore the foul magic, to push forward and show the force of Chaw steel. In the flame wall, hideous faces appeared, howling and cursing, threatening the soldiers if they did not flee to the hills and leave the spirits of the village in peace. The guardsmen were now level with Xante and Curos when with sudden swiftness the morale of one of the columns broke. By the glow of the sorceress's light, Curos saw the men of the Third Guard Ulus begin to waver. Their panic grew like a contagious disease leaping from man to man until they turned and ran, stumbling and shrieking. Weapons and shields were thrown down as they fled back to the safe darkness of the low hills.

Even as they fled Curos could hear Wan shouting to his remaining men, deriding those in flight, calling scorn on guardsmen who faltered. Unbelievably, he was leading them on to Xante's fire wall.

'He calls my bluff, Curos, and I have little left to play. If I strike down Wan, the rest would flee . . .'

'No, Xante! I want no injuries. If he wins, let him win.'

'The Chaw soldier cannot triumph over a Dryad,' she snarled with the venom which Curos was beginning to recognise only too well. As she spoke the fire wall changed and burning jets shot out towards the advancing phalanx. The ox-hide cover of Wan's shield began to flare and he beat desperately at the flames with his scimitar. Still Wan called his men forward. A soldier screamed in fear and pain, hurling away his blazing spear.

'Curos! He's lost them, Curos. I have broken Wan's grip on them. I can feel them crumbling!'

'It is enough,' Curos shouted back. 'Mount up and follow me.' Curos threw Xante onto her horse and galloped toward the Chaw detachment. He could almost smell the panic as the guardsmen crouched behind grounded shields, watching in disbelief as the dogged Wan inched his way forward, calling them to follow.

'Follow your K'tan,' roared Curos. 'Advance and kill the filth of the West who defile our land with their magic.' Curos heard a sob of fatigue from Xante as the flame wall died. He reined in his mount to stop close beside the two guard Ulus. Wan shouted in triumph and the guardsmen moved forward.

'The Dryad woman destroys the witchcraft,' shouted Curos in mock jubilation. Xante's eyes were unseeing and blank with tiredness.

Above the muted cheers of the guardsmen came the distant sound of hoofbeats. In the village dim, mounted shapes became briefly visible, slipping past the indistinct houses. The Chaw Guardsmen hooted and jeered, Chaw soldiers shouting their contempt for an enemy who would not stand and fight once their cowardly tricks had been detected.

Villagers had awoken in terror at the sound of turmoil, the shouting armed men and the fire in the desert. Now their panic slowly dispersed as they recognised the distinctive scarlet uniforms of the Chaw guard. Many came to stand and listen as Curos spoke to the Guardsmen, praising their bravery. To explain the events of the night he fabricated a story of roving barbarians spying out the land of Chaw.

Later Curos was sombre faced as he stood with Xante, watching Wan march his men off to arrange the water and food for the main army. 'Only a small sham victory, Xante, but they have gained confidence and you have shown amazing power.'

'I wish it were as easy as that,' Xante replied in a strained voice which made Curos turn and look with concern at the pale, shaking figure. 'I put out all my power, and more, to fool sixty soldiers with a trick. The barbarians' sorcerers stopped the whole Chaw army with real fire. I cannot begin to get that power, I will never achieve that power,' her voice trailed off in despair and frustration.

Without thinking, Curos folded his arms protectively around her so that her hooded face fell down onto his shoulder. 'Do not denigrate your achievement, sorceress,' he murmured. 'It was not peasant soldiers you stopped. It was the Guard Ulus of Chaw, well-trained men, led by a fanatical officer.' He looked across the plains to where the sun was rising to turn the heavens a delicate rose pink. 'You must forget the barbarians' fire. Your powers may be even more terrifying to them than fire.'

He took blankets from the horses and spread them carefully. The exhausted woman sat in the Perfect position facing the east. Her chest began to move with the rhythmic breathing of pranayam 'The Cleansing Breath'.

'Think not of fire,' he murmured from beside her. 'Think of the pink hue of the wild dog-rose and the grey of the ash tree and white shine of the birch as it grows in the forest. The colours are in the sky, reflections of the forest of the Eternal S'lan.'

With an ease which made it as natural as life Xante spoke directly into his mind. 'There is no green in the desert, Curos, nor in the sky. Eternal S'lan, the beloved of the Dryad, is filled with greenness.'

'All the greens of the forest are in the sunrise,' he replied, 'but only the Dryadin and those taught by the Dryadin may see them. You are tired indeed, my sorceress, if you see no greens of S'lan in the sunrise.'

'It is not the tiredness, Curos. Not just the tiredness. It is the distance from S'lan and the smell of the living forest.' No sounds had come from her mouth, the rhythmic breathing did not falter and her eyes did not flinch from the light of the glowing dawn.

13

From the exhaustion and trauma of the night Xante-Yani the Dryad Sorceress rested in meditation until the sun had ridden into the bright morning sky. Beside her sat Zachaw Ca'lin, K'tan of the Topaz Wind, waiting until his sorceress was rested and ready to meet the world. Eventually Xante shook her head with drowsy slowness before facing Curos with an open smile.

'Thank you for staying with me, Curos. I was fatigued and I fear my childish display attracted some penetrating attention, as if an intelligence was seeking me from afar. The Warchaw may have already sensed a new power in the land of Chaw. I may have been in some danger if I could not have drawn on your strength to protect myself from their gaze.'

He stood up and respectfully helped Xante to her feet. 'Thank you in the name of the people of the Land of Chaw for your help in extinguishing the fire of the Warchaw sorcerers,' he stated in a ringing voice for the benefit of the watching villagers.

'Oh, Curos, look, people are waiting to speak with you. They will be angry that we have kept them waiting.'

'No, they are Chaw, they wait in patience,' Curos said, not bothering to turn around. 'They expect to have to wait for superiors and it will further enhance your standing that I expect them to wait for you. You are our Queen of Sorcery, they are mere ants, the ants of Chaw.' He raised his hand and smiled as she started to protest. 'Even so we will not make them wait any longer than necessary.'

'The embellishment of the fleeing horsemen was quite inspired,' he whispered to Xante as they walked towards the village elders.

'Curos, I did not make the sounds of the horsemen.' She frowned. 'I thought it must be Bhal Morag or some soldiers riding up.'

'No, the hoofbeat was too heavy for Chaw horses. You have

no idea what was happening?' his voice trailed off in puzzled concern.

'No, Curos. I was too exhausted to think very clearly.' Now agitation had come into her voice.

'It could have been honest traders, I suppose,' mused Curos. 'Surely, there could not be Warchaw spies this far east; but I will ask the village head men.'

Briskly Curos strode over to the village elders and quickly cut short their flowery words of welcome and many deep bows.

'Please excuse my uncivil haste, honourable magistrate,' he broke in after a cursory salute. 'Time is pressing. As you no doubt know the Esteemed Dryad Sorceress defeated the attempt of barbarian wizards to burn up the soldiers of the Guard Ulus. The barbarians have fled and the Sorceress has been unable to draw them back. Have you any news of three or four strangers in the village, possibly posing as merchants? They would be tall, powerfully-built men with hard, blue eyes and difficulty in speaking our language.' The two village elders exchanged surprised glances before beginning to apologise profusely for failing to recognise the travellers who had arrived several days before. They had come with pack camels and trade goods and had conversed in Corninstani. No-one had seen such strange people before but they seemed generous and paid well, in advance. These four strange, outlandish merchants had indeed been in the village. At the height of the flames in the desert they had saddled their horses and ridden off at high speed to the West leaving their trade goods behind.

Curos considered this unwelcome information and a cold thread of fear began to develop. Already the barbarians were beginning to probe into the homeland of Chaw over a month's hard riding from the Durin Mountains and Corninstan. Scouts must be seeking out initial attack routes along the Great North Road which ran through the sparsely populated regions. The spies would be quick to recognise sorcery at work but what had directed them to Dar Tol? Any observation of sorcery, which could challenge the Warchaw's power, would be reported to the barbarian commanders immediately.

Four men had ridden from the village and four men must be captured or killed before they could reach Corninstan. Curos

94

explained the danger to the village elders and to his officers. He would need ten able and well-mounted soldiers and at least two guides from the village. Only one man from Dar Tol was willing to act as a guide: Akab was a grizzled gazelle hunter and had lived for most of his forty-five years in the saddle, hunting the sparse game of the area. A hard, bitter man, he showed little respect for either the elders or for Curos.

'Lord,' he said in a flat, irreverent tone, 'our quarry has a start of six hours. Their horses, although heavy and seemingly spiritless are strong and will have great stamina. To race after them in hot pursuit will be useless.' Curos had already thought as much himself, but was pleased that the guide showed such judgment.

'What you say rings true, Akab, but are we to allow the misusers of hospitality to escape without an attempt to hunt them down?'

'No quarry is safe from Akab,' replied the man with an evil grin, showing his broken and diseased teeth in their full splendour. 'But it is cunning, not rashness, which brings home the prize. I would suggest, K'tan, that we reduce our party to six. Instead of following directly after the fleeing filth, we exhaust our horses in a fast passage to the Arrow Riders' station at Dar Fir. There with your excellency's authority we commandeer a string of fresh horses and swing out north to pick up the trail. The spies have no spare horses and will have been forced to slow their pace by then. The rest will be a simple hunt.'

'Your plan has much merit, Akab, and if successful will be well rewarded.'

'The pack camels and goods abandoned by the Westerners would be sufficient, Lord,' suggested Akab.

Curos ignored this impertinent request, and continued, 'I will take only four mounted bowmen with us and trust to your skill. We will travel light and pick up food and water at Dar Fir. Seven to four will give us fair odds!'

The hunter looked puzzled. 'We will be but six, Lord. Do we ride to kill or capture?'

'To capture if we can,' replied Curos, 'but we are seven. Your count did not include the Dryad sorceress.'

'This is no hunt for a young girl, however welcome she may

95

be to the sleeping mat,' spat the hunter with scorn. 'Leave the woman to the care of your officers and catch up on your pleasure later!'

Akab staggered sideways, struck by an invisible blow which sent him sprawling to the hard, dusty ground. His head rang with pain. He looked up in a daze and saw that the soldiers and villagers werre staring at him in surprise. They had seen no physical blow. Only the K'tan seemed unmoved.

'Akab,' a voice cold with anger spoke directly into his mind and his body froze with fear. 'You are spared great pain and punishment only because you have some value to Lord Zachaw. I will ride with your hunt and its speed will not be reduced.' Akab was overpowered by the presence of the black-clad figure of the Dryad sorceress; beneath the veiled hood her eyes were infinite pools of dark malice and for the first time in his life Akab's courage failed him. He feared no man or animal, not death itself, but now he trembled like a child. Two gold disks landed in the dust at his feet. 'Take this, Akab. If I, Xante-Yani, am late at the kill, it is yours.'

The early darkness of the evening, two days later, concealed Xante and Curos as they crouched uncomfortably among the rocks within sight of the barbarians' distant camp fire. Silhouetted against the brilliance of the star-strewn sky, Curos could just make out the head and shoulders of the barbarian whose presence had sent them into cover. It would be impossible to attempt a long-range bowshot in such uncertain light for all the skill of his selected archers, Juchi, Munlik, Kasar and Tayan. They waited for Akab to work his way around the sentry.

Curos had set a hard pace for his party on the first leg of their ride, arriving at the Arrow Riders' post at Dar Fir late on the first day. There they had exchanged horses and ridden north according to Akab's plan. As they neared the Old North Road a party of merchants travelling to Dar Fir had been able to give them valuable information on the barbarians' progress and Akab had then discovered tracks of the men they hunted.

Xante suppressed a shiver, wishing for protection against the cold. Even the memory of the warm evening was dispersing into the desert night. 'To think only last night I wasted energy lighting a fire for your bowmen, Curos.' Xante shuddered again. 'I would that I had a little of that heat now.'

Curos voiced a thought which had been occupying his mind for most of the day. 'I have been wondering why those merchants were so far north. The route is longer and the Night Dragon Clan who inhabit this area are little more than bandits.'

'I think the merchants have little to fear from the Night Dragon,' whispered Xante. 'Have you thought how the Dryadin obtain commodities such as metal and leather? Apart from flax and wood we have no raw materials.'

'Do you trade? Aalani hinted as much, but I thought yours was a closed world.'

'It is, almost,' she replied, 'but certain merchants do enter the forest. We have flax, medicines and some precious stones which are sought after. It is in the interest of all that the trade be kept secret. The Night Dragon people take a toll from the traders but protect them as they cross this section of the plain.'

'That is one worry less, then,' said Curos. 'The merchants are no threat, although I expect they pay little tax on their trading.'

'If Akab fails,' Xante changed the subject, 'I will attempt to strike the Warchaw down by sorcery. I am beginning to feel the shape of his thoughts. He is wary and afraid of pursuit; he suspects that we are close by but cannot hear or see us.'

'Wait,' said Curos. 'Look, our quarry is moving again.' Frequently the man had stood up and moved around in an agitated way before returning to the rock he had chosen for his vigil. It was as he returned that Akab struck. Like a black, noiseless cloud he appeared behind the man, slashing oncc with his razor-sharp skinning knife. The arms flailed frantically but apart from a sickening gasp there was no other sound.

'Strange, is it not,' Akab grinned up from robbing the dying body as Curos and Xante appeared, 'not one animal will make a sound when its throat is cut, even if the windpipe is intact? He has little enough, a broadsword and a knife and a few coins.'

'Not to mention a ring and a neck chain,' corrected Xante.

'Do that later, Akab,' Curos chided as the Westerner sighed, expelling the last of his life breath. Curos shuddered and Xante realised he was visualising how his own death might have been at the hand of Aalani.

Closer to the fire they could make out two other figures sprawled in attitudes which spoke of relaxation and confidence.

'There is one man missing, if I am not deceived. One bird has flown!' said Akab. Flat open ground separated Curos from the Westerners, preventing any chance of a surprise assault. He began to despair of securing a prisoner.

'I think I can help now,' suggested Xante. 'Cast your eyes down and be ready to run forward.' Almost as Xante spoke, the air around the Westerners became charged with brilliant, luminescent energy and the camp fire burst up into a torrent of sparks and flames. The Westerners' reaction was totally unexpected. Both men shouted with joy and one rushed directly towards Xante, a smile of welcome on his face as he called out in the strange, flat-sounding language of the Warchaw. As his eyes penetrated the darkness he realised his mistake and grabbed for his sword hilt.

'Do not kill him, take one alive.' Immediately Curos sprang, and the Topaz Stone charged by Xante's sorcery unleashed a blinding flash of energy. A Jitsu cut to the bridge of the nose sent the barbarian collapsing into an untidy heap. The Topaz had energised Curos and gave added power to the blow, its impact jarring his entire arm, and he could hardly draw his sword.

Already two archers with scimitars were closing in on the remaining barbarian, cutting off his escape to the horses. He backed slowly away, threatening them with his broad-bladed sword and drawing his dagger as if preparing for a throw. Curos called out, 'Close in, don't shoot. I need this man.'

The stalking archers were penning in the luckless barbarian with a ring of human bodies and whirling blades. He leapt directly towards Juchi, swinging the heavy sword in a devastating arc. The archer attempted to parry but his lighter scimitar was beaten down and his feet kicked out from under him. Munlik's slash to the barbarian's head was defeated by the dagger and the broadsword stabbed down at the defenceless Juchi. This time Curos deflected the sword point and the huge barbarian leapt back and away from Curos' fast cut to his face. The barbarian now attacked Curos with a series of wild swings, only to turn about and drive back Kasar.

'It is like wild dogs pulling down a bull, Lady.' Akab grinned as he laid a restraining hand on Xante's bow arm. 'Do not try to shoot. Your Lord is safe enough if he keeps his head.' He laughed at his own joke and viewed the combat with evident pleasure. The Warchaw's first elation at the fight was waning with his strength. The Chaw soldiers instinctively worked in a team to counter his greater strength. A precision cut by Curos sliced through the leather sleeve of the Westerner's sword arm and Juchi landed a stunning blow to the side of the head with the flat of the sword. Still the barbarian fought on, keeping the Chaw at arms' length with his sweeping sword blade.

'He despises us,' said Xante. 'But he knows now that he is defeated. His mind races in panic.'

Desperately the barbarian looked from side to side, holding out his heavy sword as if preparing to launch a last bid for escape. Then with a scream of defiance he held the sword high in the air as if in salute and viciously stabbed himself with his dagger. The triangular blade plunged into his neck and down into his chest. Kasar was already springing from behind to grip the dagger hand as the blow descended. In his dying strength the barbarian spun him off and stood swaying grotesquely, the hilt of the dagger protruding from his body.

Curos shouted frantically to Xante, 'Can you do anything to save him?'

'Save him for questions and for torture?' Xante replied as she looked into the dying blue eyes. 'He bleeds deeply inside. I can only lessen his pain, Curos, and seek to understand a little of why they hate us so much.'

Some time later Curos was talking quietly to Akab when Xante walked over to them. She sat down unsteadily and gazed deep into the fire before speaking.

'It is not pleasant, Curos, to peer into the mind of the dying, feeling the fear and certainty of death and the growing confusion and blackness as thoughts become jumbled and memories disappear. I saw scenes from his childhood on a green, damp land, greener and more fertile than even S'lan the Eternal. Parents, friends, a happy land with no threat of famine or war – why do such as he need to come to this desert wilderness?'

'Could he speak our language?' asked Curos, breaking into her flow of speech.

'No, certainly not in his condition. I saw only pictures, visions of his life all mixed and confused.' She sat silent for some time, trying to arrange what she had seen while her own mind recoiled at the horror and fear. 'He crossed a huge expanse of water on a massive boat propelled by the magic of the wind and then rode on horseback for many days to reach Imran and Corninstan. It took over a year I would think, but memories may be distorted. I saw the town in Corninstan, a woman he thought beautiful, and the battles. He loved the battles and the fighting for their own sake – perhaps that is important. I saw also the face of a man, a man of power who directed them to Dar Tol to seek out the Chaw witch.' She shuddered. 'Their vision of me was not flattering. Even as he died he was worried that his friend who had ridden off would be caught before he could warn the Warchaw sorcerer, Val-lan-nas? Such loyalty.'

She looked up at Curos, her black eyes for once lost to him in the shadow of the veil and head cloth. 'His soul will not be reborn, Curos,' she whispered and he realised that for Xante, this was the greatest sacrilege. 'For them there is one life only and then everlasting nothing – he expects no more.' She turned away and again lapsed into thought as the fire crackled and the archers moved in near silence around the camp.

With an effort, Xante wrenched her mind away from the ideas which attacked the basis of her own Hinto belief in reincarnation. 'There is more,' she said. 'There were pictures of how the War-chaw see the Chaw and the Dryad: hordes of evil, mis-shapen, yellow-skinned men fighting fanatically with feeble weapons. They despise your people, Curos, but fear their numbers. They believe the Forest of S'lan to be the source of evil, the spawning place of the Chaw race, and the home of foul spirits who inspire the Chaw to acts of horror.' She shrugged with disbelief. 'Until the battle in Corninstan he had not seen any members of the Chaw race but his view of us both is deep-seated. It is almost as if the Warchaw believe their purpose is to rid the world of the Chaw and the Dryad.'

'Perhaps, in his dying, he was confused.'

'Perhaps, childhood nightmares mixed with recent memories,' said Xante but her voice did not sound convinced.

Tayan and Kasar carried the body of a Warchaw into the firelight and began to search for anything of value.

'Help yourselves,' said Akab, completely unmoved by Xante's words. Xante looked out into the darkness and said with some confusion, 'The first Warchaw, the one who thought I was Vallan-nas? I thought he could be questioned?'

'I fear not, Lady,' said Akab with his malevolent grin. 'Lord Curos was over-worried for your safety and struck too hard.'

'It was unnecessary,' grimaced Curos. 'His weapon was still sheathed.'

'There is still the one who fled,' Akab reminded them.

'You are sure there was a fourth man?' asked Curos. 'The merchants only saw three.'

'Merchants have only eyes for gold and profit,' spat Akab. 'The tracks say four and the lady sorceress' words confirm it. When the party stopped to rest just after mid-day the fourth man made off on the best of the horses. Like the sentry,' he indicated the third body, 'he may have sensed we were close by and decided to try his luck alone.'

'Curos, it is important,' said Xante. 'These men recognise sorcery, at first they were not terrified by my fire.'

'It terrified me, madam,' said Juchi, handing her a small bowl of tea with a bow. 'I fear no man, not even death Himself, but I, Juchi, must admit to being afraid of a woman!'

'But the barbarians thought it a jest of their sorcerer Val-lan-nas,' Xante continued. 'The man ran forward and shouted, "Hj Valanus".'

'Whatever that means?'

'It does not matter. As soon as the barbarian realised it was not Val-lan-nas he knew it was the Chaw Witch from the village. He recognised my style of sorcery, Curos, as if he knew my face.'

The import of her words was not lost on Curos.

'Yes, Curos. These spies know there is at least one sorcerer in Chaw. The Warchaw magician probably begins to suspect something already. If Akab's fourth man confirms their fears they will move quickly to destroy me before I can build up

101

sufficient skill to combat them. I am not ready for that yet. Not half ready.'

'Do not worry, lady,' chided Akab. 'You gave me two gold coins. I have earned one this night, you will get value for the other soon enough.'

Without speaking Xante stood up and still sipping scalding tea walked over to look at the three dead barbarians. They lay in the flickering firelight, their clothes disarrayed by the rifling of Tayan and Kasar. What had brought these foreigners from their own green forest and fields into the heat of Chaw? She barely noticed as Curos joined her, standing close so that his arm touched hers. She realised that he alone knew how badly shaken she was. The Warchaw were big men, a head taller even than Kasar and proportionately broad. Their skin was pale with only faces and hands browned by wind and sun. It was the hair which most surprised her: long and fair on two of the men, slightly darker on the third. One also had a thick, full beard, so different from a Chaw or Dryad. He had been strong and skilful, thought Xante, stronger probably than any Chaw. Were the Western sorcerers stronger than any Dryad?

14

Deep into the cold, cloudless night, Curos finally gave up all attempt at sleep. He slid out from the quilted sleeping sack, aware that Xante had already left the shelter of the makeshift tent, or yert, which acted as little more than a wind break.

The Dryad woman was sitting close to the glowing embers of the camp fire, her face turned slightly upwards, her eyes gazing on the brilliant desert stars. 'The water is hot enough for tea,' she murmured as he approached. 'You could not sleep?'

'No, my mind and body are still reacting to the fight and the extra knowledge we have learned.'

'. . . and mind control does not seem appropriate when there is much to be considered,' Xante replied. 'I must speak to Dromo at some time.' She shook her head as if to clear an evil dream.

'Are you unwell?' asked Curos, sitting so that he could see her face, for once uncovered.

'Yes.' She shuddered again. 'Unwell in my mind. It is not easy to pry into the soul of a dying man, Curos. He had such fear. Fear of death and fear of the Chaw people. These people are revolted by us.'

Curos moved closer and held her in a comforting embrace. They did not speak for some time until Xante remarked, in an obvious attempt to make conversation, 'In S'lan we rarely see the stars, Curos. There are always tree tops or clouds between us and the sky and it is of little importance. Now there are so many stars and they are so bright and close. When I am in S'lan, Curos, death has no meaning but in this emptiness, where the sky goes on for ever, I am afraid. I doubt everything. The sounds are different too.' She looked at Curos and smiled. 'It sounds as if every grain of sand out there is moving, moving and talking. I have heard it before, but tonight it seems louder.'

'The N'gol say it is the song of the Sky Maidens as they sing in the Heavens,' said Curos. 'The Sky Maidens are the bright stars and are the daughters of the Great God of Winds, the God of Heaven.'

'He has many daughters,' commented Xante. 'What are the smaller stars? Some seem very small, clustered like clouds.'

'They are the children of Dei Sechen, the N'gol hero, and Ren the Sky Maiden,' replied Curos. 'Of course the wise men, the astronomers of Chaw, have other explanations. There is still some time before dawn – shall I tell you of Dei Sechen and the Sky Maiden?' Xante merely nodded and snuggled more tightly into Curos, her eyes still lost in the stars.

'Many centuries ago,' started Curos, 'the world was one vast, open steppe-land with long rivers and wide open spaces of grazing land and scrub desert. There were no forests and no farmlands.'

'In our stories,' interrupted Xante, 'the early world is always totally covered by one everlasting, never-ending forest.'

Curos smiled at this remark and continued. 'The clans lived much as they do today, with each clan split into smaller family groups, all moving over the grazing lands of their ancestors. There was the same amount of fighting and raiding and feuding but of course men were stronger, women more beautiful and horses ran faster than those of today.'

'As in all old stories,' Xante commented sleepily.

'In one of the clan villages was born a boy called Sechen. He grew quickly and strongly. He could ride when he was three and shoot a bow when he was five. He was no larger than other boys but seemed to be much stronger and more skilful.

'Soon he could ride even the fastest and strongest of the clan's horses but no horse, mare or stallion, suited Sechen. One night, after a long gazelle hunt, so the story goes, he was camped far away from the yerts of his people. On waking, he found a wild mare looking down at him as a woman might look at a man. Without thinking, he leapt up upon the mare who seemed only too pleased to feel him on her back. Without trying to throw him off, she raced across the plain at a speed so fast that Sechen could barely breathe for excitement. Although he had no saddle or halter on the mare, Sechen felt as secure and as firm on her back as if astride a harnessed war-horse.

'And so Sechen and Desert Mare became as one, riding over

the plains and having many adventures. Sechen never used a saddle but he could shoot his bow from Desert Mare's back as finely as if standing with both feet on the ground. They visited many clans and the girls would cast soft eyes on Sechen, for although not a big man, his strength and skill were beyond that of any N'gol living at the time. But Sechen responded to none of these advances, thinking that until he met a woman as beautiful as Desert Mare he would remain unmarried. Many stallions of the clans were similarly desirous of Desert Mare but she was also unmoved. It was said that only a stallion who could run as far and as fast as she, would be able to make her his brood mare.

'One evening of bright starlight Sechen and Desert Mare were travelling slowly across the open plains – where the O'san Plains are today – when a Sky Maiden swept down close to the earth. In those days there were few stars and the N'gol did not know that they were the Sky Maidens, the daughters of the Great Sky God of the Winds. Rarely indeed did they come close to the earth to sing, having little interest in the affairs of men, but one of the Sky Maidens, Ren of the Red Light, had often seen Sechen from afar and had been very attracted by the manly strength of this mortal. She guided her red chariot, pulled by a massive black stallion, down through the skies until its magic wheels ran on the hard earth.

'The surprise of Sechen at the sight of the celestial chariot coming down to earth was quite swept away by the instant love he felt for the Sky Maiden. Her beauty was quite beyond comprehension by a normal mortal. Her face glowed with the crystal light of the stars and her long hair fell like waterfalls of black fire down over her shoulders. Without speaking, she descended from her chariot and released the stallion from its shafts. Instantly, the chariot was transformed into a sky dome of jewelled splendour, the goddess' yert. While Sechen and Ren the Star Maiden spent the night in this mystic place, Desert Mare and the Sky Stallion ran free across the whole length and breadth of the N'gol lands. The sound of their cries and their hoofbeats was worse than a thousand sand dragons and the earth was rent and torn by their passage.

'After the long night Sechen and Ren emerged as man and

wife and Desert Mare stood trembling with fatigue and pleasure as the Sky Stallion rested his head on her neck. Despite their love, they could not stay together. The Sky Maiden could not remain on the earth for more than one night and it was not permitted for any mortal to travel to the heavens.

'Sechen and Desert Mare returned to their clan village. As usual they were treated as heroes but there was little joy in life for Sechen and Desert Mare. Listless and without interest in the affairs of men, they spent their days sleeping fitfully so that they would be able to ride beneath the night sky seeking the Sky Woman and her mighty steed. Far and wide over the desert places of N'gol travelled Sechen and Desert Mare, becoming more and more desperate until their grip on life itself weakened.

'In the sky one star also became dim with longing and sadness. One star at first, but then other Sky Maidens also grew dim with the sadness of their sister. Soon the whole night sky became shrouded in misery.

'At last Sechen could stand his life no longer. He took Desert Mare high up into the mountains of Lune as high and as far as horse and man could travel. To the very point of the highest mountain they went by night, seeking one last sight of Ren of the Red Light and Sky Stallion. Still no vision was granted them and with a mighty leap such as no other earthly horse could make, Desert Mare leapt into the very sky of heaven. High above the mountains she soared with Sechen urging her onwards. Only then did the Great God of Winds relent and show mercy to his daughter, Ren.

'Instantly she sent Sky Stallion speeding downwards, and faster than any eye could see they swept beneath Sechen and Desert Mare to carry them up into the very star seats of heaven where Ren had her place. Together she and Sechen entered the sky dome and Desert Mare and Sky Stallion sped off through the darkness of the night sky. The light of Ren and all the Star Maidens blazed out as of old and on the earth it was as if a great sadness had been lifted.

'And so Sechen and Ren lived in the sky. Soon their children began to appear, small stars which grew no bigger and were never as bright as the stars of the Sky Maidens themselves.

'Although the girls are true to their mother and the sky world, the boy children are as the N'gol and speed through the heavens on the black horses bred from Desert Mare and Sky Stallion. Sometimes on a very clear night one of them can be seen as a flash of light as he speeds close to the ground to seek a glimpse of his father's people. If the sky N'gol see that their brothers on earth are beset by danger then they will come streaming down from the skies like the night wind of heaven, and with arrows of fire they will destroy those who beset the true people.

'The other Sky Maidens envy the happiness of Ren. Often, in secret, so as not to anger their celestial father, they fly close to the earth, seeking some mortal hero whom they could take for a husband. Sadly for the N'gol people and for the Sky Maidens, there are no warriors equal to Dei Sechen riding on the earth in these later days and the song of the Sky Maidens is sad with the loneliness of the desert. So sad that even the grains of sand are moved to echo their pleas for happiness.'

15

It was still dark when Curos finished his tale and he sat quietly with Xante, all thoughts of re-entering the yert long rejected. In that relaxed state he lapsed into a gentle doze, only to be roused by Akab's light pressure behind his ear.

'Shh, Lord, quiet,' he breathed. 'Riders are coming. Wake the Witch Woman. There may be need of her sorcery.'

The moon had set and the night darkened over. Curos' small party hastily concealed themselves in the rocks and the bushes away from the well and the dying camp fire. The bodies of the Warchaw had been quickly covered to look as if they were sleeping.

By the size of the horses and the style of the riders the new-comers were not Warchaw, but could hardly be Chaw Army either, thought Curos in some confusion. Also it was unusual for the N'gol to risk their horses by riding in such darkness, even in a raid. Silently and skilfully twenty or so men ringed the camp in a half circle and Curos could sense rather than see their short, recurved bows ready to shoot.

One of the riders came forward and called out in a confident voice. 'I am Yesugei, son of Ongul, leader of the War Ulus of the Night Dragon Clan. We are not robbers who prey on peaceful travellers. It is useless to hide from the Night Dragon who see in the dark. Come forth and explain who you are and why these people lie dead in a place of peace.'

Curos stiffened in surprise. Could these clansmen truly see in the dark as it was rumoured? He stood up and walked out into the open before proclaiming his name, his lineage and his rank; it was expected. He also explained that he had been seeking enemies of the Chaw people, foreign spies of great evilness, who had fled from true justice in the D'was.

'Then you have hunted well, Lord Zachaw,' said Yesugei, indicating the covered bodies. 'That is to be expected when one has Akab as a guide. Come out from the shadows, old friend of the Night Dragon. Your excursion into our hunting grounds is forgiven.' As the hunter led the others of the group out from their cover Yesugei said to Curos, 'We came seeking a party of merchants to warn them of new dangers in our land. There had been no sign of those we sought to protect but only a strange fire in the sky. You'll be welcome at our kuriyen to talk with my father and perhaps explain some of these mysteries.'

With the minimum of conversation and formality they all mounted and moved out from the camp of fire and death. Yesugei guided his horse close to Akab and said, 'You keep strange company these days, Akab.'

'Yes,' the hunter replied. 'Strange and dangerous, Yesugei. Lord Curos is as deadly as any man I have known.'

'I will be warned,' said Yesugei. 'But a man is just a man in the D'was.'

'And be warned also against the woman, Lady Xante. For the sake of your father and your clan do not trifle with her. No,' he stopped Yesugei's question. 'Say nothing more but treat her not as a woman but at least with the respect of an equal.'

Not far away Xante and Curos were similarly discussing Yesugei and Akab. 'I am sure we can trust them,' Curos reassured her. 'The clans are not hostile to the Chaw and this clan would seem to have a link with your people.'

'Only through the merchants,' replied Xante. 'But all is not as it seems. From within this depression the light of my sorcery could not have been seen for more than a few yetang. And how did Yesugei know where we hid? They ride in black and are closely veiled, it makes them look sinister.'

'Possibly they copy the Dryadin dress.'

'No, I am sure not,' she said and thought for a while as their horses picked up speed following the leading Clansman. She leaned sideways in her saddle to speak again. 'Curos, what is that small group there who hold back from the main party? One rides as if blind, attended by the other.' Curos could give no answers.

It was well into morning when the kuriyen of the Night Dragon Clan came into sight. Their camp was the usual circle of yerts around which grazed small herds of horses, goats and cattle. During the year the Clan would be continually moving in an almost migratory pattern from well-site to well-site; forced on as the supply of water and fodder neared exhaustion. Although tolls gathered from escorted merchants and game from hunting were welcome additions to their economy, it was their stock animals on which they most depended. All but the simplest agriculture was ruled out by the thin soil and harsh climate of the high D'was plateau. Often the younger men would enlist in the Chaw cavalry units where their stamina and horsemanship were appreciated. Of Curos' party, Juchi was from the nearby Silver Fox Clan which was not always on the best of terms with the Night Dragon.

The meeting between Curos and the headman was conducted outside his yert in the open air. The only concession to comfort was the provision of several large leather cushions. Headman Ongul and four other elders were similarly seated while the remainder of the Clan, warriors, women and children, sat respectfully on the hard, dry earth. Visitors were obviously of great interest.

'Welcome, Zachaw Ca'lin, son of Lord Zachaw Pa'lin who is known to us as the Esteemed Leader of the Chaw Army. Please accept our humble hospitality. There is koumis to drink and bread and cheese-curd. The fugitives you sought must have been important indeed to bring such an honoured pursuer into our land so close to the winter cold.'

'We did not intend to kill at your watering place, Ongul,' Curos said, 'but they refused capture and gave me no option.'

The headman dismissed the incident with a gesture. 'They were strangers who came unbidden. If you had quarrelled with them, that is your affair, Lord Zachaw.'

A woman brought large beakers of the fermented mares' milk and served Curos and Akab, pointedly ignoring Xante, who had no right to sit with the men. Akab caught the N'gol woman's wrist firmly and took another beaker. 'It does not do to be uncivil to a sorceress, woman,' he said quietly with his usual broken smile.

'On your journey, Lord Curos,' asked Ongul, 'have you seen a party of honest merchants from the town of Untin? There would be three men of substance with servants and pack animals.'

'Would you mean the merchants who travel by the old road to avoid paying taxes?' asked Curos with a half smile.

'I know nothing of taxes,' shrugged Ongul with an expressive gesture. 'But these merchants hire my men as guides. Why they travel so far north is no concern of mine provided they pay and do our people no harm.'

'Neither are they any interest to an army K'tan, even when they trade with the dread forest of Sibrea or S'lan as the Dryadin call it,' replied Curos. 'Your merchants are safe at the 55th Arrow Riders' Post at Dar Tol. They turned south to avoid the fleeing Warchaw spies.'

'I am pleased they are safe, Lord Zachaw. No doubt they will travel north again in a few days.'

'No doubt,' replied Curos, 'and they may now consider paying more for the protection of the Night Dragons.'

'There is still the question of the last of your fugitives,' said the headman seriously. 'You seek him still?'

'Yes. It is important to me that he is found. I would make a suitable gift to anyone who would bring him to me, a better gift still if he were alive and able to talk.'

'There is no dishonour in accepting gold,' replied Ongul, 'but in this case we will need no payment and there is no question of the man leaving our land alive.'

'He might die more painfully and slowly if handed to Lord Curos!' Akab suggested.

'That is unlikely. Two women of the Clan have a high claim on his body.' Ongul paused to drink his koumis before continuing with his explanation.

'Two days ago men of our clan were seeking game when they saw a lone rider on a limping horse. Thinking he might be in distress, they approached with the greeting of friendship. He replied in Corninstani, which many of us speak, asking for guidance to the source of water. It was only when Jebei of my own family was offering a drink that the stranger struck him down with a dagger. Another was then treacherously slain by the sword. His brother, Tiniujin, managed to strike the evil one and draw blood but then he too was struck down.'

'A deadly foe to kill three clansmen in such a way,' mused Akab with grudging admiration.

'A coward and a traitor who strikes the hand offering Water Friendship,' shouted Yesugei. 'None in this Clan will speak well of such filth.'

'We mean no disrespect to your Clan,' apologised Curos. 'I and four of my soldiers were hard put to cut down one of the Warchaw and I grieve for the death of your family.'

'Just so,' growled Ongul, 'but young Tiniujin did not die. He regained his horse and outdistanced his clumsy pursuer. His arm was broken or with his bow he would have avenged his brother. Even so Tiniujin only feigned flight and turned back secretly to see which way the traitor departed with his stolen horses. Already the anger of the Night Dragons is following him.'

'Two days,' said Akab sadly. 'The Warchaw has two days' start and fresh, fast N'gol horses to carry him. The autumn winds are already blowing and in the hard ground it will not be easy to trail such a man.'

'So Akab has his limits but he should know that The Night Dragon Clan have different ways,' said Ongul. 'Since the Warchaw tries to go west we have sent out scouts to cut his route and to turn him back.'

'But in the night he may slip past any such cordon,' said Curos worriedly, looking at Xante.

'It is our hope that he will try,' said Yesugei, 'for in the night nothing escapes the Night Dragon as Lord Curos has seen.'

'It cannot be certain,' answered Curos. 'I will send messengers to the other clans and my father will order out the army to patrol the line where the D'was merges with the O'san.'

'I cannot have other clans riding across our land,' stated Ongul flatly. 'There is little enough grass for our own herds.'

'I know your problem, Ongul. My own mother, the Lady Turakina, is from the Clan of the White Dragon,' said Curos.

Despite his concern, Ongul smiled briefly. 'All N'gols know the story of Zachaw Pa'lin and Turakina but even for the son of Pa'lin I cannot open our lands to other clans.'

'I speak openly before all, Ongul, so as not to insult your people but what I say must be a close secret. In Corninstan the barbarians used a great power to defeat us. I have been seeking a counter to this knowledge and it must be kept from them.'

'Men from the Clan died with the Ruby Wind,' said one of

the elders. 'We need not know your secret. Better if you were to know ours, Lord.'

'Yes,' agreed Ongul. 'Honesty brings honesty. Present Tayan to our guest.'

'This is Tayan and his father,' he continued as a man and his son approached. Both were dressed in the usual black clothing and the man was of pale skin and hair for a N'gol. The youth, Tayan, had his face completely covered and needed to be led by the hand. He was evidently unable to see clearly and stood timidly before Curos.

'The Night Dragon are renowned for being able to hunt in the dark,' said Ongul. 'But a few have the ability of Tayan; he is almost blind in sunlight but the darker and colder the night, the better he can see. Other clans cast out those with the white hair and skin but we know their true worth. For hunting or guiding at night Tayan has no equal.'

'This explains much,' said Curos. 'Is it permitted to see the face of Tayan?'

'My son is not afraid to show his face,' said the father boldly in the way of the N'gol. 'But your companion, Lord Curos, also keeps herself covered.'

'Then we will both be open to view.' Without further speech Xante removed her veil.

The boy's skin and hair were a pale, almost translucent white, even his lips held no colour. He had moved to avoid the direct sun but his eyes still blinked against the morning light. It was the eyes which were the most disturbing, pale, watery pink with no pupil; they looked unseeingly at Curos.

'I see you as a man, Lord Curos, a man of hot blood and much energy. In the dark of the Well of Sorrow I could see you as a beacon as you crouched, bow in hand.' The colourless lips smiled oddly as he continued. 'The Warchaw were almost cold and difficult to distinguish from the rocks where they lay.'

'So you see by heat?' asked Xante in surprise.

'Yes, Lady of Chaw.' Tayan looked at Xante for the first time. His face showed sudden shock and fear and he stepped back against his father. 'Protect me. It is a spirit woman, a spirit from the shades. She gives out less heat than the newly dead.' Around

113

the circle of Clansmen signs against evil were made and as women pulled children away, men reached for weapons.

'Is this your secret, Lord Curos? To raise the dead to fight the Warchaw?' shouted Ongul. 'We want no part of it.'

'Tayan,' said Xante earnestly. 'You can see a tree in the dark?'

'Leave me, I mean you no harm!'

'Tayan, can you see a tree in the dark?' Her deep voice rang with unexpected authority. 'Think and answer.'

'Only just, madam.' His voice wavered. 'Their life is so cold and slow. Often in the cold of winter . . .' His voice faltered with slow realisation. 'Often in the cold of winter it disappears and then in the warmth of the spring night the same tree will glow as a fire.'

'Then you know already that we have no need to fear each other, Tayan.' Xante smiled as he turned and seemed to peer at her. 'For the others of the Night Dragon Clan know that I am a Dryad Woman, a High Sorcerer of the Eternal Forest of S'lan.'

A hush fell on the assembly but it was not the N'gol way to be surprised or quiet for long. Questions and discussion abounded and to Curos' surprise the Clan seemed genuinely delighted to have a Dryad in their camp.

'We of the Night Dragon have often met with the Dryadin such as Aalani the Runner,' explained Tayan, 'but now a High Dryad has come from the Forest. There is so much difference in the power. Aalani is a man of note and honour but the Lady is a sorcerer indeed.'

'It is good that the magic of the Dryad has again come into the world of men,' said an elder. 'When Emperor Xan II defeated the N'gol hordes of Tinjin by destroying the water places it was the holy Dryads who restored our land and built the well places for us.'

'We have no need for ancient tales today, honoured grandfather,' cut in Ongul, 'but see, Lord Zachaw, Curos, that no man will pass the cordon of the night. Already five such as Tayan are with our horsemen as they sweep the plains for the murderer. Bringing in more men will only cause confusion and lessen the chance of success.'

'It is agreed,' said Curos. 'It is for you to hunt in your land.'

Looking directly at the headman, he added more quietly so that no other would hear, 'Now that you know the value of the sorceress I wish to protect, you will understand why I had to be sure you would be able to capture the Warchaw.'

Ongul was looking with open admiration at Xante, who was speaking to Tayan. 'As a man I understand.' He punched Curos with boisterous good humour before bursting into laughter at Curos' unaccustomed embarrassment.

16

Xante-Yani, Dryad sorceress and horse-rider, stood up in her stirrups and let out a yell of pure elation at the sensation of speed and freedom. *Was it the first time that the war cry of the Dryadin had ever sounded in Akar, the north-west province of Chaw?* thought Curos as he rode beside the tired but ecstatic woman. Not to be outdone, he answered with the cry of the Topaz Wind Riders as they covered the last yetang of the journey to Te Toldin and the Topaz Stone glowed a deep yellow at his chest.

Curos had left the main body of troops to continue their march to G'tal, the capital city, under the command of Bhal Morag. With Xante and six horsemen Curos had decided to make a rapid journey to his father's estate, Te Toldin. The Great Northern Road stretched from the Eastern Sea to Corninstan and led to the large estate of the Zachaw family, which sprawled near the western edge of Chaw. The pace of their two-day ride had gradually increased until it had almost become a long-distance race with minimum stops to rest and change the horses. Darkness was falling but Curos had pressed on, determined to reach his home without having to stop on the road for another night. It was as they passed the boundary marker for Te Toldin that Xante had made her yell of almost defiant greeting to this new land. The magic of the Dryad was equal to the hard nomad-trained horse warrior.

The fatigue of their mounts and the danger of mishap forced them to slow for the last leg of their journey. In the dusk the road spread out into a large, circular open space before continuing straight into the distant west. At the northern edge of this circle stood the ornate pagoda gate which marked the entrance to Te Toldin. Beyond the gilded archway the long, gently curving drive swept through intensively cultivated fields and orchards to the Guarded Gate of the park which surrounded the Zachaw mansion.

As Curos passed through the pagoda he struck the bronze gong of greeting with his sword hilt, and again shouted the Topaz war cry to herald his approach. He spurred the tired horse along the drive at a full run until the torchlit main entrance gate came in sight. Only then did he rein his horse and wait for Xante to catch up.

Even before she reached Curos, Xante sensed an abrupt change in him. The feelings of sheer elation were dashed into fear and despair. In the semi-darkness she could make out little of his expression but the hanging lanterns and sentries' braziers showed only too clearly the long white banners of mourning.

Two heavily armoured soldiers stood unmoving while the white tapes from their helmets fluttered lifelessly in the scant cool breeze. The guard commander, surprised by Curos' rapid progress from the outer gate, hurried forward and bowed low to Curos. It was impossible for Xante to read the black script on the banners but she realised that, like some powerful spell, they had changed the vibrant young War Lord into the dignified Chaw nobleman who now slowly dismounted from the nervous horse. She could almost feel Curos' tension as he waited impassively while the guard commander bowed again and dropped to his knees.

'Most honoured Zachaw Ca'lin, your father, the High General Commander of the armies of Chaw, the Commander of the Topaz Wind, the Master of Te Toldin, has committed his soul to the void.'

In the flickering light Curos stood motionless, his face blank and expressionless. Xante could feel the despair and grief surging up in him as he used all his resolve and strength to control his outward feelings and maintain the stoicism his father would have expected. Agonisingly the silence extended, engulfing the death-like tableau. Eventually with broken, almost inaudible, words Curos returned the guard's salute. Leaving his sweating horse unheeded, he stalked through the wide entrance courtyard of the Zachaw mansion with stiff shoulders and a firm tread. Uncertainly Xante followed behind until they ascended the steps to where the household officials waited with respectful servitude.

Only after further exchanges of greetings and condolences did Curos turn to Xante. 'I have had grievous news. My father is dead. Would you wait here while I greet my mother and brother? The servants will bring you food and prepare you a room.' Before she could answer he had left and made his way off with the elderly man who had greeted him at the head of the steps.

Xante looked around the immense hallway which was lit by many lanterns. This one room was much bigger than any tent or Dryadin long house that Xante had ever seen. This and the cold stone walls and floor sent chills of unease through her tired body. Around the walls stood stone figures and pathetic miniature trees, horribly stunted by cruel practices. For all the sorrow and grief she could feel in this venerable hall, she realised it was not a dark and evil place. It was almost like a person that grieved, but behind this were memories of joy and security stretching back into the dark of time. And something else deeper still, an echo of the forest. Her mind reeled. It was too much; she was too tired to accept these images. Without further thought, she left the hallway and returned to where a perplexed groom was wondering what to do with her meagre baggage. Easily, she shouldered the sack of personal items and seizing the bow and quiver of arrows marched back into the forbidding building.

Like a wandering storyteller, Xante unrolled her sleeping mat and sat in a relaxed pose close to the wall until a servant brought in a tray of boiled rice and tea. The confused manservant looked at Xante and then at the small alcove with its padded cushions and low tables where a guest might wait comfortably. After some moments he bowed and placed the tray on the floor before hurrying off to seek advice from the House Steward.

Despite her extreme hunger Xante ate the mixed rice and vegetables slowly and carefully. The spiced meat sauce was fastidiously ignored but she found the hot fragrant Jasmin tea delightfully refreshing. There was still no sign of Curos and the disdainfully hostile stares of the sentry and passing servants did not encourage conversation. Echoing memories, almost a hint of welcome, plucked at her thoughts but she brushed these aside and made a soft pad from her spare clothes and stretched herself out to sleep. In her vision she sent out tendrils of green snaking across the cold, brown stone, crossing and turning in a mat of awareness which would awaken her at any approach. The innermost stems writhed upwards towards the high ceiling, closing over her like a canopy of the forest. As an added precaution she slept with her drawn bronze and poison-wood dagger clasped in her hand.

While Xante slept content and secure in her self-confidence, Zachaw Ca'lin Curos, master designate of Te Toldin, was involved in a grief-laden family meeting with his mother and younger brother, Makran. In the face of his mother's tear-stained mourning, Curos' anger and frustration at his father's suicide had dispelled into sadness and concern for her welfare. But now with embraces and sympathetic statements completed and the refreshing tea of welcome drunk Curos was compelled to speak and ask bitter questions. Questions which had seared his mind from the time the guard sergeant had made his fateful report. His mother's face was now hidden beneath a white silk veil and the dim lamplight gave away no secrets from under her tear-swollen eyelids.

'Why, mother?' he asked desperately. 'Why did he need to do it, and why now? He could have waited at least one more day until I returned.'

'In your heart, Curos, my son, you must know the answer,' his mother answered sadly. 'He took his own life to atone for the disgrace of the army of Corninstan. He took his life when he did to avoid the pain of arguing with his eldest son who would try to dissuade him from the path of honour.'

'The path of honour is to fight, not to do the enemy's work for him,' growled Curos.

'It was father's choice,' suggested Makran lamely. 'He could not live with the shame of defeat.'

'There is no disgrace in defeat,' snapped Curos. 'In cowardice, yes, but none would make such a charge against Zachaw Pa'lin.'

'You do not understand, Curos,' said Turakina, his mother. 'It was not your father's own conduct he had to atone for. It was to remove the shame felt by the whole army. After the battle he sent written orders to each commander, to each K'tan, forbidding them to act against themselves. His suicide will seal that order. Chaw needs the men who have fought the barbarian Warchaw, not the suicide of its most able commanders. He was

119

afraid that they would not live with the shame of their defeat unless he bound them to life.'

'He could have waited,' said Curos flatly. 'The order of life lasts for three months. There are still sixteen days left. He need not have rushed into the void before my return. I have brought the sorceress as he requested. Now Chaw needs a man of vision and cunning to use this new power. All his experience and wisdom have gone with him. He sent me off before we could talk after the battles – I needed that conversation.' Curos was unable to keep his voice from trembling. 'I would also have bid him farewell.'

'He hands the banner of Chaw to you, my son,' said Turakina, 'but not to fight with the wild heroism of my people. He has sealed you to the fate of Chaw.'

'You have no reason to grieve for the loss of father's wisdom,' said Makran. 'As soon as you departed he summoned the Noyans of the army who had fought in Corninstan and recorded all the events of the battles, even to the number of men killed and the arrows shot.'

'I would at least have bid him farewell,' repeated Curos but now his brother interrupted bitterly.

'When the recording was complete he spent many days meditating on the events, and many hours discussing his thoughts with the generals, particularly with Po Pi who will succeed him as High General Commander. He did not want to talk with his own family or take notice of his estates or his other responsibilities.'

'His warrior son was not here,' snapped Curos. 'Would he discuss war with Makran, the farmer, or with the women of the house?'

'The heir to Zachaw is often away,' retorted Makran. 'We cannot all spend our lives riding with the wind of the desert but now you are master of Te Toldin.'

'I am still mistress of Te Toldin,' cut in Turakina authoritatively. 'For three months the order of life lasts and I will run Te Toldin for Zachaw Pa'lin. My first instruction is that Pa'lin's sons will not discomfort his spirit by arguing and by showing bitterness at their father's actions. His course over the last two months was well planned and fully considered. You will not show disrespect by questioning your father's wisdom. The time since the Battle of the Corninstan Road was a hard one for Pa'lin. It was not easy for him to relive again and again his failure and the loss of the fine cavalry army he had trained. Night after night he did discuss his thoughts with me while his shame and failure kept him from sleep.'

'So he talked to his wife but not with his son,' interrupted Makran angrily.

'Yes, with his wife, Turakina of the White Dragon Clan of the N'gol nomads,' snapped his mother. 'As Curos said, Makran, you are a farmer and a manager and we respect you as such. But I am a horsewoman from the D'was. I can still ride better than most men and know all the moves of the horsemen at war. Yes, Pa'lin talked to me and planned his actions and wrote his words of wisdom for Po Pi and Curos. It was not easy and it was not enjoyable to see such a strong man broken down.'

'And you agreed with his suicide?' asked Curos in a pained voice.

'No, I would not agree to that.'

'Neither did you agree to be with him at his hour or to accompany him into the void as is the custom,' said Makran.

'No. I am a free woman of the White Dragon Clan taken by Pa'lin Zachaw to be his wife according to our custom. I did not come to Te Toldin as a sold Chaw wife. If Pa'lin, my husband, had left his home to seek death in one last desperate attack on a Warchaw war band I would have ridden gladly at his side but I could not put the knife to my own throat. To the N'gol throwing away the gift of life is a great sin, greater still when one leaves enemies alive. Neither would I attend my husband when at the early morning sunrise he sat between the tree and the stone and took his life.'

'Did he die alone?' asked Curos.

'As he wished,' said Turakina. 'He gave the sacrifice of his life that other, younger men would live and pick up the war banner from where he had let it fall.'

'We have much to discuss,' said Makran.

'But not tonight,' replied Curos. 'I would like to see my father's body.'

Turakina gave a deep, gasping sob and slumped forward, her head almost touching the low table. 'Even that cannot be, my son. He took his leave of me in life and would not have his family see him in death. The funeral pyre was already prepared. Now only his spirit remains in this world, free to fly with the wind.'

Curos' self-control snapped at last and he staggered to his feet, tears streaming down his face. He bent briefly to kiss his mother's forehead and gripped his brother's shoulder before leaving the room. In his haste he collided with the tall, angular figure of the Steward.

'A thousand pardons, honoured master,' the Steward began to say but Curos cut him short. Trying to control his speech he said, 'From the forests of S'lan has come an honoured and powerful sorceress, come to Te Toldin at my father's bidding. She is not used to our ways and may be confused by this honoured house. Will you please conduct her to a chamber close to mine?'

'Sir, with respect,' the Steward said in a flat voice, 'your wives have the rooms on either side of your own and both expect an audience, a visit from you on your return.'

'Then they will be disappointed. Please conduct the Dryad lady Xante-Yani to a guest room. I will use another close by. Inform the ladies that I am overcome with grief and tiredness and cannot be seen tonight.'

The Steward carried out Curos' instructions with the quiet competence which he had developed over forty years in the service of Zachaw Pa'lin at Te Toldin. The ladies Hoelun and Kataln were told of Lord Curos' indisposition and the Jade Guest room was prepared for the Dryad woman. Only then did the Steward descend to the entrance hall to conduct Xante to the chamber. Crossing automatically to the annexe off the hall, he was startled to see a black-clad form stretched out asleep on a crude peasant sleeping mat. With slight indecision he crossed to where Xante lay and stood staring down at her. Despite the enveloping tunic and trousers and the practically obscured face, the Steward was immediately aware of her youth and vitality, so far removed from the timid rustic he had expected. Younger even than his own daughters, could this girl be the Dryad sorceress Lord Curos had spoken of?

Diplomatically he coughed and moved forward, triggering

Xante's defences. Instantly she awoke and sprang upright behind
the venomous dagger. Never before in his many years of Jitsu
practice had the Steward seen such a fast and fluid movement
into the aggressive defensive position. The left hand darted forward, the fingers curved back as the Paw of the Tiger. The right
hand carrying the knife was drawn back with a blade ready to
fly at his throat while the legs were perfectly placed for attack
or defence. Instinctively the Steward jumped sideways and then
realised how much too slow he would have been to avoid the
threatened attack. He dropped his arms and bowed, embarrassed
at his over-reaction as the girl said in a strange husky voice,
'Ancient sir, I fear I am discourteous as a guest in this fine
house.'

'It is I who should apologise,' replied the Steward. 'I should
not have startled you from sleep in such a harsh manner. I fear
you have been neglected, but the hospitality of this house has
been strained by the death of its master, Zachaw Pa'lin.'

'I feel that grief and pain in the very walls of the house,'
replied Xante, 'and I pray that Master Zachaw's transition from
this life into the next may be free from anguish.' The Steward
nodded sadly and begged leave to conduct the girl to the chamber
prepared for her.

Xante was amazed at the size and elegance of the room, one
personal room as large as her family's forest home. She touched
the soft, rich fabric of the curtains and stared in wonder at
the gilded cages of the lamps and the glowing opulence of the
furnishings. The large bed in the screened-off alcove was in itself
a marvel outside her dreams of experience. In a daze she washed
in the large bowl of scented water and looked unbelievingly at
the silver and glass mirror.

Soon, however, the wonder and amazement faded as her mind
again began to feel the aura of tragedy which clung like a marsh
fog around the once joyous house of Te Toldin. Even deeper
and more in anger than in sorrow, she detected the despair and
desolation of Curos. Curos whom she had been ordered to help
was in real danger from himself and his overwhelming grief and
guilt. Slowly Xante redressed. Carefully and meticulously she
arranged her own mind as she arranged her clothes. Her purpose
and resolution had to be sternly fixed in every detail before she

123

could risk touching minds with this violently disturbed man. Any indecision, any faltering could be dangerous to both of them and to the now linked lands of Chaw and Eternal S'lan.

Silently Xante opened Curos' door and allowed her forest-tuned vision to penetrate the smoke-filled darkness. Curos was sitting cross-legged on a low dais surrounded by small sticks of smouldering incense. Tears ebbed gently from swollen lids, and from cuts in his arm blood dripped down onto his thighs. His breathing was sharp and uneven as if cries or screams were barely being suppressed.

'Curos,' she said softly as she entered the shrine-like atmosphere of the room. 'Curos, this ritual is not working for you. It can never work for such as you. It will only worsen your grief.'

'Go, Xante, you are not wanted here. This is nothing to do with you or the Dryadin. I need to be alone to do things which have to be done.'

'To try to confer with the soul of your dead father, Curos?'

'There are things I need to say, woman, things I need to ask. They are no concern of yours,' he replied in a hard, angry tone.

'Zachaw Ca'lin Curos is now my concern,' said Xante. 'Your body is exhausted, your mind is gravely disturbed. In this state, disease, evil ideas or malevolent spirits could seize control of your very being. You have convinced the Dryadin that we need you, Curos. I will not see you dying, destroying yourself before your time.'

'I do not need the help of a woman, I have my own women. I do not need the help of a sorceress, doctors or drugs. Strength comes from within. After I have spoken to my father I shall be content.'

'You cannot coerce him to speak to you, Curos,' she replied with desperation in her voice. 'Your father did not wish to face your anger, he will not face it now. Only when you are at peace .and reconciled to his purpose will he seek you out. It is dangerous, what you do. You are no ordinary man to seek help from ancient half-forgotten practices. Already powerful evil forces have started to recognise you as their enemy in Chaw. In this state you are vulnerable.'

'And what would the Dryad have me do?' asked Curos bitterly. 'Seek ecstasy with my wife, Hoelun, or drunkenness or the oblivion that comes from the poppy?'

'No. You must protect yourself from what you have started. You cannot summon those dead who will not come, but already you begin to summon the spirit of those from the West who would have you dead or in their control. Sit where you are and together we will overcome this state of danger.' Fatigued beyond belief, Curos remained in his position as Xante removed her black clothing and folded gently into the lotus position. Her pale olive form was barely discernible in the gloom but he was aware that her knees were almost touching his. He could hear her slow, rhythmic breathing and make out the rise and fall of her exquisite shoulders.

'First we link hands to form a circle of power,' said Xante in a low murmur. 'Now we surround ourselves with a circle of burning fire to ward off demons and spirits. Concentrate on inner awareness. We must be as one within the circle. There is no outside, no existence beyond ourselves.'

Curos was half roused as a wall of incandescent, non-consuming fire surrounded them.

'Sustain that image with me, Curos. Now it is easy but the fire wall must be kept even as you ascend into the next level of navra. First by incantation and cyclic breathing and then by inner thought we raise the energy of your soul from its position at the base of the spine. Slowly, as this spirit rises it will lessen fatigue and bring stillness of mind. We sustain the Kama by deep yoga and breathing until our turmoil sleeps.'

Gradually Xante's hypnotic voice, the deep, slow breathing and the mental help quietened Curos until he felt he almost floated free of earth and all his troubles. Dimly he noticed the evil face of a young and bearded man whose gaze sought to penetrate the protecting fire wall. Curos felt the keen presence of the Warchaw sorcerer and the fire began to waver. But this was of no consequence, already Curos and Xante were in a new place where trees soared to the heavens and a hedge of interlocking green excluded all who were not welcome.

Curos' next recollection was of waking stiff and cold. He had been carried to the bed but the thin covering had not protected him in the cold room. Xante's dynamic presence had gone and so was any clear memory of her almost naked body; only her huddled form sleeping peacefully on the floor at the end of the room remained. The anguish at his father's unseemly and unnecessary death rushed into his thoughts again. Physically and spiritually rested, he was now able to control his emotions and to accept some of his father's logic without anger.

17

The noise and squalor of G'tal never changed or abated; their effect on Curos and ten days of constant riding from one Arrow Rider post to another did nothing to soften his view of the capital city of Chaw. Always he was shaken and bruised when he arrived at G'tal, always in a hurry, always having to leave something more enjoyable. He had planned several peaceful days in the estates of Te Toldin with Xante and had intended to read carefully the reports of his now dead father. In those words he hoped to gain full acceptance and understanding of his father's purpose. But the impelling if courteous greeting from Noyan Po Pi was more than an invitation to visit the capital.

The sweating post-horse pushed its way through the surging crowd which parted only grudgingly in response to the beast's strength and its rider's badges of rank. The human river of faded blue-clad peasants moved inexorably to the Northern Gate. The market had closed and they struggled to clear the gate before it shut at sundown. Men and women with empty baskets and carrying poles, tired, expressionless and almost silent, pressed in on Curos. The horse stumbled and lurched sideways as it stepped on a woman's foot. Her face was upturned in a scream which barely carried over the indistinct babble of the crowd. The horse recovered but before Curos could readjust himself in the saddle the anonymous woman's twisted face was swept away by the endless, streaming tide.

Curos turned east away from the mainstream and picked his way through the narrow streets which were little wider than cuttings between the packed buildings. On either side against the houses were neatly laid flagstones on which cart wheels ran and men walked. The gap between was a miniature dry canal along which horses walked or pulled and where refuse was thrown. Every fifth evening it would be the turn of this street to be swirled clean by the action of opening the main canal into the network of streets. Any large remaining items had to be carried away outside the town before the warden of the streets made his inspection the following day. The system was unique to G'tal and had been started when the city was built to replace the old imperial capital at the end of the Xan dynasty.

Another myth, thought Curos. Xan II had already started the building at the end of his reign. When Xan II had ascended the dragon throne the N'gol were sacking the old capital of Harwa on the Chew Kin river, but before his death the N'gol were crushed and the building of G'tal was well advanced. G'tal, the new city, between the arms of the yellow Lokin and the green Tishin river. Impregnable from attack, safe from the plague and destined to stand for 2,700 years.

But Xan II had died childless and had been succeeded by the tyrant Yen IV. In less than twenty-seven years, the civil wars had started, heralding the rule of the Civilian Council of Nobles and the Army Council of Noyans. Their first dishonourable act had been to annexe the achievements of Xan II as their own and to ensure that the wealth of the records and history destroyed by the N'gol hordes was not replaced. They had decreed that a new era would begin in Chaw, an era of increased stability where greed or ambition would have no place and even family loyalty would be limited.

Curos was roused from these thoughts by the sight of the city house kept by the Zachaw family – a modest frontage with a carriage arch leading into a courtyard surrounded by apartments and stables. Modest by the standard of the richer nobles, it was nonetheless twenty times larger than the usual G'tal family dwelling. Curos was not well known at the house and the groom who led the tired horse away was less than civil. Only when Curos approached the main door did an older servant recognise him and hurry forward, bowing with the expected deference.

'Lord, your presence is most unexpected,' he started to say but Curos cut him short with a perfunctory gesture.

'This is most unacceptable,' he stated coldly. 'No marks of mourning are before the gate and the porter is absent. I rode in ungreeted and unchallenged. The groom failed to recognise either my status or my person despite the badges of rank.' Again he silenced the cowering man. 'The offenders must be replaced

128

by others who are more diligent. I expect my apartment is fit for habitation?'

'Yes, Excellency. Clean and well serviced.'

'Good. I need a hot bath as soon as possible. A light meal, fruit, bread, nuts and perhaps a bean salad. Ensure the water is well boiled and flavoured by a little wine and lemon.'

'Yes, Excellency,' intoned the steward. 'Would a massage relieve the strain of the journey?'

'No. I find such attention distasteful, as you would do well to remember. Later this evening I will visit the esteemed Noyan Po Pi. Send my token to his office and enquire when it would be convenient to call. The valet will need to prepare my dress uniform. No decorations but the sash of the Topaz Wind will be appropriate.'

'Yes, your Excellency. Should mourning bands be provided for the arms?'

'No. It is not expected on military uniform, as you should know,' Curos was striving to control any display of anger, 'but for the next seventy days until the third month of Lord Zachaw's death it would be appropriate for the civilian staff to show such respect.'

Po Pi was known to Curos as a contemporary, rather than a friend, of his father. The relationship had been polite and formal as if some barrier had been erected between the two men. Many letters from Po Pi had been filed amongst Pa'lin's papers – letters explaining facets of the battle from Po Pi's viewpoint, constructive criticisms and comments on the final, massive report. There was even one severely impersonal letter advising the Grand Commander Zachaw Pa'lin that Noyan Po Pi saw no need for any one person to commit suicide as an act of atonement. It was strange therefore that with such an input into Zachaw's formal work and such apparent agreement with Zachaw's opinions Po Pi had never visited Te Toldin.

With Zachaw Pa'lin's death Noyan Po Pi had been elevated to the ruling Army Council and given command of the Western army of twenty T'sands. As yet no Grand Commander had been appointed, but Po Pi for one had achieved much benefit from Zachaw Pa'lin's death. Po Pi also retained his honorary appointment as Commander of the North-West Quarter of G'tal. He

129

was held responsible for the defence of that part of the city walls and also for supporting the Civil Governor of the Quarter as necessary.

Curos was given little time to recover from the arduous journey or to reflect on his future in the city. In less than two hours after requesting an audience he was riding to a meeting with the new member of the Army Council. Curos was flanked by two armed household retainers as custom decreed but the near-empty streets were not particularly dangerous, even for an infirm traveller. As he rode towards the Barrack Mansion of the 41st T'sand, Curos watched with amusement as two elderly Watch-Militiamen with full confidence in their authority stepped out before a party of lads off to the wine tavern. When the drinking party returned there might be a little jeering at the age of the 'Protectors of the Peace' or even at the inadequacy of the weapons but it was most unlikely that the youths would show any real disrespect or violence to the elders. The pressure from hundreds of years of reliance on order and self-control to cope with the over-population had forced the Chaw townsmen and peasants into this mould. It was this passive, well-disciplined population which had to be whipped up into a fighting force which would match the best soldiers in the world. How could these small, underfed people, conditioned from birth away from violence, be expected to stand when the Warchaw swordsmen advanced?

Without conscious thought, Curos had allowed his horse to stop rather than push past the knot of men who blocked the narrow street. Recognising his rank, they now flattened themselves back against the building. The Watch-Militiamen bowed. *Was this the army of Chaw? The men whose ancestors had thrown back the N'gol hordes and destroyed their power for ever?* Curos shook his head sadly and wished for a rebirth of the Xan dynasty.

In the centre of the large square which acted as a parade-ground stood the twin Army and Civil Mansions of power. One housed Noyan Po Pi and some three hundred officers and men, the other was the home of Admin Tuclei and the offices of the North East Quarter's civil servants. At night the Civil Mansion became silent and almost deserted but the Army Mansion's lower floors now swarmed with the K'tans and soldiers of the 41st T'sand. Many of the younger men were unmarried, others had

130

left wives in Uzan province, the T'sand's regional base. Some K'tans, even some soldiers did maintain homes in G'tal but their families were not welcome in the Mansion.

The Guard K'tan directed Curos to the Noyan's personal entrance which led via four flights of narrow stairs to the top floor and Po Pi's living area. At each landing a guard saluted after acknowledging Curos' token of identity. The Noyan's apartments were not only his home but the army administration area for the North East Sector and the 41st T'sand.

It was to one of the larger rooms that Curos was conducted. Empty except for a small writing desk and two chairs and lit by several candles, it could have been a deep cave rather than one of the power centres of Chaw. An orderly was arranging a brazier for making tea and a flask of rice wine was on a small table. The desk was piled with papers and scroll maps but there was no sign of the Noyan. Only as Curos entered the empty chamber did a plain, flat voice speak from behind him.

'Good evening, K'tan Zachaw, you are punctual indeed. I had expected to have at least another hour before you arrived.'

Curos turned and bowed to his army superior before straightening up to say, 'I plead pardon for coming in haste, sir. Your message requested my presence as soon as was practicable.'

'And to a Zachaw ten days in the saddle would be no excuse for an hour's rest!' commented the short, stocky man whose loose, casual robe did little to conceal a dynamic, powerful body. The Noyan bowed. 'May I say as a Noyan of Chaw and a friend of Zachaw Pa'lin how much I regret and grieve for his death.'

'Some would welcome the death of the High Commander as a chance to seek their own advancement,' replied Curos without prudence.

'Then those men are fools,' retorted Po Pi, 'and I am no fool.' He led Curos into the centre of the room and indicated that he should sit before the desk. 'Neither of us are fools, Curos, even if we do not have your father's wisdom.' He sighed. 'So let us ignore formality and family differences. We will have few opportunities to talk without being overheard and there is much I need to say. There is great privacy in this large, open room where none may listen unobserved.'

131

'My first words to you, K'tan Zachaw Ca'lin, must be of thanks for the help you rendered to the 41st T'sand in Corninstan.'

Curos tried to dismiss the speech of gratitude from the Noyan, saying, 'The 41st was in little danger under your admired command, honoured sir. I merely took the selfish opportunity to use my Winds' remaining arrows.'

Po Pi smiled and said, 'Unexpected help from so capable a force was help indeed.' He gazed around the large, empty room, then continued, 'You are aware that I and Pa'lin were friends from the days we were officer cadets?'

'No sir,' said Curos. 'I knew your name only and you never came to Te Toldin.'

'That is true,' sighed Po Pi. 'Your father and my sister were betrothed in a perfectly correct way. When Pa'lin snatched Turakina from her tribe in the N'gol fashion it was a great scandal.'

'Not in Western D'was,' smiled Curos, in spite of himself.

'No, I suppose not,' Po Pi replied. 'But it was in Chaw. When he then pronounced Turakina his principal wife and refused to take my sister as a second wife it was seen as a foul insult to our family. In the army, personal matters are nothing. Pa'lin and I remained brother officers but it was impossible for me to visit Pa'lin's home and his outlandish wife.'

He sighed and shook his head. 'You must be the first Zachaw in memory to make a decent marriage. Even that cold brother of yours, Makran the farmer, showed the Zachaw streak when it came to choosing a wife.' Po Pi looked up and, mistaking the cause of the look of pain which crossed Curos' face at the mention of his own marriages said, 'I am sorry, I mean no disrespect to your brother. Time is short and I ramble.' He paused to gather his thoughts before starting again.

'After the defeats in Corninstan the Councils were paralysed with shock and fear. The Noyans and the Administrators refuse to accept the true record of events that the Warchaw sorcerers intervened. Your father, Zachaw Pa'lin, was branded incompetent and a coward. The Winds are said to have failed to press home their attacks; the army panicked and fled at the outset. Any and every excuse is accepted except the truth. The section of your father's report on the effect of the sorcerers has been censored, deleted from the official record.

'And you, sir?' asked Curos icily.

'I am a hero because most of my men remained alive. I am not disloyal to Pa'lin. His last order, Curos, as a friend and as my commander, was to accept the honour thrust on me and not to dissent from the Council's view. Only in this way can I, who know the truth, remain in power and assist you in the tasks your father set you.'

A cold, icy silence descended upon the room as Curos stared at Noyan Po Pi, trying to gauge the truth and sincerity of the words. 'Am I also in disgrace?' he finally asked.

'No, it is accepted that the army needs some live heroes. Topaz Wind completed its duty, the only Wind to emerge with honour. The other Winds are disgraced and what survivors there are will be disbanded and the groups reformed.'

'It cannot be so,' growled Curos with barely suppressed anger. 'How can such brave men be labelled cowards? Sir, you saw Ruby and Emerald Winds die. You saw what truly happened.'

'I saw,' said Noyan Po Pi, 'and I say nothing because Noyan Zachaw ordered me to stay silent. For the good of Chaw, for his new plan, I keep silent. I keep silent although I saw Emerald Wind charge into the flames and perish in their attempt to reach the fiends who beset us. I also saw my second son die with them.'

'I did not realise, sir,' apologised Curos.

'He was only one of many not afraid to die. His loss was hard. But to hear him and his companions called cowards and traitors! I will not forget that, Curos. We two who survived are honoured for being alive. I have achieved my ambition to have a seat on the Army Council, but it is now a council of fools. You, my boy, have promotion to Bagatur Noyan and command of a T'sand.' Curos hid his surprise and Po Pi continued. 'I argued against you receiving the full Noyan rank and the command of the 10th T'sand.'

'Why sir, the 10th T'sand has been associated with Topaz Wind and the Zachaw family for generations. Surely it is a natural choice?'

'Again I obeyed your father's request, Curos. He felt you

needed to be at the centre of power in G'tal, not waging your own minor war in the O'san.'

The extent and detail of his father's planning was becoming more evident to Curos and he realised that he would have to work closely with Po Pi. Only he and the Noyan appreciated the true nature of the Warchaw, and Noyan Po Pi had a seat on the Army Council. It was now Curos' instinct to trust this short, powerful man, despite his previous suspicions because the Noyan had profited from Zachaw Pa'lin's death. First he and Po Pi would need to share their information. Curos methodically unfolded the story of his journey to the Dryad forest and the powers and limitations of Xante's sorcery. Noyan Po Pi listened attentively, asking few questions as Curos outlined his ideas.

'I have achieved so little,' Curos said finally, 'and now I lack the guidance of my father in how to use the power of the Dryads.'

'You have the basis of a plan that you can build on,' replied Po Pi. 'There are weaknesses, to be sure. You cannot as yet prevent the Wizards' fire from scattering our T'sands. It takes time to develop a new weapon. But take care – sorcery is almost illegal in Chaw and at this time is far from popular with our rulers.

'I suggest, Curos, that you accept your advancement to Bagatur Noyan and take command of that rabble of the 22nd T'sand. You did well with the detachment that you borrowed from them and at least a nucleus of them will accept your ideas of discipline and training. I will support the Council's plans for better military organisation and at the same time can give you the scope to develop your ideas on sorcery. If we proceed well, I will annexe command of the O'san and Western D'was which is loyal to the Zachaw family. That will give us control of a buffer area against the Warchaw. You have Topaz Wind by right and my family have traditionally equipped and commanded Emerald Wind.' Po Pi stopped his flow of words suddenly and turned away to pour wine into the small porcelain cups.

'There will be no member of the Po family to command Emerald Wind but I have the right to approve the commander,' he continued bitterly. 'Some man of note will ride under the green banner.'

'The Noyan has an elder son,' Curos started to say.

134

'An elder son whose interest is in farmland and cattle,' snorted Po Pi. 'Honourable interests of a landowner, I know. Perhaps my grandsons will one day feel the need to draw a scimitar and lead a battle Wind.'

'Perhaps a nephew, or even a son-in-law,' suggested Curos.

'Perhaps, perhaps,' shrugged Po Pi impatiently, 'but that is a detail you can leave to me. You have problems enough. The most pressing is to take command of the 22nd T'sand without incident.'

'There is an accepted procedure for transfer of command?'

'Yes,' grimaced Po Pi, 'but you do not know of the Noyan of the 22nd T'sand?'

'Noyan Chou, a name only. What is he to me?'

'That says it all,' said Po Pi. 'You do not know even the rank of your wife's close relative, her cousin.'

'It is of no consequence to me.'

'But it is to him. He genuinely feels you treat your wife appallingly. How many years of marriage and no children? And then a second wife so soon.'

'That is quite proper,' stated Curos stiffly.

'Yes, but unusual before the first wife has a child to console her, and now there is the rumour of the Dryad woman.' He looked fixedly at Curos. 'Be careful of him, Curos. He is dangerous and could use feigned family grievances to seek a quarrel. He has commercial interests in G'tal. If you take command of the 22nd he will be expected to move to the 10th T'sand in O'san which would suit him ill.'

18

It was near dawn by the time Curos returned to the Zachaw City Mansion but he had no hesitation in having the Steward wakened and summoned to his room. The half-sleeping man was given a stream of instructions and told that Curos was not to be disturbed until midday unless required by a person of Noyan or Admin rank.

The next afternoon developed into a succession of hurried interviews as Curos attempted to cut through the ingrained time-wasting politeness which impeded his progress. A representative of the Ataman of the 41st T'sand arrived with an ancient ring embossed with strange designs. This gift was to show appreciation for Curos' assistance to their regiment in Corninstan. A Bagatur Noyan from the Army Council staff presented Curos with his Warrant of Promotion and his commission to Command the 22nd T'sand as from the next day.

Bhal Morag and Chalak Konn also called as requested. As the two men entered, Curos was again forcibly struck by their dissimilarity and apparent lack of officer-like qualities. Bhal Morag was as usual relaxed and confident; tall and good-looking, he was ruthlessly successful with women and looked typical of the many indolent young noblemen who congregated in the capital. In cruel contrast, Chalak Konn was shorter and with his square face looked older and more akin to a junior civil servant than a nobleman serving with the army. Curos hurried them through the briefest of welcomes, ignoring Chalak Konn's condolences for his father's death and Bhal Morag's questions as to Xante's whereabouts. Curos wanted to learn as much as possible about the 22nd T'sand and its state of morale. But more importantly he wanted to know about his wife's cousin, Chou Ramin.

While Chalak Konn was very forthcoming about the material state of the T'sand's equipment and training, he could not bring himself to criticise the men or his commander. In contrast, Bhal Morag had no such qualms. Although he now showed more respect to Curos, he retained his over-relaxed manner as he spoke. 'Konn is too loyal to Chou, a man who himself does not know what loyalty would mean. Chou has demoted Wan Abac back to Ataman and has tried to discourage any of the training methods you instigated in the D'was. His only interest is to keep the 22nd as a garrison T'sand so that he can stay in G'tal and supervise his businesses which supply much of the army needs in this province as well as the city.'

'Is he then a corrupt bureaucrat rather than a soldier?' suggested Curos.

'He breaks no laws and trades fairly if keenly with the army, even the common footmen,' said Chalak Konn carefully. 'There can be no complaints at any level if he is to preserve his near monopoly. Also your wife's brother, Chou Yuel, has recently been appointed as a senior Admin in G'tal and would endure no taint of suspicion on the Chou family.'

'Neither is Chou a bloated idler,' drawled Bhal Morag. 'He exercises regularly in all combat disciplines and has fought more than one duel.'

'In complete disregard of army edicts,' interjected Chalak Konn. Their conversation continued until Curos had built up a full mental picture of Chou Ramin.

Curos' next audience was with Lin Sri who had been his father's scribe for many years. Curos knew the man but slightly and was surprised by his frank, almost arrogant tone.

'Sir, I see from your manner that you are in haste this afternoon. Is it permitted that I speak directly as if to your father, who was my friend?'

'A friend who says no word of remorse at his death?' questioned Curos angrily.

'No sir, I would not question his judgement.'

'To the point then, Chief Scribe Lin. Would you have any objection to serving the new head of the Zachaw family?' asked Curos sharply, ignoring the previous conversation.

'Sir, I have no employment. I was retired with a pension on completion of my last task for His Excellency. I have purchased a fine house in G'tal and have a young Corninstani woman for my wife. During my service for your honoured father I travelled with him all through Chaw, N'gol and even through Corninstan to Imran. My duties were difficult and often dangerous, for which in truth he rewarded me well. I now intend to live comfortably and to enjoy the results of my hard work and careful investments.'

'You object then to entering my service?' asked Curos, suppressing his growing anger at the man's attitude.

'No, Excellency, I object only to resuming the style of life I pursued for your father. I am in my thirty-third year and am a scribe, not a soldier. I now need an ordered life.' His smug expression and tone further irritated Curos, despite his knowledge of the man's worth.

'Lin Sri, if you sit in idleness you will be disillusioned within the year. I have another offer. I need a secretariat in G'tal which you could run from offices in this house. I need every breath of knowledge on the Warchaw collated and catalogued into an ordered picture.'

'Much of this is already done by the army Council's scribes,' suggested Lin.

'In a useless and censored manner, as you well know. I also need intelligence as to the significant events and opinions in G'tal.'

'I would need staff and a budget to buy information.'

'The details of your work will be yours to organise,' replied Curos. 'I need the results. Prepare me a paper on what you need for your organisation, how long it will take you to set up what I need. There are 100 gold hawa as an incentive.'

'I will need little time, Sir, as I have not yet disbanded a similar system I ran for your father.' Sensing he may have been too insolent, he added hurriedly, 'There will therefore be no need for any bonus.'

'There is one more thing,' stated Curos. 'If you will not travel, I will need you to train me a scribe who will have no fear of the world or its dangers. He must be able to recognise facts and record them accurately and frankly.'

'I understand,' replied Lin respectfully. 'I will choose a young man of the required calibre and train him myself.' He continued apologetically, 'Sir, I know you are in haste but the archive room in this house holds many documents which you should see.'

Curos was at last aware of some measure of contact with this independent scribe. 'Later, Lin. When I have overcome my present crisis I will spend time going through my honoured father's papers. Now I have a more pressing duty, one which may preserve my very life.'

Lin Sri, the scribe who considered himself supreme in his profession, might well have been surprised to have known that Curos' urgent appointment was in fact with two horses, Thunder-Arrow and Gentle Warrior, whom he had seen but briefly in the stables below the mansion. It was late, very late indeed when Curos finally returned to his room and the welcome bath and meal.

'I have been to the stable and exercised my two war ponies,' he told the Steward. 'Has the stable man accepted his flogging? I see he is still tending the animals.'

'No sir, he refused the lash but with the haste of many tasks I have been unable to secure a replacement. Before the end of the week he will be gone.'

'Inform him, Steward, that he may keep his post, if he wishes and if he can force himself to be more respectful.' Curos paused and added in explanation, 'The horses are in fine condition, kindly treated and well exercised. For that I can forgive much.'

As noon of the next day approached Curos, mounted on Thunder-Arrow and flanked by twenty guards from Po Pi's 41st T'sand, rode slowly into the compound of the 22nd T'sand's barracks. Like the men who waited for his inspection, he wore full ceremonial uniform. It was the first time that Curos had worn the purple and gold of a Noyan, with its exaggerated lacquer-work facings and shoulder-plates. The helmet's ornate cheek-guard gave complete anonymity, only offset in Curos' case by the yellow pendant and sash which he wore by right of commanding the Topaz Wind.

An equally anonymous K'tan in the scarlet uniform and purple sash of the guards rode forward to meet Curos. He saluted before exchanging a correct if impersonal greeting with the new commander before leading him to meet the outgoing Noyan.

Some time later Curos and Chou Ramin sat at either side of the main table with the ten K'tans of the T'sand around them. With the inspection and ceremony over it was the custom for the officer K'tans to invite the new and outgoing commanders to a meal in their quarters. Curos was aware that Bhal Morag and Chalak Konn had chosen seats to his left and right.

Each course of the meal consisted of one large dish from which the men helped themselves, giving preference to those of higher rank or seniority. The abundant supply of wine was largely ignored as a stressful atmosphere developed. Each attempt at social conversation was blocked by Chou Ramin and any effort to compliment the commander on the officers or the troops was likewise rebuffed.

Only as the silver dish which still held most of the uneaten sweet course was removed did Chou address Curos directly. 'May I be permitted to ask if my cousin the Lady Hoelun is contented with life in the provincial house of Te Toldin?'

'You may,' replied Curos lightly. 'My Lady wife was in excellent health when I left Te Toldin only twelve days since, summoned to G'tal to take up command of this esteemed T'sand.' He raised his glass as in toast to the officers present. The gesture brought no response from Chou.

One of the junior K'tans started to say, 'You have already commanded a section of our T'sand with some success I believe?' but Chou then interrupted. 'I had heard that Noyan Zachaw was to command the 10th T'sand which has long been associated with his family and the Topaz Wind. Topaz was the only Wind not to suffer great loss in Corninstan.'

'The only Wind fortunate and skilful enough to achieve its objective,' corrected Curos mildly before continuing to mention the valour of the 22nd T'sand in the D'was march.

'As I said some time ago,' Chou returned to his previous subject. 'Many in G'tal are surprised to find one of the Zachaw family being placed in command of the 22nd T'sand. Could it be that the hero of Corninstan, Zachaw Ca'lin, has used up his share of courage and now seeks a safer life with garrison troops while leaving those of us less experienced in war to face the barbarians?'

'Some uninformed persons in G'tal would say as much,' agreed Curos pleasantly, 'but I am sure Chou Ramin would not be one of them. You have heard from your own men that in the march back from the Sibrea Forest I killed many Warchaw. I have

140

fought the enemies of Chaw with the bow, with the scimitar and even open-handed. I seek only to do so again. It is the case that some on the Army Council do not wish to see one of the Zachaw family pushed into an honoured position too soon, but would have him in G'tal where he can be observed.'

'To criticise the Army Council could be called treason,' snapped Chou.

'I agree,' Curos smiled, 'but I do not criticise. Indeed, honoured Noyan Po Pi, a member of the Council, informed me plainly that he considered such a junior officer too inexperienced to command a full T'sand. He believes that my administrative skills need to be more fully tested.' He sipped his wine and added, 'I am sure the honoured Chou Ramin knows it is one thing to lead a Wind in battle, quite another to command and organise a full T'sand.'

Silence descended around the dining table as the assembled K'tans sat immobile, unwilling to join the conversation. Chou downed his dish of wine in one long swallow before again fixing Curos with his eyes. 'Perhaps I do wrong in questioning the valour of Zachaw Ca'lin,' he sneered. 'There is a certain type of man who has no lack of courage but who has other flaws. I asked after the well-being of my esteemed cousin Hoelun. She is in health, but after so long she has no child.'

'No,' replied Curos without comment.

'And the lady Kataln your second wife is also childless. A strange misfortune.'

Again Curos did not answer but turned as if to speak to Bhal Morag but Chou cut in. 'Zachaw, the situation is not flattering to my cousin.'

'I mean no dishonour to your kinswoman,' replied Curos angrily. 'My childless marriages are a personal sorrow which I would not discuss openly to embarrass brother officers'.

'It could be, Zachaw,' said Chou with deliberate venom, 'that if a false hero spent more time in his wife's bed and less time in unnatural behaviour with a sub-human animal from the northern forest, his father would not have died without a true heir.'

'Do you refer to the Lady Xante-Yani, ambassadress from the Dryadin people of the forest lands of S'lan?' said Curos, trying to control his anger.

'I know only that the Yasil Law categorises the Dryadin as sub-human animals and warns of their danger,' replied Chou, pleased that he had at last succeeded in rousing Curos. 'It is also known that the female animal sleeps, or at least spends the nights, always in your bed.'

'Chou Ramin, I congratulate you on your success.' Curos breathed dangerously. 'I had intended at all cost to avoid a quarrel but you have found the point on which I must stand. The army has taught me to ignore my own honour but Chaw needs the Dryadin more than any Noyan. I must ask you to withdraw your remarks.'

'I cannot.'

'No, you will not, you seek the alternative,' replied Curos. 'My death would remove any suspicion of your cowardice but leave you in G'tal. There is no stopping the man who seeks death. For the slur you have cast on the Dryad in my charge, I challenge you to fight.'

'My lords, please consider the T'sand,' warned a senior K'tan. 'It is not expected that brother officers should fight against each other.' Curos and Chou where now standing, facing each other across the low table, the other K'tans uncertain how to react.

'It is customary to appoint envoys to negotiate choice of weapons,' Chou stated conversationally. 'To save time I propose combat with the bow mounted on horseback, three arrows and free choice of other weapons.'

'N'gol combat to the death?' asked Curos.

'Surely you do not object? It is an uncivilised choice, I grant, but quite suitable to one of your lineage.'

'I do not object,' Curos smiled maliciously as he recognised a little of Chou's purpose. The Chaw protocol for a duel called for combat to cease the instant blood was drawn. The N'gol duel continued until the death of one combatant.

'Good,' replied Chou, 'I would not wish to be accused of seeking an unfair advantage.' He paused only to name two friends who would act as his attendants before leaving.

Curos was now Bagatur Noyan of the 22nd T'sand and the dismayed officers waited silently for his orders. 'K'tans,' he started in a pleasant tone. 'I fear my personal quarrel has ruined the elegant banquet which you have presented to welcome me as your new commander. I will not expect this duel to disrupt the T'sand. I will use the commander's quarters to change and will expect the senior K'tan to organise an inspection of the T'sand in working order. Have the T'sand scribe bring me any urgent papers.'

It was early evening before Curos left the barracks accompanied by Chalak Konn who had volunteered to command the escort, rather than pass the duty to an Ataman. The small man sat his horse confidently enough but did not seem at ease with his military duty.

'I am still surprised that Chou has chosen to fight me "N'gol",' Curos confided to Chalak Konn. 'I fear he may have some devious plan which I cannot unravel.'

'He has,' replied Chalak Konn seriously. 'But he may suffer for his dishonourable actions which are not worthy of a Noyan, or of any man of status.'

'Explain?' asked Curos shortly, not wishing Chalak Konn to settle into his customary oblique, long-winded manner of speech.

'Chou pays his servants to listen to gossip for him, in itself an act not . . .'

'Please, Konn, I am tired,' sighed Curos.

'It is well known by the T'sand soldiers that I have voiced disagreement with your words and actions during the mission to the northern forest. It was with knowledge of these low rumours that Chou sought to converse with me as to your attainments in the military arts.'

'I see but dimly as yet, Konn,' mused Curos.

'I informed Chou that my ability to judge was severely limited but that I had seen you practise with great skill the lance, the scimitar and in Jitsu. I said also that to my knowledge it was with these weapons that you had fought against the Warchaw at Corninstan and the D'was. Chou then asked of your skill with the bow and I replied that I had no personal information but that some said you were regarded but poorly by the N'gol and by the Topaz Wind.'

'Lying to your commander was a serious offence!' Curos smiled in the darkness but kept his voice serious.

'I did not lie, Excellency,' said Chalak Konn in a shocked voice. 'I spoke the truth as I knew it and repeated clearly what

143

others had said. It is just that the N'gol standards are somewhat high.' Rising slightly in the saddle, he continued stiffly. 'A man who fishes a dirty stream must beware that he may catch a diseased eel rather than a healthy salmon.'

Curos had never expected that he would be brought to laughter by Chalak Konn and they rode in an amicable silence until they approached the Zachaw City Mansion. From the shadows beyond the gate lanterns, a man stepped into Curos' path and bowed deeply. Only the slight limp and the plain N'gol clothes were registered at first but even as the guard moved forward protectively Curos abandoned all propriety and leapt from his horse. Gripping the man's shoulders he stared in amazement at the now scarred face of Khol Dalgan. Several times Curos began to speak but the futile words failed him.

It was Dalgan who spoke first. 'Bagatur Noyan Zachaw, I congratulate you on your success and your advancement. Curos, my friend, never since I first met you in the land of my Clan, did I expect to see you unable to speak.'

'Dalgan, I thought you dead. Killed as a result of my order. Even I do not expect men to return from the void without rebirth.' Ignoring the stares of Chalak Konn and the guard, he continued, 'I saw you die on the Warchaw spears, Dalgan. There is much to explain. Enter my home now and we will talk.'

'We will talk, Curos, but not tonight. News of your planned fight with Chou Ramin has preceded you. Even the men of the Sand Dragon Clan do not prepare for personal combat by sitting drinking and talking with old friends. I could not have stayed away from the arena tomorrow and I could not risk your shock at the first sight of a friend you thought dead. Kill well, Curos and we will celebrate.'

'You are confident of my success,' laughed Curos.

'Beyond confidence,' replied Khol Dalgan. 'Chou Ramin is a fool to sit a horse and trade arrows with a N'gol, even half N'gol like you. He must be weary of life!'

19

It had taken all of Curos' power of self-control to still his racing mind and compose himself to sleep. It was, he judged, just after midnight when he was woken by the faintest sound of a dragging footfall from the passage outside his sleeping room. Almost by instinct he rolled off the low bed and moved closer to the door, dagger in hand.

'Do not fear, my friend, it is only Khol Dalgan whose lame leg announces his presence.'

After the briefest of explanations the two men ran to the stable where the dim lantern light revealed the body of the groom as it lay in the blood-soaked straw. Close by another man writhed in death agonies, his voice whimpering up from the floor as his hands sought to close the gaping wound in his gut.

'The groom died to protect his charges?' asked Curos.

'No, the traitor had already administered a drug to the horses and this carrion was paying him when I arrived. In my anger I stabbed them both. I had suspected some such attempt but came too late.'

'Will Thunder-Arrow and Gentle Warrior survive?' asked Curos in a pained voice. Disregarding the mens' bodies, he moved to the horses who were already sweating and shivering as their heads tossed frantically.

'It is a drug, not a poison. In two days there will be no sign that your horses were sick. Tomorrow they will sleep the sleep of death. You will have to fight on another horse, Curos, or accept the disgrace of failing to meet Chou.'

'That is tomorrow's problem, Dalgan. First we must encourage them to drink all they can. I'll get rugs to cover them from the chill. I should get something for this wretch too,' Curos added as he walked past Chou's man.

'What, Curos?'

'A handful of salt to sharpen the pain of his wounds,' he spat savagely. 'One who makes war on horses deserves to die in more than agony.'

In the dimly-lit stable as they attempted to calm the delirious animals, Curos heard Dalgan's story of his return from Corninstan.

'My mistake was to underestimate the Warchaw footmen,' he began. 'We had thinned their numbers with arrows but they stood firm against our charge. I deflected one pike with my scimitar but a thrust from the second rank hit my thigh, here. I was then struck from Jay Bird, probably with the butt of a pike. In the confusion as our charge broke, the barbarians' pikemen pushed forward, leaving the dismounted and the wounded to the swordsmen. I could not rise but I attempted to block a slash from where I crouched on the ground. My scimitar was beaten down by a heavy straight sword and I received this gift!' Dalgan indicated the pale red scar which ran from forehead to cheek across his face.

'I was three times lucky, Curos,' he said as he sponged Thunder-Arrow's head. 'The pike head cut only muscle and left the great artery intact; the sword slash cut flesh and not bone and with the main T'sands attacking, the Warchaw did not check us for dead as they did later with those on the battlefield.'

When Dalgan had regained consciousness he had bound his leg with the topaz sash and sought for weapons amongst the dead. Of his horse, Jay Bird, there was no sign.

'I think Chou's man has died at last,' Curos remarked casually. 'How did you get back to Chaw?'

'More luck – this time from other men's greed,' replied Dalgan. 'A Corninstan farmer began to rob the dead and wounded, Chaw and Warchaw alike, when the armies had departed. I baited my trap for him with this emerald, a present from my wife's father, and lay very still. It is not easy to ignore pain and watch a host of flies settle on your blood as it seeps through the bandage. Eventually the farmer noticed the sun sparkle on the ring. As he snatched it I stabbed him cleanly; his horse did not even panic.'

Dalgan's luck had almost failed as he made his way through East Corninstan. By the time he had found a better N'gol mount, grazing riderless, Dalgan was weak and dizzy from shock and loss

146

of blood. Later when challenged by two Warchaw cavalrymen he tried to fight and paid a savage penalty. The slash of a broadsword had cut through his scimitar's fine cross guard and chopped away three fingers of his right hand. Only the speed and endurance of the N'gol pony had carried him clear of his pursuers and out into the O'san. With other stragglers he had made his way back into Chaw and then north west to his Clan's grazing grounds in the D'was.

'It was a strange homecoming, Curos. My parents in mourning, my wife with the shaved head of widowhood. The death of six men of our village had been a sad blow. You could see it in the faces of the other wives, Curos. Why should Khol Dalgan be the one to come back from the dead, why not their husband? At least my wounds show I was no coward.' He looked directly at Curos. 'Wounded as I was, my only instinct had been to return to my home. If I fight again, Curos, I will not go back defeated. I will return a hero or not at all.' He grinned in an attempt to lighten the gloom of his words. 'And if I do return home a hero there will be two children to greet me. The god of Winds grant the second is a boy.'

'I would that I could have as successful a homecoming,' shrugged Curos. 'Perhaps if I had been wounded it might have helped the Lady Hoelun and myself.'

'If my wound had been this much higher and inward, my homecoming would have been less welcome,' laughed Dalgan. 'Better for a woman to be a widow than married to an unmanned man. I would not seek wounds, Curos.'

He paused, then continued. 'I did not waste my summer days either, Commander. I can now ride well again and fight with the sword in the left hand. The bow is beyond me, but,' the twisted, scarred face grinned again, 'I can still fight the barbarians.'

'I am pleased to see you back but wish that your hurt was less savage.' Curos started on a new theme. 'You were maimed on my orders, I had thought to offer your father recompense. The same sum could be your pension from the Topaz Wind.'

'No, you read me wrongly, Curos,' Dalgan said in half anger. 'I need no pension. With the lance and sword I am still as deadly as any man. My scars harden every day. I can ride well enough to keep pace with the war band.' He smiled. 'You have been away from the clans too long, brother. What need have I for gold? I have horses and cows, as many as the grazing can stand. Would you make me think to take a second wife like a Chaw, or be richer than my father?'

'Think not of money then, but a gift perhaps.'

'There is nothing,' Dalgan started to say but hesitated. 'Except one thing . . . No, it would be too much.'

'Anything truly mine is yours, Dalgan. Try me.'

'Curos, you need a trained horse tomorrow. Due to my weakness I ride a mare who is docile but obedient and extremely swift-footed, perhaps better than an unpredictable mount of higher spirit. She is yours, my gift to you.' The lopsided scar made Dalgan look as villainous as a horse-dealer. 'And as your gift to me, I will take the black Warchaw stallion you captured at Corninstan.' Dalgan roared with laughter. 'See, even for the great-hearted Zachaw that is too much to ask. I have beaten you, Curos.'

'No, you misunderstand. The stallion is yours although you will need to be strong to ride him.'

'I doubt I ever will be.' Dalgan shrugged. 'But his breeding into the clans' bloodlines would add new size and vigour which we need. The steeds of Chaw and N'gol grow small. Rare indeed are beasts with the fire of Thunder-Arrow and Jay Bird.'

In less than an hour from leaving the stable, Curos was riding with Khol Dalgan, Chalak Konn and Bhal Morag to the exercise grounds outside the walls of G'tal. Curos had informed the Steward that an assassin had entered the stable and both the intruder and the groom had died as they fought.

Because duels were forbidden to them, the three army officers did not wear uniform but had dressed as they considered fit for the occasion. Curos, in N'gol riding gear, wore the sash and Topaz which proclaimed his heritage; Bhal Morag in his multi-coloured court clothes shivered in the early morning chill but smiled arrogantly; Chalak Konn's dark and sensibly thick riding-coat showed taste and quality on close inspection but from a distance he retained his look of clerk-like gravity.

Although dressed as if to lead Topaz Wind, Curos was seated on a borrowed and hardly warlike horse and felt quite unlike himself. He had barely considered his tactics for the coming combat, let alone the possibility of defeat. Now that the need for immediate action was past, he became aware of the fatigue from days of hard riding and the hectic day in the capital. The last sleepless night had not helped either. He must think, at least enough to have a concerted plan. Skill would not be enough: Chou Ramin had skill also.

Tiredness gripped Curos and his mind wandered back to the time he was but twelve years old. He had often spent summers with his mother's people, the White Dragon Clan, at first staying as a guest in the yert of a married cousin. The expected pleasure of his second visit had been overshadowed by the brooding anger which had grown up between husband and wife. Curos understood little of their argument but the dark atmosphere marred even the enjoyment of riding and hunting with the Clan Ulus.

On the third week of Curos' visit the wife left her home and moved to the yert of another man, a friend of her husband. It was her right to go provided the marriage price was repaid. She was a free N'gol woman who could sleep where she wished. The child would stay with her until he was five and then return to his father. At ten he would choose his own home.

Curos had been very confused and hurt at the time but now understood that this was all allowed for in the flexible N'gol customs. His cousin had no right to act under N'gol law but after two days of frustrated anger he challenged his rival to combat. The challenged man, knowing of Curos' cousin's unsurpassed skill on horseback, chose to fight on foot with heavy swords.

Despite his disadvantage of size and strength, Curos' cousin had fought long and died hard. Curos watched as his friend and kinsman was virtually cut to pieces, eventually dying more from loss of blood than from any single wound. The wife watched too, tears seeping down her face as her husband died. That night she took her own life leaving her two-year-old son an orphan.

Curos had never quite recovered from that episode in his life and always shied from close personal involvement, particularly with women. He distrusted friendship as he feared marriage, also he was left with a certain fear of fighting on foot. On a horse with bow, sword or spear he was N'gol, mobile as the wind and able to avoid or accept death as fortune dictated. On foot, as at Corninstan or the well in the D'was, he was static and vulnerable. Perhaps the two fears were related, he thought. Friendship and marriage were like fighting on foot: spiritual or physical mobility were prevented. Above all he must be Wind Free, never like his cousin, tied down and waiting for certain death, death which in its turn would bring death or misery to others.

'What you do is rash, Zachaw Curos.' The thoughts of Xante floated into his brain. 'The strong and those destined to be great are right to be rash but they cannot afford to dream or to doubt themselves. If your consciousness is too tired for thought, my Curos, you must rely on your emotion and instinct. It is too late to try anything new.' As he attempted to focus on the projection of her personality it faded and withdrew. He jerked as if waking from sleep.

'Curos!' Dalgan rode close alongside. 'Are you fit for this? You sleep in the saddle. Send a proxy, or ask for a delay.'

'No, Dalgan, it is no use,' laughed Curos, suddenly awake and vibrant with new energy. 'I cannot lose face by asking concession from Chou, and a great lady tells me I shall win. A Wind Rider of my mother's White Dragon Clan can ride all night and then fight all day, say the songs of the N'gol. Should a ruler of the Chaw nation be able to do less?'

When they arrived at the training ground it was quite bright with the light of early morning. The area had been methodically prepared by soldiers of the 22nd T'sand under Chalak Konn's direction. Two concentric circles had been marked out by thick ropes and stakes. The inner circle was about a hundred paces in diameter and the outer one some two paces from it, forming a track just wide enough for a horse to run freely without easily being able to turn around. In the desert duel there would be no track, just an empty plain and two riders, but in all things the Chaw demanded form and order.

Scattered groups of soldiers from the T'sand had arrived, eager to watch what they hoped would be a suitably bloody occasion. Chou Ramin was not popular and Curos was hardly known to them. Certainly few there would grieve for the death of either combatant.

150

To one side of the circle, Chou Ramin waited with two mounted companions. Dressed in rich but sombre civilian clothes, he rode slowly towards Curos and his friends. It was not expected that the enemies would speak with each other but it gave the attendants sufficient time to inspect discreetly for signs of body armour. There was little chance of hiding mail or bamboo under the robes of the combatants, but while the attendants went through the formal requests for a reconciliation, Curos studied his opponent. He noted the well-oiled, highly recurved bow fitted easily into the horse quiver and the three perfectly fletched arrows. Chou's scimitar was a mirror of Curos' own: sharp, light and deadly.

'No extra weight and a light bow,' Curos considered as he rode towards his position at one side of the killing track. 'A fast horse and a fast rider.' Without further thought, he leaned towards Bhal Morag. 'I'll change this for the more powerful fighting-on-foot bow and the heavy, broad head arrows,' he said, handing his traditional horse-bow to Dalgan.

'It will take more shooting on horseback,' warned Dalgan anxiously, but this remark was brushed aside.

Dimly, Curos was aware of the throng of soldiers and the squat bulk of the city some five yetang away as he guided Dalgan's placid mare into the tracks between the rope fences. Absently, he stroked the animal's head and smoothed her mane to reassure her, but his blood sang with excitement and his senses were fastened only upon his enemy. On the opposite side of the arena Chou Ramin was having difficulty controlling his more mettlesome stallion which was protesting at the constraining ropes.

A trumpet sounded a preliminary note and continued into a long, stirring trill. Curos turned deliberately, settling himself in the high, padded saddle, and carefully nocked the heavy, broad-headed arrow onto the bowstring. The mare's reins hung limply against her neck.

Abruptly the trumpet ceased and both riders kicked their nervous mounts into motion. The crowd roared. Instantly Chou Ramin was at full gallop and closing on Curos who was inexplicably riding at little more than an ambling run. Curos was hardly aware of the noise and tumult. His grip on the bow and bowstring were relaxed but sure, leaving his full attention on Chou. Instinctively he gauged the distance and the moment when Chou would shoot.

In one smooth motion, Curos' bow arm came up into position and the arrow was drawn back and loosed. Even as Curos' heavy arrow sped away Chou was beginning to draw his own bow. For one instant Curos felt as static as a figure on a scroll picture while his arrow fled towards Chou to strike home with an audible, tearing thump. Chou reeled backwards, gripping the shaft which protruded wickedly from his stomach, his own bow falling unheeded. The horse faltered and then shied in fear at the smell of hot blood which cascaded down from the rider.

Already Curos had kicked his mare up to a fast gallop. He shouted with elation the shrill war scream of Topaz Wind's battle frenzy, fitted his second arrow to the bow and flew around the circle arena towards his adversary.

Chou lolled from the saddle, desperately trying to pull himself upright while one hand clutched at the arrow. At full gallop Curos closed up behind him and loosed a second arrow before hauling the mare to a stop to prevent a collision. The impact of the shot sent Chou hurtling to the ground as with fresh terror the now riderless horse raced away.

Curos urged the responsive mare back to speed and with the precison of a dancer she ran over the inert Chou Ramin, never faltering or flinching as her shod hooves crushed into the helpless body. One more circuit and one more arrow. Curos now stood in the stirrups, legs locked into the mare's sides as he again approached Chou. Shooting directly ahead, he sent the last arrow into the lifeless body and again rode his horse mercilessly over the fallen enemy. Only as he allowed the mare to slow her hectic, blood-spattered progress was he aware of the shouting and cheers of congratulation.

Dalgan rode alongside him yelling, Morag close behind. Coming to a halt where the ropes were aready being opened for him, Curos called to Khol Dalgan. 'The Queen of horses, Dalgan! Fast, obedient and responsive. You have a bad bargain in exchanging her for the Warchaw stallion.'

'No, Curos, she was but a loan,' called the excited clansman. 'Any N'gol would sell his wife and children for her after today.'

152

'You N'gol!' butted in Bhal Morag. 'Such a victory and you discuss horses.'

As the elation began to evaporate, Curos looked sadly as the mangled corpse of Chou Ramin was carried off. 'A brave man, and skilful,' he complained to Dalgan and Morag. 'Why are we so stupid? Why should Chaw kill Chaw when a horde of War-chaw are within ten days' ride?'

'He was more skilful than I gave him credit,' replied Khol Dalgan, his face twisted into a lopsided smile by his war scar.

'Yes,' added Bhal Morag. 'Even with your shaft embedded in his entrails, his shot came close to you, Curos. If you try that trick again, remember to duck. Even Zachaw Curos of the Topaz does not have a charmed life.'

Chalak Konn rode up to the three horsemen and bowed before speaking to Curos as if to a total stranger. 'I will arrange a suitable cremation for Noyan Chou Ramin. His kinsmen in the city will surely disown him and his attendants seem particularly inept. One of them has already departed to salvage some financial enterprise, the other is dementedly cursing and swearing vengeance in a most unseemly manner. I will arrange for him to be silenced.'

'No,' Curos whispered. 'I want no assassinations or further duels.'

Chalak Konn allowed the merest hint of disapproval to show in his face. 'That will not be necessary, commander. The Army section of the Yasil code specifically forbids officers to challenge or threaten one of superior rank. I will ensure that this is made sufficiently clear to prompt an apology or resignation.' Only as he was about to ride off did Chalak Konn add, 'May I congratu-late you on your victory? A totally unexpected tactic.'

'There was a certain skill involved also,' suggested Dalgan.

'That was expected from a Wind K'tan,' replied Konn dismiss-ively. 'It is the ability to out-think an opponent that is necessary in a Noyan.'

As Chalak Konn left to conduct his self-appointed duties Dalgan said, 'I cannot understand, Curos, why you tolerate one such as that. He has no fire and no soul but beneath his formality is an insufferable arrogance.'

'Do not underestimate Chalak Konn, friend Dalgan,' replied

153

Curos. 'He is skilled in the use of weapons and has a sharp mind. Despite his deference to rules and protocol, he is more able than most.'

'Able at what?' laughed Dalgan. 'I cannot see Konn at the head of a charging T'sand.'

They had started to ride back towards G'tal. Curos started from a seeming preoccupation and replied, 'No, Dalgan, I have you to do that, and Wan Abac to keep the footmen firm and Bhal Morag here to plan and scheme. But who will feed the army and provide weapons and spare horses, carts and tents? Not Khol Dalgan of the N'gol.'

'True,' shrugged Khol Dalgan. 'We ride, we fight. What we need we take from our foe.'

'That is true of a clan war band of twenty or forty riders, but I cannot support a Tuman of fifty T'sand in that way. They would destroy Chaw and Corninstan by their very passage as did the N'gol hordes of old.'

'But that was real war, Curos: to sweep through nation after nation, fuelling the next attack from the wreckage of the defeated, using their food, their horses and their women, always to drive forward and conquer.'

'Until the momentum is checked, Dalgan. As emperor Xan II showed, halt the N'gol Tuman, deny them one victory and the attack crumbles. The ants of Chaw or the footmen of Warchaw can do that. Then you need the resolve and the resources that Chalak Konn can give.' He laughed suddenly and urged the willing mare into a faster gait. 'Even so, it is a worthy dream. If we could break through the Warchaw in Corninstan and take enough horses, we might yet have N'gol war. Imagine, Dalgan – whole T'sands of Wind Riders slicing Warchaw nations into strips, strips to be fed between the mill wheels of the Chaw foot Tuman and ground to dust!'

Curos' combat with Chou Ramin gave him instant recognition and prestige, at least among the more junior army officers in G'tal. While senior Noyans and Army council members could not publicly approve the killing of a high-ranking officer, the ruthlessness of style was privately welcomed in one who seemed destined to rise high in the army.

The civilian arm of the government showed open disapproval and Sri Lin informed Curos that the Zachaw name had been removed from the invitation lists to all civil functions for a period of two months. If the Bagatur Noyan of the 22nd T'sand was now officially banned, there still seemed an endless round of dinners at which Zachaw Curos was most welcome. Important as these social events were to Curos' need to advance his political power, they detracted from his immediate task of revitalising the 22nd T'sand. Its two most senior K'tans were too closely identified with Chou Ramin to fit easily into Curos' command. After polite but forceful interviews both resigned from the T'sand, one transferring back to his home province of Sunel, the other leaving the army to concentrate on family business.

The flamboyant Bhal Morag was advanced to Senior K'tan which caused some dissension, but more questions were asked over Chalak Konn's new role of Logistics K'tan. An administrative post responsible for considerable sums of money, it was usually retained for more elderly officers of proven honesty. Other changes were less obvious but in the long term would be even more significant. Men were posted away and newcomers brought in as a slow tide of change began to run through the T'sand. Wan Abac and another Ataman of low birth were promoted to K'tan and seemed to have little difficulty in assuming the suitable officer status, uniform and horses. Weapon training took on a new dimension. Compulsory 'morning ritual' and increasingly long marches began to improve physical fitness.

During the evening and late into the night Curos spent hours with the scribe Lin Sri in the archive room of the Zachaw City Mansion, reading through the carefully catalogued records compiled by his father, Zachaw Pa'lin. The chief work of scholarship was a frank and unbiased history of Chaw as collected by scribe Lin with copious listings of source material and interpretation. There were also maps and histories of the lands bordering Chaw, with particular emphasis on battles which marked the progress of the Warchaw. Any reports of wizardry or sorcery had been largely ignored by Pa'lin and Lin Sri's factual treatment but after Corninstan this was already in revision.

Some of the information was already known to Curos but he had never read the full, detailed accounts of the Warchaw's conquests. Little was known of their homelands to the far west, isolated by the sea and mountain ranges. They had first appeared in force some three hundred years ago, landing from a fleet of massive ships at several places along the coast of the Tyrian Empire. The massive fortified towns which had withstood countless sieges had fallen and armies which a hundred years previously had withstood the N'gol raids from the north and east had been shattered.

'I will now revise the translations,' said Lin Sri apologetically. 'Where the chronicles said "walls were destroyed by shock of fire and sorcery" I had thought it an apology for defeat. I made a similar error, here, where the original said that the "Caliph was swept away by a storm of fire." I had not considered its literal meaning.'

As the Warchaw invasions came closer to the lands bordering Chaw the history became more detailed. The fall of Imran eighty-seven years previously was covered in great length, piecing together Imrani and Corninstani texts. The course of each battle was carefully charted with comments on tactics used, particularly the long-range shooting of the Warchaw bowmen and war engines, the devastating use of shock tactics from the heavy cavalry and the solid defensive stability of the foot-soldiers.

Already Lin Sri had obtained the names of the principal Warchaw commanders and sources in Corninstan. 'Baron Renult commands the army in all things, but the policy and direction appear to be guided by the sorcerer Valanus. Renult is far from a figurehead – he organises and feeds the army and rules the conquered Corninstan nation – but Valanus is the key, the source of all major ideas.'

'But we have no idea of their purpose, their aim.'

'Unless it is to rule the world,' shrugged Lin Sri. 'Other War-chaw armies are advancing south into Hind and Warchaw soldiers in Corninstan speak of other wars.'

'The pattern of events after conquest is always the same,' said Curos. 'First to establish iron control and then progressively to reduce the population until the nation hardly exists – wanton destruction of whole cultures, whole peoples.'

'I have some information on individuals,' suggested Lin Sri. 'Renult is a typical general commander, a competent but not outstanding warrior who is able to organise battles and supplies, line of march and segregation of a whole country. A very logical and predictable man, he has one wife and two married daughters. His wife joined him soon after the conquest of Corninstan and runs his household and much of the army secretariat.'

Curos moved on to the next scroll. 'Valanus, I have heard of him – the spies in the desert.'

'He is a strange character,' said Lin Sri, 'full of contradictions. All seem to respect him. He is a High Sorcerer, perhaps the most powerful of the Warchaw. At times he shows great reverence to the ancient forms and ceremony, at others he follows his own path. He is also an accomplished horseman and swordsman and often competes in contests at the highest grade. Some believe he is only happy in the company of men, other sources point to tactfully concealed seductions, usually of high-born married women.'

They sat in silence for some time until Curos said, 'Is it so strange? Perhaps he seeks adventure at the highest level in all things, in his art, in war and with women also. And in all things he excels.'

'To excel, he must have dedication to each activity, each endeavour,' suggested the scribe. 'Study and training, practice at arms and at the least persistence with women.'

'Pride and arrogance are not mentioned but they must be there underneath, a weakness that could be exploited,' said Curos. 'I could lead him into a field of combat where he does not excel, or towards a woman who will not succumb . . . ? I know not, but we must build up a picture of these men. Even from afar it may be possible to tempt them into rashness or ruin.'

Also of interest was a series of personal files kept on the Noyans and other important persons in Chaw. In a number of cases there was even a brief character study written by Zachaw Pa'lin himself.

'Lin, this record is priceless,' commented Curos as he examined one scroll recording a long-forgotten battle by Emperor Xan II against the N'gol. 'Every item provided for the army is listed in detail – food, weapons, even glue and twine for fixing arrowheads. K'tan Chalak must study this at length if it is authentic.'

'Is is my own copy of a faded and crumbling scroll,' replied Lin. 'It is by the Emperor's chief scribe. I can recognise the brushwork and the exemplary style which I have vainly tried to equal. At the end of each section is an embellished character symbolising an open eye: the unflinching observer.'

'I see you have adopted the same symbol as your mark, Lin.' Curos smiled.

'As a disciple only. I have also retained the ancient scroll form, rather than reproduce it as a book.'

'It is good to see that you show respect to one man at least, Lin, even if he has been dead for five hundred years!'

After the fight with Chou Ramin, Curos had drafted a long and apologetic letter to the Lady Hoelun, his wife, but it was to Xante-Yani that the more regular letters were directed to report progress and the shaping of his opinions.

Curos had been some eight weeks in G'tal when two quite different communications impelled his return to Te Toldin. A letter from Dortie, his brother's wife, was almost rambling in its tone as it skirted around the points she was trying to make. The Dryad woman Xante seemed to have lost her reason and was spending whole days and nights in the massive Zachaw tree or riding alone around Te Toldin. His wives pined and fretted. His brother and mother were concerned over the fate of the estate and quarrelled regularly.

The second communication was from Xante and burst into his

mind late one evening, harsh and raw as he half dozed over Lin's scrolls.

'Curos, I have made two important discoveries which must be used. It is also necessary for you to define the future of Te Toldin and your family. Stop playing soldiers in G'tal and get here as quickly as you can.' There had been no greeting and no feeling of closeness this time, and he felt as empty and alone as he had at any time in his life.

Despite the new grasp his officers now had on the T'sand it was not possible for a Noyan to leave at a moment's notice, without permission from Grand Noyan Po Pi.

'You have certainly made impressive improvements with the 22nd,' Po Pi agreed, 'but it would seem irresponsible for you to abandon your T'sand after so short a period. However, I fully appreciate your need to continue with the sorcery aspect of our defence.' He reflected for some time and then suggested, 'This request from the elders of a merchant town may be of interest. The hills around Lokar are infested by bandits which are beyond the local militia's ability to control. Lokar is not that distant from Te Toldin – why not take the 22nd with you?'

'An admirable plan, Excellency,' Curos nodded. 'On foot it will give the men a twenty-day march.'

'At least,' agreed Po Pi. 'Particularly if some exercises are conducted on the route.'

'My thoughts entirely, sir. They will be toughened up and blaming all their misfortunes on the bandits by the time they reach the Lok hills! I can bring Topaz Wind under Khol Dalgan around from the south west as support.'

Even with the driving haste which Curos placed on the task, it took four days to get the T'sand in marching order. Four days in which the dour Chalak Konn never seemed to sleep as he arranged for the provision of stores, weapons, carts and horses for the inexperienced men who viewed his preparations with mounting concern. Their destination was kept a secret but there had been some reports of clashes between Warchaw scouts and the 10th T'sand in the O'san desert and few in the 22nd had any real desire to join in the fighting.

On the evening before their departure Scribe Lin called Curos into the archive room in the City Mansion. It was already late and the winter cold hung in the room, despite the lantern and charcoal stove. Also present was Wou, the Junior Scribe selected to act as Curos' secretary. The slim, almost juvenile, form of Wou bowed and seemed both excited and confident. He had been chosen by Lin Sri for his high attainments in examinations, his ability to ride and withstand army life and, not least, a quick wit able to sort the relevant facts from a morass of worthless characters. He was also Scribe Lin's nephew.

'Wou will be travelling with the T'sand under K'tan Bhal Morag's command,' explained Lin. 'I have therefore instructed him to gather facts about Lokar province and all accounts of the bandits in the hill region.'

At a gesture from Lin, Wou began his report. 'Esteemed Noyan, I compiled a scroll of information on the area for K'tan Bhal Morag who will organise the search of the hill, and then began collating reports on thefts.' Curos nodded. 'It became evident that only very selected thefts were being made, always from merchants or travellers, never from local craftsmen or peasants or government officials.'

'Strange,' mused Curos. 'Tax gatherers are usually the first target and isolated peasant villages are always used as a source of food.' He thought for a moment, then said, 'Unless with cunning they do not wish to rouse the local population against them.'

'It is only merchants with goods of high value who are robbed – money, gemstones, gold, occasionally spices or perfume. Significant too,' continued Wou, 'that according to the head of the Lokar militia, they know exactly which caravans to rob and often which beast or man to search.'

'Few men could give them that precise information,' interjected Scribe Lin.

'The Admin of taxes at Lokar or at Untin?' Curos suggested.

'I would not dare to suggest such an illustrious personage.' Wou bowed dismissively.

'Then you should, and will in future,' replied Curos. 'That is part of your task for me, Wou. An excellent piece of work. Obtain the names and rank of family of the relevant collectors of trade tax in Lokar and Untin. Also, any family or contacts

160

they have in G'tal. The T'sand marches out at dawn. You will need to stay another day here and then catch us up, you understand?'

Dressed in the purple-and-gold ceremonial uniform, Curos marched his 22nd T'sand out from the North Gate of G'tal at dawn the next day. Flanked by his staff officers, including Bhal Morag and Chalak Konn, and backed by Wan Abac's Guard Hund, Curos felt a renewed confidence and power.

The T'sand did not maintain this formation for long outside the city walls. Each guard Ulus returned to its parent Hund and Wan Abac's role changed to that of the combat advisor and staff assistant on the infantry. At the end of the second day, satisfied that the T'sand had settled down well into its marching routine, Curos left them under the command of Bhal Morag and set off alone for Te Toldin. At the same time, the N'gol Khol Dalgan also left with orders for the K'tan commanding the Topaz Wind in the O'san. If senior people in G'tal provided the Te Lok outlaws with information, there would be at least one surprise when the Wind cavalry joined in the hunt.

Again Curos used the post-horse of the Arrow Riders to achieve a rapid if bruising transit to Te Toldin. The latter, northern part of his journey was made increasingly arduous by the wintry conditions. Long stretches of ground were frozen hard and in some places a soft powdering of snow fell, only to be melted by the midday sun. Snow was very rare on the Chaw plain, even welcomed as preliminary to rain when it did occur. Far to the north-west snow would be falling heavily in the mountains of Lune, a valuable reservoir of water which would not melt into the rivers until the late spring monsoon rains.

Wary of another traumatic surprise arrival at the Zachaw mansion, Curos rested at a staging post for the afternoon of the last day and sent a messenger on ahead. He planned a more leisurely ride to complete his journey the next morning, timing his arrival for noon and the midday meal.

It was early morning with the winter sun still low on his right shoulder when Curos left the Arrow Riders' Post. He was hardly settled into his deep, padded saddle when a dark, sinister figure sped from the frost-shrouded orchard. Even before the shrill, alien cry echoed down the hard road towards him, his heart leapt with recognition and a message of affection reached his mind. He greeted Xante as she wheeled her horse around to come alongside him. 'Welcome, Sorceress of the hidden face, who sleeps in apple orchards and risks her person alone on the road.'

'Welcome, Lord Zachaw!' She laughed as she removed the black veil from her face. 'As I have said before, I sleep where I please.' She pointed to a dark copse which cloaked a small hill some way to the right. 'There are few I fear to meet on the road.' Curos noticed her bow was strung in its N'gol-style horse quiver.

They chatted inconsequentially as they rode until Xante turned to more serious matters. 'Curos. You hold the future of all at Toldin. Your wives and brother cannot endure much more of this tension.'

'And the Lady Dortie?'

'She is a joy and a wonder,' trilled Xante, mimicking Dortie's voice. 'She ignores and rises above all problems. Her gardens, her orchards, her farms and her children all flourish because she breathes life into them. Her husband, your brother Makran, is beset by fears and frustrations, but only when she is away from him.'

'I hope you are on good terms with Dortie?'

'Could I not be? She is never shocked, never critical. She is a Dryad of the farms, Curos. As soon as I cured the rusting disease from her rose garden we were friends for life and I had no choice in the matter.'

'It was the same with my brother, Makran.' Curos laughed. 'Dortie looked at him and her eyes said, "you tonight", and he was lost.'

'But there is more than enough trouble at Te Toldin for one man, Curos,' Xante said carefully. 'Some of which I cause. There are important things I must speak of but I can wait. Would it help if I disappeared for two days?'

'You would destroy any pleasure in my homecoming? Where would you go?'

'To the Hill of Tears. It intrigues me, Curos. Like your W'dom tree, it holds many secrets. In two days I can unlock some of them.'

'In two days you could freeze to death on the hill,' but he made no further attempt to dissuade her.

Xante turned aside from the road just before Curos reached the main ceremonial drive to Te Toldin, leaving him sufficient time to compose his thoughts for the meeting with his family.

21

Curos' family met him on the steps of the mansion. His mother, Lady Turakina, veiled and shaven-headed, gave the first greeting, the long, formal robes of mourning seeming to envelop her small, stocky figure. Hoelun, his principal wife, met his attempted politeness with cold disdain. Kataln seemed as usual permanently angry with her position as second wife and wore pale blue instead of conventional white, no doubt as a gesture of personal defiance.

Compared to his wives' hostility, Curos' brother showed genuine pleasure at the meeting but even he had an air of concern and tension. Only Dortie beamed a welcome totally free from reserve. Her tubby, probably pregnant body was draped in a white smock of almost peasant cut, its only decoration being numerous smudges and children's finger-marks. At least, for once, her childen Pa'na and Turkal must be safely confined. Their ability to disrupt any occasion was well remembered.

Each attempt at conversation with Hoelun or Kataln during the meal seemed to founder on some sensitive issue but this in some manner eased the task Curos had planned. The lack of any feeling or emotion from his mother, Turakina, was however almost painfully difficult to bear and so different from her normal open manner. She seemed totally preoccupied with the past and had no time or love for her family.

'There are important matters of expenditure I must discuss with you, Curos,' suggested Makran towards the end of the meal. 'I must plan for next year.'

'I am sure, Makran,' Curos replied, 'but our talk will have to wait until I have spoken with Hoelun and Kataln. We have much to say and the farms will wait one or two days.'

Hoelun was not at all pleased to be visiting Curos in his sparse, plain room. As she sat facing him, this distaste was quite noticeable and added even more unpleasantness to the calculated severity of her face. Hoelun had changed a lot, thought Curos.

In the five years of their marriage, she had hardened and grown inwards, leaving just a ceremonial wife-mask visible to the outside world.

'You received my letters?' asked Curos.

'May your unworthy wife first welcome her husband back to his home,' stated Hoelun. 'It is unusual for husband and wife to meet after so long as if on a business discussion, Curos.' Seeing no response, she faltered in her evidently prepared speech and said instead, 'I received two most elegant letters, husband, but I understood little of the matters which occupied your time in G'tal.'

'You do understand, I take it, that I fought with a kinsman of yours. It was not my choosing and I would not have had his death cause you sorrow if it could have been avoided.'

'If my husband considered himself or his marriage insulted, he had little choice of action. No true kinsman of mine would have spoken so, certainly not in public. I am sure Chou Ramin was only using my name to promote a quarrel. I will not let his death come between us.'

There was silence for some time during which Curos felt the initiative and his resolve slipping away, particularly when Hoelun began to speak hesitantly, 'Curos, can we not make at least one more attempt to salvage our marriage? I know I am not active enough to please you but I have been trained as a lady. I could learn to ride and . . .' Her voice trailed away into hopelessness which roused even Curos' pity. 'Could I not do something for you?' she pleaded. 'I can write well, if slowly and . . .'

Curos shook his head and sought for words which would not injure Hoelun further. 'I fully appreciate your qualities and I know you have tried to accept the unconventional nature of the Zachaw household.'

'I even feel jealous of Dortie,' interjected Hoelun, 'despite her scandalous behaviour.'

'I doubt Makran is ashamed of her,' replied Curos shortly.

'No, that is quite evident! One hardly dare enter their apartments at any time of day and in the summer they have been seen lying together in the apple orchards. At planting time Dortie goes into the fields with the peasant women, Makran rides out to take lunch with her and like the peasants they crawl away into the hay grass.'

'Please, Hoelun, I know, all Te Toldin knows.' He shrugged in annoyance. Hoelun sat angry, so embarrassed that her own frustrations had surfaced in a stream of waspish gossip. The conversation ceased and Curos was aware of a vast rift which had opened up between them. Now in her presence he felt choked by her petty attitudes and insistence on correct behaviour.

'There is very little to say between us, Hoelun, and what I do have to say is very painful.' Hoelun had already begun to resume her mask of indifference as Curos continued, 'In Corninstan I received a wound which I thought of no concern, however it has taken away all my interest in women. I am told by doctors in G'tal that it is now impossible that I could give my wife a child.' He waited for these words to register before saying, 'I know that you and Kataln suspect that I have taken the Dryad woman as a concubine, but it is not true and cannot be true.'

'I am an unworthy wife not to have known,' whispered Hoelun. 'I am so sorry, Curos, are you sure the doctors speak the truth?'

'Yes,' Curos lied again.

'I could try very hard to arouse you,' mumbled Hoelun with evident embarrassment. 'I have been reading certain love manuals written for the guidance of unexciting wives . . .' Her voice trailed off as Curos spoke.

'As I will be unable to provide an heir to Te Toldin, Hoelun, I have decided to sacrifice my life to Chaw following my Esteemed father's example. Makran and Dortie can have the estate now.'

'Then I will die with you,' stated Hoelun defiantly. 'I have been a poor wife in life but in my death I will do my duty.'

'I wish no-one's death, Hoelun. Least of all yours. I mean to dedicate my life to the service of Chaw. Your father expected you to be mistress of a vast estate and every wife has the right to expect a child. I will not be able to honour these basic requirements of a marriage contract and I feel I should offer you an honourable divorce with return of dowry to your family.'

For once Hoelun was completely stunned into a silence which stretched into minutes. Now that he had made his statement,

166

Curos wanted to end the interview as quickly as possible, but he was unable to drive Hoelun away. When she did speak, her voice was as cold and emotionless as ice.

'My father is dead and my brother, Chou Yuel, is now living in G'tal. I do not want a hurried divorce to cause scandal. With your leave I will travel to your City Mansion in G'tal and stay there while the formalities of divorce are completed.' She stood up slowly and left the room with no further comment.

A much stormier session followed when Curos spoke to Katalin. She claimed Curos' impotence had started well before the Corninstan battle and that he was casting her and Hoelun out only to indulge his perversions with the Dryad savage more freely.

'You are not half the man your brother has proved himself to be,' she shouted. 'You disgrace both our families and your father's memory. If you had died honourably in battle I and the rest of your property would have passed smoothly to Makran without shame.' She ran from the room as much in fear of Curos' anger as from her own emotion.

Left alone Curos felt suddenly relieved, certain he had acted correctly. Ignoring the temptation to relax, he swiftly rose to his feet to go in search of Makran and Dortie before news of his proposal filtered through the household. Turakina would be the last to know of his plans but in her present depressed state he doubted if she would care.

For once happy with himself and sure of his family plans, Curos found Makran sitting at the low scribe's writing desk in the paper-smelling estate office.

'Kataln has told me you are casting her off,' Makran said, looking up from his papers. 'One of your few wise decisions, brother! As you would say, if you can't ride a horse, let it run free. She has even suggested that I should take her as a second wife!' He shook his head. 'But it is not all her fault, Curos. She is twenty years old and childless. Hoelun is also extremely unhappy, although she is too much the lady to show emotion and would never admit to being desperate for a child; but I only have to see her with Pa'na and Turkal to see the truth. She reads to them, plays with them and tells the most amazing stories as well as embroidering all of their clothes.' He pushed away his

167

papers and together the brothers walked to Dortie's rose garden, a small paved area enclosed with a warm sandstone wall which provided a sun-trap and shelter from the cold winter winds. In this protected haven Dortie had planted rose beds and herb gardens to give an overpowering riot of colour and fragrance which mirrored her exuberant personality. Many of the plants had been brought from Dortie's home in southern Sunil province and she and Makran had gone to great lengths to ensure their growth.

Makran and Curos stood watching for a moment as Dortie and little Pa'na fanned life into the charcoal brazier. Curos noted the smile of happiness on her face, reflecting the look Makran gave her, a happiness that Turakina, Hoelun and Kataln would never understand. Inside the shelter of the screen walls a physical and spiritual warmth seemed to be preserved. It was as if the tensions and traumas of the household were shielded out as effectively as the winter wind.

Pa'na was dispatched to his bed with much unseemliness before Dortie said, 'I am budding a new variety of rose especially for Hoelun. It will be ice-white, small and long-flowering with a gentle scent. I feared I would lose all the stock by forcing them too hard, but Xante cured them of the white mould. Not very original, Curos, but we thought to name it "Lady of Toldin".'

' "Lady Hoelun" would be more personal,' Curos said shortly. He had not realised there was any affection between Dortie and Hoelun nor that Hoelun had shown any maternal feelings to the children. Hoelun's outburst against Dortie, he now understood, was much more in jealousy than in spite.

Soon Dortie had Makran and Curos seated on the thick, padded mats while she poured scalding water on the jasmin-scented tea with a seriousness which would have pleased Hoelun.

'It is time that you explained what is pressing down on your thoughts, brother,' said Makran, relapsing into his usual gravity of manner from which only Dortie or the children released him.

Curos selected his words carefully before explaining the changes he was planning to his life. He started by outlining the threat to Chaw and how he interpreted his father's sacrifice before outlining his plan to make over Te Toldin to Makran and Dortie. In total silence they listened without interruption, only sipping occasionally at the fragrant tea or exchanging sympathetic glances.

'We had expected something like this, Curos,' Makran stated when Curos had finished his explanation. 'Neither I nor Dortie or Turakina would wish to sway you from the path of duty. A man must live each of his lives as he sees them and I understand this is no hasty decision. The sacrifice of dedication is sufficient; there is no need to give away Te Toldin and cast off Hoelun. Chaw needs a leader I admit, but that leader need not be an ascetic monk.'

'Particularly not a celibate monk, Curos,' Dortie added. 'Keep one foot at least in the real world.'

'I am not giving away Te Toldin, even to you,' replied Curos. 'I am making it yours to run and to pass on to Pa'na. I can have no heirs and I merely anticipate what will happen and give you the full pleasure of ownership in return for your efforts.' He held up his hand to silence Dortie's interjection. 'I will need an income from the estate, a home when necessary and the family's support of Topaz Wind. Te Toldin will come to you with many obligations.'

'You have no children now but Hoelun and you are still young,' suggested Dortie. 'She is thin and withdrawn but she warms to children, Curos. In a few years all could change. Take her to G'tal with you.'

'There is also Xante,' suggested Makran. 'Where there is understanding other things may follow.' He stopped this line of argument at a single glance from Dortie and silence descended for a moment.

Curos took up his explanation with the fictitious wound of Corninstan. He hated to lie to Makran but it at least gave some linking reason to the events he planned. Dortie was not convinced and with a farm woman's total lack of delicacy for such subjects, she demanded to know details of the wound and what treatment Curos had sought. He tried to dismiss the subject but Dortie insisted.

'Curos, listen to one who knows about these matters. I have seen you look at Xante and it was not the look of a gelding. Xante says that Dryad and Chaw cannot breed but I see her eyes grow soft when she talks of you. Do not do any rash thing, Curos. Divorce and renouncement of heritage are serious matters which cannot be easily corrected. Do this and any children you may have would be landless.'

The conversation continued for some time until the darkening coldness drove them back into the main house. Dortie stayed behind to supervise the erection of the frost shutters and the placing of the braziers which would burn all night.

'You are not too shocked by myself and Dortic, are you, Curos?' asked Makran. 'For a woman she is outspoken and shows little respect but we live our life as we choose.'

'I am always shocked by Dortie, but never annoyed! You will take Te Toldin, Makran. In the end you could not refuse it and Dortie will argue conditions and contracts with me like a G'tal scribe while you sit in embarrassed silence!'

'We are not ungrateful, Curos, but gift or sale, it is too much to give up. I know there is little love between you and Hoelun but she gives all she is able.' He added with some defiance, 'Whether I take Te Toldin or stay as estate manager, she will be always welcome in my home, even if you are divorced.'

22

The next two days were both hectic and stressful for the occupants of Te Toldin. Kataln, still displaying real or imagined rage at every opportunity, departed for her father's home with bags and belongings and a personal escort. Hoelun also left but for G'tal where her elder brother Yuel was an Administrator in the civil service. Curos was sure that the divorce contract would be debated at great length and with all due propriety. Preservation of dignity would be much more important to Chou Yuel than return of dowry money, but luckily Curos could allow Lin Sri to conduct the tedious procedures. Kataln's father, however, struggling against soil erosion on a now impoverished estate, would be only too pleased to accept the return of his daughter's dowry with interest.

There were tears when Hoelun left, and again Curos realised how little he had understood the feelings in his father's house. To its inhabitants it was Curos who was wrong and unreasonable and little Pa'na refused to speak to his uncle for several days.

'I feel your actions are unwarranted, Curos,' Dortie had said, echoing Curos' own thoughts as Hoelun's carriage and escort departed down the long drive. 'Once your letter to Hoelun's brother, Yuel, is delivered there is no turning back. You will regret this day. Call back Hoelun. Wait for one year, Freu will find a way to help you.'

'Freu!' Curos laughed bitterly as he turned to walk up the mansion steps. 'The peasant's goddess of fertility! You are an educated noblewoman, Dortie!'

'Do not mock Freu, Curos. She is no peasant deity, she is all. And all women at some time worship Freu.'

'Even Turakina, my mother?'

'Yes, even Turakina, but to her it is Sh Ren, mother of stars who now sits with Dei Sechen on the moon and governs the cycles of birth and growth.'

'And Xante?'

'To Xante there is no name and no shape to the awful spirit who drives fertility. It is part of S'lan itself, perhaps just one aspect of S'lan.'

'Have you spoken much to Xante?' Curos asked in a conversational tone.

'Yes, when she is not sitting like a naked bird in the great tree or charming my roses into health.'

'Naked in the tree!'

'That's what Kataln said.' Dortie smiled. 'It was a great disappointment to Makran. The girl wore quite enough to veil the full details of her beauty but Kataln is easily outraged. You should allow Xante back now, Curos. She is quite amazingly hardy but the Hill of Tears is a cold, barren place even for sheep and goats at this time of year.'

'Your judgement, as usual, is sound, Dortie. I will take food and wine and ride out to the Hill of Tears. I need exercise and fresh air. You and Makran prepare this ruinous contract.'

'Take rather a brazier and tea with gensing,' suggested Dortie. 'Hot tea will be better than cold wine. And beware Sh Ren, arrogant Wind Rider.'

Far out across the estate as the land began to rise up towards the D'was plateau the Hill of Tears stood out like a bleak outpost of the desert. The tough grass and shrub plants which struggled to grow on the dry, rocky pasture seemed to have an even more tenuous grip on the hillside. Huge blocks of granite stood out starkly, defying the winter wind, and the twisted trees were tortured into grotesque shapes by a combination of weather and inhospitable soil. It was a place rarely visited except by the occasional shepherd who sought a straying sheep which had been hungry enough to clamber up through the miniature crags in search of food. Strange then that Xante had chosen this place as a refuge from the turmoil and confusion of the mansion. She was not a creature of the wild open spaces and preferred to be surrounded by trees.

It was not difficult to locate the shelter which she had constructed in a depression huddled back against a granite outcrop. She walked to meet him with genuine pleasure as he guided the reluctant horse up over the difficult path.

172

'The true N'gol even here,' she called to him. 'Never walk when a horse will carry you!'

'It's not the walking, it's the weight – food and stores Dortie insisted I bring in case you were dying from cold and hunger!' He jumped down off the pony and surprised her by gripping her hands in an uncharacteristic show of emotion. She started and he stepped back before continuing, 'Now, what do you wish to tell me that is so important?' He swung the saddle-packs over his shoulder and viewed the desolate scene. 'I would think there is danger of boredom as well as cold.'

'No, I have learned a great deal,' she explained, taking him to the shelter where they began to set up Dortie's charcoal stove. 'I have been trying to listen to the Great Tree of Te Toldin, but it is so old, Curos. Old and venerable like an ancient person. It tells what it will tell, not what the disciple wishes to know. It is as if it half sleeps and is near to death.' Without thinking, she stretched out her hand and lit the charcoal with a small but sustained burst of fire.

'I was out riding with your esteemed mother, Lady Turakina, when we passed by here. We must talk of her some time, Curos. She is a sick woman, sick with anger and with grief which she will not show or share. She is deliberately cutting her ties with her family, even the grandchildren she loves, piling misery on grief upon anger.'

When Curos began to question Xante, she merely said, 'Not now, Curos! Later we will talk of Turakina – I must continue. This place seemed to call to me, Curos. I could feel the pain and sorrow of this area. The next day I rode back here alone and read the memories of the rocks and the stones. There is less knowledge to filter through, and the events are clear.'

'Is it important?' he asked.

'Who knows?' She shrugged. 'There is a riddle in Te Toldin's past and I know more of it now.' Carefully, Xante explained how the whole of the hill was permeated with the roots of great W'dom trees which had died in a cataclysmic fire about five hundred years previously. The dormant seeds still lay in the soil, waiting for a spark to bring them into life. That spark would be the presence of Dryadin bringing the influence of Eternal S'lan.

173

It was the spirit memory of these ancient seeds which Xante had in part begun to understand.

The Hill of Tears had been a small Dryad enclave which had been destroyed by the great N'gol raids which had devastated Chaw five centuries ago. The Zachaw family with the estate people had centred their defence on the Te Toldin Mansion. Although the house and the Great Tree had been saved by the Dryadin, the hill community had been destroyed and never re-established.

'There are also jumbled memories of the Great Stone but to the Dryads here it was the tree at Te Toldin which was of importance.'

'Why is this important to us today, Xante?' Curos asked, spooning the dried green tea into an earthenware pot.

'Tea, Curos? I had been expecting wine! Did your time at Toldin go that badly?'

'No, I achieved my objective with the expected casualties. Hoelun is hurt, Kataln angry but happy to be released. Makran is happy at having Te Toldin but feeling guilty. And Dortie is sad to see Hoelun go, blaming me for the ruin of my marriage; but even she makes some errors. She thought you would like hot tea instead of cold wine! So you have tea.' He poured on the water with a flourish. 'What is the importance of this discovery?'

'These half-memories were imprinted here as messages to the future by those Dryads. They spoke of hope and purpose, not of the death and fire which destroyed their community. The tree's Wisdom did not grow except by the purpose of Eternal S'lan and I believe this hill was to be the start of a new arm of the forest. For all the importance which they attached to this work, the preservation of Te Toldin and the Great Tree was much more vital. There is a link between the Zachaws of Te Toldin and the Dryadin which was strong then, but during the N'gol wars and the destruction of the D'was that link became severed. To save Chaw and defeat the N'gol it was necessary to reverse centuries of patient Dryad work in the desert, a difficult act for us to forgive. The hill also proves that even a sacred place with W'dom Trees and Dryads to protect it can fall to axe

174

and sword if unsupported. This may reinforce my people's will to help you.'

'Perhaps.' Curos shrugged, unimpressed. 'Should not Ze Dryadi know of these facts already?'

'Yes, the knowledge is in S'lan if Ze Dryadi were to seek it out but he has many other cares and responsibilities which keep his mind from our problems. All this is of the past, however, most important is the knowledge that shows that Dryads could live here and could re-establish a small community, an outpost of S'lan. Give this hill to me and I will bring four Dryadin. Ze Dryadi could not refuse.'

'What do I get in return,' Curos laughed, 'or what does Makran get? It's his hill now!'

'With the Dryadin you get trees, Curos, trees fix soil, hold water, encourage rain. This could be the start of a belt of new vegetation stretching out into D'was.'

He sipped his tea and surveyed the bleak winter-gripped hill and its stunted vegetation. 'Your visions do you credit.'

'This is not a girl's dream, Curos, or a game to fill in time. The Dryads would live, at first, in the orchards and timber copses out over there closer to Te Toldin.'

'I feel there is a second plan afoot here, Xante. You had better continue slowly. This Chaw's brain is slow with the strain of the last two days.'

Xante explained that she had also detected at least one Chaw person with potential to learn sorcery. He lived in the village of the Yellow Stones half-a-day's ride from the Te Toldin Mansion, and seemed to be a successful fortune-teller, judging from the wealth shown by his horse and clothes. His name was Gron Fa.

'Gron Fa,' agreed Curos. 'I know of him, tall and wears blocked shoes. Makran and Dortie dislike him because he takes too much for poor medicine and superstitious predictions.'

'But there is a spark, Curos, a weak spark of ability. Gron Fa is probably genuine in his belief of himself. He may not be eager to change his way of life, but if there are others of similar ability and Dryadin to train them then you may yet have your one hundred sorcerers.'

'If Gron Fa is of use to me he has no choice. The army can call on all men, or women, to repel an invader.'

175

'I did not mean to suggest punishment or coercion, Curos. He should be persuaded to help save his land and his people.'

'Such as he have lived off the people long enough, now they will serve the people. Would your Ze Dryadi give free choice in such matters?'

'There would be no need to give free choice, Curos,' she said stiffly. 'As you have seen, any Dryad would immediately realise the path of duty if S'lan required it, we have no choice.'

Curos handed her a second bowl of tea and leaned back against the granite. 'I need rapid conformity, not slow recognition of duty. Has Gron Fa any family?'

'No.'

'A great shame. Some weapon will come to my hand when we speak with him.'

The possibilities of Xante's plan began to take enthusiastic root in Curos' mind and he was quite unable to contemplate a return to Te Toldin without first visiting Gron Fa.

It was late afternoon when Curos and Xante rode into the farming village of Yellow Stones. A few of the peasants retiring from bedding down animals for the night or from work in the cold fields recognised Curos and bowed low as a mark of respect. The community was quietly prosperous. Tidy, solidly built houses with attached outbuildings, well-dug garden plots and a clear street all showed the result of stability and good harvests. Te Toldin had been luckier than most areas with adequate rainfall over the last five years and the paternal estate management of the Zachaw family had been given new impetus by Makran and Dortie.

All thoughts of Makran and Dortie quickly slipped from Curos' mind as he and Xante stopped outside the house of Gron Fa. A village girl, who acted as the self-styled Magi's servant, recognised Curos and led them with much bowing and trembling clumsiness into a well-furnished room, explaining that the Master was meditating.

Shortly after, the same girl returned and invited Curos and Xante into a second, dimly lit chamber. The walls of the room were hung with macabre occult trappings of theatrical sorcery: masks, bells and skulls which stared out grotesquely in the flickering lamplight. Incense smoke drifted densely in the still air, adding a further layer of obscurity.

Gron Fa sat at a small table, and with unbelievable arrogance did not rise as Curos and Xante entered but waved them towards floor stools with a grave gesture. Curos' anger flared uncontrollably but Xante respectfully bowed and sat as the fortune-teller requested.

'I have been conducted here by Lord Zachaw,' apologised Xante in her deep, husky voice, 'to seek guidance as to the future of the esteemed Lord and myself.'

Gron Fa murmured at the wisdom of her choice in seeking such a skilled fortune-teller and turned his haughty gaze onto a disk of crystal. The single flickering lamp cast evil shadows down over his face and showed glimpses of macabre objects hanging from the walls. Curos was well aware of the frightening effect that Gron and the carefully planned room would have on simple villagers.

'I see long life and many sons,' he intoned in a bored voice, but stopped abruptly as the view into the crystal changed into a blazing fire and then into a green mass of writhing tendrils. Shocked and afraid, Gron gasped and slid the crystal away across the expensive, highly polished surface. 'Your case is difficult and confused,' he said in a theatrical voice.

'I seek only the Magi's guidance on how I should act to certain proposals made to me by Lord Zachaw,' replied Xante in a timid voice.

Now on firmer ground, Gron flashed Curos a lewd smile. 'I am sure Lord Zachaw's proposals to you are just and to your benefit, madam. In matters of importance it is best that I should consult your hand.'

Xante removed the black glove and held her hand palm upwards for Gron Fa's inspection.

'Ah! So obvious!' Gron said. 'A novice could see as much.' His voice failed as his eyes actually registered the shape of the long, thin hand with its flat, featureless palm, the clawlike fingernails extending into wicked, curved claws.

As Gron flinched and drew back, Xante said coldly, 'You are a fraud, Gron, who prostitutes what little ability he has for money. You felt my power but you refused to accept it.'

177

Gron had now stood to his full height and pointing an accusing finger at the seated woman shouted for her to leave his house.

'Sit down,' she ordered with an irresistible authority. Gron struggled, held his head and staggered before collapsing down into a slumped, defeated heap.

There was no speech and no sounds intruded into the room from the village. Gron looked up and gathered the last of his courage. 'Begone, witch! Do not trifle with me. I have powers no woman can comprehend. I will summon demons and spirits to my aid if you do not depart.' He stretched out a hand for the lacquered rune staff which lay on the table but it flew from his fingers, shattering into shards and splinters. On the prayer table the ornate dagger rose into the air as far as the very ceiling before plunging down to split the polished wood, its hilt burning with green fire.

'Like you, Gron, I can invoke the trappings of sorcery to impress,' Xante said. 'Mere tricks that even you could manage. You have some latent ability. Instead of study and exercise you choose deception and trickery to achieve unearned riches.' As Gron cowered back she continued remorselessly, 'Now another path has been chosen, so that you may serve Chaw.'

With weakening defiance, Gron muttered sullenly that he was a free man, not a peasant to be ordered by either Lord or Witch.

'Your first lesson will be to show due courtesy and use the correct forms of address.' Curos spoke for the first time. 'Any man, or woman for that matter, can be ordered into the army in time of danger to the land.'

'You must learn also,' said Xante, 'not to judge evil with your eyes only. The setting of this room is your making. Viewed like this, would I still seem fearful?' As she spoke, the three of them were surrounded by a mirage of the S'lan forest. Dappled light shone through the trees, water flowed nearby and birds sang. Even Xante herself had changed. Her black robes were now as fine white silk and her unveiled face shone with pure beauty. 'It is still the same woman, Gron. Reject sight and logic and ignore your fear. Use only the emotions which come from your mind. If you truly feel evil in me then you will be unable to learn the skills we need.'

Curos wrenched his eyes away from the vision before him and

178

turned to Gron. 'You are fortunate that your insolence is so rewarded. I would have taught you respect with a whip, and then to fear the real evil which threatens our land.'

'That also will be done, Lord Zachaw,' came Xante's words floating into his mind, 'but the message may be painful to you too. Close your mind to it if you wish.'

Curos did indeed close his mind to the vivid pictures which he knew so well. Shutting out the images of the fire wall and the destruction of the Wind Hunds, neither did he see the bearded face of Valanus which peered into Chaw, seeking its new leaders. The display sent Gron into a spasm of shock and abject fear which rendered speech impossible.

The visions cleared. Xante with the merest of gestures lighted more lamps around the room and Curos shouted for the servant to bring tea. The symbols of fake sorcery were swept away and the burnt dagger was pulled from the table. Only as Gron attempted to steady his hands to take a bowl of tea from the maid did Curos resume the conversation.

'You see now, Gron, a little of the true power of the Dryad Lady and the evilness of the Warchaw sorcerers who threaten us.'

It was now important to allow Gron Fa to recover a little of his composure. Xante's revelation had in minutes destroyed his cosy, ordered world. The shock was still in Gron Fa's words as he mumbled, 'This humble man is wretched at his stupidity and rudeness. I feel the power of the enemy and tremble with cowardice, Lord. A pathetic worm such as I can be of no use to yourself and the Queen of Sorcery.'

'It is too late to crawl away, Gron.' Curos shrugged. 'Already the Warchaw prepare to invade Chaw. They rule by sorcery and by their army. Any who like yourself have some ability for magic, however small, will be sought out and destroyed.'

'Either killed or corrupted,' Xante added, sipping her tea. 'Full sorcerers like myself will be struck down violently but such as you may well suffer even more dreadfully.'

'Our enemy is strong beyond belief,' Curos explained. 'In sorcery or force of arms they excel us as the tiger excels the ant. Chaw's only advantage is in numbers. As the soldier ants will drive out the tiger, so shall the ants of Chaw drive off the

179

Warchaw. We have one sorceress but she is a Queen who will train countless others. You are the first chosen, Gron, and cannot reject the honour or the duty.' He paused as he felt Xante smile, but in only a slightly more circumspect style he continued, 'Tomorrow you will appear at Te Toldin and will be enrolled as Sorcerer to the 22nd T'sand. As a privilege you will have the equivalent rank of Ataman and draw the same pay. Your training will begin at once.'

'Lord, forgive me,' cried Gron fearfully. 'I cannot. I have my house, my servant and there are affairs to settle.'

'Your duty is all that is important to you. The servant girl who is not without sense will care for your house, or the village headman will sell it as you wish. Your officer will be K'tan Bhal Morag, the principal warfare officer of the T'sand. Gron, in twenty days' time I lead the T'sand against the rebel bandits of Te Lok. By that time you will have learned to speak from afar to Lady Xante by sorcery. That is your first task. Obey and you are rewarded by life. Fail and your brain will burst with the power she will direct towards you.'

23

Following Kataln's hasty departure to her father's estate and Hoelun's more lamented leave-taking, the Zachaw household assumed a more relaxed atmosphere.

Turakina had not seemed interested in Curos' plan but when pressed seemed pleased that the management and ownership of the Estate was to be settled. She counselled Curos to make a very careful contract with Makran such that they would know and understand each other's expectations. In times of prosperity there was little to contend with, but if times grew hard, or if Curos did eventually have children, she feared the brothers might quarrel. Many N'gol family feuds were started by acts of generosity which later turned sour. She insisted that scribes should be appointed to draw up a legal deed and sat in on several of the discussions to ensure that her sons treated the matter seriously. The widow's robes were now discarded but the deep-set eyes, even more than the shaven head, proclaimed her continued distress. Much of her time was spent riding with Curos or Xante and most often with her youngest grandson, Turkal.

Although cold, the winter night was dry with little wind and the hard, black sky seemed brilliant with stars. The oppressive sadness and tension of Te Toldin made it difficult for Xante to relax and she had wandered out into the enclosed courtyard where a huge, ancient tree grew beside and leaned protectively over a boulder of volcanic rock. Protected from the cold by the Dryad clothing and a leather N'gol riding suit, she sat some distance from the tree and began to play the long, hardwood Dryad flute. Its husky tones mimicked the lament of two estranged lovers. The music was cold and without hope, the perfect accompaniment to the words of a hopeless love story.

A second shape stole into the garden with cautious step which only a Dryad would have heard. The shadow advanced but Xante finished the lament before looking around to Turakina.

'You suffer, too?' asked the stocky, hard-faced woman who carried with her the aura of death.

'Not as you do, madam,' Xante replied respectfully. 'The tears of those who have never known love cannot be as deep as those of one who has lost the lover that they lived for.'

Turakina sat down and looked up at the sky where a thin winter moon was beginning to rise. 'I have had my life and my sons,' she said. 'Please continue playing, if you will.'

Xante considered several tunes but strangely her fingers disobeyed her and the tune was far from what she had intended. She stopped and tried again but once more was pulled into a wild N'gol ballad. Turakina gave a gasp of surprise and Xante stopped playing.

'I am sorry, Turakina, the tune slipped into my mind and commands to be played. I have never heard it before.' She peered at the N'gol woman through the darkness and was aware of tears glistening on her face. 'I meant no offence. My music is poor, I cannot seem to remember.'

'There is no offence, Dryad, but that is the ballad of Turakina and Pa'lin, my husband. It is sung with joy and pride in the D'was, not least in the clan of my people, the White Dragon.'

'It is not fitting,' Xante murmured. 'I will lay down my flute for this night.'

'I will say what is fitting,' snapped Turakina, who was now openly crying. 'A song will not be stifled when it comes of its own will and I will sing it myself. You appear to know enough of the tune.'

In the silent darkness Turakina sang each verse of the long epic ballad which told of their love. From the first hot glances exchanged between Zachaw Pa'lin and Turakina of the White Dragon Clan, through all their adventures until after three months they rode back into the kuriyen of her father as man and wife. It told of the riding, the stealing of her brother's horses and the jokes they had played on the tribesmen and the Chaw Cavalry who pursued them. How Turakina had crept into Po Pi's tent and stolen his trousers and how Pa'lin had exchanged her father's wine-flask for another filled with horse water!

Curos had also entered the garden and stood apart in disbelief. His mother was singing as if about two strangers and their deeds long ago. Since his father's death Curos had been unable to make any contact with Turakina, and try as he might he could not reconcile the hard face and the harsh, impersonal voice with his mother. At the evening meal tonight she had not bothered to change from her N'gol clothes into her Chaw robes as was her custom. Sitting flanked by her family, amid the miniature trees and the polished surfaces of rich furnishings which reflected the flickering lamplight, she looked like a stranger who had arrived uninvited. Desperately, Curos had tried to fix this new scene in his mind, convinced that this would be the last time Turakina would sleep in Te Toldin.

Now as she sang on and on tears flowed freely down her face, her voice growing hoarse. Each change of wording and the tune of the accompaniment came with a natural ease which was belied by the tension in the singer. Curos wanted to hold her, speak some words of consolation, but this was a private ritual between Turakina and the memory of Pa'lin. He was excluded, shut out from this section of their life. The song ended and Turakina stumbled off to her room while Xante continued to play. For once she did not want to talk to Curos, the music and the sadness had left her too vulnerable.

Curos left the garden and Xante was alone, utterly alone. She had grown away from Dromo, probably even before she had left the forest, and now with her burden of knowledge and power, her affinity to her father and the forest had been stretched thin. She was becoming estranged from the Dryadin, N'gol and all but one man of Chaw. Thankfully he was unaware of her weakness tonight. There were times when she was frustrated by his lack of interest in her, times when any interest or affection he did show roused her to anger.

'May S'lan the Eternal protect me from Ki Freu and Sh Ren,' she said aloud and only the Tree and the Stone listened. Curos and Xante must run as two horses harnessed side by side, with one speed and one direction. 'If ever we touch, really touch, there will be a flash of passion rarely seen. A disaster for our two peoples, possibly the final disaster.'

Curos tapped on the door of his mother's room and heard a guttural assent. Inside, Turakina was packing spare clothes into deep pack-horse panniers.

'You heard tonight,' she said, her throat as hoarse as her eyes were sore from tears. 'You were in the garden?'

'Yes, mother, I heard.'

'Then you should have sung with me. There was a message there for you as there was for me. Pa'lin, my husband, your father, was there in spirit, Curos. He is not angry that I seek death in my own way but by the song he reminded me of love and of life and bade me not lead too many young men and women to death with me.' As she turned towards him he caught her in his arms as a N'gol would have done months ago.

'Mother, you read too much into a tune. Your grief is real – it needs time to heal.'

For once she did not push him away immediately. 'No, I will not heal, I am one with myself and my purpose. And we are both proud, very proud of our son. I know you and Pa'lin made peace a long time ago and he sees how you build on his plan.' As he stood in disbelief she moved away from him, her face smiling. 'I know men do not speak of agreements and friendship, they ease into them. Father and son do not need to speak, husband and wife do.'

'There are things we need to discuss, mother.'

'No, I have my plan. Tonight I move outside into a yert to live as a N'gol and go back to my people.'

'Your home is here.'

'Not now. I have stayed too long. I will form my own war band and slay Warchaw. I will kill my enemies until the D'was is made fertile by their blood or until I find my own death. You will ride with me in the morning, for the last time as my son?'

Two horses thundered out of the thin morning mist and wheeled in a new path parallel to a line of man-sized straw targets. Neither rider needed reins but used hand and arms to shoot the short, highly recurved bows of the N'gol. Arrows thudded into straw and the horses turned away in a wide circle before attacking again. The horsemen were hardly recognisable beneath the leather riding clothes and steel war caps but subtle points of style or riding and shooting were now obvious to Xante. Physically, Turakina was not as strong as her son and her line of attack approached the targets more closely, too close, Curos had said.

She had a fire and urgency in her practice that complimented her preoccupation with death and war. Curos, stronger, and possibly even more skilful, could not match the venom of his mother's shooting. They walked the sweating horses back to the target area and reviewed the effect of their numerous attacks.

Xante joined them. 'Your shooting is exemplary, Turakina, in style and in accuracy. Few arrows have missed their mark.'

'I lack power,' replied Turakina. 'I am too old to pull a heavy bow and must compensate by closing with my enemy.'

'Against Warchaw armour no bow is strong enough,' said Curos. 'Speed and accuracy of shot are vital.'

They retrieved their arrows and remounted before Turakina spoke again. 'He shoots well, does he not, Xante, for a half-N'gol? With the sabre he is better, better than any. He was bred as a N'gol, you know, that is what makes him so. Pa'lin journeyed to the far side of Imran to spy on the Warchaw and I accompanied the party. Curos was conceived and born before we returned. Like a N'gol his feet never touched earth until he was three years old and he was suckled in the saddle. Even at night the floor of the yert is covered by horsehide. Great houses cut out the wind and stifle the spirit of children – Makran was born in a house, you see. My only mistake with Curos was to allow Pa'lin to give him a Chaw wife. A N'gol woman who could ride the wind with him and ride again two days after giving birth would have drawn him back to the clans. He would have rivalled Tinjin of old and scattered the Warchaw . . .' Her voice trailed off.

Several times Curos had tried to explain to Turakina the plans for his life and for Te Toldin but she had showed little, if any, interest. Most often she sat in silent inattentiveness when he spoke to her. What speech she did utter was a confused mixture of recriminations against the duty her husband felt for Chaw or happy reminiscences of their journeys into strange lands or of time spent with her people. Always she returned to the idea of revenge against the Warchaw and a need for her to ride and to practise her shooting. Te Toldin was now her prison.

She turned suddenly to Curos and said, 'It is time we talked, you and I. Enough time has passed and I prattle like an old woman.'

185

'I have tried to explain,' Curos started to say, but Turakina cut him off.

'You have left Te Toldin to Makran, that is good. As I said last night, you and I have no place here now. Pa'na is like his father and will be tied to the land with Makran, but in little Turkal the blood flows with the fire of a Wind Rider. One day Topaz Wind will be proud to be led by him. Inheritance and succession are all accounted for. You can follow the path of duty and I shall follow the Death Wind.'

24

Turakina left Te Toldin and returned to her clan, leaving her sons more than concerned for her welfare but able to do little to change her intentions. With the estate now legally ceded to Makran there was little to hold Curos to Te Toldin and he was ready to depart for the merchant town Lokar where he would meet with the town leaders and the Chief of Militia before rejoining Bhal Morag and the 22nd T'sand.

Travelling with Curos were Xante and Gron Fa, the latter showing signs of marked physical and mental strain. In keeping with Gron Fa's honorary rank of Ataman, Curos had insisted he achieve a higher level of fitness than suited his sedentary nature. This, however, was almost a minor problem compared to that imposed upon him by the mind-training from Xante. It was not the mere effort required which had taxed Gron Fa but the realisation of how feeble his powers of sorcery were when measured against the young Dryad woman.

'It is very difficult for him, Curos,' Xante had explained. 'From a position of supreme confidence in his own ability he has been humiliated and forced to submit to the regime imposed by a woman.'

'As we have agreed before, life is hard. If it is hard for Xante-Yani and Zachaw Ca'lin, why should it be easy for Gron Fa?'

The ride to Lokar was a leisurely progression to Xante and Curos, but almost too strenuous for Gron Fa. As he lagged behind, Xante explained to Curos their difficulties in mind-communication.

'Strangely,' she told him, 'there is a basic discrepancy in the way the Dryad and the Chaw think.'

'Think!'

'Yes, the clue is in your written script,' she explained. 'You write in a series of pictorial characters, thousands of them. We use twenty-one runes which define sounds. Gron Fa tries to

187

communicate to me in a series of pictures; I expect a flow of ideas.'

'No, stop, Xante! It is too subtle for me! Who but a Dryad would have discovered such a difficulty?'

'It was Makran who suggested the idea to me.'

'Perhaps an illiterate Chaw would be a better choice for sorcerers.'

'Unlikely.'

More seriously he added, 'I do not mean to advance too quickly, Xante, but there is a chance to test our ideas against the Te Lok outlaws. Could you not use a simple code as we use for signal flags?'

'More pictures, Curos?'

'Yes, but only twenty. Soldiers are simple people. Some, even of Noyan rank, cannot read more than one thousand characters.'

To the south, on their right-hand side stretched the weather-worn limestone hills of Te Lok. Its seemingly endless valleys and ridges were interrupted only by tussock-like outcrops of volcanic granite. In other places deep pits filled with water marked the site of quarries from which better quality stone had been taken to build Lokar city in ancient times.

In the heat of summer, Te Lok was dry and brown as water evaporated or drained quickly through the porous stone. Now in winter the dull vegetation was sprinkled with thin snow and the edges of the streams were rimmed with ice. It was no wonder that Te Lok was sparsely inhabited. In scattered villages, farmers attempted to terrace the thin soil or to graze the hillsides with hardy sheep and cattle. Te Lok had been a haven for outlaws and fugitives from times before Lokar was built but only recently had this well-organised, well-informed band threatened the trade roads to any significant extent.

The fabled merchant city of Lokar when it came in sight after several days of riding was always a disappointment. There were no towering pagodas or palaces and the ancient, now crumbling walls, were surrounded by a shanty town which the administration had long since accepted as inevitable. Recently more substantial buildings, warehouses and mansions had been constructed until Old Lokar was now almost a separate city within the sprawling growth of the unplanned new town. Set firmly astride the Lokin river and commanding the Northern Road, Lokar lived only for trade and commerce. Undefendable but unthreatened, it was rich and old but still vibrant with the energy and wealth of a thousand merchants. The taxes collected, even if only a fraction of what was legally due, were important revenue to the Civil and Army Government of Chaw.

Bypassing the main town, Curos followed the south road for some yetang. Beyond the narrow strip of farmland which bordered the Lokin river, on the barren eastern edge of Te Lok, Bhal Morag had camped the T'sand. Nearly one thousand men, foot-soldiers, guards and light horsemen, made up the fighting strength with yet more under Chalak Konn to provide cartage and other services. They were tired and footsore from the ardour of the long march from G'tal but to Curos' relief still in good order and good heart. Chalak Konn, meticulous as ever, had established the camp in accordance with the precise army guidelines and arranged a formal welcome for the T'sand's commander with the scarlet-clad guards now drilled to perfection by Wan Abac.

In the officers' enclosure Curos, Xante, Bhal Morag, Chalak Konn and Wan Abac met to discuss their progress. There had been one new development since Curos had left the T'sand. A violent robbery on the north road between Untin and Lokar had caused the federation of merchants to raise their offer of reward.

'The Certificate of Tax issued at Untin values the gems and precious metal goods at 10,000 gold hawa,' explained Chalak Konn precisely, 'but the thrifty merchants are offering an equal amount for recovery of their property instead of the usual one quarter.'

'No doubt due to their remorse over the death of six hired guards,' added Bhal Morag with accustomed irony.

'It is widely believed that the full inventory of goods was worth six times the official figure,' continued Chalak Konn, 'and that the guards were murdered by the merchants after the raid so that they could not reveal the true extent of the goods carried.'

The next day, leaving Bhal Morag and Chalak Konn planning their search routes of the Te Lok hills with the aid of hired local guides, Curos and Xante turned back into the town. Soon he was being swamped in an endless series of formal meetings with the mayor, civil administrators and leaders of the merchants' federation. Only on the second day did he achieve an interview with Ho Bek, the lowly Militia Commander who Lin Sri had suggested would be the best source of local information.

Xante was introduced as Curos' personal scribe, and with her almost covered face and dark clothes attracted little attention. Soon Ho Bek was explaining his energetic if fruitless attempts to search for the Te Lok outlaws with the few militiamen who could be spared from Lokar. For all their concerns over the outlaws on the trade road, the city elders were still insistent that most of their militia resources should be used in keeping order and guarding against crime on the city itself. After many long rides, and many equally long drinking sessions with village elders, Ho Bek had not been able to uncover any significant trace of the outlaw band. Although the villagers probably gave no active help to criminals, they took little interest in their capture either.

Ho Bek was enthusiastic to join Curos. He was convinced that the outlaws often left the Te Lok hills for months at a time until summoned back by their informant. The most recent robbery indicated that they were again active. Curos did not explain that his scribe, Lin Sri, had in fact organised by devious means the attractively rich caravan from Untin to Lokar.

When Curos had suggested that tax officers in Lokar or Untin could be the source of intelligence for the outlaws Ho Bek had been quite sceptical. Part of his duties was to audit the tax gatherer's accounts and he had never found any trace of corruption. To support his point Ho Bek produced a ledger submitted by a tax gatherer of the Fifth Grade.

'An educated man from his calligraphy,' commented Curos at the unexpectedly neat and well set-out accounts.

'Yes, indeed Lou Chi only failed the final scribe's examination due to sickness. Sickness which also struck down his father and mother, leaving him penniless. His chest was still weak and he was forced to take any clerical employment he could find. Tax collecting has a poor salary and with a wife and two sisters to support he is near destitution. There is also a small child, two years old, as I remember.'

190

'He is honest?'

'Impeccably so, and the villagers hate him.' Ho Bek smiled. 'They say nothing is safe from Lou Chi – he can smell a goat hidden behind ten hills. He is both diligent and surprisingly hardy, considering his past sickness. If there were justice in the world he would have been promoted long ago but without patronage . . .'

'I would like to meet with this strangely well-educated tax gatherer,' commented Curos. 'A man who can keep such careful accounts and ride over Te Lok for days on end could be well employed in my army . . . his health must have improved.'

It was some time before a messenger returned with the tall, seemingly frail man. Curos merely nodded when Lou Chi entered, bowing with utmost servility. Lou Chi then seemed to falter and looked wildly around to where Xante sat beside the window.

'A thousand pardons, madam, Excellency,' Lou Chi stammered. 'I did not realise at first.' He bowed to Xante and closing his palms as in prayer made a second obeisance.

'Lou Chi,' Ho called angrily. 'Do not turn from Noyan Zachaw with such rudeness. The Noyan is here to investigate links with the Te Lok outlaws and desires his scribe should examine your scribbled records for evidence.' Lou Chi became more confused and dropped to his knees, apologising to Curos.

Curos was disappointed at the action of Lou Chi, who did not appear suitable for army service. After a few words from Curos, Ho Bek dismissed Lou Chi to an anteroom where he could discuss his tax records and observations in the hills with Noyan Zachaw's scribe. As soon as the door was closed behind them Xante removed her face covering and looked directly at the confused Lou Chi.

'Lou Chi, you have powers of sorcery,' she stated without preamble. 'You detected my abilities immediately. What other skills have you mastered?'

'Madam,' Lou Chi again bowed to his knees, 'I apologise for my stupidity. I assumed K'tan Ho and the Noyan were aware of your identity.'

'The Noyan Zachaw is well acquainted with my power but that knowledge is not for all. What do you know of me?'

Lou Chi seemed unsure of what to say and looked uneasily towards the door and windows. 'Very little, Lady Xante. My wife, Suzin, and I have some small skill, madam, and occasionally meet others with similar ability in Lokar. A rumour has spread that a powerful sorceress, a Queen of Sorcery, has arrived in Chaw. Previously there had been other, darker stories of barbarian sorcerers, the Evil Ones who destroyed our army in Corninstan. Some of us have felt their eye travelling over the land, searching for a source of power. We now believe that they may seek Q'ren Xante in order to destroy her.'

'Then let me tell you the truth, Lou Chi, and put an end to rumour. But first let us sit and talk like civilised people. Your stories are in part true. There are evil sorcerers of the Warchaw race who threaten Chaw but I am no Queen. I am merely a sorceress with similar but more developed skills than your own. Now I and Noyan Zachaw seek other Chaw to form into an army of sorcerers to oppose the barbarian threat. Tell me of your skills.'

As his reserve and fear began to dispel Lou Chi appeared as a man of true scholarly wit and humour whose conversation was embroidered with elegant jokes, usually against himself. His particular power, he explained, was to be able to detect and divine objects or people from a distance.

'He also claims,' Xante explained later to Curos, 'to have a complete empathy with his wife, Suzin. She has an awareness of what he thinks and what he sees, an immediate effortless transfer.'

'I pity him greatly,' Curos smiled. 'How could a man live without secrets from his wife?'

'It is not a burden to Lou Chi but when I think of the effort it takes me to converse with Dromo or the other Dryadin I feel almost jealous. As I understand it they do not converse, they just share the same thoughts. They would be perfect communicants, Curos, but Suzin has another skill which we will test when we visit their house tonight.'

The house of Lou Chi was a small, threadbare dwelling of two rooms. Kept scrupulously neat and clean by Suzin and Lou Chi's younger sisters, it possessed nevertheless an air of poverty seldom felt in Te Toldin village homes or even the cramped, jumbled yerts of the N'gol. Lou Chi greeted Curos and Xante with a repeat of the morning's extreme politeness and at Xante's request introduced his two sisters. He explained that Suzin, his wife, was attending their child, a two-year-old boy who was troubled by his new teeth.

For some time Curos conversed with Lou Chi and like Xante was struck by his intelligence and well-mannered humour. Curos again touched on the threat of the Warchaw and how Xante had proposed to train Chaw sorcerers.

'I would truly welcome such a chance to serve Chaw, Lord Zachaw,' Lou Chi replied, 'but I doubt I am able to meet the physical standards necessary for Ataman rank.'

'You are not needed to fight, Lou Chi,' commented Xante. 'The infection of the lungs which afflicted you is quite healed although the scars are deep.' She frowned as if looking into his very chest. 'I must talk to your wife. Rarely, if ever, can such grievous infection be healed without strange aid.'

'Women hold up half the sky, the proverb says.' Lou Chi smiled. 'But when Suzin nursed me back to health after my parents' deaths, she supported more than her half. Despite her father's fear and anger, she moved into my honoured parents' large and prosperous house. The servants had fled in terror of the sickness and the business declined until only debt remained. I was too sick to halt the ruin of the house and could only sit with Suzin. At our betrothal we felt a sudden drawing together and affection but it was only when she came to dwell in my house that we discovered our similar powers of sorcery. It was by that she dragged me back from the very brink of the void. For days we sat together breathing as one the Cleansing Breath as she taught me.'

'A remarkable woman indeed,' commented Curos. 'You were formally betrothed, you say?'

'Yes and on my recovery we married, against Suzin's father's wishes and without dowry.'

'What need of dowry for a woman who gives a man his life and a son?' Curos said wistfully. 'I would see your esteemed wife, Lou Chi, and learn of this special skill which Xante says she possesses.'

193

'Then you only need to look closely,' murmured Xante. 'I fear Suzin is too embarrassed to speak.'

'My foolish husband shames me with too much praise and I could not speak before,' said a female voice. Curos turned and stared at the blank wall less than two paces away. The air assumed a vague shimmer and then he could see the figure of a young woman sitting with a small boy on her lap. Her face was that of a young noblewoman, cultured and refined, but thin and marked by great suffering. He was immediately struck by her appearance of inner strength and stillness. Curos started in amazement and looked questioningly at Xante.

'She has been there all the time, Curos,' Xante smiled at Curos, 'and her son copies his mother's thoughts, although he has little power. Even I, who knew where Suzin sat, could see her but dimly.'

'How is this done?' asked the astonished Curos, staring openly at the pale though attractive woman as she stood up to bow to him without any loss of composure.

'I do not know, Curos,' said Xante. 'I truly do not know. Suzin could carry her beauty through the camp of your villainous T'sand unheeded. Even by sorcery I would find it hard to detect her from any distance.'

'Please fetch tea for our guests, Suzi,' said Lou Chi gently, 'and bring the small sweet cakes.'

Anticipating such ill-afforded hospitality, Curos and Xante had come prepared with food and sweets which were now presented as gifts to the house. As Suzin and Lou Chi's sisters retired to the diminutive kitchen Curos said, 'Would the hunters of the Night Dragon Clan see . . .' he was still unable to be reconciled to the reality of Suzin.

'I don't know, I think not. It is not as if Suzin confuses sight or hearing; it is as if she slips out of your consciousness.'

'Like a spirit?'

'Please, Excellency, do not speak so. There is nothing ghost-like about my wife, she is no spirit woman, but we have been too close to the spirit world to speak of it lightly.'

'I myself cannot explain,' Suzin apologised as she knelt to set out small cups on a plain tray and arranged cakes and sweets in a pleasing pattern. 'It is a strange gift to live with. Occasionally if I am embarrassed or afraid I forget, and confuse people. I even considered theft when we were very hungry. I would welcome a chance to join my husband in using my skill honestly.'

'Then I do believe you will be the first woman Ataman in the 22nd T'sand,' said Curos. 'N'gol women fight, now Chaw women will be in my army, as sorcerers.'

'First Lou Chi and Suzin should go to Te Toldin,' suggested Xante. 'When Dromo and the others arrive they will investigate her powers. Perhaps what Suzin can do instinctively, another can learn with effort.'

It was a pleasant, relaxed family evening with Lou Chi and Suzin, but as Curos and Xante rode back toward the T'sand's camp Curos became tensely silent, the cold, dry winter air seemingly reflected in his hard face.

'You did not say that Dromo was one of the Dryadin who would come to Te Toldin,' he remarked after some time.

'No, I am sorry. It will not be easy for either Dromo or myself and he brings his wife. They have no child yet but one will be born next year. There will be another couple with them.'

'A strange choice.'

'No. Dromo is a teacher and the others have the qualities to rejuvenate the Hill of Tears. I did not ask for Dromo to come, Curos. Perhaps now all will be well between us, and he is by far the best choice for this task. No other would be so able at understanding Suzin's ability. If he can understand, he can teach it to me and perhaps to others. Our minds are quite attuned.'

'I understand.'

'I do not think you do, Curos, but then I don't think you want to,' she said bitterly. 'In certain directions your mind is quite tramelled into lines of conventional lust and jealousy. You look on the happiness of Makran and Dortie or Lou Chi and Suzin like a young bird looks out from a tree but even when the opportunity is there you lack the courage to step off and fly.'

195

25

On one of the long downs which characterised the western edge of the Te Lok Hills was a small camp of three tents. Heavy frost hung on the sparse heather as the winter sun slanted over the close horizon of the surrounding hills.

Smoke was already rising from the struggling camp fire into the freezing air. Noyan Zachaw Curos had risen to perform his morning exercises and the semi-frozen guardsman who had taken the last night-watch crouched over his fire like some strange, smoking ham.

It was three days since Bhal Morag had set off with the long cordon of the 22nd T'sand crawling among the Te Lok Hills. Each twenty-man Ulus kept close together under their Ataman and maintained contact with the Ulus to the left and right. A light cavalryman rode with them or led his horse as the terrain allowed. The outlaw band was quite large and with its goods and semi-permanent camp should be detectable, but Curos was already becoming concerned that it might split up and try to slip past his searchers.

Instead of accompanying Xante to join Topaz, Curos had decided to use Lou Chi as an additional seer and to allow Bhal Morag and Khol Dalgan to act independently. This would prove a much more stringent test of using sorcerers for communication.

Lou Chi had made good company for the first few days but Curos had gradually become bored with the tax gatherer's polite, refined conversation. It was also noticeable that Suzin appeared to resent any time Lou Chi spent talking with Curos, although through her veil of formal good manners it was impossible to tell if this was due to dislike or mistrust.

Xante had expressed something similar. 'It is strange, Curos, that I can hold mind communication with Suzin so easily. Although messages can flow freely between us, there is no tuning of thoughts or sympathy of feeling as there is when I speak to Dromo.'

There was always a barb when Xante mentioned that name but Curos had asked, 'Does she dislike you, then?'

'Yes, I believe she does. Not particularly as a person but as someone violent and alien. Also she feels betrayed by her parents who would not support her when she honoured her betrothal to Lou Chi and withdrew dowry payment because he was destitute. This and her husband's lack of promotion, despite his abilities, have convinced her that Chaw society is worthless, and she has turned completely inwards to her own family. The facade of breeding and cool manners remain but it is only a protection against the outside.'

They had proceeded to discuss Suzin's relationship with Lou Chi, which disturbed Curos.

'I still cannot understand how two people can always share their thoughts,' he had said. 'Surely every man and wife must quarrel on occasion, even Dryad couples?'

'Indeed, Curos,' she had replied. 'Dromo and I had the most furious of quarrels. But consider, if love and need for reconciliation are present then that is visible too. When one withdraws their thoughts from the other then it is clear that love has died. When one refuses to open his thoughts to his partner it is clear that love has not begun.'

Strange relationship or not, there were two of them in the tent to keep each other warm, Curos thought as he attempted to cast off the Te Lok cold. He looked again at the carefully marked-up map on which he had recorded progress. Also shown was Lou Chi's prediction of where the outlaws were camped. Weak evidence, but if the villagers said that Lou Chi could divine one hidden sheep from behind ten hills, maybe he could detect twenty outlaws.

Curos had spent some time hunting but the only game was rabbits and hares which were more effectively snared than shot with arrows. He had also ridden across the nearby hills to check the actual terrain against his map but dared not move too far from the camp. As his boredom increased so did his annoyance at the placid composure of Lou Chi and Suzin. On several evenings he had even descended to playing dice with the four soldiers who accompanied the party.

197

It was on the fourth day of this strange vigil that Suzin approached Curos with her habitual deference.

'Lady Xante has news from Gron Fa,' she said. 'One of Bhal Morag's groups has discovered a permanent campsite with huts like a small village. It has been recently deserted and another search group has detected a party of horsemen with a cart who are making their way westward.' She indicated on Curos' map. 'Topaz Wind are moving around to camp here and Bhal Morag is swinging his men along these hills.'

Suddenly excited, Curos resented not being able to take a more active part in the search. He became anxious that Bhal Morag might be pursuing an innocent party of travellers and allowing the true quarry to escape. It was one thing to allow Khol Dalgan and Bhal Morag freedom of action but quite another to have to sit and watch them make mistakes.

'He should keep his search more open until he is sure,' he said half to himself, and then added to Lou Chi, 'Can you explain that to Xante?'

'Surely, Lord Curos, but Lady Xante cannot speak easily to Gron Fa, she can only read his simple messages. Her power bruises his mind.' Suzin smiled in a somewhat superior way. 'Do not concern yourself, Lord Zachaw. The village was close to where Chi, my husband, predicted, I am sure your soldiers are hounding the correct people.'

If Bhal Morag were staking his whole game on one throw, Curos could do no less. He decided to move his own small camp due south to the hilltop overlooking the outlaws' probable route. When they struck camp and moved off it was at an easy pace with Suzin sharing her husband's horse. One of her first lessons ought to have been in riding, Curos thought, and in the four days they had been in the Te Lok hills she could have made some progress rather than sitting painting or reading poetry. It never occurred to Curos that since her marriage Suzin had had few opportunities to practise the accomplishments she had learned as a wealthy merchant's daughter.

The next day from the new camp Curos could view the steep water-cut sides of one of the minor river valleys with its mixed gorse and heather cover. Snaking erratically around stone out-crops and occasional trees, the single-file track which followed the stream looked broken and little used. On such a path the advantage of speed could well belong to the smaller party, although the outlaws would be hard pressed to negotiate some of the turns with the carts which carried their belongings.

That evening, Curos' loneliness was heightened by thoughts that Xante and the good company of his Wind Riders were only a day's ride away to the west. There was also the frustration of enforced idleness when others were so close to success. From the detached peacefulness of the hillside camp it was difficult to imagine Bhal Morag and Chalak Konn driving on their straggling Ulus of foot-soldiers, trying to keep them in line as they traversed the low hills.

The next communication from Xante confirmed the outlaws' progress. The band was larger than expected, about twenty men with several spare horses. Since sighting the T'sand scouts they had abandoned their baggage cart, and had increased their speed. Morag was convinced that it was no unplanned flight and suspected the outlaws had been warned in sufficient time for them to leave their village-like camp in an orderly fashion.

As Curos considered the long message he smiled to think of the effort from Gron Fa and the patience from Xante which had made it possible. Gron Fa's head must be aching like a thousand hangovers by now, but the message system was working and Topaz Wind had been guided into position by the barely trained seers.

'How many people can you conceal with your strange gift?' he asked Suzin suddenly.

'I am not sure, Lord. Two at least.'

'I can echo Suzin's thoughts,' added Lou Chi, 'and add to her power.'

'Good,' Curos smiled. 'We will move again further along the ridge until we can see Topaz Wind's camp. We can then command that path, see any possible escape routes. It is not shown on the map and I doubt Morag will know of its existence.'

By mid-morning the next day Curos caught his first welcome sight of a distant yellow banner, Topaz Wind. The N'gol horsemen had chosen to camp where the valley began to open out and give flatter ground to favour light cavalry warfare if they needed to fight.

'Lord Curos,' Suzin interrupted his thoughts. 'The Lady Xante has noticed us and sends you her greeting. 'She also warns you, Lord,' Suzin faltered with embarrassment. 'In her words, do nothing stupid and let Dalgan and Morag have their day.' It was not just the bright winter sun which sent a flood of warmth flowing through Curos.

When Curos saw the approaching outlaws he realised that down in the valley the ground was even wetter than he had expected. The horses were tiring in a virtual canal of mud and several men had dismounted to lead distressed animals. Further back still, along the main track and following side paths invisible from this distance, he sighted the faded blue field uniforms of the 22nd T'sand – horsemen and footmen driving on, trying to close the gap on the fugitives. Bhal Morag and Chalak Konn would be hoping to capture the outlaws outright, not just drive them into the clutches of Khol Dalgan and Topaz.

One of the soldiers addressed Curos respectfully and pointed back along the ridge on which they were standing. Swarming over outcrops and ploughing through the peaty bogs, a horde of red-clad figures had come into sight.

'See, Excellency.' He spoke excitedly. 'K'tan Wan drives the Guard Hund this way. Soon his red guards will turn to brown ants.' It was quite true. The scarlet uniforms of the guards were already dulled and mud-splattered by days in Te Lok and their rapid progress across the worst of the countryside.

'Why did he not have them wear field uniform?' said Curos without thinking.

'Pride,' growled the soldier, for once forgetting Curos' rank. 'To be a guard you need a big head with no brain and enough pride to support it. "Iron Man" would wear red in a storm of arrows! Today he wants the rest of the T'sand to see how far and how fast his guards can move.'

Curos recognised the grudging respect from the soldier and realised that Wan had, in so short a time, turned the Guard from a symbol of oppression to an elite. Now he was attempting to cut off the escape of the men below.

'They are indeed like ants,' said Lou Chi. 'Frighteningly like ants.'

'It is so unfair,' murmured Suzin. 'An army of soldiers hunting those few pathetic men, they are so exhausted.'

'You are wrong to waste sympathy on such murderers!' Curos exclaimed. 'Such as they eat the heart out of Chaw. Have they pitied those that they robbed and killed? This is not sport, it is war and the only need is to win.' As they argued it was hard to realise that neither the guardsmen nor the outlaws floundering below were able to see Curos' party standing openly on the hillside. Even when deep in discussion with Curos, Lou Chi and Suzin were effectively screening them from sight. In amazement he watched as Wan Abac and over fifty guardsmen jog-trotted past less than a hundred paces distant. In the faces of the closer guardsmen, strained with exertion, Curos clearly felt their grim pride in the red uniform and superior training.

The forced march along the hill tops brought Wan Abac and his guards to the head of the track from the valley floor almost as the outlaws started to ascend: their one possible escape route. One look at the formidable line of red-clad figures was enough to deter that course of action and the outlaw leader turned back. The time wasted on the detour had, however, brought him into full view of the main party of his pursuers and a ragged shout of triumph rose from the blue-clad T'sand soldiers.

'Can I relax now, Excellency?' requested Suzin in a pained voice. 'I fear I weaken.'

'Yes. They are well past.' Curos spoke with preoccupation. 'I can hardly believe what happened! K'tan Wan is well known to me but even he did not see us. If he had been an enemy I could have shot him down so easily.'

'It was far from easy for us,' complained Lou Chi. 'The energy needed was much higher than we would have expected.'

'Perhaps it is Lord Curos' violent nature,' suggested Suzin. 'There is much to conceal.'

Below in the valley the outlaw leader now realised the hopeless nature of his position. As the valley opened out into a flatter, wider space he had seen not freedom but the line of Topaz Wind's horsemen screening off any hope and even up on the hillside Curos could hear the Wind's shrill battle-scream. On the far side of the valley more T'sand soldiers were now visible

201

as they scrambled across gorse- and heather-covered ridges to complete the enclosing ring.

Bhal Morag had achieved much to get nearly three hundred men into position and co-ordinated with Topaz. Now it was only necessary to draw in the cordon, slowly and carefully to avoid any combat with the desperate and violent criminals. Curos wanted prisoners and information, not a massacre, but neither the footsore 22nd T'sand nor the Topaz Wind would be disposed to mercy.

Swiftly, Curos started to descend through the ranks of Wan Abac's guards. The surprised men bowed in salute to their commander, amazed at his sudden appearance without warning. Wan began to walk beside Curos' horse, forcing himself to speak as if nothing unusual had occurred.

'Welcome to the kill, Noyan, but beware advancing alone. Ki Dug, the Mad Dog of Akar, is with the scum below. He will not surrender.' Wan Abac looked down from the flash of anger in Curos' eyes. 'I mean no disrespect to your skill, Excellency. You are but lightly armed and the horse is not to your usual standard.'

One of the outlaws was riding purposefully to the centre of the line of Topaz Wind. Curos could just distinguish the mounted figures of Xante and Khol Dalgan. 'What is happening, Lou Chi?' he shouted to the seer who was vainly trying to scramble his horse down the hillside after Curos.

'Madam Xante is alarmed, Excellency,' he gasped as he completed the last fifty paces on foot, leaving his fretful horse with Suzin. 'Ki Dug has challenged Khol Dalgan to combat.' Curos swore. He did not need to be told that Dalgan would accept. He was still too far away to intervene and could not have Dalgan humiliated before Topaz by ordering him not to fight. Unfit as he was, Dalgan would rather die than refuse a challenge.

'Suzin, inform Madam Xante that if Ki Dug wins or even looks as if he will win she must shoot him down. I will have no outlaws escape.' He silenced the protest. 'I know it is not chivalrous, Suzin, I will not explain again. Do as you are bid.'

Khol Dalgan had ridden away from the group of T'sand horsemen to a position where he could face Ki Dug's charge from the far side of the available flat space. Curos could half see, half sense the high-stepping, responsive mare Dalgan rode and knew the animal was well rested and in good condition. They were to fight with lances: the sharp pike of Chaw pitted against the hooked cutting lance of N'gol. He saw the black form of Xante give an exaggerated wave in his direction. Her bow was now strung and ready. Ki Dug might possibly win his combat with the weakened Dalgan but he would not live long enough to boast of any success.

'Suzin,' Curos began as he forced his attention away from the scene below. 'Inform Bhal Morag to advance his men closer to the outlaws while they watch the fight. Talk directly to Gron Fa.'

'I cannot, Excellency, and it would hurt him.'

'I give orders, woman. I do not listen to excuses. Madam Xante has other tasks.'

'I will try to help,' said Lou Chi, angry at Curos' tone with Suzin.

Ki Dug and Khol Dalgan were now charging. The sun sparkled on Ki's lance point and then Curos reacted with combined anger and concern: his friend was charging with only a blunt, unheaded lance-pole. Curos had ordered Topaz to take prisoners, and the N'gol was obeying to the point of absurdity. The combatants closed, then Dalgan rolled over in his saddle, away and under the lance before swinging back to strike his own blow into Ki's ribs. With a headed lance it would have been a killing thrust but the hard wooden end only bruised and stove in ribs. The outlaw staggered in the saddle and dropped his lance, but remained upright. With the shock of the impact Dalgan was betrayed by his maimed leg and rolled from his horse's back in an untidy heap and splashed into the boggy ground.

Wincing with pain from broken ribs, Ki Dug turned his horse and drew his sword. Curos was guiding his own slithering mount down the crumbling track. Xante had moved closer to the fighting men but did not shoot. The outlaw ran his horse bodily at Khol Dalgan and wheeled slightly to strike with his sabre. Dalgan leapt aside and despite stumbling struck at the horse's fore-feet with his lance-pole. The horse shied up but Ki kept his seat and turned safely away.

He returned to attack more swiftly, intending to use his horse's speed and momentum to better effect. Instead he received another stabbing blow to the ribs which sent him spinning from his horse. Now using his pole like a long club, Dalgan attacked Ki Dug, striking him again and again as the outlaw attempted to rise and draw his dagger. Only when he lay completely senseless and bleeding did the furiously angry N'gol relent. To be unhorsed was an unbelievable shame, to fall off was beyond contempt.

As Dalgan threw down his shattered weapon the T'sand soldiers whistled and cheered his victory and the Topaz Wind shrilled out their battle scream in salute. The defeat of one outlaw, even Mad Dog Ki, did not however mean the surrender of the outlaw band. They were all wanted men and many like Ki were named felons who would undoubtedly go to the block if captured. Swords in hand, they were measuring their more numerous assailants while their leader decided in which direction they would attempt to break out.

It was now that Xante decided to take her own action. Intending to dazzle and cower the outlaws, she projected a vivid flash towards them. Curos' Topaz pendant was already charged from Lou Chi and Suzin's sorcery. It reflected Xante's power with amplified force, surrounding the hapless outlaws with yellow light which it further sustained by their own emissions of terror. The T'sand soldiers saw a streak of fire flash from Xante towards the group of outlaws. As it struck it flared up in an explosion of yellow light, completely obliterating men and horses. Brilliantly incandescent in the dull winter light of Te Lok, it cleared as suddenly to reveal shying horses and blinded men falling from their saddles, covering their eyes and screaming in terror. The leader was permanently blinded, others would not regain their sight for many hours.

Unheeded by anyone, Gron Fa slipped slowly from his horse in a faint of sheer exhaustion, his inner senses suffused with a yellow fire he had been forced to contribute to. The amber Topaz on Curos had stripped energy from every available source and hurled it to Xante's aid. Lou Chi and Suzin sat slumped on the ground but they at least had been able to resist the topaz in some measure – Gron Fa had been emptied like an upturned pail. The astonished Chaw soldiers were greatly impressed and

204

cheered Xante in similar fashion to Khol Dalgan. Many had expected to see charred bodies when the light of sorcery cleared.

Soldiers seized the blinded outlaws and forced them to their knees as Curos approached. Arms twisted violently up behind their backs, the sixteen men and two women were forced face downwards into the soggy ground before the T'sand's Noyan.

26

The soldiers of the 22nd T'sand of Sunil province camped for the last night in the Te Lok hills. Those who had been close to the point where the outlaws were captured had sufficient time to choose half-dry tent sites while those who struggled along later, exhausted from their less productive endeavours, had to camp wherever tent-pegs could be driven into the rocky ground with its covering of soggy soil.

By the time the last of the foot-soldiers were arriving, Curos had completed all the obligatory duties of a successful commander which included congratulating his men and receiving brief verbal reports from his officers on the success of the mission. He had also reprimanded Khal Dalgan for his rashness and commended him on his skill and visited Gron Fa who was prostrate with exhaustion. In a N'gol-style tent with a lamp and small charcoal stove to keep the temperature comfortably warm he could relax with Xante while they ate a frugal meal.

'My days with Lou Chi and Suzin have been a great strain,' sighed Curos. 'It is not that they lack stamina and energy, those two; they are just too patient, too polite.' He shook his head sadly. 'I have never met anyone who could be so disapproving and say so little as Suzin.'

'Poor Curos. You would have been happier with the grumbling Gron Fa or the uneducated N'gol of Topaz.'

'At least they have some fire and enthusiasm and they are not all N'gol – half are Chaw and many are quite literate.'

'I know, but they feel they have to behave as savage tribesmen, like the war bands of ancient N'gol, but it is really no more than half a game. It is also tiresome to be treated as a Queen and I fear after today that that aspect will get worse.'

'It was a most impressive display,' said Curos. 'Unfortunately the Topaz Stone will not be controlled.'

'Not by anyone but yourself, Curos,' suggested Xante. 'I had merely intended to dazzle the outlaws and permit their capture without further fighting. I had not realised the Topaz was so charged with energy, nor that it would strip all the power it could from the other sorcerers to aid me. Perhaps that is a technique I may need sometime, but all I achieved today was to blind Mingas permanently and to attract the attention of every Warchaw sorcerer in Corninstan. Truly, if you were to learn to use the full power of Topaz, it would be a formidable weapon indeed.'

'No doubt, but I will leave sorcery to you; I have the problem of the outlaws' interrogation to consider and I fear there is no easy solution.'

'You take any reason to avoid your own ability towards sorcery! But no, we will not quarrel tonight. Are you sure there is no other way to gain information?'

'Officially I could avoid the responsibility and deliver the entire band to the magistrates' prison in G'tal,' replied Curos, 'but then they would be tortured by those who enjoy inflicting pain rather than seeking to acquire information. Also, as soon as news of the capture is known, those who helped Mingas will flee or construct alibis. No, I need to know all of the truth within two or three days at most.'

'More could be achieved by subtle questioning coupled with traces of hallucinogenic drugs,' commented Xante. 'It does take longer but is also more reliable and does not result in maimed bodies and broken spirits.'

'Attempts at such methods in Chaw merely break minds instead of bodies, but how long would it take to interrogate a forceful character such as Ki Dug?'

'Twenty or thirty days,' she answered, 'too long. And must it be Ki Dug? He has some potential ability and we could possibly train him – he is a man who has knowledge of weapons and war.'

'The main outlaws have all been named felons,' said Curos. 'Those such as Ki Dug and Mingas Yi will die at the block in G'tal. Ki Dug is accused of at least seven murders and a score of serious robberies. No court in Chaw could show him mercy; he has the reputation of an unpredictable madman. I doubt he would yield any worthwhile facts under torture until he was in such pain that no reliance could be put on his words, but only he and Mingas Yi would know the principal informants.'

'For all of Ki Dug's crimes, he has been loyal to his leader and to his wife and daughter,' mused Xante.

'That is his weakness!' exclaimed Curos. 'He would never yield himself, but could he resist the screams of his daughter's anguish?' He paused, then said, 'I dislike my own reasoning, Xante; all must face death at some time but to deliberately extend pain and suffering is not to my liking – if I reach that conclusion so will others. Ki Dug's daughter is only fourteen years old but that will not protect her from defilement and agony in the dungeons of G'tal.'

'So at last the Iron Sentiment of Curos relents!' said Xante. 'Why treat women more favourably than their menfolk? We must seek to arrange the pieces of this dreadful puzzle to gain your information and my sorcerer without more pain than is necessary.'

Early in the cold of the next morning the whole T'sand was mustered in formation. At first Curos commended them on their success and fortitude in succeeding in the capture of Mingas Yi's band when all others had failed. When the reward money for recovery of stolen treasure was distributed there would be a small portion for each man. He then continued to state that two guardsmen had flouted his instructions and taken food from a hill village. Despite their own ample rations, they had stolen from the peasants instead of protecting them. Although only two chickens had been stolen, it was a firm order that had been flouted and the only suitable sentence was death. The penalty had been swiftly enacted and the T'sand dismissed.

It was then the turn of the outlaws. Mingas Yi and Ki Dug were brought before Curos, who sat with Bhal Morag and Chalak Konn while Wou, the junior scribe, was present to record the interrogation. A flat outcrop of rock had been covered with cushions and acted as a slightly raised dais so that Curos, although seated, was slightly above the level of the outlaw leaders and their guards. Ten of Wan Abac's picked men in hastily cleaned red tunics were stationed around in a half-circle to pen the captives while two more stood between them and

Curos' party. Each carried the large shields and short, straight swords which the K'tan had introduced to improve the effectiveness of the guards at close-quarter fighting. An impressive array of fighting men to guard two prisoners, but all guard K'tans seemed to have an instinct for ceremony, and in this aspect, Wan Abac was no exception.

K'tan Wan Abac and one of his Ataman stood close behind the manacled figures of Mingas Yi and Ki Dug, forcing the outlaws to kneel on the boggy ground and bow until their foreheads were wet with mud. Some distance away a ring of the more usual faded blue field uniforms of the T'sand's common foot-soldiers marked where the other outlaws were being guarded. Curos imagined their fear and despair at capture. Ki Dug's wife and fourteen-year-old daughter huddled together with the wife of Mingas Yi as if for warmth. Perhaps it was indeed for warmth; the biting wind cut even those flushed with success. Curos became aware that Xante was not to be seen.

'You are two worms who eat the heart out of Chaw and weaken our nation in the face of its enemies,' intoned Chalak Konn. 'There are others of high rank in G'tal, Lokar and Untin who guide your crimes. It is important to the Noyan Zachaw that these too are punished.'

As Chalak Konn paused to draw breath the blind but still defiant Mingas Yi muttered in correction, 'He is only Bagatur Noyan . . .' but before he had finished speaking, K'tan Wan Abac's hand shot forward, gripped under Mingas Yi's nose and heaved him backwards.

Blood pumped from torn nostrils and the K'tan shouted, 'Resume the position of subservience and show respect to the T'sand commander.' Unsteadily, Mingas Yi knelt upright, his head bowed with pain.

'The Noyan has declared martial law over Te Lok and has the authority to act as judge,' continued Konn. 'For your crimes both Ki Dug and Mingas Yi can expect only death. All property and proceeds of your crimes will be seized and your family condemned to slavery.'

The full rigour of the Yasil code was rarely invoked and the possibility of these clauses being used had evidently not been considered by Ki Dug. 'Excellency, my wife is blameless; also my daughter.'

'They knew of your crimes and shared your evil profit,' retorted Chalak Konn. 'If, however, you were to provide evidence against those in G'tal who are your partners, then only your own life will be forfeit. How say you to this?'

'Speak now, when you are bid,' snarled Wan Abac threateningly from behind Mingas Yi.

'Say nothing, Ki,' called out Mingas Yi. 'Trust no words from rulers or judges. They have this morning executed two men for trivial crimes but it does not increase our fear. We live and we shall die by our own honour.'

There was silence for some little time until Curos spoke for the first time. 'Then I will be forced to use torture. You are outside the law and may not claim its protection.'

'I have been tortured before.' Mingas Yi shrugged. 'If you are to be kept alive by your tormentors the pain will be borne. If not, within one day or two death will eventually end all pain.'

'So I have heard,' replied Curos, tight-lipped, 'but the screams of one's friends are more difficult to bear. You will listen carefully to the death of Ki Dug. During his torment he will tell us a little but it will be too garbled to be of use. If you are still resolved to protect those who betray you, then Ki Dug's wife who is your sister will suffer next. If that is not sufficient to break your resolve, you will listen to the violation and death of the girl. As soon as I have my information and it is corroborated, the women can go free.'

'You have no right to torture the women,' pleaded Ki Dug.

'My power gives me the right, and they are also outside the law.'

Mingas Yi and Ki Dug waited impassively as soldiers constructed a crude torture bench and then strangely erected a canvas screen around it. The two wives were brought to kneel beside their husbands and the young girl sobbed and clasped her arms around her father. A black-hooded executioner and two soldiers approached Ki Dug and the scribe, Wou, took his place with paper and writing materials.

'Are you both resolved to silence?' questioned Wou almost pleadingly, his face ashen white as he sat, writing-brush gripped in a trembling hand, beside the screen. There was no reply. The soldiers seized Ki Dug, and giving him no chance to stand, dragged him from view. Already he was gasping from the pain of the ribs and arm broken by Dalgan.

'You have one brief chance,' stated the executioner in a voice distorted by the hood. 'I will employ the torture by Introduction of Injurious Substances to the Nine Orifices of the Body. Once I start the law commands I may not stop. No man has survived past stage seven. My assistant is melting lead and the poisons are mixed.'

At the first hideous scream, Ki Dug's wife threw herself flat onto the muddy earth, clasping her hands over her ears. As the whimpering cries subsided, the scribe asked in shaking voice, 'Criminal Ki Dug, name those who are your accomplices.'

Relentlessly the torture continued, Ki Dug's broken voice babbling disconnected names and facts which Wou recorded as best he could. Curos and his senior officers and the captain of militia from Lokar sat impassively. The whole camp fell silent. Soldiers went about their tasks with hesitant steps and the prisoners shivered with more than cold. When Ki Dug could scream no more, subhuman gasps slowly died away into the final silence.

The hooded torturer emerged from the evil domain, bowed to Curos and reported with flat unconcern, 'He has died, his heart failed him. Shall I now take one of the women, Lord? Their bodies can endure pain of a higher level than those of men.'

'No,' replied Curos. 'Mingas Yi is a hard man. Bring the girl, Ki Dug's daughter. She is condemned by her father's guilt and deserves no clemency. Perhaps her younger voice will better penetrate his feelings.'

The women shrieked, begging Curos for mercy and remonstrating with Mingas Yi. Only when the terrified girl was dragged towards the enclosure did Mingas Yi shout. 'Curse on you, Zachaw, you would do anything to gain your ends . . .'

'Anything, Mingas Yi. I have learned at a hard school.'

'I could not shame Ki Dug by submitting for his release,' whispered Mingas Yi, his voice almost lost in the gusting wind. 'But I will betray anyone if it gives half a chance of life to the girl who is guiltless.'

'Can you trust a man who speaks out under torture?' hesitantly asked Ho Bek, the chief of militia from Lokar who was standing beside Curos.

'No, but Mingas Yi speaks to save others and knows that if he lies I will only resume when these lies are revealed. Do not leave, Ho Bek, what is said will be of interest to you.' Already Ho Bek was beginning to show fear, fear that was heightened as he realised how closely he was guarded.

Mingas Yi spoke clearly and slowly, giving sufficient time for the shaken scribe to record his words. He explained how information on caravans was collected and how stolen goods were dispersed. Most significantly he named the names. Customs officials in Untin, Lokar and G'tal. Merchants and dealers of precious stones in almost every trading city in Chaw. And controlling the whole organisation, the revered, rich Admin Ci Shen, member of the ruling Civilian Council.

'There is yet more,' sighed Curos. 'But Wou, cease that scroll there, leave space for the signatures and seals of those who heard Mingas Yi's free confession without application of torment. Now on a fresh scroll we will start anew. There are more names I must have.'

'Yes, there are many minor names,' said Mingas Yi desperately. 'I cannot remember all, over so many years.' He waited but Curos did not speak. Finally he said, 'The last name you already know? Ho Bek, leader of the militia of Lokar.'

'That is good, Mingas Yi. Now for each name you will provide as much detail as you know. The scribe will then cross-check your statement against Ki Dug's ravings and against what your other men know. Speak well, Mingas Yi, and you will die easy under the block leaving a rich widow. If the gods smile, your children may never even learn that their father died a felon.'

As Ho Bek was pinioned and Mingas Yi continued to give information to Wou, the wife of Ki Dug crawled to Curos and begged to be able to take charge of her husband's body. He nodded to a guard who helped the distraught woman to her feet and led her towards the improvised torture chamber. The daughter followed unnoticed. Then one last, terrible woman's scream cut through the cold winter air.

Inside the enclosure, trembling with shock and fatigue, his

mind broken with stress, sat her husband, Ki Dug. Unseeing eyes looked blankly at her without recognition as she wrapped him in her arms, sobbing uncontrollably. Physically, Ki Dug was unharmed but mentally he had suffered great hurt.

'He felt every agony in his mind,' explained the Dryad voice of the executioner. 'Instead of the punishment of death he has paid for his evilness in a way more useful to the Noyan Zachaw. He is deranged now but will recover and his body is whole. Officially Ki Dug died this day under torture, only Zachaw and I know differently. You will stay with him until we break camp, and then make your way secretly to your home in West Akar. I will know when Ki Dug is recovered. He will then be summoned to Te Toldin and begin his new duties.'

'I will accompany him to that place?' asked the woman hesitantly.

'If you wish, and at first he may need you; after he is trained it may be different.'

'I have learned long ago,' sobbed the woman with bowed head, 'that I must accept what happiness the wind blows to me and not question tomorrow.'

27

'There can be no mitigation and mercy,' stated Curos to Ho Bek. 'You are well aware of the law and penalties.' The two men sat solemnly outside Curos' command tent while the T'sand was hectically mustering for the return to G'tal. As far as Ho Bek knew, Ki Dug's wife and daughter were transporting the shattered body home for cremation and Curos' scribe was preparing indictments of arrest for all those implicated by Mingas Yi.

'I admit my fault and will sign a full confession,' pleaded Ho Bek. 'I will take my own life and accept disgrace if that is necessary. Spare the livelihood of my family, truly they are innocent of all crime.'

'Knowingly or not, they have prospered due to your evilness, Ho Bek, and the law is quite clear, as I reminded Mingas and Ki Dug. Only in the case of benefit to the Chaw nation is the magistrate able to mitigate punishment.'

'I have nothing to offer. Mingas Yi knew much more than I. Mine was a private agreement with him alone. I was only to divert the searches from his camps.'

'And so you were not known to Ci Shen?' suggested Curos.

'No, neither did I aid him in any way.'

'That is of little importance, but it could be that your position is of use to myself and Grand Noyan Po Pi. You see all that happens in Lokar and meet and speak with many of the town merchants and those who pass along the North Road. You have some wit and ability.' He paused as if in thought as he felt Xante's humour at his leaden duplicity with Ho Bek.

'Ho Bek, if you are permitted to live you could be of some use to myself and my attempt to ready Chaw for its struggle with the barbarians.'

'I would do anything you ask, Excellency.'

'Do not be rash, Ho Bek. My demands may be high.' Curos studied him intently, trying to gauge how far he could trust the corrupt militia man. 'You will have three tasks, all of which will be checked by others in Lokar.'

'You have informants there?'

'Several,' lied Curos easily. 'How else would I have detected your corruption? I only needed Mingas Yi's word as corroboration. You will be but one of those who report to my chief scribe Lin Sri, but you move in higher circles of the towns. You will also place the training of your militia on a firm army footing and increase its size to five hundred men, but your first task will be to render reports of all that occurs in Lokar.'

'But Lord, the town only budgets for three hundred militiamen?'

'Do not tell me of your problems, Ho Bek. I expect five hundred fully trained militia in Lokar by the new year. Thirdly, you will at your own expense act as a benevolent ward for the sisters of Lou Chi who is now with my T'sand. Food, clothing, education and ultimately dowry will be provided from your purse which has been filled by corruption. In the town you will be respected as a charitable man, but the secret testimony of Mingas Yi and your own signed confession will bind you to me.'

Ho Bek considered the proposition for some short time before looking directly up at Curos. 'What you ask, Lord Zachaw, is no great thing and can be borne with little dishonour and no ruin. I will comply with your request but go no further.'

'That is fair,' replied Curos. 'But take special care with your duty to Lou Chi's sisters. Their remaining childhood needs to be happy. I cannot have Lou Chi concerned or distressed for their welfare; he has important duties which need his full attention.'

Some time later, when Curos and Xante were alone, she said, 'We have gained one man each. One sekar and one spy.'

'Sekar? I am not familiar with this term.'

'It is how we Dryadin refer to junior sorcerers,' Xante explained.

'At all events, the gain was at great cost to you, I fear: the infliction of torment on Ki Dug cannot have been easy. However, I believe two of the tax gatherers denounced by Mingas Yi could also be persuaded to act for me, one in Untin near the O'san and one in Lokar to check on Ho Bek.'

'I believe there is more also,' she forced a smile, 'a further turn to your web of cunning.'

'I hope so. It is not removing Ci Shen that is important to me, but who replaces him. Ci is on the Civilian Council where I have no influence as yet.'

'Ah, I see. A young, bright civil servant, well disposed to the Zachaw family. It could be too obvious.'

'Not necessarily. He has denounced Ci once before for corruption but being but a recently appointed Admin, his words were ignored and his own career was placed in doubt. It needs more thought, Xante, but I am sure Makran's brother-in-law Shekar Lotol will welcome advancement to a new post.'

'Is that the work of the day done?' asked Xante quietly as she stood up and surveyed the barren hills.

'There are a few details to check,' he replied. 'Chalak Konn will expect me to inspect his inventory of the recovered merchandise – it is an extremely rich haul. I must then ensure that scribe Wou's record of all the confession is accurate and consistent and that no suspicion of Ho Bek is indicated.' He looked at Xante and asked, 'Have you any plans?'

'Yes, I need to exercise my legs rather than my horse. My mind is pained and confused with doubts and dark thoughts; clear air and toil will sweep them away. I thought to run down the valley and up over to that hill.'

'A good distance on foot,' he replied, following her gesture. 'Going and returning it will take until evening.'

'I have time. Gron Fa, Lou Chi and Suzin are much too exhausted to practise sorcery and I need to be free of soldiers and tribesmen.'

'You need solitude like the N'gol,' he smiled.

'The Dryadin need solitude from people, and the company of trees. But I would enjoy the company of one person.'

'Good, I will endeavour to be my most treelike! I will ride and you can run. I would run with you,' he lied blatantly, but I need the horse to carry a minimum of food and a few other things. If the mist descends quickly in these hills, it is cold and dangerous.'

'I will speak to our sekars, you complete your duties and we will depart.'

'I do have one more onerous duty this evening,' complained Curos. 'Tonight the Topaz Wind is celebrating Dalgan's victory over Ki Dug. As commander of Topaz it is expected that I attend and,' he grimaced theatrically, 'I can feel the hangover now. I have no head for wine.'

It was a carefree afternoon. Curos' horse picked his way up crumbling slopes and trotted heroically to catch up lost ground, while Xante ran like some wild ibex, seeming to defy gravity and fatigue as she covered ground as effortlessly as a hunting wolf. The view from the hill they had chosen took in most of the Te Lok, and in the dry, clear air they could see as far as Lokar and imagine their distant, invisible homes of Te Toldin and S'lan.

The return journey was more leisurely. Changed into dry clothes and refreshed by the packed meal, Xante was happy to walk beside Curos or share his horse depending on the roughness of the path. They talked and laughed and joked until as darkness closed in they reached the campsite.

'I suspect it will be less unpleasant than you fear,' Xante suggested as she viewed the preparations in the Topaz Wind's section of the camp. 'Shall I prepare to cure you of the wine sickness?'

'I fear the after-effects of koumis, the fermented milk. After the first drink I will forget caution and drink with the rest. The remorse comes later. You are lucky that women are not invited.'

'To the Topaz and the T'sand I am not a woman, Curos. I am Qren Xante, Queen of Sorcery. I am invited and I will attend. It was suggested by Dalgan this morning that I should ignite the big fire.'

'Oh no, so secret are our plans.'

'Modesty bids I refuse, Curos, but I will dress as a Dryad for festival.'

'Then at least cover yourself a little more than you did in S'lan.' A little bitterness crept into his voice. 'Some of us may forget that female Dryadin are not women.'

The large cooking fire blazed in its full splendour by the time

Curos and Xante arrived at the Topaz celebration. Rabbits, hares and several small sheep had been jointed and were roasting over the hot fire. Dalgan and his comrades of the Wind sat with Wan Abac and Bhal Morag, who had also been invited. Jars of wine and koumis were circulating freely as the men drank with the restrained dedication of those intending to continue throughout the night and get very drunk.

The smell of scorching meat mingled with those of sour milk and sharp wine was almost overpowering to the near-vegetarian Xante. Curos felt her flinch as the solid wave of odour struck her, but she smiled convincingly. The firelight flickered through her thin veil, showing up the white dots and spiral patterns which decorated her bare arms and face. Even without drink it was difficult for Zachaw Ca'lin Curos to remember that female Dryads were not true women.

As the night and the eating and drinking progressed Curos' reserve quickly dissolved into an alcoholic haze. He joined in the group songs and cheered as one by one the principal guests and officers were asked to perform. Bhal Morag achieved much honour when he rendered a particularly obscene version of the song of 'The Soldier and the Fox Woman'. Wan Abac gave an unbelievable display of sword spinning with the short sword he had introduced into the guards. Curos, as commander, was not asked to perform, and due to his weakness when drinking did not offer.

It was totally unexpected when Xante stood up, flute in hand. The flowing rising and falling of the Dryad music with no pauses for breath or individual notes was much more akin to the music of the N'gol than to that of the Chaw. Her swirling tune which spoke of the wind in the trees of the Forest of S'lan was probably wasted on the half-drunken Wind Riders but to Curos who had visited that land it invoked all the atmosphere and tranquillity of that other world.

The song died away and the wine jars and the koumis beakers were passed around.

'It is a great pity, Dalgan,' said Wan Abac, 'that there are none here who could have written a song for you. The "Defeat of Ki Dug" would make a good title.'

218

'It was a little matter not worthy of a song, but well worthy of drink,' Dalgan laughed, filling Abac's barely sipped beaker.

'Time will tell,' said Wan Abac, 'but Ki Dug had killed seven men of note in combat. To take him alive for questioning was not without merit.'

'What chance had a mere Chaw from Akar against a true N'gol?' yelled a drunken tribesman. 'Khol Dalgan is from the Sand Dragon Clan, most skilled in horse combat.'

'No, I disagree,' shouted back Abac. 'There was more to Dalgan's victory than breeding or training. He was unhorsed but still achieved victory.' Wan Abac drained his beaker of koumis and laughing again slapped Dalgan across the shoulder. 'I never expected to see a N'gol, at least a sober N'gol, fall from his horse, Dalgan.' Unheeding of the change in atmosphere, Wan Abac continued. 'I must confess, Dalgan, when I saw you splash into the boggy ground I thought you finished. It was a marvellous fight back, well worthy of a song.'

'Your words are ill chosen,' snarled Dalgan. 'Some things are not spoken of. Victory is victory.'

'I agree,' shouted Abac drunkenly. 'I drink to Dalgan's victory. This sour milk has made me feel as drunk as he looked when he rolled from his nag's saddle.' Wan Abac never drank wine or beer for reasons of deep principle; the potent koumis was new to him. 'You had us well fooled, Dalgan. Were you drunk or was it your crippled leg which betrayed you?'

Sitting in a dream-like state of alcoholic contentment, Curos was quite unaware of the developing situation. Vaguely he followed the thread of the song by a staggering, swaying N'gol who appeared close to collapse. Distantly other words cut into his befuddled brain.

'Fight Dalgan, how could we fight?' Wan Abac was laughing.

'Men of honour take no account of laws,' Dalgan shouted angrily.

'Law, Dalgan, who heeds laws?'

'Then you accept my challenge?'

'Dalgan, how can we fight on anything like terms? On horseback I am a buffoon by your standards. On foot with the sword you are a cripple . . .'

'You dare call me a cripple,' shouted Khol Dalgan. 'A cripple.

219

My wounds were inflicted as I fought for my people while cowards slept in idleness.'

'Others fought in Corninstan too, N'gol, and they also lost much!'

'Stop,' cried Curos. 'Stop this stupidity!' His mind strove to find reason through the enveloping fog of drink-induced lassitude. 'Would men of Chaw kill each other senselessly while our enemy gather and laugh at our stupidity?' He fought again to compose the next sentence. 'Be silent, the men enjoy their feast. I forbid you to fight. Our land needs you both. It is time the T'sand officers withdrew to leave Topaz to celebrate in its own fashion. Wan, Bhal, you will escort Q'ren Xante to the tent. I will stay . . .'

Curos did not remember stumbling back to his tent or fumbling his way into the sleeping sack. But when he awoke, the pain and agony he had predicted were only too real. Quietly, Xante spoke to him.

'So you are awake to reality and duty, commander. Is it only when your mind is dulled with wine or with the thrill of speed or combat that it flows free?'

'Xante, please, I am too ill for H'tao philosophy. Order me fragrant tea from the servant, I need hours of quiet and peace, not philosophy.'

'You have no time for either my philosophy or your rest,' Xante said seriously. 'Dalgan and Abac are preparing for combat.'

'No, not that senseless quarrel of last evening?'

'I am afraid so.' She laughed as Curos grimaced at the tea which was already at his side. 'Drink it slowly and breathe deeply, or your anger will increase the pain.'

'I should execute Dalgan myself,' growled Curos. 'Attempted murder of his commander by poisonous beverage. How will I keep him alive? How do they fight, and when?'

'Late afternoon with swords on foot. It is Wan's choice, Curos, and he is a hard man.'

'At least he has some sense of self-preservation. With the short sword he will flay Dalgan; no, it will be one thrust. Through the brain, no doubt.'

'The brain?'

'Yes, here,' replied Curos, indicating his lower body, 'where Dalgan keeps his brains.'

'In the same place as most Chaw men!'

'By the god of winds I ache all over.' Curos' face creased in pain and he gripped his throat before hauling himself to his feet and lurched unsteadily from the tent to vomit loudly.

'That is good,' commented Xante. 'I was unsure if the emetic would function with so much evil fluid in your stomach. Now, drink the second part of the cure.'

'Never.' Curos gagged weakly. 'You betrayed my trust, woman. I will only need pure water.'

'That is what I have for you, warm boiled water to flush and purify.'

'I am flushed already.'

'You can order them not to fight?' Xante questioned.

'Yes, but Dalgan would not accept the order for long. It would fester in him until he had goaded Abac into combat.' Curos sat down slowly and rested his head on his knees, a picture of abject self-pity.

'There is more you should know of last night, if we are to be open with each other.'

'What?' he groaned.

'While you were poisoning yourself with your savages.'

'Against my will.'

'As you say, but the effect is the same. Bhal Morag conducted me back here while Wan returned to confront Dalgan.' She chose her words carefully. 'He made me a proposition few Chaw women would have refused, I am sure. He has a certain charm.'

'What! He proposed marriage?'

'Not exactly,' she laughed, 'but the results may have been similar.' Curos swore silently under his breath, his face hard with anger, his hand moving unbidden to his dagger.

'There is no need for anger, Curos, and no need for action. He was quite complimentary and I politely refused him,' she added archly, 'for the time. Until that point I had enjoyed the celebration as an equal, the nonsense of Q'ren was forgotten and I was still flattered to know that at least one man remembered I was a woman.'

'That fool seeks death also!'

'Neither of us were in danger, Curos. I would not have harmed him.'

'It is danger from me that he should fear.' Curos leapt up and stalked out from the tent.

'Curos, you will not be stupid. If you kill each Chaw who looks at me you will decimate your army! I should not have told you.'

'No, I will be civilised and sensible, and you did right to speak freely, Xante.' He stopped walking and rubbed his head, embarrassed at his condescending tone. 'Was there madness abroad last night? Are all my officers mad?'

'Yes there was madness, an honest madness of success. You have gathered together four spirited horses, Curos, and when your grip on the reins relaxed they ran wild.'

'Then the grip on the reins will tighten. How is Dalgan?'

'His leg is weak. The fall strained the damaged muscles of his thigh and he is in some pain.'

'He will feel more.' Curos called a guardsman over. 'Summon scribe Wou to my tent.' And then to Xante, 'I will send letters to Makran and to his brother-in-law, Lotol – a good task for a Wind Rider like Dalgan. Then he will rejoin Topaz in the O'san without any chance of meeting Wan.'

'And for Wan Abac?' Xante smiled.

'A forced march by back roads to H'war to post a writ of arrest on Admin Ci's property and to search for stolen goods before news of the outlaws' capture is known. They will need to leave immediately.' He smiled evilly at the thought of the two officers trying to shake off hangovers as they started on their long journeys. 'When they have calmed down, in a few months I will forbid them to fight by personal order. I will forbid them to train together in any combat, even the obscure, harmless forms of Jitsu, even by finger wrestling!'

'You have some punishment in mind for Bhal Morag?'

'A year's map-making in the O'san? Guard to a monastic order of desert hermits, five days' ride from the nearest woman? There are many possibilities and I have no need to hurry. At least Chalak Konn is reliable.'

'Reliable, yes, but then so was your brother, Makran, until

the Chaw goddess Freu breathed softly in his ear and showed
him Dortie!'

28

A mixed party of Warchaw cavalry and foot-soldiers trudged along the northern pass through the Lune mountains down towards the land of Chaw. The thin air of the high pass had left them weak and breathless and even the most hardy of the archers and pikemen had been pleased to take advantage of a chance to ride on the baggage and provisions carts pulled by tough Corninstani hill ponies. In their turn the cavalry had found it necessary to change mounts often, resting their heavy-footed war-horses as much as possible.

Instinctively, Cedric of Hereford, Grand Master Bowman and Commander of Archers in Corninstan, checked the width of the pass, the line of sight along the valley floor and the best position for defence if it proved necessary. A veteran of a dozen pitched battles and more skirmishes than he could remember, Cedric was continually alert to the possibility of sudden attack. Higher up in the pass where only one or two carts could pass on the rough road there was little danger, now in the wide, flat-bottomed valley there was the chance of a full-blooded attack or an ambush from one of the many half-hidden side openings.

A party of horsemen who had been scouting ahead galloped purposefully back up the pass and, noting their urgency, Cedric and Sir Sigmund, Knight Commander of the expedition, rode out to meet them.

'Chaw soldiers guarding the valley, about two miles ahead, sir,' the leader of the scouting party reported. 'They appear to be aware of our approach and are preparing to fight.'

'Numbers?' asked the Commander impatiently.

'At least two, possibly three thousand, sir. I counted their horsemen quite carefully before we were spotted: I estimate eight hundred.'

'You exaggerate,' stated Sigmund emphatically. 'I doubt they could support that number in such an inhospitable place. We will let their cavalry charge into our arrows before I lead our men and sweep the way clear.' Dramatically he wheeled his palfrey away to where a groom and squire rode with his war-horse.

Cedric caught the scout's eye and waited until the Knight Commander was well clear before asking, 'Your numbers are true, Mark?'

The younger man was flushed with anger at the tone of Sir Sigmund's rebuke and answered, 'As I breathe, and it is Sir Mark if you please, Bowman.'

Cedric shrugged and smiled blandly. 'It is Sir Cedric of Hereford, Grand Master Bowman of the Eastern Army if I wish, but I value your opinion of our enemy more than my title or even . your respect.' With deliberate smoothness Cedric turned his horse so that he and Sir Mark could walk slowly back to the main body of men. An appearance of coolness before the troops was important.

Of all men in the Eastern Army Mark Longfeau respected Cedric of Hereford most, and was annoyed at showing childish anger. Cedric had fought in three wars and had risen to be an honorary knight and Grand Master Bowman by his combination of skill with the bow and sound understanding of battle tactics – a man any young knight could learn from with honour and profit.

In turn Cedric was pleased to hear the young knight speak clearly and confidently, 'The enemy's cavalry are mainly mounted bowmen, regular soldiers, not tribesmen; some carry lances and seem a separate group. About eight hundred, slightly less than one full Chaw battle group.'

'How do you rate them?' interrupted Cedric.

'Well disciplined and skilled but second-rate compared to the nomad tribesmen. Their maximum effective bow-cast is hardly more than fifty paces.'

'But dangerous if they get too close,' agreed Cedric. 'And the foot?'

'As I said to Lord Sigmund, at least two thousand. Regular soldiers with small groups of the Fanatical Red Guards. No javelin men that I could see.'

'That is significant?' questioned Cedric.

'I believe so, Master,' replied Mark, now happy with this form

225

of address which showed due respect without compromising his feudal position with one of common birth. 'At the Yanix river crossing a regiment of Chaw with javelins, led by Red Guards, were particularly difficult to defeat.'

As Mark of Longfeau joined the main body of horsemen Cedric divided his forces into two groups on either side of the pass, with a gap of about one hundred and fifty paces between them. His numbers were too few to form an effective barrier over a wide front but he knew he must counter the usual tactics of mounted bowmen to surround their enemy. Funnelled into the narrow gap, the Chaw would bunch into an easy target and then be vulnerable to a massed charge from the knights. There would be a good chance of crushing the horse attack which was the main danger; after that it was up to Sigmund's cavalry to 'sweep the way clear!' as he claimed they would. Cedric grimaced. In practice it never seemed that easy.

In position Cedric checked his equipment, particularly the leather of the shooting glove which would protect his fingers from the bow-string. He fanned out his arrows, inspecting for true shafts and sound fletchings, teaching those around him by example. In a loud, confident voice he called out his instructions.

'The little sods will ride in open order to make killing difficult. We shoot down the left-hand side of the pass, starting at two hundred paces, so they bunch up in the middle. Bill's lads on t'other side do similar.' He paused, the rest would be obvious. He cast his eye surreptitiously over the archers with approval. Most of them were 'good lads' who kept themselves fit and practised regularly. Unlike the knights and the swordsmen they wore no uniform, except for the tight leather jerkin which fastened oddly on the right-hand side of the body. Its smooth, polished brown leather was tailored not to snag a bowstring. Some wore mail, some a steel cap, most did not bother. For personal weapons the short Italia sword or the northern hand-axe found favour. One of Cedric's greatest concerns was to stop them getting mixed up in hand-to-hand fighting.

'When I shouts "fast", stop shooting, not a'fore – understood? And afterwards don't take anything from a dead 'un until you cut his neck through. I don't want anyone killed by a Money Mary playing dead.' Already the Chaw horsemen were drifting around the turn of the pass in that loose, open formation: horse archers used plenty of space for the horse to run, plenty of space for long-range arrows to fall. Across the valley he could clearly see Bill of Asham sweeping aside small stones with the side of his boot and choosing a firm footing. Cedric nocked his first arrow and waited. The first Chaw passed a red rock in the valley floor which he had chosen as a marker at one hundred and eighty paces.

'Shoot!'

Each man drew up his bow in his own time to shoot at will; good individual shots, not timing, was what Cedric called for – dead was dead whenever it happened. On the other side of the valley Bill of Asham drew up his bow in one smooth, perfect action. Instinctively, Cedric's eyes followed that shot; the arrow was away, soaring and high without a tremble in flight. A purple-clad Chaw horseman ahead of the rest staggered in the saddle and fell. Cedric swore under his breath. The last thing he wanted was to stop them this far out – why wouldn't Bill listen to orders?

Fortunately the Chaw were too disciplined to falter because their commander had died. The other Western archers followed Cedric's instructions, raining arrows down on the left and right wings of the charge – high, soaring arrows falling steeply at extreme range, only one in four hitting. It was enough – the valley walls meant the horsemen could only swerve inwards to avoid fallen companions. At eighty paces a solid mass of men and horses propelled by its own momentum had formed into the perfect bow target. They could not miss. Shoot a bit low, hit a horse; shoot high and the arrow hit the man behind. Arrow after arrow after arrow. Excitement added to the speed of shooting, the skill was burned in from hours of practice. Cedric was as breathless, with tension and fatigue as any of his 'lads', breathless, excited and proud. This was what it was all about! Fifty paces. The horsemen had stopped, a mass of dying men, hardly able to shoot an arrow back. A bright Western trumpet sounded; Sir Sigmund was working the knights up to the charge.

'Too early, too bloody early! Keep shooting!' Each arrow was hitting, if only he could direct the shots to the back of the Chaw group. He turned to watch the knights charge, gauging the time and distance. 'Fast! Fast!' Others took up the cry and the merciless rain of arrows stopped. Heartbeats later the first of the long lances and heavy horses smashed home. Speared, knocked down, trampled underfoot, the Chaw virtually disappeared and the knights rode clear.

'Pikemen, forward!' roared Cedric. Now was the important time to clean up the mess, and make sure no remaining Chaw escaped. Standing between the bowmen, the swordsmen and pikemen had been waiting for a chance for hand-to-hand fighting. They worked together, spearing and gutting men, blocking terrified horses with shields, hamstringing others. The knights turned in precision but were called to a halt by Sir Mark to hold them back from the frantic killing area. Bowmen left their stand to join in the fighting and take any chance to loot the dead. Cedric did not stop them, although he would have a reckoning later.

Up the pass the Chaw foot-soldiers were padding in that knee-bent, shambling trot that Cedric so hated. The last of the Chaw horsemen were still dying, but already Sir Sigmund was forming up to charge the footmen! He was always hasty, believing that one furious charge could sweep away all opposition but there were only two hundred knights and three hundred foot in support.

Cedric ordered the bowmen to recover any serviceable arrows and formed up the foot-soldiers in a supporting block. The first Warchaw charge smashed into the leading Chaw foot regiment with devastating effect, long lances, heavy war swords and the sheer bulk of the chargers destroying the front ranks. But they did not run; small men with flimsy spears and pikes held firm, absorbing the impact, struggling over dead bodies to cut at the horses or prod at the riders. Sigmund turned his riders away and allowed the archers to shoot until the arrows were gone. The Chaw stood and died and another regiment moved forward to absorb the next charge. They were forced back but would not break.

'Perhaps our footmen could force a passage,' suggested Sigmund to Cedric.

'It would be unwise, Lord. Once mixed with the enemy we could not retreat. They still outnumber us five to one and one regiment has not yet been used.' It was impossible to argue with the commander and the footmen had advanced as ordered, shields and swords pushing the Chaw back, pikes thrusting forward between the swordsmen. Again ground was gained, but the advance was bogged down and Cedric's archers resorted to shooting used arrows over the heads of his swordsmen to allow them to disengage from the fight. When they retreated the Chaw let them go. They would stand and fight but their savaged formations had not the will to advance.

Cedric and Sigmund stood on a small rise sufficiently clear of the valley floor to get a better view. They had pushed the Chaw a mile back down the pass and the flat ground was appreciably wider. Without the protection of the valley walls there was a real danger that the Chaw could surround them.

A new batch of about a thousand Chaw were moving up, and on the wings fresh horsemen had appeared: horsemen in brown leather and brilliant silk sashes, an unruly mix of warriors with bows and lances who could ride faster, shoot further and exploit any advantage to a greater degree than the more numerous regular soldiers.

'It is not a time for heroics or chivalry, Lord Sigmund,' said Cedric. 'You have lost thirty knights, less than a hundred are fully fit and they ride windblown horses. My archers are weary to exhaustion and have few sound arrows. The footmen have lost badly; they cannot defend, let alone attack.'

'Master Bowman, *I* command here, and one last charge could win us the day.'

'More likely it will lose us the battle completely. Count the dead – we have killed over one thousand men and still the Chaw will not retire from the field. New horsemen have arrived; if they close the battle to us we could be destroyed utterly and they would have a free march into Corninstan. Our duty compels us . . .'

'I do not need you to spell out my duty to me, Bowman!'

'Then we should fall back to the narrow high pass which we can hold safely, even in the dark.'

'It is so. We have the advantage; they have been well bloodied and will not attack. A thousand killed for less than fifty, a victory to be proud of. March the men back, Master Bowman, and I will form a rear-guard.'

229

Cedric hated this man; he never counted the dead footmen as important and at least a hundred swordsmen had been lost in the senseless mêlée he had ordered.

Weeks later in the dark, smoke-scented atmosphere of the New Inn two men sat in near silence studying the flickering of the firelight on their pewter ale pots.

'So you've decided, then,' growled Cedric of Hereford.

'Aye, I have,' replied William of Asham. 'Me mind is made up.'

'Bloody fool, you, Bill,' said Cedric. There was a hint of resignation in his voice.

The New Inn had been built outside the city, free from any smell or sound of Corninstan. New wood and quarried stone had been used to construct a massive building divided into several drinking rooms. Only beer or wine of traditional western origin were sold and the food had no hint of eastern spices. The beer was not too bad, Cedric reflected, but when the yeast settled down and the hops began to crop locally it would be improved. The wine, which he never tasted, had to be imported as yet but no doubt the lads from the south would find a way to grow their traditional vines. It was important to keep all the traditions going.

'Look, Bill. It's as clear as day. I'm nearly forty-five years old, in my prime I know, but I can't go on for ever. In ten or so years' time I'd seen you taking my place. You're the Master at Archery as it is. I need you to train up the lads, keep up the standard.'

'You trained me, Cedric, and I don't have the head for giving orders. I just shoot arrows.'

Cedric remembered back to the last skirmish. Bit of a panic really, and there was Bill kicking away any loose stones so he could get a firm, flat footing. That really instilled confidence in the lads. And that first shot over a hundred paces and as clear and straight as target day on a village green. Unbelievably, he'd dropped the Chaw cavalry leader dead in the saddle.

'Look, Cedric, I know you take it bad, but I need a change. Valanus is forming a band, a company of masters to undertake a quest. They're all good lads. There's Sigmund the knight . . .'

230

'A dreaming idiot, full of old stories of chivalry! He knows nothing of war,' growled Cedric, 'nearly finished us in that last scrap in the mountains.'

'And Hosca, the Northman.'

'By the Gods, he's naught but a madman with an axe. Bill, they're not your folk. Valanus is a good hand with a sword and a lance but it's not his trade – he should keep to sorcery and keep out o' fighting. I've heard that Batan the Elf is joining the company, he's not bad, but then they're all dreamers in their way.'

'Chance that's it with me, too, Cedric. It's the skill and the flight of the arrow that's important. I've no real interest in the wars or the killing. I don't even hate these people.'

Cedric snorted and they sat in silence deep into the night.

29

No amount of description or warning could have prepared Xante for the reality of a Chaw city the size of G'tal. Lokar, for all its wealth and importance, was like a village in comparison. Lokar's open areas, crumbling walls and shanty towns gave it an almost friendly manner compared to the packed unfriendliness of G'tal. The sheer numbers of people seemed to close down on her like a pressure of human water. Always there were hints, like multiple whispers from other minds, which made a muted background not easily ignored.

The result was a growing sense of tension which caused fatigue and made Xante irritable and bad-tempered. She found it difficult to control her sorcery practice and even the adept Suzin now at Te Toldin had been hurt by the erratic force of Xante's thought projection. The City Mansion servants regarded her with great respect and fear while the soldiers of the 22nd T'sand truly believed she was the violent and terrifying Q'ren Xante of whom Gron Fa so often spoke in a reverent tone.

There were no parks or gardens in G'tal; poor houses often used their flat roofs to grow meagre salad vegetables but the great mansions with their high pagoda tiling were even denied this greenery. When Curos was engaged with the administration or training of his T'sand, which was often for days at a time, Xante would ride outside the city to leave behind the ant-like whispering of G'tal. The ordered, over-farmed countryside with its straight-edged fields on the wide, flat plain were hardly to her liking but at least her mind could be silent.

Despite the cold winter winds and the occasional sleeting rain, she could ride or run through the farmlands for exercise or would shoot her bow at the military training area which was but infrequently used in poor weather. The Masters of Archery were intrigued at the female figure with her strange bow who practised so regularly at the butts beside the drill grounds. In the worst of the weather it was often only the drenched, black-clad figure of Xante shooting methodically and the Guards of the 22nd T'sand under Wan Abac who occupied the vast open area.

Curos was quite aware of Xante's frustration and unhappiness but there seemed no immediate solution. He needed her in G'tal to help him sift the records of Scribe Lin for hints as to the purpose and methods of the Warchaw sorcerers. Her instincts coupled with Lin's intelligence reports were also invaluable in discovering the intentions and opinions of civilian and army personnel in the government. It had also been hoped to locate more potential sorcerers in the enormous population but this had proved fruitless, despite many visits to magi, seers, fortune-tellers and others who were all proved to be frauds and charla-tans.

A surprising friend to Xante during this time was Curos' first wife Hoelun, who had taken up residence at the Zachaw City Mansion while Lin Sri negotiated the divorce arrangements. By the time Curos had arrived from Te Lok, Hoelun had dismissed the steward and many of the other staff and had established a benevolent despotism which had resulted in a model household. The tall, thin figure still glided demurely in the approved fashion of an aristocratic lady but now with a new-found purpose a steely core was revealed. If Hoelun spent long hours playing her flute or painting exquisite transparent water-colours she was content that the house ran as orderly as a beehive – a credit to both her illustrious husband and the training from her mother.

It was on one depressing afternoon when a damp winter drizzle clung to the very walls of G'tal that Xante returned from an early ride and heard the plaintive beauty of Hoelun's flute. In desperation, she bathed and dressed in Chaw fashion before approaching Hoelun who sat playing in the large reception room. Hoelun looked up as Xante entered and smiled austerely; she now understood a little of Xante's feelings. For a Dryad, exile in G'tal was worse than ever her own imprisonment at Te Toldin had been.

'You play so sweetly, Hoelun,' Xante murmured. 'I wondered if I might join you.' She indicated her own long flute fashioned from heavy dark wood. 'The silver of Chaw may mix well with the black of S'lan.'

A look of suppressed horror crossed Hoelun's face before she answered apologetically. 'So sorry, Xante, but it would be too difficult. Our instruments differ in pitch and in tuning and the music of Chaw is like tinkling raindrops compared with the hurricane wind of the Dryad.'

'Such a challenge, then,' laughed Xante, sitting cross-legged opposite Hoelun's higher cushion. 'Much of our music has the rush of wind, like that of the N'gol, but we too have our laments and love songs.'

Hoelun considered this and said, 'Then let us both be as children and start our music anew. I will play a simple nursery song and you can follow. Then you will teach me a Dryad tune. Perhaps a new style or form will be born.'

It took many hours of deep concentration before the seemingly discordant instruments were able to blend together and even longer before the first composition was completed. During these sessions however Xante was able to shut out the pressures of G'tal and return in spirit to the deep, green forests of S'lan or the orchards of Te Toldin.

Curos' first act on returning to G'tal from the Te Lok expedition had been to send to the High Admin Ci Shen an elaborate parchment letter penned by the scribe, Lin Sri. In flowery, apologetic language it collated the evidence obtained from the outlaw leader, Mingas Yi, and the corroboration discovered by Wan Abac at Ci Shen's estate at Zantu. Curos begged the esteemed administrator for an interview in which the errors of these findings could be explained so that the evidence need not be placed unnecessarily before the Army Council.

The fact that his crimes had been discovered was quite evident to Ci Shen, who wasted no time in denials or bluster once he gauged the strength of Curos' resolve. The High Admin was in his seventieth year and still possessed of the faculties which had served him in a distinguished career. He was well aware that Curos would have a price but also knew that the young, ambitious commander could have denounced him without this elaborate charade. Ci Shen claimed that the deeds had been organised by some miscreants in his staff but that he would accept full responsibility to the point of taking his own life provided his family could be shielded from shame. He therefore

234

invited Curos to the Ci family Mansion in G'tal and discussed the matter with apparent frankness.

'I fear you take this matter too grievously, Excellency,' suggested Curos with exaggerated deference. 'I cannot believe the words of a condemned outlaw are to be trusted but I cannot either, in justice, let the matter rest. Might I suggest that Your Excellency retires temporarily and appoints a successor to your Department of Agriculture to investigate these matters?'

Ci Shen considered Curos' words gravely, then said without a hint of a smile or irony, 'Has the Noyan anyone in mind?'

'I hardly dare to presume,' replied Curos, 'but the honoured Admin Shekar Lotol is due for advancement and has been critical of your policies. It would show greatness of spirit if you were to appoint him. I am sure that after examination of your files and papers he would clear your name and unmask the viper who has dishonoured you.'

'Is Admin Shekar a relative of yours?'

'By marriage only, and not on good terms with my family due to a certain scandal between my brother and his wife, Dortie.'

'The Chou Ramin duel,' murmured Ci Shen.

'Not my personal choice, but he is regarded as just and comes from a very ancient Sunil family.'

'Just so,' said Ci Shen, nodding with a sardonic smile as he perceived Curos' plan to obtain influence in the Civilian Council.

The Admin called for tea and the formal part of the interview was ended. 'I have enjoyed the tone of our conversation, Noyan,' he said easily. 'I like meeting an agile mind and bear no recriminations.'

'The pleasure was mine, sir, I assure you.'

'I never met your honoured father but now count it a loss. Do you, in truth, believe that the Warchaw threat is as severe as some think, or is it a ploy to gain influence and power?'

'By all that I revere, my parents' honour, the duty of my command and my love of Chaw, I have no doubt that the Warchaw, if not checked, could sweep away all that we love in our nation.'

Their conversation continued for some time, and at its close Curos considered that he might well have been better advised to retain Ci Shen as his ally on the Civilian Council.

235

As Curos suggested, Ci Shen petitioned the Civilian Council to appoint Admin Shekar as his successor. Fortunately Shekar Lotol, advised by Makran, was already travelling west to visit G'tal and rapidly took up his new post. Within days of starting his investigation he issued a statement absolving Ci Shen and indicting two Junior O'tans who had feloniously used the High Admin's authority. Shamed by such corruption in his department, and no doubt to dissuade any further investigation, Ci Shen took his own life. His letter thanking Curos for the diplomatic and civilised way in which the matter had been arranged was a masterpiece of calligraphy and prose which even the sceptical Lin Sri was forced to admire. Ci Shen had died but his reputation and more importantly his family's fortune remained intact.

Noyan Po Pi, Curos' army superior, was quite amused by the reaction of the High Admins of the Civilian Council. To show no ill-feeling towards Curos they pressed the Army Council to elevate Curos to the full Noyan rank. His evident tact in handling such a delicate matter and his organisation of the investigation and capture of the Te Lok outlaws were cited as evidence of sufficient maturity for the post.

'It is ironic that the men on the Civilian and Army Councils who owe you most, Lotol and myself, are those who speak against you,' said Po Pi.

'One needs friends at high level,' suggested Curos, somewhat perplexed.

'Yes, and it is necessary for friends to stay their hands until they are needed. I knew my objection to your promotion would be outvoted and so I felt safe in suggesting caution. Shekar Lotol also feels it necessary to demonstrate no gratitude to you – at least for the time.'

Before a promotion to Noyan the candidate was required to be examined by the Army Council. This process could be a brief formality or a gruelling interrogation. Few candidates failed but those who did were expected to resign from the army in disgrace.

One other candidate was being presented to the board on the day of Curos' interview. Moi Tek was several years senior to Curos and came from the province of Sin Shi in the far south.

236

His family was of the highest rank and with a quick ability and many good sponsors his promotion had been assured from the day he finished training. Although his self-confidence bordered on arrogance, it was hidden in a pleasant, well-bred manner and his skill as a horseman and swordsman made him popular with the younger element of the army.

Moi Tek and Curos arrived at the citadel before dawn, as custom decreed, to await their audience with the Army Council. The citadel had been designed as the fortified palace of Xan II but had subsequently been adopted as the seat of the ruling Councils. The squat, tower-like building was the tallest in G'tal and was made ominous by its massive bulk. Beneath its foundations were vast subterranean reservoirs which were fed via gravel filter-beds from the Tishin river. As a result the lower rooms always felt cold, even in the height of summer. Now with spring still some weeks off the lower waiting room where Curos and Moi Tek sat was as bleak and as damp as any mountain cave.

Both were dressed in the full purple-and-gold ceremonial uniform of their rank. Each carried a highly decorated regulation sword and dagger. For once the thickness and warmth of this clothing was quite welcome. Moi Tek greeted Curos pleasantly and contrasted the temperature of G'tal to that of his home province of Sin Shi.

'The southern uplands of Sin Shi are reputed to be the most beautiful in Chaw,' commented Curos. 'Warm in winter, cool in summer, fertile as the garden of Freu herself.'

A slight shadow crossed Moi's face. 'So it is said,' he replied, 'but the spring rains have been light these several years and the crops have almost failed. While harvests have been good in the north, Sin Shi is not far from famine.'

Their talk drifted to discussing Moi's prospect of winning the light-sword championship for the fourth year running and Moi complimented Curos on his victory over Chou Ramin.

'Your second victory in a duel to the death, I believe?' asked Moi.

'Yes, but I take little pride in either. You have more victories?'

'Four, all with swords in accordance with the strict code. It requires a certain skill to make the cut for "first blood" also a

237

killing cut. I take great care,' Moi Tek smiled, 'that my opponents are not members of the army. Killing a "Brother Officer" is frowned upon, as you have experienced with Chou Ramin.'

Before the conversation could proceed further Moi was summoned to the interview room at a higher, more comfortable level of the building. The odd, damp room took on a new feeling of emptiness with just Curos and his uncertain future.

In a very short time the servant reappeared to conduct Curos before the committee of the Ruling Council. Evidently Moi's promotion had been a formality soon dispensed with.

Only seven of the eleven-man Council were present. The post of High Army Commander was not filled and four other members were either not available or like Po Pi had declared an interest in the candidate which might affect their impartiality.

Six of the Council Noyans sat on a raised dais while the venerable Council President occupied a central position, slightly elevated above his peers. The Council members did not wear uniform. Their age ranged from fifty-three to the President's sixty-eight. The first general impression was of ageing serenity and a contented lack of energy. Curos bowed low to the President and was bid to kneel as a scribe read out a synopsis of his lineage and personal history.

With the first question from the esteemed President, the impression of dull senility was dispelled and the presence of sharp, agile minds revealed. Each Noyan seemed to have prepared set questions on some aspect of Curos' career but often his answers were interrupted by another Council member who probed some principle or detail of Curos' actions or opinions. The interrogation was particularly sharp when covering the battle of Cornistan Road.

At one point Curos found himself declaring with severe formal politeness, 'I cannot accept, Excellency, that the men of Ruby Wind were cowards. I saw them with my own eyes ride into the heat of the flame barrier and many died. No one man in T'sand or Wind band turned away from the attack until the battle was lost.'

'But the attack failed?' asked the President.

'Yes, Lord, but failure does not mean cowardice. A man could do no more than die.'

'And so you believe in this preposterous notion of magic power?' snapped another.

'I am a soldier, not a philosopher or priest, Lord, but I do know that the fire was real. It burned and it killed and it destroyed the impulse for our attack.'

'It could have been caused by some alchemy unknown to us,' suggested another Noyan.

'Possibly, but whatever its source, its deployment against us was most rapid.' The Noyan smiled and seemed to accept this possibility. He nodded sagely, any explanation of the defeat was better than the truth.

The Civilian Admin who sat with the board then said, 'It has been noted that you dealt cleverly with the matter of the Te Lok outlaws and the scandal of Admin Ci, surprising in one of your war-like temperament.'

'I wished to avoid any unnecessary disgrace or contention,' Curos said dismissively. 'These are difficult times for our nation and the people must not distrust the governing Councils.' The Admin's smile suggested he fully understood Curos' motives. A man aspiring to high office would be expected to use any legal advantage.

'It is perhaps unfortunate,' continued the administrator, 'that you have been less than tactful over the rewards offered for recovery of the stolen goods. Certain merchants claim they have been threatened with law and forced to pay vast sums which have been distributed to the common soldiers.'

'I have issued no threats,' replied Curos, 'but letters written by my Scribe Lin Sri are rather too direct. He is more used to the blunt language of the army and being no lawyer has possibly been less than civil in his tone. I will point out his error to him. No merchant has paid more than he offered as reward and Lin Sri's letters only pointed out anomolies in tax paid and goods recovered.'

'And so your soldiers are rich.'

'Not rich, but each benefited by ten gold hawa – a fortune to a foot-soldier. The money was distributed according to the Yasil code but the K'tans elected to return their reward to swell the soldiers' portion.'

Having avoided direct argument and contention, Curos now faced the greatest test when he was asked to explain his campaign in Te Lok. It was necessary to introduce his idea of the use of sorcery to the Army Council if it was to be used more widely. Curos had discussed this with Po Pi at great length and they had decided to use Xante's word 'sekars' to denote junior sorcerers and to liken them to fortune-tellers. Curos would give credit for their use to Po Pi himself and would lessen the importance of the role played by Xante.

The explanation had been made to sound quite credible and the phenomenon was a long way removed from the violent sorcery attributed to the Warchaw. Several Noyans were quite enthusiastic; others demanded to see a practical demonstration. The President of the Council astonished Curos with his sudden interest, wanting to know how fast sekars could be trained, and if it were possible to allocate one to each T'sand. Evidently he fully grasped the potential of controlling a 100,000-man Tuman as closely as one regiment. He also suggested more strategic uses of the method.

Curos felt safe. There was now no question of him being accused of using unnatural witchcraft. The Council's only concern was over the time it would take to extend the system.

The interview was at its natural end but unexpectedly the previously silent Noyan Qunin from the extreme south-westerly province of Zantu raised the question of Curos' illegal duel with Chou Ramin. As Curos desperately tried to think of an effective reply, aid came from an equally unexpected quarter. The civilian Admin coughed politely and begged to be given leave to speak. He had taken the step of investigating the matter and had taken a deposition from Admin Chou Yuel, Hoelun's brother and kinsman to the slain man. Basically Chou stated that Curos had been unbearably provoked by vile insults to his marriage and to his esteemed wife, the Lady Hoelun. There was also evidence, only now coming to light, claimed the Admin, that Chou was a corrupt profiteer in army contracts who had sought Curos' death for his own ends.

This long but effective statement removed Curos from danger.

He evidently had two civilian sponsors to counter the enmity of Noyan Qunin on the Army Council. Curos was however warned most gravely by the President against similar infringements of discipline.

When Curos later mentioned the line of questioning to Hoelun she was most dismissive.

'I had taken some small trouble to speak to my brother on the matter but it seemed that a wife's simple duty was too trivial to concern my husband. I pointed out that had Chou Ramin's accusations been correct then I would be dishonoured as an imperfect wife. My wishes take some precedence with Yuel.'

30

Punishment of crime in G'tal was swift and severe and was carried out in public, at one of the major market places. In serious cases, as with the Te Lok outlaws, senior officials who had been involved with the detection or investigation of the crime were required to attend and verify that justice had been correctly enacted.

It was for this reason that Curos and Shekar Lotol, Dortie's younger brother, were riding together through the city to the North East Market Square, attended by a formal military guard. As on most occasions, Xante rode as a silent, hooded figure following closely, veiled eyes probing the crowd, senses alert for any hint of attack. Within the square the law decreed that no trading take place until the punishments were complete. The major stall-holders could prepare wares and the peasants could lay out their produce but they were forced to wait while their potential customers thronged the execution area. Above the crowd the two stark stone pillars with their crossed beam and the scaffold platform were clearly visible from all areas of the market place, but most of the people pushed up to the barrier for the best possible view.

The crowd's hushed voice rose in pitch as Curos and Shekar Lotol arrived to mount the official dais at one side of the scaffold. Scarlet-uniformed guardsmen surrounded the scaffold and the pen-like enclosures which held the prisoners, but it was the town Militiamen in faded blue uniforms who supervised the winching of the crushing stone to its required height and conducted the executions.

A Law-Scribe read out the crimes of each of the Te Lok outlaws and their accomplices, who included tax gatherers and civil servants from the department of Admin Ci. Each level of guilt was carefully defined in the ancient Yasil code of law and the prescribed punishment listed. Once guilt was determined there was no scope for interpretation or mercy. A plea of poverty, coercion or even madness was not accepted. As the Law-Scribe completed his address Curos nodded to the K'tan of militia and one by one eight minor criminals were brought forward to receive ten lashes of the heavy chabou. Several lost consciousness and needed to be carried away to begin their year of labour for the city. Six more were both flogged and branded, marked as City Slaves for life to repay their debt to the people.

The crowd grew more excited as a more serious offender, one of the outlaw band, was brought forward to suffer mutilation of the foot. At first the man watched impassively as the huge, bronze-shod stone block was winched up by a rope suspended from the wooden cross-beam linking the two stone pillars. As the militiamen began to lash the outlaw's foot to the iron grating beneath the crushing stone he started to struggle and scream. Patiently the militia K'tan waited until the outlaw was safely restrained before releasing the catch.

The massive stone fell with ponderous swiftness to pulverise the trapped foot and an ancient punishment, adapted from Chaw's barbaric past, was completed.

Now a surgeon worked with speed and skill to amputate and cauterise the shattered lower limb. This civilised doctor was often well bribed by friends or family to ensure the convicted man's survival. The criminal was free to leave, often only to live as a beggar or to hobble to Felon's Point on the Tishin river bridge and his last journey.

Three more mutilations followed before Mingas Yi was assisted to the scaffold. Still partially blind from Xante's sorcery, he was now hunched and frail, a ghost of the man who had once commanded a feared outlaw band. Defeat and sentence of inevitable death had reduced him in spirit as in stature until he seemed little more than some decrepit beggar hauled from the streets. Curos had seen the progressive deterioration in Mingas as investigation and trial had proceeded to sentence and execution. Worse than a malignant disease, it had wasted away all trace of the original man.

With passive submission the outlaw leader was pinioned and his head placed beneath the suspended stone block.

'He wishes death,' whispered Lotol in awe. 'They say he never

243

recovered from the death of his friend, Ki Dug, and only wants to seek Ki in the void of death.'

'He will wait long,' Curos muttered in reply. 'Pity him not, Lotol, he has murdered a score of innocent men, young and old. Mercy was unknown in him and he does not deserve it himself. Think more of his victims, or the widows and orphans created by the actions of Mingas Yi.'

Curos stopped speaking and signalled to the executioner. The stone fell again, crushing all that had been Mingas Yi. The headless body convulsed and blood spurted against the stone block which had pulverised the man's head. The noise from the crowd was that of a vast, collective sigh, with no hint of a roar or cheer.

The last prisoner was dragged forward. An O'tan from the department offices of Admin Ci Shen who had been implicated by Shekar Lotol's investigation. Young and with a promising career before him, he had probably been obliged to obey orders from his corrupt superior, Ci Shen, as he had claimed in his defence. To the last he proclaimed his innocence, until gagged by the executioner's assistants. The block fell and the Law-Scribe declared justice complete. Trading began in the market and Curos was able to lead his party away.

'A sickening spectacle for a civilised land,' Lotol apologised to Xante as, white and shaken, he rode beside her on the return to the City Mansion.

'Yes, but much more rapid than in my land,' she replied bitterly. 'Our people can die in prolonged agony for crimes trivial in comparison to Mingas Yi's murders or the O'tans betrayal of authority. I know one who, when she had to die, would have welcomed the Block of Chaw rather than the Execution Tree of S'lan.'

31

Following his promotion to full Noyan, Curos took his place on the planning committee which was run for the Army Council. Po Pi was its senior member but had so far been able to instigate little action in the undeclared war.

The plan proposed by Curos was however much more dramatic than anything Po Pi could have expected. His idea was to move sections of the N'gol tribes west from the D'was and down into the even more arid O'san desert which separated Chaw from Corninstan. They would exclude the Warchaw and be in a position to raid over the Lune mountain range when the opportunity appeared.

'Your Excellencies will realise,' stated Curos at the end of his address to the full Council, 'that any battle for Chaw should be fought in the O'san, where the enemy can advance over nothing but rocks and barren waste. We must deny the Warchaw all access to the O'san until we are ready for war. There we can fight on our terms. If the Warchaw ever reach the populated areas of Chaw we will be hampered by our own fleeing peasants or townsmen.'

The plan was no vague idea, but had been fully researched by Bhal Morag, Chalak Konn and the O'tans of Shekar Lotol's agricultural department. While the Army Council could see the attraction of a larger, more effective force in the O'san, the Civilian Council was concerned over its existing small population who would need to be displaced. These people, although only several thousand in number, would have to be absorbed into a land already overcrowded and starving. A suggestion that it would be preferable to allow the Warchaw to invade and slaughter the farmers and then to reoccupy the land with N'gol was not entirely spoken in jest. Curos often wondered in later years if it was a sense of misguided spite at Moi Tek's easy success that made him suggest resettling the people in the southern province of Sin Shi.

The simultaneous endorsement of moving the N'gol into the O'san and the rejection of Noyan Qunin's plan to invade S'lan was a double triumph for Curos. While he and Bhal Morag finalised the detailed military planning, the once reproachful Chalak Konn became a regular visitor to the City Mansion where he worked often with Curos, Lotol and Lin Sri on the administrative details.

Hoelun's musical evenings and dinners became the temporary highlight of G'tal society. Curos' notoriety and that of the strange Dryad were contrasted with Hoelun's exquisite propriety and compliance with formal practice. The first performance of Xante and Hoelun's new music was greeted with utter disbelief but soon other, more accomplished, composers were rushing to hear and then to write their own pieces in the 'Style of the Tree'. Chalak Konn was also revealed as an admired player of the large flute, with an established reputation as a composer of minor works.

Despite Curos' frustration at the waste of time involved in attending the gatherings Hoelun organised, he was quite aware of the importance of social contacts and the need to avoid any risk of annoying the influential persons who now flocked to his home. On one such evening there was a recital of music of the Single Dropping Raindrop, music of infinite slowness in which single notes seemed to sound and linger in the air. Xante, introduced as an Honoured Dryad Lady, Xante-Yani, had dutifully played a love lament transposed into the Chaw style but now sat in some detached trance as one of Hoelun's acquaintances played with exquisite precision or to some, such as Curos, agonising boredom.

Curos found himself gazing at Xante. From his position slightly to one side of her, he noted the vacant eyes and expressionless profile which showed in silhouette through the thin silk veil; in public she still preferred the anonymity of the covered face. He wondered where her mind was now. Was she running through the desolate places of D'was under the infinite bowl of night which frightened and enthralled her? Or was Xante-Yani back with her own kin in the enfolding forest of Eternal S'lan as Xante, daughter of Yani?

None of the people Curos was assembling to save Chaw had

an easy life. Khol Dalgan was always on a tight rein; Bhal Morag was never allowed to sink back into his philandering, pleasure-loving indolence and Chalak Konn was being driven to the limits of his propriety. Even Lotol had been sucked into Curos' schemes. For none of these, however, was life as hard and as cruel as it was for Xante. The simple Dryad of the trees of S'lan was being transformed into Xante Q'ren of Sorcery, Xante the mysterious associate of Zachaw, Xante the leader of a T'sand of seers. Worst of all she was Xante the exile, who no longer walked under trees or saw the faces of her own people. Slowly her face turned and the now-living eyes looked directly into Curos'. She smiled, he knew she smiled, although with the change of light he could only see the blank veil.

'Pity not Xante of S'lan, Curos. You are Lord Zachaw, the man of destiny who has no feelings, but I thank you for the warmth of your thought.' Curos stiffened with surprise at the words that formed directly in his mind and then the communication was lost. He saw Xante shake her head slightly and then point to where two new army guests had just arrived.

Quietly and without fuss, Curos rose from his seat to greet the two men. Yi Janisu, a young but rich nobleman from the north west province of Urtish, and a tall hawk-nosed Corninstani. The Corninstani's height, darker skin and turban marked him out from his Chaw sponsor and indeed from the rest of the company. Curos indicated for the newcomers to follow him into the small anteroom where he could provide them with wine or spirit without interrupting the recital.

'Fraud!' Xante's voice sounded in his mind. 'You seek any means to leave.'

Yi Janisu introduced the Corninstani as Raja Pata Sing, a Hill Raja from the north of the occupied country. A friend of the previous Corninstani ruler, he had supported the claim of the legitimate juvenile King and had followed him into exile. Pata Sing had been repeatedly frustrated by the lack of any Chaw action and by the way the Corninstani royal family had been monopolised by several senior Civilian Council members. Now he had used his friend Janisu's invitation to Hoelun's party to seek out Curos. Curos did not want the Corninstani's critical words to be heard by the other guests and assumed an impassive

247

mask of indifference to the man's complaints, whilst plying him with a vicious mixture of rice wine and distilled spirit, flavoured with fruit juice to mask its fiery nature. Pata Sing drank deeply without pause or taste and Yi Janisu steered the conversation to the safer areas concerning the hatred of the Warchaw.

Pata Sing presented himself at Curos' office the next day, none the worse for the night's heavy drinking, and explained the latest developments in Corninstan to Curos. The Corninstan traitors had initially succeeded in effecting some control but now the Warchaw had relinquished all pretence of assistance to them or acknowledgement of the sham government. Corninstan was being turned into an armed camp where the town people were little more than slaves and the once-free farmers were peasants. Only in the Lune mountains which separated Corninstan from the O'san plain did some villages have any vestige of freedom.

Pata Sing saw these villages, particularly the ones in his own northern province, as springboards for guerilla raids and then the liberation of Corninstan. Curos listened intently, noting Pata Sing's detailed knowledge, and called in K'tans Bhal and Chalak to join the discussion. Sing's enthusiasm for action and his hatred of the invader were extreme but his lack of any real plan horrified Bhal Morag; the Raja had no idea of how to launch a sustained campaign.

Evidently, Sing expected Curos to instigate immediate action and he became increasingly annoyed by the detailed questioning of the Chaw K'tans. He declared angrily, 'When the Warchaw came you Chaw fled before them. Now you worry over trifles, or do you seek some excuses not to fight?'

'When the barbarians cross the Lune mountains into our land we will have reason to fight,' drawled Bhal Morag.

'How many Warchaw have you killed, hand to hand?' asked Wan Abac with sudden anger. 'A man seeking help should first draw his own sword.' The Raja's hand flew to the hilt of his weapon but stopped when the two door guards inched forward.

'Please let us not fight each other,' Curos said lightly. 'We all have a common enemy. We should share our knowledge and efforts.'

'My honour has been questioned,' replied Raja Sing hotly.

248

'As has mine, and that of my commander,' retorted Wan Abac. 'Lord Zachaw killed Warchaw barbarians in Corninstan as did I on the banks of the Janix. We fought not for our land, Raja, but for yours. Many of my friends died, good companions left for the crows or the Janix crocodiles while Corninstan stood and watched. I expect no thanks, but I will not accept scorn.'

Curos was more than surprised when the arrogant Raja backed down sufficiently to apologise. But much more surprising was this outburst from Wan. Even the Iron Man could be moved to show emotion!

It was several days later, mid-morning, and Curos occupied his huge office on the top floor of the Army Mansion of the 22nd T'sand. He was discussing with Wan Abac the latter's proposals for changing the sword training of the T'sand in order to bring the basic foot-soldiers in line with the guard. The use of shorter straight swords and the idea of a shield was quite foreign to the Chaw infantry, who traditionally relied on long, slashing scimitars or the knife-headed khol spear. Wan had adopted the Warchaw practice of equipping half the footmen with large rectangular shields and short straight swords while the other half carried heavy pikes and javelins without shields.

'I am sure it will be effective, Wan. The remaining problem is our bowmen's lack of power. They are but a feeble shadow of our enemy's archers.'

'I know little of the bow, Lord,' Wan frowned, 'and even among the champions of Chaw there are none who could match the power of the Warchaw. In battle it is not simply accuracy that tells but the number of shafts and the cast of the bow. I have seen Warchaw arrows penetrate thick leather and kill at two hundred paces.'

Curos had no answer and sat silent for some time before changing the topic of conversation in an easy tone. 'I had not realised until recently, K'tan Wan, that you had fought in Corninstan. The 22nd did not leave G'tal?'

'No, Lord, they were not highly regarded by the Esteemed Commander, your father. I served with the 35th from my home province.' He paused as if considering his words, but then said only, 'I had much time to study the barbarians' technique.'

Curos was well aware that the 35th T'sand, the pride of Yec Min province, had been almost annihilated at the Janix. It had held its own section of the river bank until forced to withdraw by the rout of the 37th on its southern flank. Acting as a rearguard, the 35th had then borne the full weight of the Warchaw attack. At one stage a counter-attack led by the Guard Hund had even forced the Warchaw back but their javelins had been no match for the longer range of the enemy bowmen. When the army had finally crossed the Lune mountains into the O'san desert less than one tenth of the 35th T'sand remained alive. It had been disbanded and its survivors allocated to other T'sands.

'At one stage I thought the 35th had broken the Warchaw,' Curos prompted.

'Yes, the guards of the 35th carried javelins and the Warchaw's front rank was shattered by our surprise volley. They were tired and we had advantage in numbers. If we could have kept the fight closer . . .' He stopped the fruitless speculation and added, 'Once we allowed room for their archers to shoot, we were lost. Without shields or effective bowmen of our own, we of the Guard were swept away. Only the Warchaws' lack of arrows saved the rest of the T'sand.'

'And you were promoted to Ataman in the field?'

'Yes, an Ataman of five men, all wounded!'

'I remember the exploits now – were you not also awarded the Gold of Valour? You do not wear it?'

'No, Lord. How could I wear gold when the families of my fallen companions starve?'

'You have sold the medal?' asked Curos in surprise.

'Yes, Lord, for a price better than its weight in gold; authentic Golds are much prized. Money is more important than badges of honour in the lower ranks.'

'I understand, K'tan, but I do not approve. You also take money for sword lessons, which is not expected of an officer.'

'I only take payment from those who can afford it, Lord. There is no dishonour in taking payment for what is earned.'

'You are not poor, Wan; in addition to your K'tan's payment I make you an extra personal allowance for uniform and officers' expenses.'

'I accept that as additional payment, Lord. You once had the best Guard Ataman in the Chaw army. To promote me to be the best Guard K'tan you needed to pay my expenses.'

'Money is that important?'

'To a peasant, only second to food. I take money from K'tans and even a certain Noyan for sword lessons but at the School of the Ataman I give lessons for free. I also profit a little from side bets placed by my friends on combat sessions, though they get but poor odds.'

Curos knew of the notorious School of the Ataman where men from the lower ranks of the army fought bruising battles in thick leather armour with blunted swords. Originally started as a training centre, it now chiefly existed as an unofficial combat arena in which vast sums were wagered on Sword or Jitsu combats.

'And you as a K'tan still hold Top Sword?' Curos asked.

'No,' Wan smiled uncharacteristically. 'There is no Top Sword. Three of us in G'tal are equally matched and train together often. To fight together would destroy speculation and profit.'

An alarm trumpet sounded from the courtyard below. There were clashes of weapons and then a wall of smoke streamed up the wide staircase and eddied through the open double doors. At Wan's shout the ten reserve guards poured into the large office. Two others with smoke-stained faces and burned hair retreated from the staircase, swords in hand. Then came confused shouts of 'We are attacked! Sorcery! Protect the Noyan!'

As the huge iron-studded doors were swung closed and barred, Wan turned to Curos. 'Lord, the back staircase.' He pointed calmly. 'Your Guard will block the pursuit or die in delaying it.' Shouts and more trumpets were mustering the T'sand but crashes on the stairs heralded the progress of the attacker as doors were thrown down. 'Lord, protect yourself,' pleaded Wan. 'Do not risk the future of Chaw by staying.'

Already Curos had strung his bow and was hurriedly strapping on the archer's arm bracer. 'No man dies for Zachaw while he flees,' he replied. 'Form a line and ready your spears!'

'Front rank, keep your shields up.' Wan now spoke to the guards, realising it was useless to argue with Curos. 'There will be jets of fire but it is an illusion. As it clears the second rank

251

will throw javelins into the door opening – do not wait to aim. Draw swords, men. Charge at my order. Our enemy will expect confusion and terror, not bright steel and solid guardsmen.' The K'tan's commanding voice had an immediate effect and the guardsmen now stood as still as on parade. Curos felt the panic of immobility and foot combat rising within him and then at the edge of his mind he felt a laughing hint of derision; someone was mocking these preparations.

They heard the muffled hoof-beats of a horse stumbling as it ascended the carpeted staircase. Smoke eddied under the door, which seemed to tremble. Curos nocked an arrow onto his bow-string and flexed his fingers. He felt kinship with a guardsman who was carefully wiping perspiration from his palm before grasping the javelin in a new grip. Silent tension hung in the air with the smell of smoke and fear.

With a huge explosion the massive doors burst inward, the locks and hinges flying across the room. The men reeled at the noise made even more deafening in the confined space of the echoing hall. Flame and smoke rushed in but did not reach the guardsmen who crouched, swords ready, behind their large shields. Recovering from the shock, the second rank were poised to hurl their needle-sharp spears.

'Fast, hold!' shouted Curos harshly, lowering his bow. 'Hold, do not throw!'

Such was the discipline of the Guard that the order was obeyed, but strained, surprised faces turned to Curos and men still gripped weapons in readiness. The smoke cleared and the black-clad figure of Xante strolled forward, leading a fretful riding horse.

'You must be proud indeed, Noyan Zachaw, to have so many brave men ready to die to protect you!'

32

In the Forest of S'lan the Dryadin would be celebrating the coming of spring and Xante had been increasingly fretful in the constrained atmosphere of the city household. She was also aware that at certain times Hoelun preferred solitude or the company of another musician, Chalak Konn, to herself.

In an attempt to release her growing tension, Xante had decided to take one of the more spirited horses for a long exercise gallop through the countryside and, knowing that Curos had few duties that day, she would suggest he accompanied her. Xante was, she knew, risking danger to be with him at the time of a Dryad 'ceremony' but the unexpected mental contact she had achieved at Hoelun's recital added to her wish for his company.

With N'gol clothing and weapons she rode the horse through the people-infested streets of G'tal and by the time she reached the T'sand barracks her flesh crawled and her head rang with the multitude of whispering mental echoes. At the gate, the sentries ignored her as she rode past; she was well-known but her status was unclear. Usually this lack of recognition did not irritate her, but now she fought to control a rising tide of emotional anger. In S'lan, the music of spring would be playing and the people would be coming together to celebrate the end of winter's hardship and to release the tension which had been locked away during the dark months.

The horse walked easily across the courtyard towards the side entrance, the private staircase of the Noyan. With unbelievable arrogance an Ataman stepped out before her, his hand grabbing the rope halter she used in preference to a bridle. Instantly, the bronze dagger appeared in her hand.

'A pretty toy for a girl,' the man sneered. 'No women are allowed in the barracks but if you uncover your face your luck may change.' Her instinct was to rip open his arm from elbow to wrist. Her teeth clenched with the effort of restraint but

253

still the Ataman staggered backwards, his ears ringing from the concussion she had inflicted.

'I am Xante-Yani, Sorceress of S'lan,' her own voice roared in her head. The wild music of the forest was playing. 'I will not be treated as an inferior.'

She now directed the agitated horse towards the wide main entrance and its closed ceremonial doors. A Dryad would choose her own path. The two impassive guards inclined their spears across the entrance and another Ataman stepped forward with the full arrogance of his duty. Her anger gripped the Ataman and threw him aside as she had once thrown Curos from their tent in the D'was. The guards crumpled. For a heartbeat Xante considered the huge closed doors and then blasted them down with the full force of her sorcery. The release of energy made her spirit soar. The blast of incandescent fire which had burst the locking bar ignited wood and melted the metal rivets. In the grip of her anger, and the frenzy of the forest, she gloried in the destruction.

Inside the building a wide, gently curving staircase led upwards from the vast reception hall. The horse shied but she reassured him, urging him forward to gallop across the fine wool carpet with its patterns of warriors and dragons and begin a clambering climb up the shallow stair-treads. At the top of the first staircase the guards attempted to close the protective gates. She dazzled them with a flash of brilliance which reflected off the crystal pendants of chandeliers and lit up the eyes of long-dead Noyans. The way clear, she ascended again, half aware of alarm trumpets sounding and the rush of booted feet below.

Higher up the doors were protected by Wan Abac's scarlet-clad guards, men who had seen sorcery before. Without wasting time in speculation, they slammed the last set of iron-studded doors and swung down the heavy bars. Her anger was passing and now with more perception she was aware of the general terror she had caused and, yes, the blank wall of a man with no fear, Wan Abac. Then Curos, that surge of energy when he faced danger, or when his other emotions were roused. The guardsmen were terrified indeed but she sensed the swords and javelins, Curos' bow. It was too late to act reasonably. She imagined: impact, smoke, fire, shattered metal hinges and it was done, in a sudden last release of pent-up frustration. She almost laughed aloud.

She heard Curos call 'Fast!' – he had recognised her. She paused just a moment to allow the smoke to clear and for the stressed guardsmen to regain full control. Xante dismounted and led the horse forward. 'You must be proud indeed, Noyan Zachaw, to have so many brave men ready to die to protect you!'

She felt Wan Abac's iron will as he controlled fear and any trace of emotion. With apparent unconcern he called his men to attention and to the salute to show his great respect for the Lady Xante. The guardsmen either grounded their spears or clashed swords on shields before bowing to the woman.

These half glimpses of Xante's ability had convinced Wan Abac of her power and the necessity of her aid to the Chaw army. To Wan Abac she was the forest girl who, in a few short months, had forced herself into a position of power. Abac had little respect for rank as such but he did recognise ability; and even more than ability he respected that drive and determination which forced some men to the top while others were cast aside or thrown down. If Xante invariably slept in Curos' room or had claws on her hands and feet, it was of no interest to K'tan Wan. Any person who could drive off barbarian sorcerers, as at Dar Fir, or who could organise communication between distant army units, was worthy of a full salute.

Wan Abac dismissed his guardsmen and turned to Curos. 'A superb exercise, commander. I will have the men at the entrance below punished for not responding more quickly.'

'Your guard behaved commendably, K'tan, there is no need for reproach,' replied Curos in a stilted voice as he glowered at Xante. 'Pass on my appreciation and have K'tan Chalak organise a replacement door.'

'I fear the one on the third landing is also damaged, Abac.' Xante smiled. 'I over-estimated the force needed to break the lock.'

There was a strange tension between Curos and Xante, thought Wan Abac as he bowed and left the large office. He hoped they did not vie for ultimate power. Since Xante's arrival Wan's own career had fired up like a rejuvenated flame, and

255

instead of just personal perfection in arms he now saw the need to lead and command. His revered mother had no respect for rank, but she would have been proud of her son's rapidly improving fortune. He must not think of his mother. Such thoughts brought weakness.

He descended through the wreckage of the smashed barrier doors on the staircase to the courtyard outside. There, he questioned the dazed soldiers who had been on duty and dismissed the guard Ulus which had assembled, awaiting his orders, before turning to the Ataman in command.

'Ataman, you are fortunate indeed to be alive,' snarled Wan. 'You have insulted the Lady Xante-Yani, Queen of the Dryadin of the Northern Forest. The Lady is equal in rank to a Grand Noyan and called on our commander to invite him to ride. It is your duty as an Ataman to recognise persons of rank.' (*Particularly ones who have the power of destroying you*, he thought inwardly.) 'Ataman, have your broken arm set and then report to the guards for a punishment of ten lashes!'

Wan Abac turned and walked swiftly back to his own quarters. He had planned a rare evening of recreation with distant relatives in G'tal but as he began to remove his uniform he thought first of Xante's display of sorcery and then his earlier discussion of his past with the Noyan Zachaw. Usually he blanked out all possible thoughts of the past but now memories crowded in unbidden.

Wan Abac had been born in a peasant village in the province of Yec Min. The province had no major rivers and the land was hilly and lacked the deep, fertile soil of nearby Sunil. The local lord was as poor as his peasants, and like them regarded tax collectors second only to drought as the worst scourge of the gods. Abac lived with his elder brother, mother and father in a small, one-roomed house. Although one of the finest in their village, it would have been regarded as little more than a hut in the prosperous estate of Te Toldin. Similarly his father's land holding was impressively large but on the thin, rocky soil the crops were always poor and each year was a struggle.

In late spring the rain storm was welcomed like gold from the gods. Rivulets which would have swept the soil off sloping fields were dispersed or dammed. Wells and cisterns were filled and flat terraces flooded. The Sunil said that the only time you could see a man from Yec Min smile was when he stood in the rain. During the summer, crops were tended with infinite care before autumn brought the harvest; locusts and mice starved in Yec Min after the women had stripped the fields. Despite this constant worry and toil, Abac remembered his parents as smiling people who did not age as other villagers seemed to.

In his thirteenth year the rains had been light and the winter cold and hungry. The next year was worse and many old people and sickly children died even before the cold set in. By the spring poorer women were boiling tree bark into bitter soup and sifting the arid soil for grass roots and dormant insects. The rain came early and the people rejoiced.

Too soon the rains stopped and gave way to a blisteringly hot, dry summer which shrivelled rice and wheat alike. Bean pods withered and the deep-rooted apple trees around the house failed to fruit for the first time in memory. There was no harvest feast and no brewing of wine or beer; fear haunted the villagers of Yec Min. Late in the autumn the Wan family like many others were aware that they had insufficient food to last the winter. The last family valuables were sold to buy rice from Sunil but already prices were rising well beyond reach of the village peasants.

In the next house the small daughter died in her sleep from an overdose of poppy syrup. She was not strong enough to survive the famine and the food she would eat was too valuable to waste. Abac felt fear for the first time, although his family were strong and healthy. Up to now their home had been happy, their only regret being that mother had no little daughter to dress up and teach to be a woman. Now mother thanked Freu in her wisdom for not granting her wish.

They held a diminutive harvest sacrifice and thanked the gods and spirits of the house for what they had provided. While Abac's brother fitfully slept he could only lie and listen to his parents' whispered conversation coming through the darkness from the far side of the single room: did father still love her, would he love her now before he grew weak and she grew ugly? Abac felt a warm thrill. He liked to hear mother and father like this and to know they still loved each other. There would be no mysterious deaths in this house, he knew.

He drifted into half-dreams and imagined walking high into the bleak hills and finding stands of wild rice or edible bamboo, possibly a colony of rabbits. Perhaps he could walk into the town and try his luck at combat with the local boys. He was broad-shouldered, strong and exceptionally quick of movement. An old soldier in the village had shown him several advanced Jitsu moves which would make him invincible. In time of famine, city dwellers would gamble on anything, father had said. Abac would come home rich and make the Wan family proud. The boy had drifted into sleep, possibly the last happy sleep he had known.

He and his brother had leapt from their beds at the demented scream of grief from his father. There were no further sounds until out in the moonlit garden beneath the apple trees they found him sobbing silently over the body of their dead mother. She had left her husband sleeping after their last lovemaking and crept silently into the garden, where she had opened the veins of her wrists. The unusual and slow suicide had left her face and body unmarked, her mouth almost smiling in death. In a sudden spasm of hopelessness the man kissed away the tears he had shed on the dead face and carried her back into the house.

Starvation for four, or survival of three. Was that the only solution?

In a land bereft of trees few funeral pyres were now possible, and many villagers were forced to lie in shallow graves awaiting full release of their souls. In one last act of tribute, father had stripped every piece of non-essential wood from the house and the farm. The low beds, the sparse furniture, even the family altar to the house gods had been collected to make the final offering.

There was no song, smile or laughter in the house from that day. No love, no whispered night conversations and no happiness. There was only basic survival. Survival to live and living to survive.

Thanks to the sacrifice they all lived through that long, hard, lonely winter and worked in the spring rains until the planting was complete. Wan Abac took leave of his father and brother

258

and set out for the city. All love in the world had died on that autumn night and Abac could not desecrate the memory of his mother by letting her spirit see him living without love. His father was tied to the land, his elder brother would inherit the lease but there was nothing for Abac. He walked through the hills of north-west Yec Min and into the southern town of Yecel Li. From valley to town he travelled until he reached the provincial capital where the 35th T'sand had recently returned from garrisoning G'tal.

At the ancient palace which now formed the headquarters of the T'sand, a Guard Ataman who had seen too many starving peasant boys try to enlist in the hope of army food attempted to turn Abac away. Defiantly Abac stated his right to be considered. As he was about to be thrown out a K'tan was attracted by the argument and sauntered over with half-bored interest.

'Are your family noted as soldiers?' he asked as the young Wan Abac bowed low.

'No, Lord, but an elder of my village has taught me a little of the Jitsu Art and I seek to improve further.'

'Would you turn such a budding warrior away?' The K'tan smiled at the Ataman.

'We are not recruiting, noble K'tan, and I need no starving peasant boys.' He smiled evilly. 'But he can fight for my dinner if he wishes. Ataman's Rules.' Wan Abac fully understood that Ataman's Rules meant no rules and also realised how slim his chances of victory would be against a hard, experienced soldier.

Abac smiled idiotically and bowed low from the waist, his back straight and arms locked into his side. The Ataman gestured derisively at the formal Jitsu salute and began a mocking comment to the K'tan. With instant speed Abac charged. Two powerful steps sent his shoulder into the older man's groin. As the Ataman reeled backward Abac grasped his thigh and heaved upwards, thumping him flat onto his back on the hard-packed earth.

The boy leapt nimbly back from any counter-move and again bowed.

'Best of three!' cried the Ataman, scrambling upright.

'But he already wins your dinner, Ataman Aki.' The K'tan laughed. 'What will you wager this time, a place in the T'sand?'

'No, there is no need,' the Ataman replied, rubbing his back and dispersing his anger. 'He has a place in my Guard Ulus for that throw. Boy, you were lucky and I too complacent. In the next training session you will teach me that unorthodox throw and I will teach you respect for your master.'

And so Wan Abac had joined the 35th T'sand, the Tol Ze, the Stone men of Yec Min who never moved under attack. The Tol Ze whose javelins had later halted the Warchaw and almost turned the Wind at the battle of the Janix. But even the mighty 35th had retreated in the end, retreated and fought and died every blood-spattered, arrow-strewn step of the way back from the Janix to the O'san. Through the cornfields and the orchards, along the roads and the mountain passes Guardsman Wan had fought until his entire body was numb.

One by one his friends of five years in the 35th had died, even the indestructible Ataman Aki had finally succumbed to one of the long, chisel-pointed arrows. By this time Wan was blind to grief or feeling. The killing machine fashioned by Aki slew until his hands were slippery with blood, and finally his scimitar shattered on a Warchaw helmet. Like some ancient hero of old he had leapt bareheaded at a Warchaw swordsman, smashed him down despite his greater stature and seized one of the deadly straight swords.

He had been promoted Ataman, Under-Officer of five battle-fatigued wounded men and later awarded the prestigious Gold of Valour. How could he keep what other men's lives had bought? It was only fitting that it should be sold and the money distributed to the families of those who had paid with their blood.

K'tan Wan Abac awoke from his reverie and continued removing his scarlet ceremonial uniform. He hoped his revered mother, she who had sacrificed her life for her children, would understand that that was money which had no right going to his own family.

He ground his teeth to prevent tears from falling and leapt up. His mouth called out for wine, his mind clamoured for release, however brief, from the harsh, cruel, evil world.

'No!' Wan Abac could not condone the waste of grain to make wine when a woman had shed her own blood to save food for her children. He pulled on his faded blue field-uniform tunic and descended angrily to the exercise ground, seeking a hard opponent. Swaggering before him was the tall, arrogant shape of Pata Sing.

33

It was dark, quite dark and the ant-run streets of G'tal were completely empty except for an occasional scurrying townsman or the ever present night watchman. Xante and Curos walked side by side, leading sweating horses so that they could cool down before reaching their stalls. The madness of the forest which had threatened Xante that morning was quite gone and in the day of almost silent companionship words had been largely redundant. Now inside G'tal a different reality had begun to reassert itself until the joy of movement and freedom had evaporated and only the sense of beleagured friendship remained.

'I fear I have acted very rashly today, Curos. I have developed dangerous levels of power but sometimes I am still ruled by my emotions.'

'What is there to be regretted?' asked Curos. 'A broken door, a dazed sentry or more rumour?'

They walked on for several streets, until Curos said, 'I know this is a hard life for a Dryad. Do you think I would not like to ride in the free open spaces, or even walk with you in Eternal S'lan? Our lives are not destined to be joyous like Makran and Dortie. If many days are sad and drab then days like today will have to pay the price. If I were to retreat into the plains of D'was and you into the trees of S'lan we would enjoy only brief happiness. The eventual slavery under the barbarians would be only the more difficult to bear.'

'I know, Curos. There is no need for you to remind me. I fight for the children of Dromo that another woman will bear, perhaps you fight for little Pa'na or Dalgan's children. The fact that our role is necessary makes the barrenness of our lives justified but it is no easier day by day for all that. Once our path was chosen we could not return to normal life. Dalgan, Morag, Abac and even Lotol are others who have no choice in their destiny.'

Again there was a period of comfortable silence between

them, eventually broken by Xante. 'I believe Abac has taught our new man, Pata Sing, a little of reality?'

'Yes, Pata Sing was eager to accept a training bout with our Iron Man and has now changed his attitude somewhat. With blunt unpointed swords and padded leather practice armour he saw war as Abac wages it.'

'Tell me, Curos.'

'There is little to tell.' Curos laughed openly. 'His first slashing cut was avoided, and Abac's counter-thrust into his stomach felled him. Abac seemed in a strange mood and allowed the Corninstani to fight ten bouts with him. Not that it took long, but Pata Sing was a mass of bruises under the leather armour. In ten bouts he had not touched the Iron Man once.'

'A serious blow to Sing's pride?'

'Yes, but he was man enough to admit Abac's superior technique. It was a hard lesson – I hope he bears no ill will.'

'Stop! Curos, there is danger. I feel we are the attention of hatred. In the alleyway to the left.'

Curos' immediate reaction was to throw himself onto Thunder-Arrow's back. 'Mount, Xante!' he called, drawing his sword which rang and glinted in the sparse starlight.

'No, some force defies me, dares me to use my power.' The dark-bladed Dryad dagger was balanced lightly in her right hand as she crouched defensively, staring into the pit-like darkness of the alleyway.

'Sow born of sow!' spat a voice full of evil hatred. 'Sow, who sees in the darkness, see now your death approaching.' Three menacing shrouded figures spread out, cutting off any flight down the narrow road; two carried curved scimitars, the third a long knife. One swordsman held back slightly and seemed to be the commander. From the height of Thunder-Arrow's back Curos detected a dull red glow at the man's chest.

'Kill the woman first,' the commander shouted as the strange tableau burst into action. 'Show the witch woman the agony of death.'

Curos ran Thunder-Arrow past Xante, slashing downward at the first swordsman's arm and shoulder. The knifeman leapt at Xante with vicious speed, combining a kick and a sweeping knife-thrust in one deadly move. Curos felt the jar of contact as his sword bit home. Xante swayed sideways and countered her attacker's move with a knife-slash that brought a rake of blood from his cheek. In the darkness, the red glow from the stone hanging at the leader's chest flared menacingly, and in its aura the shape of a bearded sorcerer appeared. Curos felt the responding surge of power from his Topaz.

'Curos, cover the stone, do not let it react,' screamed Xante, her concentration waning from her own combat as she warned Curos. The assassin who faced her seized his chance for an unorthodox counter-attack: a left-hand fist strike which sent the girl reeling away like a broken doll, but she had left her dagger firmly embedded in the thick muscles of the knifeman's thigh from a blow which had been invisibly fast. He staggered and attempted to close to where the dazed girl was rising to her feet, taloned hands advanced in the defensive Jitsu position.

Curos had turned the pendant to face his body and covered it with the palm of his hand. Now using Thunder-Arrow's bulk rather than the sword, Curos charged down the assassin leader, riding the trained war-horse over his body. He wheeled the horse and saw two men running towards the combat from the far end of the street. Xante stood dazed and shaken over her fallen victim, his body arched backward, his mouth twisted into a fearsome rictus of agony.

Savagely Xante snatched her dagger from the dying man's thigh and turned to meet the second onslaught. Eyes glazed with near concussion, she leapt with the fury of a wounded tiger towards a third swordsman. Her dagger caught his sword-cut and she struck with a clawing left hand which left his face a sheet of blood. Again deflecting the swordsman's weapon, Xante stabbed up into his arm and smashed her knee into his groin.

The last assassin backed away, keeping against the wall and using the high curb as protection against Curos' horseback attack.

'Surrender, you cannot escape!' Curos shouted.

'Kill him, Curos, kill him quickly before any others come.' The man edged further away, turning slightly to look for some courtyard doorway or alley which would aid his escape. Curos leapt from Thunder-Arrow's back and advanced with sword in one hand, the other still grasping the pulsating Topaz.

In the darkness and with uneven footing they were equally matched but Curos' confidence gave him an increasing advantage as the fight progressed. Clashes of swords rang out loudly with sparks off tempered blades streaking through the night as Curos pressed his opponent hard and the cross guards of their swords locked. His instinct was to kill, to stab deeply with the triangular bladed dagger and leap back. Instead he struck hard with the pommel of his sword at the man's jawbone.

Curos ran back to where Xante stood looking down at the unconscious form of the assassin leader.

'Are you injured?' he gasped.

'No, only bruised, the penalty for indecision and over-confidence. I hesitated between sorcery or combat and then realised I had to warn you to control Topaz.' She shook her head, which still rang from her blow. 'My veil will cover an ugly face tomorrow, already my cheek and jaw swells.' She waved him away. 'Please, it is nothing, Curos, turn this one over before he recovers.'

As the trampled body of the man was heaved over by Curos' foot they both saw the dull red glow of the stone at his throat which shone with more than moonlight. His fine-boned face was partially covered by a pointed black beard.

'A man from South Imran – what does he do in G'tal?' asked Curos.

'Curos, that stone has some power, like your Topaz. He goaded me to try sorcery on him.'

'For the stone to counter . . . ?'

'I know not.' She rubbed her forehead vainly and flexed her bruised face. 'I am dazed, Curos. I can't think. It has no power, no personality. Hand it to me please, my head spins.'

Curos bent to snatch the stone off the thin chain which secured it around the assassin's neck.

'No! Curos, stand back.' She pulled at his arm but already he was springing away as the stone began to glow a brighter red. The brilliance increased and burnt to a dazzling white flame. Both the stone and the body of the wearer were consumed, leaving little more than ash and a vile smell of sulphur and burned flesh.

'It destroys itself, Curos, to avoid detection. Could it have

265

been a spy stone, a stone by which a Warchaw sorcerer could see?'

'If you had used sorcery then all your power would have been revealed?'

'Revealed and destroyed. I feared the Topaz would react to counter the Red Stone and reveal you as a source of power. The Imrani had no fear, Curos. He wanted me to use sorcery against him and believed he was protected.'

'Or was he only testing you? A way to show your power to the Warchaw? To check if the rumours of a Dryad sorcerer were true?'

'And if they were untrue there would just be a dead girl in a filthy alley. A life of no importance extinguished!'

They stood considering this before another thought occurred to Curos. 'Xante, where is the Watch? There should be two on this street at all times. They stand down there in the archway for shelter.'

The man Curos had stunned was beginning to recover. Dragging him to his feet, Curos and Xante retraced their steps to the arched entrance to a shuttered courtyard. In daytime it was the Place of Physicians, now it was in deathly darkness.

Inside, sprawled across the flagstones in the shadow of the wall, were three more bodies: two elderly watchmen with cut throats and beside them a young woman who lay whimpering pitifully, her hands flicking ineffectually at the deep wound in her stomach. Even as they ran towards her with sickening hearts she gave one last shuddering breath and died. Close by her was a basket and an overturned jug of still-warm soup which she had brought to the Watchmen.

'Who did this foulness?' cried Curos, rounding on his captive.

'Lie to Q'ren Xante and your mind will boil in torment,' hissed Xante in her deep voice. 'Lie to me and the torments of Ki Dug, the Te Lok outlaw, will be as nothing compared with the agonies I can visit on you.' Every market gossip, every tavern raconteur had his own version of the torture of Ki Dug and the assassin squirmed at the thought of what might be planned for him.

'It was Korian, the Imrani, who killed her with his own sword,' he said in a rush. 'She begged for life because she was with child. Korian thrust his sword through her stomach and laughed at her

266

pain. I had no part in it. I learned to fight in the army. I only wished for more payment for use of my skills. I am but a poor man.'

'A poor man who sells his soul to evil.'

'I am not a leader, I only obey orders.'

'The men who cause evil can only function because tools such as you exist. You will suffer until you reveal all. The longer you resist, the greater will be my gratitude at your suffering.'

'No, please. I am not strong, the Imrani who paid us works with the Noyan Qunin. I learned this when I escorted him to an inn in the South-West Quarter. They met there secretly. I know not their purpose but Qunin is the name you need.' Curos turned to Xante with an unspoken question and disbelief in his face.

'He speaks true, I am sure. His terror leaves him no skill to lie. His mind is full of the name.'

Before Curos could reply a hasty footfall approached. A young man clutching a staff appeared in the archway. He faltered and said, 'I seek my wife who brought food . . .' His words broke off as his eyes recognised the dreadful truth of the scene before Curos. He stumbled forward with a barely audible cry of grief and cradled the dead woman in his arms. Xante turned away, Curos felt his own stomach and eyes revolt at the cruel reality. The assassin slumped to his knees, his head bowed in shame.

'Why! Why was she killed?' the demented husband screamed at Curos. 'She did nothing to deserve violent death! She was in her sixteenth year, only one year married. The sweetest life with a bitter end, my . . .'

Curos and Xante stood silently as the man's tears flowed down onto the face of his dead wife. Any words of comfort would have been too shallow.

'The others I cannot explain,' sighed Curos. 'All who partook of this deed are dead except this living carrion. You, as the woman's husband, have the right to his life.' He held out his sword to the sobbing man who took it without thought.

He looked at the weapon with disgust and surprise at what he held. 'In her short life my wife harmed no living creature,' he sobbed. 'Should I kill now and profane her memory? This morning we spoke together of a new life we had created. Now her soul is crying in the void of the dead with that of our unborn child. My only wish is that we be together.' With a desperate violence the young man thrust the sword into his own ribs. Curos grabbed at his arms but the dying man fell forward, driving the sword deeper into his body.

'Will there be no end to the violence of this night?' Angrily, Curos retrieved his sword. 'Did you realise what he intended?'

'Yes,' Xante said softly. 'He could not bear the grief.'

'But why? He was young. Years would dull his pain and the memory. He might even have found a new wife. Why did you not stop him?'

'Curos, I think he knew all of that. The fear of forgetting her love was as bad as the loss.'

'We can do little here. I will say the Watchmen died in trying to help us. They will receive due honour and some compensation will be found for their families.' He heaved one of the Watchmen's swords from its scabbard, stiff with dried grease and lack of use, but its point was still sharp. Without warning Curos thrust the sword into the kneeling assassin and twisted the blade. The man died almost silently.

'An easy death for such a criminal,' Curos spat venomously. 'I will bloody the other watchmans' sword,' he commented in a flat voice, 'before I call the Militia.'

'The men I fought are already dead,' Xante replied. 'My knife is poisoned.' She held out the dull-coloured bronze blade. 'See, this ceramic insert contains a mixture of paralysing poisons.'

'From the forest paradise of S'lan!'

'Yes, from S'lan. You claim that we fight a war, not a contest of sport. When the need is to kill, then Dryadin too can be very efficient.'

'With talons also?' he asked bitterly and his memory returned to that night of madness when in the grip of Ki Fru Xante had threatened Aalani with the same extended talons and her poisoned dagger.

'They are not decorative, Curos. Would you rather I had been killed? Mercy is not a luxury one can afford when one fights for life.'

'Or to protect the Forest of S'lan the Eternal,' whispered Curos, quoting the words of Aalani-Galni. 'For it is the purpose of the Dryadin to protect the forest.'

34

With all Curos' rank and prestige it was still no simple matter to explain the carnage of the Street of the Physicians. Stage by stage Militia, Ataman, K'tan and Noyan were summoned until the Admin of the city quarter was called from his bed. Crowds gathered at either end of the narrow street and physicians whose practices occupied the courtyard dwellings arrived from their more luxurious homes. Relatives of the watchmens' families howled with grief.

Militiamen held up torches while scribes meticulously recorded the details of each corpse. Positions, nature of wounds and weapons were all set down in the curtailed civil service script. Finally Curos was conducted, with all deference, to the Civil Mansion to record his own statement of the happenings.

He explained in simple, succinct phrases how he and the Lady Xante had been attacked and would certainly have been slain but for the intervention of the gallant watchmen. These ancient but valiant protectors of the law had paid for their bravery with their lives. A young couple, bringing food to the watchmen, had also been caught up in the fight and been slain wantonly by the attackers who were obviously led by a Corninstani Warchaw spy.

It was near to dawn when Curos and Xante finally completed the bureaucratic formalities and arrived back at the Zachaw City Mansion. Hoelun had retired to sleep early and was unaware of their late return. Hastily Curos awoke Scribe Wou, and dictated yet another account of the events of the bloodstained night, this time for his army superior Po Pi.

Xante left them to forage in the deserted kitchen and had collected up a meal of exceeding robustness – broken hunks of bread, a few fresh leaves of pe-tsai, cheese and wine still in the storage jar. She sat slumped at the kitchen table, her bruised face rendered more livid by the flickering lamplight.

'Join me in this repast of simple elegance, Lord Zachaw. Eat, if you would not rather summon a scribe to first record the menu!' He crossed to the table and examined her face closely. She winced and pulled away. 'No sympathy, please, Curos. I feel wretched. This morning I craved for excitement and the release of unused energy, my body resenting that it could not follow the rhythm of the forest. Would that I had that energy now! I have not killed men before, does it grow easy with practice?'

He tipped wine into a beaker and topped it up with water before sitting opposite her. 'The fighting does. The thrill of combat can even become like a drug but such as we saw tonight is never easy to bear.' Curos regretted the use of the word for he was sure that in the defence of the Forest, the Dryadin would use the drug of madness to give added venom to their combat.

'Part of me cries out with disgust at the violence and the blood under my nails, Curos. At the same time my fury urges me to summon my skill and attack Noyan Qunin, now, before the traitor knows he has failed. That girl's death pulls at my soul, Curos. She died simply because we walked that way. The assassins would brook no interruption and no delay.' Xante stopped speaking and instead drank deeply of the undiluted wine.

For what was left of the night Xante slept in Curos' room, curled into her Dryad sleeping sack on the hard floor. Curos forsook his bed to lie near her, close enough to give a sense of comfort without contact. Like every warrior, he too had once looked violent death in the face for the first time. In the heat of battle the spirit soared and exulted in victory. Afterwards in the cold night the reaction was savagely chill, especially if one counted dead comrades or, as in this case, innocents who had died unnecessarily.

The next day Curos, Xante, Lin Sri and Bhal Morag met with Po Pi to discuss the reasons why Noyan Qunin should have plotted assassination. Po Pi and Lin Sri considered that Qunin must hold some grudge against Curos, and the scribe had investigated all possible family links between Curos and persons such as Ci Shen and Chou Ramin whom Curos had harmed. Po Pi saw possible cause for a hidden feud in the most distant family associations but found it difficult to convince Bhal Morag.

'You reflect your own virtue of loyalty to Chaw onto all of our class,' stated Bhal Morag. 'Forget Qunin's position and possible motives and first consider the facts alone.'

'I fear Morag is right,' agreed Xante. 'The only answer is that Noyan Qunin is in league with the Warchaw. The assassin we captured was convinced Qunin was their leader and the Imrani was obviously a Warchaw tool.'

They sat in deadly silence. Recognition of the truth did not mean an easy solution. How many more high-ranking Chaw saw personal advantage in alliance with the barbarians?

'We know our enemy. He plots against us all and commits atrocities beyond all common laws,' stated Xante. 'We are people of action and must not shrink to strike at him!'

'He will be extremely well guarded,' commented Po Pi.

'Not against my anger,' replied Xante. 'A Dryad is permitted to kill to protect the Forest. I have reason enough and in my anger I have the power.'

'You are quite right, madam,' argued Lin Sri softly, 'but we know not the Noyan's allies. If he were struck down by sorcery they would accuse the only known sorceress of power in Chaw.'

'That would lead to division, even civil war,' said Po Pi. 'Some would side with myself and Curos, others would condemn sorcery and listen to agents of the Warchaw.'

'The arch sorcerers would use condemnation of our sorcery to divide our nation and then destroy us,' murmured Bhal Morag. 'The irony of the situatiuon is unbelievable.'

'The key is still Qunin,' stated Curos, who had taken little part in the discussions. 'We need to discover his motivation, and how far he supports the Warchaw. Possibly he only seeks their help in securing power for himself, and does not realise the danger.'

'As did the traitors in Cornistan,' replied Bhal Morag. 'Pata Sing can explain the danger of such a course if Qunin would listen.'

'Then he will listen to me!' said Curos. 'I will confront Noyan Qunin and ask the question we have voiced today and seek to learn his purpose.'

'You speak like a Dryad,' said Xante angrily. 'Talk, discuss and conciliate. You have taught me to be Hinto and have shown

271

me that evil must be destroyed. He who condones the death of children and the destruction of a living forest is beyond hope in this life and must be committed to the void to contemplate his sins before rebirth.'

'Save us all from such religious conviction!' said Bhal Morag in his lazy, drawling voice. 'But I doubt any will be able to save Qunin from your anger!'

It was, however, Noyan Qunin who contacted Curos first, summoning the younger man to an interview at the Mansion barracks of the T'sand which Qunin commanded. Suspecting some further assassination attempt, Po Pi declined on Curos' behalf. Message followed message until finally it was agreed that Noyan Qunin would visit Curos in the 22nd T'sand Mansion for a private conference.

Noyan Qunin entered the large conference room followed by a ceremonial guard of five men commanded by a K'tan. These waited just inside the entrance and Qunin advanced to meet Curos in the centre of the room. Curos' own Guard, commanded by the belligerent Wan Abac, waited along the opposite wall, their ceremonial spears replaced by needle-pointed javelins. Hidden behind the wall-length embroidered tapestries along the sides of the room, Xante and three other picked archers completed Curos' defence.

Curos and Qunin bowed to each other and seated themselves on low cushions on either side of a polished table on which stood an ornate flask and two diminutive cups.

'May I command your precautions against attack, Zachaw,' said Qunin with a gesture that indicated the hidden bowmen as well as the Guard.

'One learns to be cautious.'

'Just so. I must also congratulate you on your escape from the attempt on your life. The reputation you have as a man of arms is well founded.'

'It was nothing. I was well assisted.'

'There is no place for false modesty between us, Zachaw. We both know that the Watchmen were already dead when you were attacked. The girl, for all your previous claims to the Council, could have been but little help. It was an heroic fight on your part. Win Li, the dagger man, alone was a deadly foe and the Imrani was a master of the sword.'

'You know a great deal of my assailants, Qunin.'

'Please take no offence, Zachaw. It was necessary to test the rumours of power which surrounded the Dryad Woman, if woman is the correct term.'

'You admit then, that you organised the attack and that you are in league with the Warchaw?' It was difficult for Curos to keep his voice quiet and mask his anger.

'Of course. I am sure you have already extracted that information from my men. You have a certain reputation for subtle persuasion!'

'Then why do you enter my domain and risk your life?'

'I am sure there is little risk. You have no evidence against me and would not attack me in an open fashion. It is however important that I ask you to join me. Join me in a bold plan that will rejuvenate our land and free us from the clinging weakness which threatens all Chaw's peoples. I will explain, Zachaw, and then I am sure you will understand.'

When Curos did not answer Qunin continued. 'There are two types of men in this life, Zachaw. There are those who have vision and energy, the leaders and the heroes, the organisers and the rulers. They are few and are surrounded by thousands of others: peasants, townsmen, beggars and idlers who have little worth. Can you imagine a world where such worthless people as those have been reduced to a minimum? The air is open and clear, free from the smell of filth and rotting population. That is how Chaw would be, as the other lands of the Warchaw have become. That is my ideal and you could be part of the new order that I plan.'

'You seem sure of my response,' Curos replied angrily. 'Why do you think I would betray our land to invasion?'

'What land? What people? You are a lone hero in your own eyes; the man who fought Chou Ramin and who slew the best assassins I could muster. What affinity have you with the slum-dwellers of G'tal or the peasant farmers? In others' eyes you are a leader, a man of destiny. With me you could lead Chaw to a new era, a new empire.'

'Did you betray my father's campaign?'

273

'No. I waited to see its outcome. When it failed I returned to my estate in Zantu and from its sea ports I sent a ship to Imran and sought ambassadors from the Warchaw. I found they spoke of a future of which I had barely dared to dream. I have conversed not only with the Warchaw but with the Imrani and Corninstani who have benefited from Warchaw rule.' Qunin returned to his previous theme. 'I have watched your progress, Zachaw, and believe you could be one of us. You have carefully built on the ashes of your father's career. You have duped that fool Po Pi. Created a myth of the Dryad sorceress. Fought a carefully chosen duel with an unpopular man of equal rank. Captured the Te Lok outlaws and achieved the disgrace of Ci Shen. The soldiers see you as a hero, the civil administrator as a politician and the Noyans as a future supreme leader – it has been masterfully done!'

'You do not believe then that my sorceress is real?'

'No. I had my doubts but I needed to know.'

'And now you are sure?'

'The Imrani goaded your woman and her life was in danger. If she possessed powers she would have used them in her own defence.'

'And what then, Qunin? Would your new masters have ordered her destruction and mine?'

'I have no masters. I am no man's slave, Zachaw. The Imrani's stone was thought powerful enough to destroy any unnatural sorcerer.'

'Destroy any power which would one day develop to challenge the Warchaw,' replied Curos. 'Now you believe you can corrupt me to your masters' ends. You will find, as those in Corninstan did, that only the weak and subservient will be allowed sham power when the Warchaw rule. They have no time for the conquered. The very philosophy you spoke to me gives no rights to the weak.' Desperately he tried to explain, 'All our people have some right to life and destiny, whatever their poverty. Only by our numbers can we hope to escape slavery under the invaders.'

'The land cannot support such numbers, Zachaw. Drought follows drought and famine is always near. The Green Plan of the Agriculturalist, Galtar Paft, required a reduction in population but it would be too slow-acting to save us.'

'And what has caused drought? The Warchaw disrupt the lands, they occupy and fell forests indiscriminately.'

'Forests are foul places, full of evil,' Qunin stated. 'The light and air must enter to sweep away that evil. The northern forest of S'lan and its hideous Dryadin people must be cleared next.'

'Can you not see that the Warchaw fear the forest only because it opposes them? All that resists their conquest is swept away. It is destroyed, whatever the effect.'

'It is man's destiny to conquer the earth and control nature,' Qunin shouted angrily. 'Your reason is warped, Zachaw.'

Curos was suddenly aware of Xante's rising anger at Qunin's blasphemy against the forest and his attention wavered. He saw images of flame jets and speeding arrows.

'Do not!' his mind screamed. 'Not yet.'

'I can see you reject my offer, Zachaw,' Qunin was saying as Curos regained his composure, 'but it remains open. I cannot be deposed and I fear not your fake sorcery. I will struggle against your ideas in Council and I will have the Chaw T'sands descend on S'lan. At any time when reality dawns in you, you will be accepted into my party.'

Dismayed by the corrupt ideas of this man who had such an important position in Chaw, Curos watched as Noyan Qunin rose and prepared to leave. Only his concern at how many followers Qunin had and the ever-present need to prepare for the Warchaw threat kept Curos' hand from his dagger hilt. As Po Pi had said, they could not risk civil war which would throw Chaw open to invasion. Qunin had to die, of that he was sure – die or be defeated in the politics of Chaw life. Neither seemed possible.

Outside, the first of the cold spring rains were lashing the pagoda roof of the mansion. Curos and all right-minded Chaw were praying that the rain would be heavy and long. How evil was Qunin? Was he praying for drought, for disease and plague to weaken Chaw until he could take control of the land at the head of a barbarian army?

Noyan Qunin's manner showed a perceptible change and had become more aggressive. He had come to the meeting offering conciliation and friendship to a junior. Faced with a stark rebuff he would revert to enmity. Curos feigned indecision and walked with Qunin towards the door.

'Your words are of great import, Excellency, and treat of matters I had not considered.' Curos paused as if for thought and slowly changed to a selfish personal point of view. 'I need time to consider your proposals. There would need to be assurances, safeguards given with respect to family estates. My ties with the nomad peoples are important.'

Qunin departed with words of shallow friendship and hope that Noyan Zachaw would change his attitude to the Warchaw. As soon as Curos returned from bidding his visitor farewell Xante stalked up to him angrily.

'We must talk, you and I.'

'We must all talk: Morag, Abac and Konn. The only counter to insidious treachery is openness. I will tell all my comrades what was offered and what I replied.' He started to move towards the door but she seized him by the shoulder and he felt the grip of her nails.

'You consider trifles. Qunin should now be dead by our hands but he lives. That is your decision and you rule here. There are other things as important,' her voice softened and her face was a curious mixture of emotions, 'important for you and me.' Curos was surprised; he had thought her blind to everything but her rage at Qunin's actions and words.

'I do not understand.'

'Your mind spoke directly to mine for the first time! I was about to shoot Qunin and you stopped me.'

'Is it that important?' he asked quizzically. 'It was only due to the urgency of the situation. I doubt I could do it again.'

'No, and why make the effort?' she retorted, with the sudden blaze of anger which the season left her unable to control. 'Sometimes I forget you are not Dryad. Mutual mind contact means nothing to you.'

35

Curos had called a conference of his colleagues, reporting what Qunin had said until at last he completed with, 'And so I chose to show indecision and doubt of purpose. I can see no way of removing Qunin quickly and hoped to stay his hand.'

'I could have removed him easily,' said Xante. 'My bow was drawn and I had chosen a point of aim.'

'One cannot kill an ambassador,' stated Chalak Konn.

'The Warchaw have killed those we sent to them,' replied Bhal Morag, 'but I agree, the time was not well chosen.'

'I agree with Lady Xante,' said Wan Abac. 'Direct action often serves best and a traitor is no ambassador. Our commander had the right, even under law, to strike instantly once Qunin's words of treachery were uttered!'

'I need time to manoeuvre and develop our plans,' explained Curos. 'I will plead sickness and return to Te Toldin. Qunin will think I consider his false words.'

'And Red O'san?' asked Bhal Morag.

'Will continue! It will appear our company is dispersed and that I have abandoned my plans but I will be meeting the N'gol leader at Te Toldin and driving Red O'san forward. Qunin has no doubt informed his masters of our intention; we must therefore act rapidly to deny time for any possible counter.'

'When will the new Red O'san start?' asked Bhal Morag.

'Tomorrow! When I leave for Te Toldin. I will speak to Po Pi now and seek his agreement to bring the arrangements forward.'

'I will tell my staff that all the maps and plans for the N'gol have been destroyed by the Noyan.' Morag smiled. 'I will curse over wasted effort and spend several days seeking consolation with certain women I have neglected of late.'

'Agreed, but take care. Qunin may seek to assassinate others of our company. Lotol and Dalgan must be warned.'

'I will also feign lack of duties and spend more time at the

School of the Ataman,' laughed Abac. 'If we are soon to depart for the desert I must ensure I take my share of fools' money.'

The gathering had dispersed amicably and now with cold spring rain falling in sheets, Curos and Xante's horses picked their way out of G'tal in the dark of early morning. At the prospect of leaving G'tal, Xante's spirits had risen like the flight of a sky lark and she was quite undaunted by the atrocious weather conditions. She warned Curos mischievously, 'You have relaxed your grip on the reins again. Are you not concerned at the possible outcome?'

'No, this is different. It is like releasing hunting dogs, each performs their task. Po Pi and Chalak Konn will act as a restraint on Bhal Morag.'

Xante disagreed and said seriously, 'You know little of your men, Curos. By the end of the week they could all have given Po Pi cause to have them banished from G'tal. Wan Abac will have beaten ten men to death in illegal contests and one of your other K'tans will have completed his seduction of the wife of a senior official.'

'You should know the tactics of Morag! If an older man cannot amuse his young wife he deserves to be cheated,' laughed Curos.

Xante started to reply but instead smiled to herself, thinking that Curos would know of events all in good time. The weather made further conversation difficult and they rode on in rain-lashed silence.

At midday Curos and Xante were well away from the capital when a covered coach left the Zachaw City Mansion. Inside Junior Scribe Wou lay back on the thick cushions and contemplated the irony of a boy from the slums of G'tal riding in a coach flying the standard of a full Noyan. Despite the six-man escort of guardsmen following behind, he kept his own personal weapons close at hand. The long, needle-like dagger and the broader-bladed throwing knife were unlikely to be effective in a battle but any assassin who tackled Wou at close combat would need to be wary indeed.

The journey to Te Toldin was one of the worst Curos could remember. The rains were heavier than any he had experienced and had already begun to cause alarm among officials and peasants. The horses were always tired, always reluctant and slow

278

no matter how many changes Curos made at Arrow Rider posts. Progress was disappointing, damp and miserable. It was tempting to rest up at an inn for a week or so until the spring rains slackened.

Good rainfall was essential, but now every river, stream, reservoir and flooded field was at its maximum level. In every province Curos and Xante saw that the workers had left their sodden fields and were struggling to keep water channels free of debris or to shore up banks and terraces which were in danger of washing away. Even Curos felt a strange urge to join in the work which meant the difference between a heavy harvest and calamitous flooding and landslide. He visualised his rain-drenched brother Makran, in shirt and cloth trousers, shovelling mud as hard as any peasant during the day only to return home to produce instructions and plans for the village headman to execute. Dortie, probably with little Pa'na, would work with the women preparing the fields for planting rice.

By the time the mud-encrusted travellers reached the estate of Te Toldin the rains had reduced to sporadic drizzle. Due to the weather the journey had taken a week longer than usual but Curos had avoided the traitor Qunin and hoped that the letters he had despatched from G'tal before he himself departed would have travelled ahead of the heaviest rains.

At the Toldin estate, Curos and Xante's arrival was barely noticed. Every effort was being directed into planting or conserving the extra rainfall. Curos' mother, Turakina, had departed to her own people of the White Dragon Clan and with Hoelun now in G'tal, the travellers were like exiles in some deserted palace from which Lord and servant had fled. In the evening Makran and Dortie struggled in, too exhausted for conversation – the most demanding of state affairs being trivial compared to the progress of the spring sowing.

The next day clear skies and warm spring sunshine propelled Makran and Dortie from their bed with rejuvenated enthusiasm. With some difficulty Curos enlisted the services of several household soldiers to act as back-up messengers to the northern clansmen.

Xante and Curos now prepared to visit the Hill of Tears where the five Dryadin had established their home. It was the first time

279

for many months that Xante had met any of her own people. Her attitude and her very existence had changed and she felt some fear of how they would perceive her. Although continued practice ensured that mind contact with Dromo was easily achieved, their communication was now formal, almost distant and there had long since ceased to be any warmth in their relationship. She had expected this but was now concerned that she might be estranged from others of her people.

The Dryadin had established one long, low hut on the leeward slope of the Hill of Tears. A strange, dark structure, it was raised up on short piles to allow circulation of air and freedom from damp. Surrounding it in small plots were a multiplicity of plants and seedlings which had been brought from S'lan and would be transplanted to the hill itself as spring progressed. Most surprising to Curos was a deep pond which had been dug out to trap some of the water which cascaded from a spring at the foot of the hill. The marshy ground created by the rain and the excavation was also dotted with plants, and the surface of the water rippled with the movement of small fish. As the five Dryadin came down the trodden path to meet them Curos pointed to the pond and asked Xante, 'Is it a fish farm?'

'No!' she laughed. 'It is for the F'gar. They have brought eggs of the Flying Guardians of S'lan with them.' Curos looked horrified. 'It will be safe enough, Curos, they will be but few. The pond will also act as a reservoir and allow us to grow some plants more rapidly.' Curos could only see a vision of hideous dragonflies carrying off lambs or children in their extended teeth.

The Dryadin were all dressed in the enveloping black trousers and tunics which Curos now only associated with Xante. From politeness, Curos dismounted and walked to meet the Dryads. Bowing low, he greeted them as esteemed friends and ambassadors to the land of Chaw.

The leading Dryad responded equally formally but continued, 'Your welcome on behalf of the people of Chaw is most generous, Zachaw Ca'lin Curos, particularly as the leaders of either the Military or Civilian Chaw Councils would be much angered if they learned of our presence.'

'Great men are often overbusy, Aalani,' said Curos with a smile as he recognised the deep, husky voice of the Dryad and his sharp humour. 'They wish only for results. I will not burden them with trivial details which they could not understand.'

'I had not thought this task suited to your noted talents, Aalani,' said Xante as she stepped forward to hug the assassin. 'Your presence was well concealed from me!'

'Ze Dryadi is as cautious as ever, Xante-Yani, or is it now Q'ren Xante? I fear I may have to show deference to my niece.' He hugged her back in a fatherly way. 'Our leader realises that some things may be kept from him and would have a Council member to act as his eyes and ears. I can take my turn with tending growing things, or digging ponds. I can also use other less honourable skills if need arises. Ze Dryadi believes it best to be wary of new friends until friendship is proven.'

The other Dryads had now uncovered their faces and Curos' gaze was drawn to a tall figure who stood with a shy, pregnant woman. He recognised the Dryad to be Xante's previous lover, Dromo, and watched Xante as her eyes met those which had once loved her. The tension between them was almost tangible, like a sinew stretched to the point of breaking, but still possessing a little of its former strength and power. Curos was now half-aware of flitting mind contacts between the Dryads as silent introductions were made. He, the momentarily excluded outsider, waited for the same to be rendered into words.

Xante touched Dromo's cheek in greeting, and even Curos felt his reaction. She repeated the action to Wylow, Dromo's wife, and then placed her hand on the woman's stomach to greet the unborn male child who could have been her own. The other Dryad couple, Okal and Hyli, were cautiously friendly to both Xante and Curos.

It was these two, however, who had led the push to recolonise the barren hillside. Curos' tentative congratulation on their progress, and questions on the type of tree being planted, unleashed a torrent of enthusiastic explanation. All pretence at formality was washed aside as he was swept first to the pond and then to every plain and crevice of the Hill to view the progress. Curos struggled to understand as Xante and the Dryad 'fanatics' exchanged views and explanations which left him bewildered. This was a side of Xante he had but rarely glimpsed, the true Xante-Yani who had been trained to use her vast skill in the service of growing things in the forest of Eternal S'lan. Hyli swept her hands towards the barren expanse of land to the north and west where the D'was plain was now shimmering with the new green growth of spring grass. Curos had been given an insight into the woman's vision of a new land where stately trees and clumped bushes would stabilise and enrich the soil.

Curos noticed that when Dromo spoke to Xante he smiled too widely and laughed too often. He wished to make an impression which she had declined to see but Curos was concerned that she might still retain some spark of love for this man. He considered Xante and Dromo in light of his own broken marriage with Hoelun; after that one emotional scene in Te Toldin, Hoelun had ceased to make any attempt to recover their marital relationship and they were now better friends than before. It was a selfish wish, but he hoped that Xante and Dromo would become completely estranged. Close by, Dromo's wife also watched the couple, her face a mixture of wretched sadness and anger.

Close by the Dryad camp was the small village which housed the Sekars who were being trained. While Xante remained to talk to her own people Curos descended to meet Lou Chi and Suzin. They were genuinely pleased to meet him, and Suzin's previous animosity had evaporated. Gron Fa was annoyed that Xante had prolonged her visit to the Dryad area instead of accompanying Curos to the village. He had established himself as the leader of the sekar village, making up for lack of sorcery talent with a new-found purpose and ability to organise. His humiliating lack of physical fitness in the Te Lok campaign had caused him to instigate a strict training schedule for himself and the other sekars. Without any true authority he had organised riding lessons and conscripted one of the Te Toldin household soldiers to give basic weapon training.

To Lou Chi and Suzin's obvious but restrained amusement he had convinced the other sekars that some distinguished uniform would be essential. Closely modelled on the Dryadin costume, his own was decorated with mystic gold symbols of sorcery which Gron Fa considered added to his prestige. He spoke openly of Xante as the Q'ren of Sorcery and used her name only in the most reverent of tones. As Curos toured the sekar village he

282

constantly reminded himself to beware the fanatic, particularly the religious fanatic who had found a new goddess to worship.

In addition to Gron Fa, Suzin and Chi there were now eleven others who had sought out the camp or been directed to it by Xante or Lou Chi. Most had brought their families, husband or wife and children – even one grandmother had struggled into Te Sekar, as it was now called, following her mature son.

Lou Chi confided to Curos. 'When Lady Xante called on all our energy to assist her in disabling the outlaws in Te Lok, it left Gron Fa totally exhausted, and I believe near to death. Instead of being outraged at the action, as I must confess Suzin and I were, Gron Fa considered it a great honour. The humble Gron Fa was called on to assist his new deity. He dreams only of making the ultimate sacrifice when Q'ren Xante will draw on all her sekars to provide energy to annihilate by fire the War-chaw. He instils the same idea into each new entrant to our cult, Lord Zachaw. It is dangerous. The men, as soon as they are touched by Lady Xante's mind-power, worship her as a goddess, almost as Freu herself. The women set her up as an idol, a beautiful pattern to be emulated.'

'Is there anything wrong in this?' asked Curos.

'Of itself, no, Lord Zachaw,' replied Suzin, 'but it is unnatural and could be corrupted. Men and women in this camp, sleeping in the same bed,' she blushed, 'both dream of the Q'ren. For the men it is "I would worship the Q'ren", for women it is "I would be as the Q'ren".' The thin, deceptively frail-looking woman who possessed great physical and mental strength looked Curos full in the face and continued, 'I am a plain woman, Zachaw, plain of face and slim of body. I admit to feeling an envy of the Lady Xante who has so much more than I. The only exceptional thing in my life is the love of my husband and the gift of a son.' Unconsciously she reached out to ruffle the boy's hair as he stood silently behind her. 'Even in envy I can recognise Xante's simplicity of purpose and her incredible power. For those who have neither love nor children and who, like Gron Fa, seek only contact with a goddess of power, Xante is a dangerous substitute for real life.'

'You must realise, Lord,' added Lou Chi, 'that many people such as we have a lonely life. Their skills, their insights or

283

abilities mark them out from other people. Subtle differences make it difficult to establish relationships. Some are incredibly lucky, as are Suzin and myself; others are destined to a life where no-one can make the contact they crave.'

'Like Gron Fa?'

'Like Gron Fa. The girl who kept his house and shared his bed in the village of Yellow Stones worshipped him, but without a spark of sorcery she could not meet his needs.'

Curos thought for a while, then said, 'In Te Sekar, Lou Chi, there will be many of your people. Will they not form friendships which will ease this ache?'

'Yes, that is my point, Lord. Some men and women would be able to ease this loneliness when they meet in Te Sekar, but not if Gron Fa overlays everything with the spectre of Q'ren Xante.'

Dromo had been able to understand Suzin's strange gift of invisibility. Other sekars were able to master the trick but never with the same perfection as the tall, thin woman. Despite this, Cloaking had become a routine exercise until five or six sekars could obscure the movement of quite large numbers of people.

Curos and Xante's return journey from the Hill of Tears to Te Toldin was silent with foreboding as each struggled with their own fears for the future. Only as they dismounted and handed their horses to the elderly groom did Curos speak.

'Xante, you are surrounded by an aura which glows like a red fire. I had thought your meeting with your own people would be an occasion for happiness.'

'It was until I spoke alone with Dromo.' She walked ahead for several paces before saying, 'He treats me like a child, Curos. He criticises my actions as if he were still my teacher. My power is now so much above his that I could hurl him into that new pond without any effort if I wanted.'

'Aalani does not disapprove of you.'

'Aalani does approve. He is a realist, yet he has some humanity. He has been an uncle to me all my life – he would excuse almost anything I did.'

'He is not a weak character.'

'No, I did not mean that. I have too great a respect for Aalani. It is just that Dromo angers me. I know he has a new wife and a child forming but we meant much to each other once and I had hoped we would at least meet as friends. Now he hates me and what I have become. He is so self-righteous, so confident. I could hurt him just to show him what hurt is.'

36

The now-decrepit coach of the counterfeit Noyan, Scribe Wou, and his mud-spattered escort finally arrived at Te Toldin. On the rain-softened roads progress for wheeled vehicles had been inexorably slow. Although the escort riders suspected that they had been followed for part of the journey, no threats had been made to the party and Wou's greatest danger had been unrelieved boredom. For several days the pragmatic and down-to-earth Wou had even attempted to compose what he recognised as abysmal poetry.

As Wou was explaining his uneventful progress to Curos a smaller, covered coach drawn by a single draft horse slithered along the narrow streets of G'tal. The horse's hoofs slipped and splashed in the rutted centre of the road which was flowing like a small mud-laden canal, swollen with water of week-long rains. The driver and the coachman were drenched and miserable while inside the two dry passengers were jolted from side to side as the wheels slipped yet again on the flagstones.

Admin Shekar Lotol, brother of Dortie, cursed the unnecessary precautions recommended by Curos, his brother-in-law, and the paranoid guardsman, Wan Abac. In this appalling weather a brisk ride on horseback and a change into dry clothing was preferable to being carted around like a feeble old man afraid of the rain. Across the carriage the studious clerk sat, head bowed as he cradled the ancient leather-covered scroll on his knees. *What a companion!* thought Lotol. *A man of one steadfast idea and no humour or conversation. I must ask Bhal Morag where more lively entertainment can be found.*

The horse stopped yet again and the coachman leapt down to explain that they had reached Lotol's rented house but the flagstones had been displaced by the storm. Admin Lotol would have to cover the last few paces on foot. In the remaining daylight Lotol could see all too clearly the cratered and flooded road. After the delay of the ride he would be wet-footed and rain-drenched all the same!

The coachman flipped down the hinged step, opened the door for them and advanced towards the heavy door of the house courtyard. The scribe jumped out with a shade more enthusiasm than Lotol could have mustered. As Lotol began to follow, he heard the driver shout a warning and saw the dejected coachman become transformed into action. The heavy cloak was thrown off and a short sword and dagger appeared in his hand.

Instantly he leapt towards two attackers who were advancing purposefully from the archway of the rented house. The scribe slid gleaming blades from either end of his scroll case and rushed to join the deadly combat. Lotol drew his own sword but the driver barred his way protectively. With outstretched arm and protective sword he stood as a human shield before the uncertain administrator.

The scribe plunged one dagger into an adversary and slashed viciously across the man's face with the other. A spear-butt felled the coachman as he slipped in the treacherous mud. Instead of pressing home his attack, the assassin stepped back and threw his javelin with unswerving venom. Untrained in combat, Lotol had no time to avoid the throw but was charged over by the driver.

Dazed and winded, Lotol tried desperately to move, cursing the driver's weight which held him down in the mud. The driver was babbling, blood running from his mouth, and he attempted to scream as Lotol rolled him away. A javelin was embedded the full depth of its pile into the man's side.

The assassin who had cast the javelin had now drawn his sword and was beating back Lotol's counterfeit scribe with a series of thrusts and cuts which would have earned praise from Wan Abac himself. Lotol groped in the muddy water for his sword and cursed his own lack of skill with the weapon. With a shout of triumph the assassin laid open the scribe's arm from wrist to elbow. In desperation Lotol hurled his sword, spinning it in a deadly flashing arc. With the quickness of a born swordsman the assassin moved aside and parried the unexpected attack. From the ground the injured coachman stretched up and stabbed at the assassin's thigh. Blood still pumped from the scribe's sword-arm as he attacked vengefully with a dagger, turning inside the wounded assassin's guard to stab at the stomach. With a spray of water Lotol arrived to deliver a stunning, knuckle-breaking blow to the neck.

In the fading light Lotol looked desperately at the dead and dying. He screamed for help and snatched up the sodden, mud-covered cloak discarded by the coachman. The scribe had sunk onto the flagstones, his feet lost in the water which was red with spilled blood. The coachman, like a primeval mud-coated spirit, his own face bruised and bleeding, was gripping his companion's arm in an attempt to stem the blood loss. With a skill learned in tending farm accidents, Lotol bound the gaping wound.

To his amazement the scribe laughed out loud at Lotol's concern. 'Fear not for me, Excellency, it takes more than a scratch to kill a guardsman of the 22nd T'sand. Men who can laugh in the face of sorcery will not die at the hands of gutter scum.'

'Gutter scum who nearly did for us, friend,' objected the sham coachman through bruised lips. 'That second man was a fighter indeed.'

'Victory is victory and we are alive! He will die at the block! Turn him over and let us see his face.'

Air and water bubbled from the assassin's mouth as the guardsman turned him over. Rain water and blood smothered his stomach and legs. He gasped and spat, his eyes opening and staring in disbelief as his stunned mind sought to understand what had happened.

'Yi Lin!' gasped the fake scribe. 'As I bleed, it is Ataman Yi Lin of the 35th T'sand. The Master Sword of Yec Min. Why, Ataman? Why do you attack your old companions in the street?'

'So you are also of the 35th T'sand. A scribe and a coachman! Now I recognise your face.' He grimaced with pain. 'Defeat is not so bad when it is at the hands of men I have trained. It was a sorry day when men who defied the barbarians were branded as cowards by commanders who sat safe in G'tal.' Tears ran down his face, mixing with the rain. 'I would not serve those who disbanded my T'sand; now I am forced to fight as an assassin and you to act as guards to a civilian. At least your charge is a man, he joined the fight.'

He swallowed hard as a spasm of pain gripped his stomach

and said, 'I am dying, friend. It was a good thrust. Young Wan Abac teaches you as Aki taught me. Abac has done well. I have watched his advancement with pride.'

'Help me bind his leg, guardsman,' whispered Lotol. 'It is too wet to stand here talking and he bleeds to death.'

'Why bind his wounds, Excellency? He will only go to the block. Let him die here and preserve the honour of the 35th T'sand.'

'No, that is not justice,' replied Lotol.

'Please, brother?' asked Yi Lin. 'A soldier's death as on the field of battle. As brothers of the old 35th T'sand, help me bury my shame.'

'No!' Lotol shouted as the counterfeit coachman picked up his dagger. It was too late, the dagger plunged down into Yi Lin. Through the left shoulder to the neck, it severed arteries and punctured the heart.

'That's the way with street scum who shame our city,' shouted a Watchman as he splashed up the street in answer to Lotol's call.

'Still your tongue, old man,' growled the scribe from where he sat, hunched in pain. The numbness of the wound had now gone and the pain had stripped him of his bravado. 'They who come late to the fight should not comment on the dead. Better you should run to K'tan Wan of the . . .'

'Leave messages and details to me, friend scribe,' Lotol silenced him as the heavy doors were belatedly opened by two terrified servants. 'I will arrange a surgeon for you and inform your commander.' He smiled dryly. 'He will know all of the truth you would wish him to know. You may conceal what you will. I know nothing of combat or regiments.'

289

37

Curos had been tempted to visit each of the N'gol clans in turn and organise the movement of tribesmen into the O'san region. This would have taken too long and made it impossible to keep in contact with events in the capital. He was therefore forced to rely on messengers sent to each of the main N'gol tribes but he feared that suspicion and enmity would prevent rapid, cohesive action.

His first success had been with the Sand Dragon and the White Dragon Clans of Western D'was. Curos was well known to both leaders and his mother, Turakina, had originated from the White Dragon Clan. They trusted Curos and were quick to seize the opportunity to expand into areas where there was new grazing for their herds and a chance of profit from the coming war. Nearly a fifth of each tribe – men, women, children and their herds – were preparing to depart on the long trek westward and then southward to occupy the southern areas of the O'san, moving in as the Chaw peasant farmers were displaced.

Pynar, the Headman of the White Dragon Clan, had known the O'san region well from the days when he had ridden with the Chaw cavalry T'sand. He had seen the opportunities and called together the headmen and elders of the groups who made up the White Dragon. He explained that there were areas of good grazing along the sluggish rivers which spread from the deep gorges descending from the Lune mountains. Well back from the mountain passes they would have good warning of any Warchaw attack and could move or fight as they pleased. To the south they would be protected by the impassable soft white sands of the Hajar which stretched to the foreshore of the ocean north of Xantu Province. To the north, the Topaz Wind and The Sand Dragon Clan would be camped along the waters of the disused grain canal. Only from the west could an attack come.

The Headman had agreed that only one-fifth of the White Dragon Clan should move into the O'san and that families should be drawn from each kuriyen. These were already chosen but there was a constant trickle of adventurous individuals who had left posts in the Chaw army to seek a place with the O'san party. It was therefore no surprise to Pynar when he heard that a party of N'gol, of no specific tribe, were approaching the kuriyen. Twenty or thirty people, well mounted with spare horses and pack animals – it appeared too well organised for the usual group of hotheads seeking a temporary home and a chance to encounter the Warchaw.

The leader of the party was a small, thick-set woman of about forty-six years who rode in the easy, economical style of one who could live in the saddle. The Lady Zachaw Turakina was returning to her people after nearly twenty-five years as the wife of one of Chaw's most powerful Noyans. Already her mind was clouded by one oppressive purpose: to revenge herself on those who had caused her husband's suicide, and in doing so to quit this life and seek reunion with him in the void of death. Beneath this blanket of hatred, old emotions and feelings scuttled like small insects, sometimes surfacing in moments of realisation, sometimes guiding her path in to a less fanatical course. With her rode twenty-two others who had cause to hate the Warchaw: men who had lost sons or brothers, women whose lives had been shattered by a loss which they could not accept. Like an evil breeze, the news of Lady Turakina's Death Wind had reached these people and just as softly as that breeze they had left their kuriyens to seek her out.

For Turakina there was a surge of emotion as she recognised the triple horse-hair standards of the White Dragon which had been planted at a gap in the ring of yerts. From the time she had left the Clan with Zachaw Pa'lin, she had always returned in his company – a free N'gol with her husband – and often with her proud, skilful, war-born son whom the people loved. Now she was nothing, a woman whose life had ended.

As she approached, she sensed the shock of the White Dragon N'gol in reaction to the dress and manner of her companions: white standards, white sashes and the blank faces of those who see nothing. Previously, kinspeople would have run out in greeting, horses showering up clouds of dust, voices shrieking the clan call and the names of Pa'lin and Turakina and Curos. In a daze she saw the same people, the same old friends, but her mind could not cut through or push aside the silken veil of sorrow which cut her off from them. She asked to speak formally to Pynar, the Headman, and noted their surprise – she was Pynar's niece and there was no need for her to ask to speak to him.

While other headmen were summoned, and those of the Clan who were close by gathered in a wide circle outside Pynar's tent, Turakina and her companions pitched their own small camp with silent efficiency. People stared openly and more than one spoke in awe of the sinister Death Wind.

Pynar was appalled at the death-like faces of the twenty men and two women who sat behind Turakina as she outlined her plan for a total war on the Westerners. She spoke well but he did not really listen, the words and the ideas were as old as the N'gol people and their resistance to order and civilisation. This sweeping, raiding war of destruction was made credible by the ideas Turakina had absorbed from the Chaw military. Phrases stuck in his mind – 'lure the cavalry out into the open plain', 'drive them from the water places', 'strike back down the passes into Corninstan' – it was so easy when there was no care for survival.

'Their numbers are few and their horses slow and heavy,' she was saying. 'We will avoid direct contact and use our bows to wear them away as the sand of the desert wears away the rocks.' It was madness, Pynar knew, but as he looked around he saw only shining eyes and enthusiasm. The young would be heroes with vast herds in a new open land; the middle-aged would have one last hour of glory and die honoured by rich children.

The glowing faces were looking at him, awaiting his approval as Turakina ended by saying, 'I have been away from my people for many years, but I have never ceased to be a daughter of the White Dragon. I visited often, and many of you here came to Te Toldin as young riders to learn reading, which the Chaw respects much. Free from the need to herd or to hunt, at Te Toldin you trained until you were better than any in Chaw or in any other clan. Pa'lin gave you much, now it is time to restore the honour of the N'gol and repay that debt.'

'I have no need to prove my courage or to speak of honour,'

292

said a tribesman, and Pynar was grateful for time to think. 'I fought in Corninstan and will wait until the Warchaw come into this land before I fight them again.'

'The Warchaw will kill our brothers and laugh at us as cowards!' replied another.

'The Clan is not ours,' said the elder. 'The Lore teaches us that the Clan stretches from the past to the future, we are only guardians now. If it is destroyed by some foolish act, where would the souls of our ancestors be born – into the homes of Chaw peasants?'

The arguments flew backwards and forwards and to Pynar's dismay there was a growing split between those for and against Turakina's plan. At last he spoke.

'No,' he said firmly, 'it is not to be. There is no need for the White Dragon Clan to become the Death Wind of Turakina. We are a living people, not seekers of revenge and death.'

'We are free people, we ride where we choose.'

'And I am Headman, chosen by you to guide us all. If the people do not accept my advice, choose another – but remember the Clan which reared you and supports you. All of you here have accepted that support and must, in honour, pay back that debt before you throw your lives away.'

'I have paid and paid more than enough,' growled Turakina. 'I have raised sons and served my clan, even if I lived far away.'

'We acknowledge our debt,' Pynar replied, 'but should young men die before they have given their wives children and added to the herds of their fathers? Should a woman leave before she has reared a child and taken her place to protect the kuriyen in war? You are not leader here, Turakina, and should not challenge the advice of the Headman and elders of your people.'

Pynar realised he had goaded the woman too far. Her eyes were locked on him with a fury and malice he had not believed possible. Silence descended except for the sound of the breeze and the animals. Turakina had come as a friend and a kinswoman and he had hardly noticed that her bow lay across her knee. The speed and venom of her arrows was legendary and he realised she would be able to draw and shoot before any could protect him. Pynar was not a great warrior, not particularly brave or wise. He had been chosen as Headman for his balance and good sense, and his knowledge and feel for the love of the people. He enjoyed the prestige it gave him and had thought the duties of little hardship. Now he faced death if he did not accept Turakina's plan which would destroy his people.

Turakina's vision was narrowed to Pynar's face. He had defied her, insulted her. Her mind was filled with the sequence of his death; one arrow, nock, draw up the bow and kill. She could take the White Dragon people and unleash them as one mighty Death Wind on the Westerners. But it was not right, he was her Headman, she must not split the people, must not break the Lore. He was speaking again.

'This is not right, Turakina,' his words echoed her thoughts. 'The Lore is clear and we do not fight each other. It is a good plan but not for a whole people. Those who would go with you must go but I cannot support you.'

The words filtered through to her and she realised the horror of what she had said and what she had nearly done. Her intention to invite any of the White Dragon Clan who so wished to join her Wind had become twisted and evilly distorted in her mind even as she spoke. Pynar's words of caution had brought her to contemplate killing him, her Headman, her kinsman. She bowed to him in the manner of the Chaw. She would never be able to explain or apologise for what she had nearly done.

'I hear your words, Pynar, and accept the decision of my Headman. I seek only leave to rest here for one night and then I and any who will ride with me will go.'

From beside the nearest yert, Pynar's eldest son lowered his bow and trembled. Pynar alone detected the movement and felt a wave of affection for his son, a dutiful son. He was sure Turakina was mad, quite mad. That night he and the other elders toured the yerts, speaking of duty to the Clan and promising normal war to those who sought vengeance or glory. Despite his efforts, and a night of cool reflection, Turakina's band had grown in size when she left at dawn. There had been no words and Pynar watched her go with sadness. He was sure that none of her Death Wind – including the four men and two women who had joined her – would return.

By the time Curos' messengers reacted, the clans of the central D'was – the N'gol of the Silver Fox, the Blue Wolf and the Grey

Jackal – had become aware of the movement of the elements of the Dragon Clans and were also anxious to seize any new territory in the O'san. Their combined leader, Konkurate of the Blue Wolf, quickly negotiated safe passage for large groups of tribesmen through the Dragon Clans' grazing land and began the migration of his people. He pretended to accept that the occupation of the O'san was temporary, but believed that once the N'gol had seized the land it would be difficult for anyone to reclaim it. Similarly to the Dragon Clans, he sent complete family units, ostensibly to establish a balanced presence, but saw it more as a colonisation than a military force. The rains in the D'was had been good over several years and the herds were increasing. The departure of a fifth of his people even for a few years would relieve the pressure on the grazing.

The next development was most unexpected: the clans of the far east, whose lands bordered the ocean, combined to despatch a powerful force to North O'san. The Rainbow Clan and the Golden Horde had been concerned that they would not be included in the coming Great War. Their warriors had broken every horse they could ride or steal in a long dash across the continent. They called themselves the Sunrise Horde and were determined to take their share of any honour or plunder which the war offered, particularly the mighty Warchaw horses.

Sechen, their leader, had sent a message to Curos saying. 'Let the Warchaw know that we of the Eastern N'gol fear them not. Our Sunrise Horde races across the length of the world to give them battle.'

Curos knew little of these people. Their warfare was based on fanatical, almost fatalistic, bravery in which hand-to-hand combat was essential and the bow hardly used. He feared they would suffer badly if pitted against the heavier Warchaw cavalry.

One clan leader, Ongul of the Night Dragon, had visited Te Toldin in person, with his son, Yesugei and a small group of riders, to speak with Curos. The N'gol were, Curos believed, as anxious to speak with Aalani-Galni and the Dryads at the Hill of Tears as they were to speak with him. The Night Dragon had strong, if secret, links with the Dryadin and Aalani's poisons were often applied to their weapons. Ongul explained to Curos that his whole clan was moving westward into an area of the

O'san chosen by their advance scouts. The Night Dragon had chosen a large, fertile area at the head of the valley which led deep into the central Lune mountains. It was good grazing but none felt it prudent to dispute its possession with the entire Night Dragon Clan.

'Your people take a great risk, Ongul,' Curos had said, 'for the Warchaw are deadly in war and your whole clan could be destroyed.'

'The Night Dragon are a small people, Lord Curos, we cannot be divided. Either we send a small band of thirty men or our whole clan moves to the O'san. Despite the slightly better rains of late, ours is a dry, arid land and our numbers always decline. We have decided to stake all on one last throw – we have little to lose. Only a few warriors will remain to escort and guide the traders and merchants who seek the Forest People.'

'Are the other clans afraid that if they leave their ancestral lands then the Chaw farmers or the Dryadin from the north will take their place?' suggested Xante.

'We have no fear of the Dryadin,' said Yesugei, Ongul's son. 'The dark go to the dark and we have helped the Dryads trade with Untin for generations.' He bowed slightly to Xante. 'Any who take our land will live a hard life there until we return, and then will die a hard death.'

'It is true our people are allies,' said Xante, 'and I know that you have visited the Eternal Forest many times, seeking for what cannot be yours despite all your passion for a Dryad woman, Yesugei. The Dryadin will watch over your land and under their care, and without the horse herds, much may be done.'

Ongul and Yesugei stayed only one night in Te Toldin before leaving to join the Clan as it moved westward.

'The Night Dragon are brave people,Curos, and our friends,' said Xante. 'The Dryadin have counselled them against this venture – surely a war band would be enough?'

'All clans move as family groups on long journeys,' said Curos, 'it is an extension of their nomadic life. No woman wants her husband to return with a female slave, or worse, decide to stay with a new woman in a new land without her, so she goes with him and tends the herds and fights as necessary. The kuriyens of the N'gol will become like moving fortresses in the desert.

The Night Dragon Clan seems more closely knit still, like one large family. I agree with your concern, but they will not join open warfare; by day they vanish, at night they hunt. Their presence in the Valley of the River's Tears will deny it to any Warchaw raiding party and the risk to them should be low.'

'They have chosen a place called the Valley of Tears?' asked Xante. 'I hope it is not their tears that are shed.'

38

Bhal Morag arrived late one afternoon with letters and messages for Curos.

He read of the attempt to murder Dortie's brother, Shekar Lotol, which had been thwarted only by Wan Abac's guardsman. Lotol himself wrote of the lack of rain which had fallen in the southern provinces. He saw grave risk of famine in the south, but already the peasants from the O'san were being driven in that direction. It was too late to divert them but food would be even more scarce. He had written to Makran explaining the need for the northern provinces to grow the maximum amount of staple food to aid the south.

'Already his request cannot be filled,' Makran said sadly. 'It is too late to rip up cash crops and plant grain, even if the provincial councils would agree to give instruction.'

Lin Sri had intensified his surveillance of Noyan Qunin and had acquired by devious means several letters destined for persons in Corninstan. He feared the Warchaw had already been warned of Curos' plans. Bhal Morag also confided that two of Qunin's more capable followers had been robbed and murdered in the streets of G'tal. After the attacks on Curos and Lotol, Wan Abac had reacted predictably and a grim feud was developing in G'tal.

There was also a very ornate and formal letter, jointly penned by Lin Sri and Chou Yuel, Heolun's older brother, announcing the end of Curos' marriage. Sudden as this final agreement was there was more to come. In a private letter to Curos, Hoelun informed him of her intention to remarry immediately – to Chalak Konn.

Curos was almost speechless with anger, anger that was fanned by Xante's and Bhal Morag's amusement. Back in G'tal he, Xante, Konn, Morag and Abac had sometimes dined at his city mansion, occasions where they could act freely while Hoelun, the perfect hostess, supervised the continual flow of food and drink. Often Chalak Konn had begged to be excused part way through the evening. Khol Dalgan and Bhal Morag had then seen free to voice their opinions on their companion and his suitability for the army. Bitterly, Curos now recalled one such occasion.

'I have said before,' Khol Dalgan had stated, 'much as I like Konn, he has no fire and no soul for a fighting man. He should have been a civil servant or a gentleman.'

'He is a younger son, and until the campaign in the forest where he first met the Lady Xante,' Morag had bowed to Xante with just a hint of a smile, 'he intended to spend only two years in the army for experience before leaving for the civil service. He takes no pleasure in the company of women or men.'

Xante and Abac had disagreed. 'He rides as well as you, Morag, and shoots the bow with skill,' Abac had said. 'He always gives me a good bout with the sword. Not a champion, but an adequate performance.'

'And do not measure a man's interest in women by his words or his visits to whore houses.' Xante had smiled. 'The music of the "Falling Raindrop" gives ample time for a man to contemplate his mistress' beauty as she plays.'

The words now took on a more significant meaning. 'You knew all of this?' Curos asked Xante angrily. 'How long?'

'I did start to mention it before, several times,' she smiled, 'but you seemed uninterested. Do not begrudge her happiness, Curos.'

'When will they marry?' he asked Morag.

'Immediately. Konn would have waited the full three months deemed by custom but Hoelun believed this unnecessary due to the reasons for the divorce. Since the reason for the divorce was that there could be no child expected from the previous marriage,' added Xante with arch innocence.

Despite the concerns from the south and his amazement at Hoelun's plans to marry, uppermost in Curos' mind was the treachery of Noyan Qunin and how best to counter it. Bhal Morag had informed him that after the attack on Shekar Lotol and Wan's counter on Qunin's men, Qunin himself had left G'tal for his estate in the south-western province of Xantu. This left the

299

capital as a site for war by proxy with both protagonists in their country estates safe from harm or blame. With the added evidence obtained by Lin Sri, Curos was now convinced of Qunin's links with the Warchaw.

In the secluded oasis of Dryadin culture at the Hill of Tears Curos explained the problems to Aalani-Galni, as the leader of the Dryadin in Te Toldin. He dealt factually with Qunin's threats to the forest and the lack of any simple solution to this mutual danger.

'I could possibly use Topaz Wind to destroy Qunin's estate,' he suggested, 'but even if it succeeded, my part in the affair would soon be known and the nation would be split into two factions. That would serve our enemy's purpose equally as well as Qunin himself.'

'Xante's sorcery could be effective?'

'Possibly, but Qunin's agent did have a talisman of the western sorcerers. If Qunin had the same, Xante's power would be revealed. There is also the possibility that people in Chaw would turn against her.'

'Natural death by illness seems to be required,' Aalani smiled evilly. 'I have solved similar problems when certain Chaw merchants and officials attempted to block trade between your city of Untin and the Dryadin. We will need to give the matter serious thought.'

Curos was able to speak to Aalani as if to a friend but Xante's discussions with Dromo were far from easy. Despite her intentions, Xante found herself becoming increasingly annoyed and then angry at the man's unfriendly, self-satisfied manner. Even her congratulation at his understanding of Suzin's Cloaking technique had been brushed aside with an air approaching arrogance. And now she sat in anger and disbelief, unsure of how to proceed. She had hoped to remain at least on friendly terms with Dromo and had made every effort to include his wife, Wylow, in that friendship. Instead they regarded her as an outsider, as if contaminated by the world outside S'lan. The other Dryads, Okal and Hyli, treated her with respect but they showed little interest in her or her work.

She became aware of Dromo's voice saying, 'Do my words now have little meaning, Xante?'

'I am sorry, Dromo, I fear my attention wandered. I had expected too much from this meeting with my own people and disappointment does not help my concentration. My days in S'lan now seem long ago.'

'You have grown away?'

'Perhaps, and we too have grown apart like branches of a tree which once started from a single point.' The attempted smile was very brief.

'No, it is you who have changed. Your whole nature seems to have become violent, aggressive. I could not believe you would kill another person, Xante, even a Chaw assassin.'

'I have explained that to you before, Dromo. Although my actions should need no explanation. What would you have done?'

'There could have been defensive techniques for one of your power,' he said, stressing the last word. 'You grow to be like the Noyan Zachaw who believes killing answers all problems.'

You are jealous of my power and of my friendship with Curos, she thought bitterly but she kept these thoughts closely guarded from Dromo. 'You saw only what you wished to see, Dromo, when we were together. My nature has always been the same. Some facets were not needed in S'lan the peaceful.'

'Anger is never needed,' he retorted loftily. 'For a H'tao there are other ways.'

'Possibly, but H'tao does not win wars; it did not protect the Dryadin who were here,' she indicated the Hill of Tears, 'and it will not protect S'lan the Eternal.'

'You must attempt to resist this violence within you, Xante,' Dromo pressed on. 'You must give up the hideous weapons you carry which can only kill.'

'When I draw a weapon, prepared for me by Aalani, it is because all else has failed. I cannot risk attempting to wound or restrain. The arrows I carry now are also poisoned.'

'You are not a hunter or an assassin, Xante. You are a sorceress whom I have taught.'

There was another silence before Dromo burst out angrily, 'It grieves me that we should argue in this way. I wish I could help you more but you have other friends.' He reached into his jacket for a long length of thin chain. It was dull silver in colour and

301

although as long as Dromo's arm it was light and fine, almost as if fashioned to support a pendant or medallion. 'This was given to me for my protection, Xante. It will bind an attacker, even the strongest. Stand up and I will demonstrate.'

'Yes, teacher Dromo,' she replied sarcastically, rising to her feet.

Dromo balanced the chain in his hand and seemed lost in thought for a moment before he swung the chain at Xante's ankles. As if possessing a life of their own, the fine, steely links spread out in flight and then wrapped around her legs in an imprisoning bond.

'It is controlled by mind power, which I am sure you can master easily,' Dromo stated. 'A useful alternative to the dagger!'

'But slow as you use it, Dromo, too slow. Remove it!'

'Ask more civilly, Xante!' He tightened the grip of the chain.

'Release your toy, Dromo. This is too childish.'

'I too have a little power, Queen of Sorcery.'

'Yes, but too little,' Xante shouted. The chain unwound and flashed towards Dromo with glittering speed. Before he could react it encircled his chest in a grip which drove the breath from his lungs and threw him backwards.

Aalani dashed from where he was talking to Curos towards the sudden disturbance which assailed his mind. Curos followed and saw Xante standing over Dromo, the air sparkling with violent energy. Instantly Aalani was halted as if by a hidden wall. Invisible tendrils lashed out, seeking a grip on his mind. Despite the shock he reacted calmly, feeling his way into the barrier, extending pacifying thoughts, seeking to reach Dromo, undetected by Xante's anger. Behind Aalani, Curos had also stopped but the Topaz glowed in sympathetic understanding with Xante's defences as if remembering Aalani's attempt on Curos' life. The barrier disappeared, the energy vanished and Dromo sucked at the life-giving air in a sickening gasp. Xante attempted to help him to his feet but he shook her off angrily, striding away without a word.

'I am sorry, Aalani, truly I am. In my anger with Dromo I set my defences to react at any attack. I meant you no harm.'

'Most impressive,' replied the assassin with a mixture of

humour and respect. 'If you and Dromo had remained together in S'lan it would have been a stormy pairing.'

'He has become insufferable! So pompous and conceited with his virtues!'

'And perhaps you hoped too hard to recapture what is no longer there, Xante. Dromo may be less than satisfied with his life,' Curos interjected.

'I believe you said as much before, Lord Zachaw, and as then it is not your place to speak on such matters.'

They stood in embarrassed silence until Xante said, 'I have behaved as a girl when there is no place for such feelings. We have our own tasks and our own duty.' She picked up the chain and knotted it loosely around her waist. 'Cunning, although I doubt it will be an effective weapon. Dromo meant well in giving it and I will take it. If nothing else, it will remind me that I am tied to my new life as he is tied to his.'

'Now!' she said with a new spirit. 'Enough of my stupidities. What have the illustrious Noyan and esteemed assassin concluded from their long discussion?'

'Little of practical use, Xante,' replied Aalani, casually resting his arm on Xante's shoulder as they walked away from the village towards the Hill. 'I fear Dromo will disapprove, but we have decided that we must hasten Noyan Qunin along his cycle of life and death.'

'May this violent person ask how?'

'You may ask,' answered Curos. 'But for once I have no answer. While I lead my nomad army into the O'san I hope that Aalani will discover a solution.'

'For that reason,' said Aalani gently, 'we require you to transfer all the information Curos has on the Noyan Qunin from his mind to mine. Looks, aura, habits, details of Qunin's mansion in G'tal, his estate in Xantu, anything which could aid me or one of my people.'

Xante pulled a face of mock horror as she regained some of her humour. 'What you ask is not easy, my uncle. Looking into a mind like Curos' is not easy, even when he presents the information. It is like seeking in a nest of worms when one probes his devious thoughts. Seriously, I need to be calm and prepared.'

303

'Were you honest, you would say you fear to reveal too much of yourself,' laughed Aalani. 'Tomorrow will be soon enough.'

As they walked along they approached the Dryads' miniature lake which was now well stocked with small fish and numerous other water animals. Curos peered in, searching for any sign of predatory dragonfly nymphs.

'I truly hope the Dryads will control these horrific creatures that breed here,' he remarked.

'They are no danger, really, Curos,' Xante said and then hesitated before saying. 'Dromo did have some news today which will heighten your fears of our F'gar. But it will also relieve your concern over the Warchaw spy.'

'The N'gol and that villain Akab seek him still. Ongul, the leader of the Night Dragon Clan, assures me the spy has not escaped to the West, but he has not been found.'

'I am afraid he has, Curos. In the forest. We believe he entered S'lan in an attempt to bypass the Night Dragon.'

'And?'

'Some of our folk on the south border of Eternal S'lan felt a warning from the F'gar and rushed to the place indicated. The Warchaw had tried to fight the Flying Guardians with his sword and had killed two before they destroyed him.'

'If he had remained still or submissive he would have lived,' added Aalani.

'I find that hard to believe.'

'It is true. It seems that our hunter, Akab, was close behind the spy. Although they were in a frenzy and actually devouring the Warchaw the F'gar did not attack Akab. When the Dryadin arrived they found him backed up against a tree, petrified with fear as the F'gar circled around him.'

'For once I feel sympathy with the rogue,' Curos commented. 'How long had he been "treed"?'

'Less than half a day,' Xante smiled, 'and all that time he held my gold coin – remember I gave him two in the D'was. He held it to act as a talisman against the evils of the forest.'

'So our Warchaw spy is dead,' said Curos. 'A good omen! Qunin believes you are a fraud, Xante, and the Warchaw have learned nothing from their Imrani assassin in G'tal or their spies in the D'was. They know nothing of our Queen of Sorcery or her trained band of sekars.'

'But Lord Zachaw, they will know by now who is the Warrior King in Chaw,' said Aalani. 'If they suspect no Queen in play they will attack the King relentlessly.'

'Then our assassin's brain will need to find an answer quickly before they succeed.'

'There has been a change,' said Xante quietly. 'Now the King and the Queen stand or fall as one. They have both cut free from the distractions of their personal lives. At all times they must be together, one protecting the other.'

39

The open plain of Western D'was opened out before Bhal Morag as he followed the Great Northern Road towards the distant O'san. To his right small occasional smudges appeared to be moving over the land as it glistened a brilliant green from the spring grass: groups of the Sand Dragon Clan migrating south with their herds and their families in a new cycle of nomadic life. Slightly to his left, and more than a day's ride ahead, was the provincial town of Be Kin Kar Small River where he would wait for Curos and Xante and collect a small party of local army horsemen who had been released from the 9th T'sand for duty in the O'san.

His only companions were an escort of four soldiers and one of Xante's more junior sekars who had been recruited from Sunil province. A remarkably quick and able girl of eighteen, she was however both overawed by Bhal Morag and very untrusting of the escort soldiers. Morag's expectation of lively conversation and a flirtation as mild or serious as the girl could wish had foundered under shy, downcast eyelids and stammered sentences. The girl's very name Li Lue lacked any sense of vitality! The vast, sweeping landscape, open sky and near-solitude were not to Morag's taste. Austere army life was tolerable, but best kept to short periods of time interspersed with the not-too-civilised pleasures of civilisation. He craved for company, conversation and amusement even to the limited extent which a town like Be Kin Kar could provide.

While Bhal Morag endured the monotony of his journey, another equally effective commander was exalting in the thrill of his first victory since the battle of the Corninstan Road. Wilff of Arren and forty picked men with spare horses, food and weapons were speeding eastward down from the pass over the Lune mountains onto the Northern Trade Route. The break through the pass had been a masterly feat of arms which had not required any assistance from the Wizard.

It had been explained to Wilff that the Chaw people had discovered a leader of note who threatened to organise the vast population into a mighty army. Like many successful soldiers, he regarded all defeated enemies with contempt, particularly the small 'Monkey Men' of Chaw, and thought it unlikely that a new leader could pose a threat. The superior strength and skill of the Warchaw, coupled with judicious use of sorcery to balance the disparity in numbers, was sufficient to defeat any Chaw army. Even so, he was delighted to be given the chance to lead this raid deep into enemy territory.

The existence of a Chaw spy, a Noyan Qunin who had supplied reliable maps and troop dispositions, further pointed to the corrupt dissipation of the Chaw civilisation. Using the Chaw maps and other information, a large party of footmen had been able to climb over minor passes in the Lune mountains to outflank the Chaw army camped across the brow of the main trade route. With them had gone Wizard Valanus, a mighty fighter as well as a potent sorcerer, but his magic powers had not been needed. Valanus' only contribution had been to send a blue firebolt high into the air as a signal for Wilff's cavalry to attack. The Chaw had formed up in a soldierly fashion but the surprise volley of arrows from the hidden archers crippled their left flank. As the Western swordsmen had charged out of the ambush, Wilff had hurled his knights at the Chaw centre.

Surprise had been complete and the shock of that one charge had been sufficient to break the Chaw infantry. Keeping in tight order, Wilff had maintained his momentum to smash through the Chaw cavalry who were in support.

After such a quick, decisive victory it was tempting to turn and annihilate the pathetic Chaw who offered so little resistance but that was not in Wilff's instructions. He had left Valanus and the main force of men and started his own headlong dash into enemy land with a small detachment of men. His purpose was simply to reach some barbarically named estate, many days' journey eastward, and to destroy all the people of rank and as many tree-dwellers as possible. His order contained both names and descriptions of important individuals but he could neither speak the language nor distinguish between the flat, featureless Chaw faces.

So far he had made two diversions to the south of the Trade Road to destroy minor villages and give a false impression of a raid. Each time, however, the detachment had returned to the main route and after changing horses, continued toward the objective. It was essential to rest the powerful war-horses as much as possible and to rely on captured steeds for basic transport. An added triumph had been the massacre of a caravan of merchants carrying luxury goods – a fortune in gold and gemstones protected only by five lightly armed guards. Each Warchaw raider was now rich – an incentive for survival when they turned north after they had destroyed this War Lord and his estate. Of all the Chaw forces, the nomadic northern bowmen were the only real threat to Wilff's mobile force but it was most unlikely that they could be sufficiently alerted to hinder his return.

Quite unaware of Wilff of Arren's progress, Bhal Morag entered the Be Kin Kar garrison to an enthusiastic welcome from the senior K'tan of the 9th T'sand who commanded the small force. The frail-looking Li Lue was immediately whisked away by the K'tan's wife in a flurry of over-concern which amused and relieved Morag. Li Lue rode her horse as well as any man, but Morag was pleased to see her drawn into the protective woman's house.

After a hot bath followed by a simple meal with the two K'tans of the 9th who were stationed in Be Kin Kar, Bhal Morag realised that the men were bored with the town and each other's company to an extent that any visitor was a heaven-sent diversion. As he planned the night's entertainment for himself and his two accomplices, Bhal Morag was still ignorant that less than a day's ride away Wilff of Arren was drinking sparingly of excellent looted wine and congratulating himself on his success so far.

Bhal Morag's dreams of debauchery were soon shattered by the arrival of a desperate Arrow Rider. Warnings from the commander at the mountain pass had been sent to Untin, and to all the minor towns of the province. The rider himself had barely escaped alive when a staging post had been attacked. He was now able to add his own graphic account of the Warchaw to that of the message he carried.

At first Morag considered that the town of Be Kin Kar itself was in danger but by the time Li Lue had been summoned he had realised the purpose of the raid. The Warchaw were too few to destroy even small towns or to terrorise the countryside. They were aimed at one strategic objective and that could only be Te Toldin. To destroy the mountain garrison, to strike fear into the province or to gain intelligence of the Chaw land and its defences were mere secondary benefits. Only the removal of a key figure such as Curos or the destruction of the Dryad enclave could warrant such an effort and risk.

'Ataman Sekar Li Lue,' he said to the girl. 'You appreciate the gravity of this threat. You must contact Madam Xante and warn the Noyan.'

'I am unable,' replied Li Lue in a feeble voice, her head bowed. 'I can only converse with the Q'ren when she addresses me herself. I have not the ability to make contact.'

'The correct form of address is Madam Xante,' Morag retorted with near despair. 'You had best go into a darkened room and balance an apple on your head or a candle in your navel or whatever you sekars do, until you can! Fail this and you will be back in Sunil and married off to some pig farmer who needs your dowry.'

'My intended husband died fighting in Corninstan,' snapped Li Lue with unexpected spirit. 'And I am sure Q'ren Xante will easily destroy these savages if they approach Te Toldin.'

'Not if she is surprised before she can act,' said Morag. 'All power is limited and this is a serious threat. A Warchaw sorcerer may ride with the party and even if that is not the case, Noyan Zachaw will not wish to advertise the secret strength we are building at the Hill Of Tears.'

'I am sorry, K'tan Bhal. I will depart and attempt to make a warning to the Q'ren.' Li Lue turned to leave, the sudden flash of vitality expended.

'The correct form of address is Madam Xante,' Bhal Morag reiterated. Now there was a hint of sympathy in his voice. 'There are no Queens in Chaw. You were sent with me because of your skill, Li Lue. I am sure you will succeed.'

It was necessary to give a brief explanation of the role of the sekar to the two bemused K'tans. Bhal Morag asked them to bring a map of the region and began charting the route of the barbarian raiders. The open plains and the few forces at his disposal would make it difficult to block their progress. As he explained his dilemma, the younger of the two 9th T'sand K'tans pointed to an area of high land on the map.

'This ridge is covered with broken rock,' he explained. 'The North Road twists through the hills here. There are several villages clustered around the springs at the foot of the ridge.'

'How wide is this pass?' asked Bhal Morag.

'It is too open to be called a pass,' said the other officer, 'but it would funnel the raiders into a known area unless they want to ride their horses over these hills.'

'Good. We can evacuate the villagers for their own safety and station them along these hills to appear as a defensive force. I need scouts out on the road and will leave one hundred T'sand foot-soldiers and the militia in the town. We will camp the rest of your footmen here in the pass with your fifty horsemen on each wing.'

'Odds of five to one at least!' The elder K'tan smiled. 'I doubt they will attack when they see our strength.'

'They will attack and attempt to break through,' replied Bhal Morag, still studying the map. 'Your men have never fought a war. These Warchaw will be picked horsemen, chosen for a vital task. On this wide front they will have a chance to use their disciplined charge and heavy horses to break our line. I will need a mobile reserve behind the foot.'

'It will take our footmen two days to reach this pass,' the K'tan pointed out, 'and then they will need rest before they can fight.'

'Then we must commandeer carts for men and supplies and make all haste. Noyan Zachaw has few soldiers to protect Te Toldin.'

Li Lue burst into the room, flushed with excited success. She stopped in mid-stride and composed her face into a passive mask as the men looked up.

'I have contacted the Lady Xante,' she reported, 'and have explained the disposition of the enemy. She will consult with Curos, sorry, Noyan Zachaw, before sending new instructions.'

'Please look at this map, Ataman Li.' Bhal Morag smiled. 'And visualise the troop dispositions I plan. Relay them to Madam Xante and explain that I desperately need good horsemen to act as a mobile force.'

With the use of every horse, cart and carriage which could be seized it was still the evening of the second day before the bulk of the foot-soldiers reached the wide, flat col in the low ridge of hills. By that time the surrounding villages were deserted, the herdsmen and farmers camped high on the ridges for their own safety and to deter the raiders.

Curos had used Xante and Li Lue to pass his agreement with Bhal Morag's plan and had indicated that the Death Wind commanded by Turakina was not far off to the north. Because the Death Wind had no sekar attached to them Bhal Morag was forced to despatch a messenger whom he hoped would make contact. At the same time the scouts from the 9th T'sand in Be Kin Kar spied on the Warchaw raiders and confirmed their progress along the North Road. Two small, unsuspecting Sand Dragon family groups had been massacred before they could be warned but there were no other diversionary raids.

It was an intense relief for Bhal Morag when Turakina led the Death Wind band into the improvised camp. They were a silent, dour-faced group who rode with purposeful, close-knit precision and confidence of purpose. Each rider wore a white sash of mourning bearing the name of the person they had vowed to avenge. While her small force rapidly set up camp, Turakina sought out Bhal Morag to ask what role had been assigned to her command. She neither questioned his plan nor offered any advice but seemed withdrawn, almost remote and indifferent. As she returned to her own people Bhal Morag watched her retreating figure with a measure of disappointment; even a tacit agreement to his strategy by a woman who was so experienced in N'gol warfare would have been reassuring.

The desert night fell quickly, leaving Bhal Morag sitting under the brilliant star-studded sky gazing into the void of the bowl of heaven and racked with indecision. The two K'tans from the 9th

311

T'sand were with their own men, leaving him to consider and reconsider his plan.

'May I join you, Excellency?' asked Li Lue timidly from where she stood unnoticed. He indicated a cushion and without thinking poured tea into one of the spare cups.

'Thank you.' Li Lue bowed as she accepted the hot drink and sat down, hugging her knees to her chest. 'I have not been close to a battle before,' she explained nervously. 'I have seen several bandit raids but never a battle.'

'I am quite the same,' he confessed. 'Fighting a dozen ill-disciplined bandits is not the same as facing a fully trained Warchaw raiding party. We will all learn more about ourselves tomorrow.'

'Do you wish me to fight?' the girl asked hesitantly. 'I often travelled with my father's merchant caravan and can use the short scimitar.'

Morag glanced at the small but razor-sharp sword which was little larger than a long, curved dagger. The thought of the frail Li Lue attempting to trade blows with a Warchaw swordsman made his blood run cold. Some way off one of Turakina's N'gols started to sing in an eerie wailing chant the 'Song of the Dead'.

'No.' Bhal Morag shook himself. 'You will stay back with me and the small reserve of T'sand cavalry. If I enter the fight you will wait to receive any message from Lady Xante. Sekars must protect themselves, but it is not their role to fight.' A second singer from Turakina's band had taken up the song, a deeper, mellower voice which gave added resonance to the grief expressed.

'They prepare to die.' The girl shuddered. 'They all have the sickness of spirit which makes them seek death and they have great courage.'

'Chaw does not need this wish for death,' snapped Bhal Morag, echoing Curos' sentiments. 'A soldier needs to have the desire to live. His duty is to kill the enemy, not be killed.' He moved his position to allow the girl to lean against him and gained as much from the physical comfort as she did. For once in his adult life, Morag was not moved to attempt any amorous advance.

At dawn the camp was roused as the scouts arrived to report that the Warchaw would reach the pass before midday. Men checked weapons and equipment as they moved into their positions. Horses were fed, saddles and harnesses adjusted and readjusted. On all sides a tangible air of fear developed as men untried in battle waited for the arrival of the foe.

The Death Wind, in contrast, were quite composed and tranquil. All fear, all doubt, seemed to have been exorcised by their ritual of the night. Like religious zealots awaiting a solemn ceremony, they moved as if in a dream, many actually smiling in expectation. When Bhal Morag spoke to Turakina it was as if her spirit had already partially departed. Her smile for once showed the dazzling beauty of Turakina, the young woman of the White Dragon Clan, who had enchanted Pa'lin Zachaw.

The enemy column came into sight and halted in indecision as its leader observed the Chaw force arrayed before him. Bhal Morag looked again at his own men: the block of infantry flanked on each side by cavalry, his mobile reserves of T'sand horsemen and the Death Wind. He imagined the thoughts of the Warchaw commander. Should he attempt a breakthrough or try to ride up over the low hills to left or right? Should he charge the foot or the horse who opposed him?

'K'tan Bhal?' came Li Lue's voice.

'Yes?'

'Would it be worth the effort of using our carts and carriages as a barricade before the footmen? They seem quite nervous.'

Bhal Morag cursed himself for not thinking of this before. 'Yes, Li Lue, but we will have our barricade behind the footmen. If the Warchaw break through they will be slowed and that will give us time to close in around them.'

By the time the wall of carts and carriages had been dragged into position, the Warchaw were in clear view. Each man had changed mounts and now rode one of the large, powerful warhorses. They advanced in a small, dense group, less than fifty men against Bhal Morag's near-three hundred. Even so, the foot-soldiers slowly inched back unbidden until they could shelter behind the protective wall.

'He will not charge us now,' thought Bhal Morag. 'He will try to detour up over the hills or turn back.' He looked up at the

313

ridges which were lined with local peasants and farmers. A thin screen, but sufficient to hold an attack until help arrived from the main force in the pass. The Warchaw commander would know he must keep his force tightly together if he was to have any hope of success.

'They are turning back?' asked Li Lue from beside Bhal Morag.

He squinted into the distance, trying to resolve the detail. 'Possibly. No I see, they are preparing to attack.' This much was now evident to the footmen of the 9th T'sand who despite their orders were slowly retreating further back behind the line of upturned carts and carriages. Bhal Morag positioned his own small force behind the right cavalry wing and Turakina's smiling death-seekers behind the left.

Already the Warchaw were advancing, working the huge war-horses up in speed from a walk to an earth-pounding run. The sound of their hoofs on the hard, rocky earth was like rolling thunder to the quivering Chaw T'sand soldiers. The K'tan was shouting orders but the men were inching back. The packed wedge of horsemen began to swing away from the centre line towards the Chaw left, long lances levelled, until the horses were at full gallop. The Chaw cavalry should have been charging but it was all the commander could do to keep them at their station. A few ineffectual arrows flew out from the Chaw ranks, shot too soon and too weakly. Bhal Morag was scarcely able to breathe.

The Warchaw lancers smashed into the Chaw line where the infantry and cavalry forces joined. Speared, sabred or thrown down bodily, men and horses screamed and disappeared under the weight of the devastating onslaught. The heavy Warchaw horses did not flinch from using their own bulk to clear a path. With no check in speed and no significant loss, the Warchaw had broken through. Their discarded pack-horses milled in confusion before following.

The Death Wind's fanatical horsemen raced to meet the War-chaw. As Bhal Morag waited for the inevitable outcome of the collision, the first rank shot their bows and wheeled away out of danger and left the second rank a clear passage. Several heavy horses fell, others slowed as riders were hit. The Warchaw opened out their line to guard against a similar attack but instead Turakina's second rank pressed home their own charge with lances or sabres. Aiming for gaps in the Warchaw ranks, they avoided direct collisions but still paid a heavy price at the hands of the enemy.

Turakina's bowmen completed their circle and now returned to join the hand-to-hand fighting, some still using the bow at close range, including Turakina herself. Now that the pattern of the fighting was defined Bhal Morag urged his detachment forward, picking up speed to strike obliquely at the Warchaw line. The broken Chaw cavalry of the left wing had recovered from the shock and turned on the enemy.

Li Lue was one of the few people who could follow the whole action. Slowed by Turakina's counter-attack, the Warchaw were being bogged down as first Bhal Morag's reserve and then the main cavalry closed in on them. Even some of the foot-soldiers were joining in the fight.

For Bhal Morag the viewpoint was considerably narrower, as he hacked desperately at Warchaw mail in an attempt to land a lethal cut. His scimitar glanced off across the steel rings, merely beating down the sword arm. From behind him a pointed lance thrust out and punctured the barbarian's side. He struck again, aiming at the wounded man's shoulder, a bone-snapping blow which still did not cut through the ringed armour. The man sagged over his horse's neck and was then swept from his saddle by a slashing blow from a N'gol hooked lance. Several men stabbed down at him as he fell between the trampling hoofs of the frightened horses, where peasant soldiers hacked at him on the ground like foraging ants in leaf litter.

The rest of the Warchaw charge had dissolved into similar local fights; the heavy horsemen were swamped by the sheer numbers of the Chaw. As Bhal Morag turned away from the fighting to view the situation, two barbarians burst free and sped clear. Blood-smeared sweating horses raced in the direction of the solitary figure of Li Lue. Bhal Morag urged his own horse to a frantic gallop but he was easily outpaced by the slim figure of a girl on a magnificently fleet N'gol pony. Guiding her horse by knee pressure alone, the White Sash flying behind her like a personal banner, she closed on the nearest barbarian and shot a needle-pointed arrow into his back.

He reeled in agony but as the woman passed him he struck out backwards with his heavy war sword. The blow hacked her from the saddle to send her rolling on the hard earth, a blood-washed broken doll. It was the barbarian's last act of defiance; he hung grimly to his horse's neck, the sword falling from dying fingers.

Bhal Morag rode past him, sword outstretched like a spear as he tried hopelessly to catch the second barbarian. Like a frightened rabbit, Li Lue sat immobile with fear as death sped towards her. Slowly one hand lifted to her mouth. Morag whipped the horse with the flat of his sword but the beast could run no faster.

Something small and bright sped from Lie Lue and she exploded into action. Her horse dived to one side and sprinted out of danger as the barbarian charged past screaming, blinded with pain which made him unable to follow the girl's flight. He fell, writhing in agony. Bhal Morag approached the barbarian's body which was arching backwards with spine-snapping paralysis. From the fallen man's cheek projected a dart shot from the blow-pipe which Morag had mistaken for a flute.

'Poison?' he asked Li Lue unevenly, revulsion showing in his voice.

'Yes. My father, Merchant Li, insisted that I be able to protect myself. Some cities he traded in were quite violent. The Lady Xante supplied the most effective poison.'

Bhal Morag turned away to return to the main combat but all fighting had now ceased. There were no prisoners and no barbarian cavalry had been allowed to escape from the last, desperate charge. While the men of the 9th T'sand scrambled and pushed to loot the bodies of the slain, the survivors of Turakina's Death Wind seemed dazed and disappointed to be alive. They assembled their pitifully small numbers; nearly half were dead or too mutilated to survive. The body of the beautiful Cyli was almost cut in two by the swordstroke which Morag had witnessed so helplessly.

As Morag thanked Turakina, Li Lue slipped from her horse and walked to the dead girl.

'She sought her dead lover,' someone commented.

'And so shall I,' replied Li Lue. 'I faced death today and was not afraid. I felt the spirit of someone dear to me.' She unwound the bloodstained sash from Cyli and bound it around her own waist. 'I will add Cyli's name to it later,' she explained, 'and that of another.'

'Welcome, sister,' came the voice of Turakina as she finished speaking to Bhal Morag. 'The Death Band now has its sekar.'

'Eighteen people is hardly a band,' commented Bhal Morag bitterly. 'One more Chaw victory, Lady Turakina, and your band will not exist.'

'Our numbers will grow beyond counting. The ghosts of our companions will ride with us and others will join as Li Lue did today.'

'The barbarian pig whom Cyli shot still lives,' announced a warrior in a flat, dead voice. 'I will show you now how the Night Dragon treat people who break water friendship in the D'was.'

'It is well known!' exploded Bhal Morag. 'Li Lue, come with me. You have work to do before you ride off with the seekers of death.'

Bhal Morag led her to where the barbarian lay, Cyli's broken arrow projecting from his back close to the spine.

'Ask the Lady Xante what we should do.'

'You are well, Li Lue?' To the others it looked as if Li Lue was transfixed and a crease of pain showed on her brow. Xante's voice had sounded in Li Lue's mind as if the Dryad was at her elbow.

'Yes, madam,' she replied.

'Please explain the events if you are able. I feel that your own life was in danger, and your mind seems changed or disturbed?'

'I have taken a great resolution and my mind is now more at ease than at any time since I lost the one who was dear to me,' Li Lue replied before beginning to explain to Xante all that had happened at the battle of the pass.

When she had finished there was a long pause while Xante considered her words and no doubt conversed with Curos.

'Li Lue?'

'Yes, madam.'

'Are you strong enough to touch the mind of the dying barbarian?'

317

'Yes, madam. I am now quite strong.'

'Place your hands on either side of his temples and try to make your mind blank. Do not try to do any more, I will probe into his mind.'

To Bhal Morag it appeared that Li Lue almost lost consciousness as she touched the barbarian. For a long time she stooped over him until she murmured, 'Yes, madam. I am unharmed. I have seen dark things.' Tears ran down her face. 'I will recover, madam, and I will have strength to carry out my resolve to join Lady Turakina.'

It took some great effort from Bhal Morag to recover the weapons of the Warchaw raiders as Curos wished. Every man in the pass wanted some item to be able to boast over when he returned home. The younger of the two 9th T'sand K'tans had been killed in the fighting and his men milled in confusion and uncertainty. Carts had to be righted and men reorganised for the journey back to the town. Turakina's people were invaluable in herding up dispersed pack-horses turned loose by the Warchaw prior to their desperate charge. The piles of dead and the huddled groups of wounded gave a frightening testimony to the effectiveness of the Western horsemen. One hundred and sixty Chaw had died in this vicious skirmish, over three times as many as the Warchaw force.

A disturbing number of men were following Li Lue's lead to join with Turakina's Death Wind – men who had lost friends or brothers in the fight and a N'gol whose family had been slaughtered as they herded goats close to the North Road. A cavalry Ataman whose son had been killed in the final mêlée gave Bhal Morag special concern.

'How can you think of deserting your Ulus and the Army?' Morag asked him. 'Such as you are needed greatly.'

'How could I return to my home and explain that I live while my son died?' the man replied bitterly. 'Better that my wife and his wife believe me dead also. Execute me for desertion if you wish, K'tan. I seek death, it has no fear for me now.'

Bhal Morag organised the return to Be Kin Kar and then waited in the town for Curos and Xante, before preparing to start his journey back to G'tal. His task with Wan Abac and Chalak Konn would be to move the 9th and 22nd T'sands into

318

the region bordering the O'san. From there they would act in support of the N'gol tribes which were moving down from the north.

His report to the Army Council was carefully worded as a preliminary statement and cited several rumours that Te Toldin had been attacked and Noyan Zachaw killed in the fight before Bhal Morag had destroyed the invaders. The true situation would eventually have to be reported to the Council but Curos hoped that it would be believed that the raid had been successful.

40

Several weeks later Curos and Xante crossed a tributary of the Antin River which flowed south into the province of Xantu. The Dryad woman removed a large glass flask from her saddle-bag and poured the contents into the swollen stream. 'Go with luck, little people of S'lan,' she murmured. 'Your life will be hard and short but you serve S'lan the Eternal and will be born again with honour.'

'You believe they will succeed?' Curos asked doubtfully.

'A small chance, Curos. As small as that of Aalani who travels by an equally difficult route.'

A month later still, the Great Noyan Qunin was back at his immense estate in Xantu. Most of the peasant farmers had been driven inland to the inhospitable O'san and the land had been progressively converted into a huge pleasure park. Gardens, a hunting chase and a delightfully cool lake had been constructed in place of the cultivated farm plots. Despite Qunin's expressed hatred of forests, many small clumps of trees had been planted to shelter game and give shade around the lake. Those few farms essential to provide food were far distant from Qunin's palace-like mansion.

In the heat of the summer the Noyan stood at the stern of a small boat, slowly rowing across the glass-calm surface of the lake. Reclining beneath a huge fixed parasol was his favourite mistress who, barely clothed, was playing expertly on a lute. Guards responsible for the Noyan's safety were concealed discreetly around the shore of the lake, far enough distant not to intrude on the pleasures of the great man.

This interval was a celebration at the success of his plan to dispose of that dangerous young fool, Zachaw. Qunin congratulated himself again at the ease and effectiveness of his simple plan to persuade the Warchaw to raid Te Toldin. He had realised that Zachaw would never join his cause and he had retained doubts about the true nature of the Dryad. His informants in the 22nd T'sand were convinced she was a genuine sorceress and despite the disbelief of the Warchaw, some disturbing events had been reported from the Te Lok expedition. Moreover, the destruction of the armoured doors was far from an illusion. Much of Qunin's success was based on ruthless attention to detail, and he had too much to risk now.

The lascivious smile from the girl banished all such thoughts from his mind. His wealth and power could buy him a dozen such women but pleasure too must be taken seriously. He smiled back and eased the boat's prow towards the decoratively planted island with its fragrant shade and cascading fountain.

Through his anticipation of satiated lust he detected a distant buzz of insect wings. Strange how anticipation heightened all the senses – his hearing as well as smell and touch were particularly acute.

The girl screamed, a shrill shriek of warning, as she pulled the coloured shawl up to her neck as a desperately ineffective protection. Qunin spun round, sending the small craft rocking. Huge, multi-faceted eyes stared at them from the face of the grotesquely huge insect which hovered almost close enough to touch. Two others hung motionless in the air and seemed almost to be seeking recognition.

The face pushed forward until the long, mobile dragonfly jaws were fully extended. The beat of the iridescent wings increased in speed until the F'gar's body was almost obscured. Frenziedly, Qunin released his oar from the stern hook and brandished it at the flying monster which now darted towards him. The wooden oar was splintered by the power of the creature's jaws but its body had little momentum and was pushed downward. The frantic wings struck the surface of the lake as Qunin attempted to push the F'gar under.

In his moment of triumph the Noyan was attacked by the other two Flying Guardians. One seized his arm, the other bit deeply into his side. His reaction to the tearing agony more than any force from the impact sent Qunin falling from the boat. The girl's voice was growing hoarse in one long scream. The two creatures attacked her master again and again as he floundered in the water. When his movements had ceased the third F'gar climbed onto his floating body to shake dry its wings.

Guards from the lakeside hurriedly launched their own boat and paddled hastily out to the decorated craft which drifted aimlessly, in the slight current. By the time they arrived the F'gar had flown off, leaving the savaged corpse of Noyan Qunin and a demented, half-mad girl who raved and shrieked of flying monsters the like of which had never been seen in Chaw.

41

Aalani-Galni of the Dryadin Hunters sat in the old market place of Se Bekin, less than a day's travel from the Chaw capital, G'tal. The shade of an enormous fig tree and his dark hooded robe shielded him from the sun and any prying eyes. Before him lay a small wooden begging bowl and a holy man's staff of hard wood, his only visible possessions. Alternately sleeping or sitting cross-legged to chant mantras, he had passed many days in many market places during his journey from Te Toldin towards the great capital city of this alien people. Beneath the deep cowl his face broke into a hidden smile as an elderly woman bowed and placed a morsel of cooked rice into his bowl. These strange people were quite beyond his understanding. Many were desperately poor, often near to starvation. They all toiled unbelievably long hours, yet they were generous to an idler who sat under the shade of a tree singing songs or contorting his body into ridiculous poses.

Aalani had been barely sixteen years old when he had first left the forest to travel with the Night Dragon to the merchant city of Untin. The Dryad had been increasingly concerned that a cartel of merchants in the city were blocking Dryadin trade to increase their own profits. The merchants who traded in secret with the Dryad explained that there was little that could be done in law; to trade with the Dryadin was virtually illegal, and no tax had ever been paid. Neither the Night Dragon warriors nor the merchants could take direct action.

At that time, Aalani was increasingly being noted for not conforming to the customs and the ceremonies, and although hunters were an unusual people allowed more freedom than most, his existence in the forest was far from assured.

His suggestion that he accompany the Night Dragon caravan was motivated partly by desperation, and partly by a desire to see more of the lands outside the forest. Hunters were only really needed in winter and early spring when other foods were scarce and the near-vegetarian Dryadin were forced to resort to culling forest animals to live. His departure therefore removed, at least temporarily, a problem from the Ze Dryadi's concern and Aalani set off on his first trek. The first setback had been his deep antipathy to horses, which had made him resort to running or walking if at all possible. The second was his total lack of knowledge of city life.

For two months he had stayed with a merchant as a guest and had discovered a gift for understanding languages and a weakness for women and alcoholic drinks. Aalani became most efficient at understanding how the traders operated and two mysterious deaths of 'unsympathetic merchants' had been sufficient to unlock the trade restrictions. The skills which Aalani had developed to become an assassin were also used for other purposes, and he had undertaken many clandestine amorous expeditions across the roof-tops at night. Fortunately, there could be no children between Chaw and Dryadin but when Aalani returned to S'lan hearts were close to breaking on both sides.

From being an awkward youth of little value to the forest, Aalani had become a valued hunter worthy of consideration. He loved the forest as much as any and served it diligently; now twenty years later he was a full Council member but an opportunity to leave for a period as envoy, observer or assassin was a welcome release from its stifling order.

As the heat of the early summer sun abated into a warm evening Aalani, feeling suitably fed and rested, made his way slowly to the city gates. Eyes cast down and with shuffling, deferential manner, he passed out onto the deserted twilit road and began moving towards the capital.

Only when full darkness fell did Aalani strip off the long-hooded robe and bundle it into a pack through which he passed the unneeded staff. Wearing no more than his fibre-soled shoes, a loin-cloth and a sparse shirt, he eased himself into the loping run which had covered so many miles on previous nights. The venerable mystic had been completely transformed into the Dryad hunter-assassin.

Never before had Aalani felt such personal fitness and well-being as he pounded the last stage of his journey. Travel by horseback would have tied him to the post-horse system or required provision of stabling and fodder. The farmed plains of Chaw were far different from the open grasslands of the N'gol. Often he had run throughout the night and begged a ride on a cart or carriage the next day, not as fast as an Arrow Rider but faster than many other travellers and completely unnoticed. With each stride he had shed the pressures of S'lan. Aalani the Council Member, Aalani the Solitary One who avoided festivals and friendships lest he betray his true feelings, was now quite gone. In a month or two he would feel the forest call him back, but now he was as free as any N'gol.

It was almost a disappointment when the massive bulk of G'tal came into view against the early morning south-eastern sky. The euphoria of his epic run was over and it was a sad anticlimax to resume the dark, sweat-stained robe and join the small knot of people waiting for the city gates to open. Merchants, peasant farmers with food to sell and other unidentifiable travellers sat or lounged in the patient way of the Chaw people.

The interlude allowed Aalani to compose his thoughts and to recall the carefully learned route to the Zachaw City Mansion where he would spend the first of his days in this city. His own sight, smell, hearing and senses of perception were acute but not as wide-ranging as those of Xante. Unlike her, he felt in the massive capital only a sense of life and vitality with none of the overbearing pressure which bore down on her sorceress' mind.

Some time after the city gates opened Aalani stalked up to the Zachaw Mansion porter with a feigned arrogance mimicked from Chaw merchants and noblemen, stated his name and demanded to be taken to either the Lady Hoelun or Scribe Lin Sri. Although Hoelun still acted as mistress of the mansion for Curos, she resided with Chalak Konn in his town-house and was not yet at the mansion. Similarly the hard-working Lin Sri was rarely at his office at this early hour. The steward ushered Aalani into a suite of guest rooms, and summoned a maid to prepare a bath from warm water kept in the roof tank and sent hasty messengers to summon his superiors.

Aalani viewed the surroundings with interest, the confusion

with amusement and the maid with pleasure. On his journey his visits to Chaw dwellings had been brief and limited to a few disreputable inns. He was however no stranger to the houses of the Untin merchants which, although not as large or rich as this mansion, had been comfortable and accommodating. Instinctively he took an interest in the maid which would have surprised those who called him 'The Abstainer'. He began by feigning intense fatigue and requesting the unsuspecting girl's assistance with his bath. Only when he had received a partial commitment to wash his back and massage his neck did Aalani strip off his old man's robes to reveal his athletic body and begin a subtle flirtation. He made great play of his claw-like nails, and flexed his hard, hunter's muscles. He also achieved a great deal of playful splashing which almost soaked the now-giggling woman. She was quite unused to such attention in the Zachaw household but was obviously not shy of men. Soon Aalani was lounging back in the small but deep bathtub passing outrageous comments on the maid's charms while she massaged his soapy neck.

Fortunately for the two concerned this was soon to be interrupted by a discreet tap on the door and a message from the steward that the Lady Chalak Hoelun had arrived and that an early breakfast had been prepared. While the maid shied in terror at the risk of discovery, Aalani leapt dripping from his bath and whispered instructions on how she should apply the towel. He was soon seeking advice and assistance in the range of toilet preparations supplied and the clean Chaw-style clothing. Hoelun was more than a little surprised at her first meeting with the Dryadin Aalani-Galni. Prepared as she was for unconventional behaviour, she was totally astounded by his mature good looks and flamboyant choice of clothing. She had expected a polite if friendly greeting and sombre black; instead there was a hunter with a smile that reeked of danger. Even as she bowed and murmured formal words she was making a mental note to ensure that the Honoured Dryad guest would be kept as far as possible from the younger female staff.

It was quickly evident to Aalani that this austerely beautiful lady had assumed that all Dryads had the same status as the sorceress, Xante. His plans to indulge in good living would need to be carefully regulated to preserve the Dryad mystique without

326

limiting his pleasures. The light, meatless meal was a slight disappointment but he took the opportunity to stress the arduous nature of his journey on foot and the consequent need to increase the meat in his diet in order to regain strength. He also believed that a pleasant Barley Beer was rich in nutrients essential for a rapid recovery of muscle-tone and fitness.

Scribe Lin Sri arrived at the mansion later in the morning. News had just arrived in the capital that the Grand Noyan Qunin had been killed on his family estate in Xantu. The cause of death, which concerned Lin Sri only if Curos was implicated, was not known. The message came as a relief to Hoelun, who had feared for Chalak Konn's safety, but was bitter indeed for Aalani whose sole purpose in G'tal was the assassination of Qunin.

His heroic run across Chaw, the excitement of this new way of living and even the seduction he had planned would seem hollow if there was no purpose to his being in the capital. While Aalani had been toiling down the North Chaw plain his quarry had been quietly eaten by an overgrown dragonfly! True, the idea to unleash the F'gar on Qunin by introducing their larvae into the river which fed the pleasure lake had also been Aalani's, but it lacked the personal involvement he had expected.

'So there is no reason for my continued stay in G'tal,' he said helplessly.

'Surely you will reside here to recover?' said Hoelun without conviction, 'and there is no need for such a hasty return journey.

'I believe there may still be an important task for one with your skills,' suggested Lin Sri.

And one special skill that would be best well away from the Zachaw Mansion, thought Hoelun privately.

Aalani was conducted to Sri's suite of rooms where two junior scribes were studiously collating information. In a separate room Sri produced a detailed plan of the Qunin Mansion and indicated a small upper chamber where the Noyan was believed to keep his more important papers. The scribe had been informed that several packets of papers had recently arrived at the mansion and would be lying there awaiting Qunin's return from Xantu. Now that he was dead it was most likely that an accomplice would have them destroyed.

Aalani's heart sank deeper. Was he, Aalani-Galni, to be used as a common thief? Despite his misgivings, he could see that the task was possibly worth his effort, and if it were to be done it would brook no delay. With a flash of inspiration, he requested a guide to conduct him to the Noyan's Mansion and innocently suggested that were he to be accompanied by a woman he would attract less attention in the crowded streets.

Lin Sri shrugged dismissively. 'That is your business, honoured Dryad, but do not let yourself be distracted by planning two successes!'

Dressed in his pilgrim's robe, with staff and halting step, the infirm Aalani made his hesitant way through the streets of the city. With hooded face and bowed head, he leaned heavily on the woman who assisted his progress.

He kept up a constant whispered conversation with May Tang. Every woman was compared unfavourably with May Tang's exquisite beauty, and he questioned her as to the identity of her many lovers.

'Ah, surely that arrogant young guardsman strutting along must have been captivated by your charms?'

'Shush, Aalani, please, he will hear. He would never look at such as I, a divorced and childless woman!'

'He is one of the N'gol then who prefer the company of horses? Or he is one of those who is so blind he cannot penetrate your disguise.' He squeezed the unresisting woman through her enveloping cotton tunic and was rewarded by a compliant response.

Later, back in his room, Aalani fought to compose his thoughts regarding the serious matter of the evening. The Qunin Mansion might not be occupied, but it was vigilantly guarded and posed interesting problems. He excused himself from an invitation to an evening meal with Chalak Konn and Hoelun and ate sparingly in private, his mind empty of all distractions. Unfortunately, the prime distraction did not understand the nature of his mental preparation and repeatedly projected her image into his thoughts.

It was past midnight when he roused himself from self-induced sleep. He washed carefully, eyes, ears, mouth and nasal passages

328

receiving ritual attention to enhance the physical senses. He then began to envelop himself in the thought-cloud which would dull the response in others. Fleetingly he begrudged Suzin and similar sekars the skill of invisibility, so different from his own. An over-active mind and a body such as his would never be able to achieve the passive tranquillity necessary to master that technique.

Like a sinister black cloud, Aalani advanced through the deserted streets. Watchmen dozed undisturbed as he passed and awoke with a vague sense of unsubstantiated fear. Dogs growled half-heartedly at the shadow which had already passed, and sleeping beggars settled deeper into their slumbers. At the Quinn Mansion, he avoided the forbiddingly barred entrance gate and skirted the building to where he could scale the courtyard wall unseen. Extended, claw-like nails and swift dexterity carried him up over the fitted stone blocks and into the branches of a sweet-scented cherry tree. Several deep, calming breaths, and Aalani was feeling his way upwards and onto the roof of the building. The window of the room he sought looked out directly into the tree branches, but as Lin Sri had suggested it was securely barred.

Squatting on the roof, Aalani used his bronze dagger to prise off tiles which he stacked carefully. Soon he was able to cut through the felt layer beneath and lower himself into the roof space before breaking through the panelled ceiling into the room below.

This was Noyan Qunin's most private chamber, where only he and his scribe ever entered. Often, Qunin had sat in the dappled shade cast by the tree outside and read his reports or planned his future successes. Now, a strange intruder had entered and drawn the thick curtains to obscure the light of his secretive lamp. Knowing little of locks, Aalani broke open cabinets and drawers by skilfully applied force, seeking sealed packets of papers which had arrived in Qunin's absence. The other handicap for this unlikely burglar was that he could not read the pictoral Chaw script, so different from his own people's runic letters. His first prize, however, required no reading ability, being a handpainted love manual of great imagination and detail.

329

This was hastily stowed in the, as yet empty, backpack and would not be presented to the scribe Lin Sri.

Emptying drawers of documents with indiscriminate thoroughness, Aalani smiled with anticipation at May Tang's reaction to the explicit pictures. He advanced on the last cabinet which was of the most solid construction. Its stout brass locks defied all attempts to lever the drawers open. Abandoning what little caution he had shown so far, Aalani seized an antique ornamental halberd off the wall and prised viciously but silently at the locking bars where they entered the wooden plinth of the cabinet. Several attempts were necessary before a bar fell clear and the first of the box-like drawers could be opened.

Hastily, he scooped up handfuls of gold coins and choice stones from a decorated box. The second drawer contained letters sealed with Qunin's ring which lay side by side with other stout packets sealed by another hand. Aalani collected the whole contents of this drawer into his pack. The final compartment had its own separate lock which again took considerable effort to force. Fearful of the noise escaping from the room, Aalani listened intently for sounds of footsteps outside the locked door but all was silent and presumably still.

Returning from the door, he glanced quickly at several opened letters, some in a strange script more akin to Corninstani or Dryadin than Chaw. Wasting no time in fruitless examination, he scooped these up and turned his attention to a large, inscribed gold box. As he stretched out his hand towards it, he felt unnatural emanations of power quite alien to his experience. Before they had parted at Te Toldin Xante had warned him of the Red Stone carried by the Imrani. A thrill shot through his excited body. Indecisively his hand hovered over the lid, then caution prevailed and he drew back to consider the possible actions he could take. Almost immediatley he felt an increase of activity from the unseen object. Mentally, he moved away from the presence, aware that his own skills would have little effect here.

Furtive footsteps were approaching. There was no time to reach the opening in the ceiling; already a key was being inserted in the lock. Aalani leapt across the room to the concealment of the long window curtain as the door began to open. A small, hunched man peered rat-like into the room by the light of a large, upheld lantern: Noyan Qunin's scribe. His eyes rapidly cast around the room at the shattered and ransacked furniture. Aalani's extinguished lantern and the hole in the roof clear through to the dark night were too obvious to miss. Assuming the thief had left, the scribe rushed to the heavy cabinet and swore violently when he saw the papers were gone.

From his hiding-place, Aalani noticed that the scribe's anger did not prevent him from snatching up the remaining jewellery and handfuls of coins. The large, deep drawer was still partially open and timorously the scribe looked inside. He had no key to this section of the cabinet and had never seen what his master kept there. Unaware of any danger, he snatched open the lid of the heavy treasure box. With a strangled scream the scribe recoiled back as the room was filled with a fiery red glow and inexorably a shape began to form. A man's head, life-size with strange features and long, flowing hair and beard, glowed with a spectral presence. The face was not old, nor evil – almost boyish except for its immense impression of strength. Aalani was instantly aware that his hunter's defences would be totally futile and that he was almost as helpless as the small Chaw grovelling on the floor in abject terror.

An unnatural voice filled the room. 'You are not the Noyan Qunin. Who are you and what do you do?' The tone was deep and flat, the accent quite unlike any that Aalani had heard before.

'I am the Noyan's scribe,' the Chaw began to say but was silenced.

'Qunin is late. Where is he, and what is your purpose in consulting the stone?'

'The Noyan is dead, Lord. Killed at his estate in Xantu by a water creature.'

'You are sure that this is true, and that the Noyan was not murdered by Zachaw?'

'No, Excellency. The woman has been put to torture and, despite having one hand crushed, she maintains that the Noyan was attacked by flying creatures from the lake. Her mind has been unhinged by the horror.'

'If not by the torture.'

'Also, it is reported that Zachaw is dead, killed in the battle with the raiders that you sent to Te Toldin.'

'I grieve for the loss of so many of my good soldiers, but there was no alternative.' Aalani detected genuine concern in the voice as it spoke of the deaths of its own people. The sorcerer, possibly Val-an-us himself, was a man, a man with feelings.

There was a silence for some time until the foreign voice said, 'There is no further use for the stone or my contact with this place. You will close the lid of the box and drop it in the deepest part of the river where it will not be found unless I need it again. This is your last instruction, which must be obeyed.' The red glow began to fade and Aalani breathed again.

'Scribe,' the voice returned, but not the vision. 'What employment have you now that your master is no more? Will his son or family require your services?'

'I fear not, Lord,' came the quavering voice, but with a trace of hope. 'I could act as your agent in G'tal.'

'And what would a mere scribe learn which could be of interest to me? I fear in your poverty you could be tempted to seek the fool Po Pi or those who remain of Zachaw's party.'

'Never, Lord. I will be true to the oath I gave to Noyan Qunin.'

'I am sure you will,' sighed the voice. 'I am sure you will. Pick up the box and obey my command.'

Hands trembling in feeble hesitation, the scribe stood up and reached out towards the dying red glow. Without warning, the stone burned up with added power, filling the entire room with intense light. A scream of pain and terror rang out.

His strength multiplied by desperation, Aalani ripped aside the window-bars and leapt headlong for the friendly branches of the tree outside. Ignoring bruises and abrasions, he skidded to the ground as lurid flames exploded from the window and the roof of the room. Better to fight an army of guards than attempt to survive the inferno above. Reaction flooded his body with a wave of weakness and with sickening realisation he saw that unseen flight was impossible.

Soldiers and servants were running into the courtyard. A steward attempted to quell the disorder and organise the panicking staff into a fire party.

Aalani placed his pack more comfortably and began a purposeful and unhurried walk towards the gate. Casually, he lifted aside the two locking bars and the ground bolt. A sleeping, drink-dazed guard shuffled from the gatehouse and viewed the scene with incredulous amazement. Seeing none of his companions, he called to Aalani simply, 'What's happened?'

'A thief overturned a candle.' The wide gate swung open.

'And who are you?'

'I'm the thief,' laughed Aalani, recovering all his confidence in the face of the open-mouthed guard. 'Buy a barrel of wine for your friends.' He threw several heavy coins which sparkled in the light of the fire as they spun towards the dumbfounded Chaw.

Aalani had escaped. He had seen the Warchaw Wizard face to face and had avoided detection. He had his pack of papers for Lin Sri; emeralds and diamonds for May Tang if she were wicked enough to deserve them. His blood sang as if he had been in combat. Running over roof tops, or skirting half-sleeping watchmen who were unaware of the distant fire, Aalani hastened back to the Zachaw Town Mansion. Dawn was still some way off as he clambered back into his room. He threw the pack onto his bed and shed the borrowed black trousers and tunic before drinking heavily from a pitcher of beer he had saved for his return. Euphoria at his own survival still masked all other thoughts. Selecting massive stones, one crimson, one deep green, he opened the chamber door and followed all his hunter's instincts towards the attic room where May Tang slept unsuspectingly.

It was well past dawn when the exhausted Aalani awoke in a strange bed. With a satisfied smile, he rubbed teeth-marks in his shoulder as memory flooded back. May Tang had left him sleeping when she went to her duties. On the small side-table two glittering gemstones reflected the strengthening morning light.

As Aalani's eye was caught by the warm red of the ruby, a cold, intense fear seized his stomach and washed away every hint of joy. Valanus, Valanus the sorcerer of such immense and awful power, was just one of their enemies. Possibly not even the strongest. And while he scampered across Chaw and through the streets of G'tal to conduct his petty theft, while he lay in the arms of the gullible May Tang, another Dryad prepared to fight that awful power.

He rolled across the narrow bed and sat slumped and dejected. Remembering the aura of that projected presence was like a foretaste of death. The hunter's senses were numbed and he had no warning of May Tang's approach until her concerned arms wrapped around his sagging shoulders. In despair he pulled her to him and hugged her like a child seeking consolation from a nightmare. Xante-Yani, for all her skill and title of Q'ren of Sorcery, was still a girlish Dryad to Aalani, his niece, the daughter of the only Dryad he had loved. Was Xante to pit herself against this dreadful power alone?

42

The Great Grain Canal was one of the highest achievements of the Chaw ruling Council, but now it was deserted of traffic and its barges lay idle. From the Lune mountains the artificial waterway led in a seemingly endless path across the O'san desert until it joined with the Tishin river. The work of nearly fifty years of planning and excavation, it had provided a lifeline of food from Corninstan to Chaw. To Xante it seemed impossible that this canal, with its weirs and changes in level, could be man-made.

'It is really a splendid failure turned to good account,' explained Curos. 'The original plan, some three hundred years ago, was to divert a number of west-flowing streams in the Lune mountains and turn them eastward to irrigate the O'san. That in itself was a mammoth task, but the waterflow was still too little and the O'san soil too poor to make any useful result. After ten years of toil and death, all that could be seen were a few fields surrounding our fortress of Bec Tol.'

'Many years later, Corninstan was attacked by the armies of the Shah of Imran. He sought to extend his realm eastward, taking advantage of a devastating civil war in Corninstan which had left the country almost helpless. Civil wars grow in Corninstan as well as corn. In desperation they called on the Chaw to come to their aid. For once the councils of Chaw acted rapidly; fifty T'sands and twenty thousand N'gol cavalry were mustered and the Tuman crossed the Lune mountains. The Imrani army was battle-trained from previous conquests. It was claimed that the mounted archers were skilled and disciplined and that its foot-soldiers were as a moving stone wall. For all that, the Chaw Tuman swept them away as a wind scatters dry grass. Their horsemen were swamped by the arrows of the N'gol and the Chaw T'sands bore down their footmen with an irresistible weight of numbers.

'Even in its seemingly devastated state, the land of Corninstan seemed rich in food to the Chaw. It grew more grain than ever the people would need and had exported much of the surplus to Imran and to southern lands by way of the Janix river and the sea. And so was born the idea of converting the ineffective irrigation dyke into the grain canal, a vast trade route between the two nations.'

Curos stood in his stirrups to indicate the long sweep of the waterway. 'This is the result. Until a year ago it was covered with barges which were hauled by men from one weir to the next. The grain would be lowered downwards while Chaw trade goods – steel, porcelain, silk and perfume – would be lifted up to fill the boats which had been unloaded. It worked as an endless exchange from the end of the Corninstan harvest until the canal's waters became too low in mid-summer.

'The men who worked the canal lived in villages with their wives and children. Leakage from the canal acted as irrigation and provided the green fertile strip you see. Now the barges are idle because there is no trade.'

'Willows grown in the desert,' remarked Xante, 'along the banks of your canal. More than the canal itself, that is an accolade to your people!'

'The fertility you can see now was built up over two hundred years of occupation,' said Curos. 'The trees are quite recent. Ten years of war, or even ten years of the N'gol, and this will revert back to the desert.'

'Spread the nomad people out and forbid them to cut the trees, and it could last much longer,' Xante suggested. 'Ten years free from farming and cropping would even see the green band widen if the N'gol do not overgraze it.'

They followed the canal upstream past the endless series of weirs. At each one the exported cargo from the barges had been winched up to the next level, using the full sacks of Corninstan grain as counter-balances.

'So much work, Curos. Was it necessary?'

'Necessary and profitable. In years of poor harvests in Chaw the Corninstani grain saved whole provinces from starvation. To have shifted a tenth of the quantity by cart would have been impossible. For two centuries the Chaw engineers have sought to find ways of moving full barges up over the levels without unloading them but it is too difficult.'

At the head of the canal they finally came to Bec Tol. The ancient fortress was as strange and impressive as the canal itself, rising monolith-like from the flat landscape. The huge, tapering circular wall was smooth and featureless with its only opening, a narrow, horse-wide door, set high up above the level of the plateau. The sole access to men and animals was a sturdy but collapsible ramp which led up to that strange entrance. Within the wall, but set back from it, barracks and storehouses were built like radial spokes of a wheel. Bec Tol always had a strange aura which, in addition to its isolated location, made it an unpopular place to garrison. Merchants and the workers who unloaded the Corninstani grain carts onto the first barges of the canal seldom entered the forbidding circular walls. Now with the granaries and the warehouses empty and the workers' village deserted, Bec Tol was even more desolate.

'It is a place of strange power,' remarked Xante as she stood, hand outstretched to touch the smooth wall. 'A current of energy seems to circulate within the stone.'

'It is a very ancient site, although its name has changed many times,' explained Curos. 'These walls were completely rebuilt after the last Corninstan wars only four hundred years ago, but the foundations date back to the time of the Dug people. In those days streams flowed eastward into the O'san throughout the summer and the land could be farmed, after a poor fashion. Now they flow only in the spring months, except for the canal and its feeder channels which the Chaw constructed long ago.'

Inside Bec Tol, at its very centre, was the swirling hot spring of water which never faltered and never failed.

'It can provide water for two hundred men without change of level,' said Curos, 'but large cistern tanks mean that a full T'sand would stand siege for a year. There are also storehouses and armouries below ground. Note how the buildings stand clear of the wall like disconnected spokes.'

'The spring and the stored water circulate in a constant motion, Curos,' commented Xante. 'It is as if this motion has induced life into the circle of the wall. Some skilled sorcerer must have felt this force and designed the wall with its shape and deep foundations to amplify it.'

She looked at Curos with new realisation in her face. 'This is completely original, Curos. I have seen sorcery as a power to help growth in plants and as a means of protection in war but this means of giving dynamic strength to a building has never occurred to any of my people. Now I think of the plan of your home, Te Toldin. It could be that the symmetry of the north garden was meant to give such an effect but the new buildings destroyed the balance and the force. The Tree and the Stone would have given the power which I can still detect.'

'It is as well, then, that we have never built onto Bec Tol,' remarked Curos. 'I fear its strength will one day be sorely tested.'

Bhal Morag and Pata Sing had already taken up residence in the bleak stone barracks, and the four hundred men of the 22nd T'sand, as well as the fifty Corninstani irregular groups, augmented the existing garrison. Indeed, the T'sand cavalry and the Corninstani preferred to camp outside the forbidding walls and draw their water from the fast-flowing canal feeders.

While Xante prowled in continued exploration, Bhal Morag, Curos and Dalgan discussed plans for their first raid into Corninstan. The Army Council had eventually agreed to Pata Sing making limited forays into the occupied country. Despite his almost rash enthusiasm, Sing had been persuaded to mount his first attacks in the south where he could use Bec Tol as a base and be backed up by the Sand Dragon Clan if the Warchaw mounted a vigorous response.

Rather than follow the guarded main pass, Pata Sing would mount his horsemen over tortuous, hidden paths to attack a village which the enemy had annexed. The Warchaw were attempting to recruit and train Corninstani soldiers to swell their army for the invasion of Chaw; to destroy this centre would have a double significance for those who opposed the Western rule.

It was late in the evening when Curos approved the final arrangements which would include a diversionary attack by the Topaz Wind and the Sand Dragon Clan. He now sought out Xante and found her high on the parapet of the fortress wall, standing as if listening to hidden sounds. Silhouetted against the light desert sky, her beauty burned into his senses like a brilliant star or the fragrance of forbidden fruit which could never be tasted. He watched her silently until she turned to greet him.

An innocent but devastating smile seemed to illuminate the evening gloom as she explained, 'I feel an attraction to this place. It has a power of its own which I could increase to make the fortress impregnable. Can you not sense it? Don't think of me like that; try to use your other senses for once.'

He suppressed the smile which was indeed forming on his lips and tried to feel what she meant. Instead he caught only the slightest sound of a snore some way off.

'That is only the guard sleeping, Curos, not the force of Bec Tol.'

'Guards who fall asleep on duty do not wake up in this world,' growled Curos with sudden anger as he drew his dagger. 'The punishment for a sleeping sentry is death.'

'There is no danger, Curos, you are too harsh.'

'It is when all seems secure that we need to be most vigilant. Those camped outside have no sentries because the fortress is near, but our guard is asleep. A sudden raid from the mountains could wreak havoc on our men and the supplies stored in the warehouses by the canal head.'

'Stop lecturing and I will punish your sleeping man. I need practice.'

Carefully she eased her concentration towards the unsuspecting soldier, feeling the pressure as he slumped against the hard stone. His senses were dulled by wine or beer and he hardly stirred as the Dryad sorceress levitated him into the air; even his slackly held spear stayed at the same angle. With infinite care, the sleeping figure was floated out over the wall to hover fifty paces from the hard plain below.

'No!' hissed Xante in alarm as the soldier began to drift along the line of the wall. 'He is caught in the force of Bec Tol, I cannot pull him back!' She clenched her teeth in effort as the man drifted further away with increasing speed. By now he was quite awake to the terror which gripped him and he writhed and tumbled in frantic desperation.

'Let him fall, his punishment is death,' commented Curos, unconcerned at the plight of the hapless soldier who was now completely out of sight. Other men appeared on the wall, rushing to their posts with alarm at the sudden shouting. Arms were pointed in wonder and fearful comments passed.

Xante mustered her power and gradually forced the sentry higher into the air until he was visible far above the line of the parapet. She had ceased to fight the circulating force but was deflecting the man's path higher until he was almost clear of its effect. Finally she drew him back inside the ring of the wall. The soldier landed in a bruising skid close to where he had recently slept in peaceful dereliction of duty. With a sob of pain and relief, he kowtowed deeply to Xante, his face pressed hard against the cold stone, as much for reassurance as for any sign of submission.

'Stand up and salute correctly,' shouted Curos. 'Stand up as a Chaw soldier and thank whichever gods you worship that you are still in the same life! Is this subservient wretch typical of those I would have defy the Warchaw?' The soldier was far too shocked to stand unaided and Curos waited for the Ataman of the guard to take the pathetic man away.

'I did not mean it to be that traumatic, Curos,' said Xante apologetically. 'I thought a sharp fright would be better than execution.'

'For him it is,' Curos reassured her. 'In a day or so he will recover enough to tell of Q'ren Xante's power. He should thank you for being alive; you have no need to reproach yourself.'

The next day Curos decided to visit the tents of an Untin merchant of precious stones who was passing by Bec Tol. The merchant traded in some of the richest jewellery in Chaw and had featured in Lin Sri's reports of gems recovered from the Te Lok outlaws. Only recently had Curos realised that many of the raw gemstones used in Untin had originated in the forest lands of S'lan, traded by the Dryads for more practical commodities.

Under the simple tent awning Curos and Xante were welcomed with as much reverence as the pleasantly self-confident and independently minded merchant could show. A vigorous, strongly built man of about forty years, he had little of the subservient nature of a G'tal market trader and his wealth and success were quite able to compensate for any lack of traditional social status. They sat sipping scalding tea and thimble-sized cups of rice spirit as Curos began to explain his business.

'I need to purchase a small birth gift. It may be long before I can visit civilisation again.'

'To buy a birth gift before the birth is said to tempt fate,' replied the merchant. 'And of course I can never know the gender or the appropriate birth-stone. However, I do have some fine Corninstan gold work which would cover all circumstances.'

'I agree with your reservations, but Lady Xante-Yani assures me that the child will fare well.'

'As you wish, Lord. May I ask who is the lady who expects the joyous event?'

'His wife,' said Xante archly.

'Ah, I had no idea. May I express my congratulations!' He looked questioningly at Xante.

'He is not the father, and I can assure you I am not the mother,' replied Xante, and added, 'There will, of course, be two children.'

The merchant looked more than confused and a trifle embarrassed.

'The lady plays with you,' explained Curos. 'The Lady Hoelun was my wife but has remarried following our divorce.' He addressed Xante. 'But who else is expecting a child? Not Dortie again?'

'No, the Lady Hoelun will have twins, one boy, one girl. At my advice she and Konn have already selected the names of the children.'

'One can hide nothing from a Dryad, friend Curos,' laughed the merchant and Curos found to his surprise that he did not object to the familiar tone.

As the jewellery was carefully selected and delivery to G'tal arranged the merchant noticed that the pieces were to be a joint gift from two people whose separation and closeness were as enigmatic as any relationship he had witnessed.

'Before your visit ends I must compliment you on your choice of antique jewellery, Lord Curos,' said the merchant. 'The Topaz of the Wind which hangs over your chest is a famous piece, well-known from the time of the emperors. The ring is however of

341

very unusual design. Although plain gold, it has a certain similarity of style to the Topaz.'

'I do not normally wear ornaments,' remarked Curos. 'The Topaz is a badge of rank and respected as such by all fighting men. The ring is a mark of gratitude from poor soldiers, even if one of their number cheated it off an officer with loaded dice!' Seeing the other's interest, Curos slipped off the ring and handed it to the jeweller, who turned it in his hand.

'Too light for solid gold.' He tapped it with a thick, strangely pointed fingernail. 'Slightly hollow with perceptible movement inside.' He looked up at Curos, a hint of excitement in his eye. 'May I open it?' he asked.

'If you can. I have tried but would not risk causing damage.'

'You lack the skill perhaps,' the merchant said absently as he brought out a small roll of tools from within his embroidered jacket. 'Ah!' he unscrewed the flat, engraved top of the ring with a flourish which belied his care. 'See the secret of centuries!'

Inside the ring was a small, disc-like cavity. Resting in this were two tear-drop shapes interlocking to form the universal sign of Light and Dark. One, black as jet, was inscribed to reveal a single white dot, the other was white with a corresponding black cavity. The merchant reverently tipped the stones into his palm. 'Topaz, both are topaz. They are cut from the same rare piece which must have had alternate black and white layers.'

'Intriguing – what can it symbolise?' asked Xante, instinctively picking up the dark shape to examine it.

'Light and Dark, equal in size and power, both essential, both everlasting,' replied Curos.

'But why hidden in a ring?' said Xante.

Curos shrugged and took up the white symbol. As soon as his fingers touched the stone, Xante gave a gasp of surprise and shock.

'What is it, Xante, are you ill?' said Curos in alarm, steadying the woman's shoulder.

'Can you feel nothing?' She grimaced angrily.

'Now what is there to feel? More magic?'

'I feel an extension of my power. I can see through your eyes, feel your heartbeat. I am linked to you and to the yellow topaz of fire and can feel your intentions and your strength.' She placed the Dark symbol back in the ring and sighed sadly. 'I feel so much and to you it is nothing! Why will you not try? The tree grows over the stone and draws nourishment from it, but the stone feels nothing!'

'The Light and Dark,' said the merchant. 'The white of the air and the black of the earth; the bright light of N'gol and the darkness of the forest. There is much symbolism in these stones and perhaps much that is still hidden.'

They sat for some time until Curos said, 'These things have no meaning to me, but I will add to the riddle. The valour of the Topaz Wind Riders led to the giving of the ring, so let us put a yellow topaz disc in the cavity. Then Xante can wear the Dark symbol and I will wear the Light.'

'Do not laugh at me, Curos.'

'I do not laugh. I do not understand, but I have been taught to treat such things with respect by my Q'ren of Sorcery. If these stones can add to your power, then we should take one each. I felt an instinct to give you the stones as soon as I saw them; now I follow my instincts.'

'To have any effect it must be held, not worn on the cloth, Curos.'

'Then our new friend will encircle the stones in filigree and fit them to ear studs. My ears are pierced, as are those of all N'gol boys.'

'So I have noticed, but Dryadin do not have holes through the ear lobes!'

'It only needs to be one ear that is pierced, unless we find further heirlooms,' laughed Curos. 'If symbols of fire and water exist, they are hidden still.'

The next day it was Xante alone who collected the modified jewellery from the merchant. He delicately fitted the gold ear stud into her left ear and asked quietly, 'Does he really know so little? Can any man of his ability know so little?'

'He knows of armies and horses and strategy and nations – all that is important to one destined to rule – he need know little of other things.' There was sadness in her voice.

'You could rule as Q'ren Xante,' the merchant whispered, almost inaudibly.

'No, I lack the resolve and it is not the way of our people to rule. You, who are part Dryad, should know this.'

'There are many ways to rule, Q'ren.' He half bowed to her and said, 'You rule many sekars already and they could become a great power. You could command the heart of this merchant, as you well know.'

'You would soon find that willingness to be ruled is not the same as being ruled. Do not judge Curos harshly,' she continued. 'Already he could seize Chaw if he wished. His N'gol would follow him through the gates of the void, and half the Chaw T'sands would follow without thought. His agents and spies give him knowledge to subvert all rivals. I suspect that only I know his full power.'

'Yet he stays his hand?'

'He does not even think to strike. He thinks of a united Land, Chaw, N'gol and Dryad, which will stand as a rock before the invaders of the West.'

'And over the rock grows the tree?'

'No, beside the rock grows the tree. As Dryadin we all stand at one level with our feet on the soil of Eternal S'lan. Any one person's significance is very small.' The woman smiled girlishly like a beam of sunlight through the dark trees and the jeweller's bones turned to water.

43

Pata Sing's raiding party set off over the high passes through the sombre Lune mountains. The forty Corninstani were accompanied by Curos and a personal escort of ten Wind Riders. Xante had selected two sekars who were adept at the cloaking technique of Lou Suzin. It was hoped that these sekars would conceal the presence of their companions from chance observation. Pata Sing was far from happy to have any Chaw present in his force and feared that Curos might annex command or take any credit.

During the journey Curos and Xante usually rode close together, following the main body of Corninstani who were led by the taciturn Pata Sing. The Topaz Wind Riders formed a loose-knit rear-guard. A sekar was positioned at either end of the long file of men to render them virtually invisible. To Xante, who had never been in the high mountains before, it was unbelievable how far one could see in the clear, thin air. This and the massive scale of the landscape made perception of distance difficult and seemed to dwarf their ant-like progress.

Several times they detected groups of riders, Warchaw or Corninstani, who occasionally patrolled these mountains to give warning of any attack. At such times the whole party would stop and dismount before slowly moving into any available cover. The advantage given to them by the sekars made certain that they were not discovered, but even this practical assistance seemed to annoy Pata Sing. He would willingly have forsaken the aid of the sekars and relied on capturing the Warchaw patrols, despite the risk of losing the advantage of surprise.

At first the high passes crossed a barren landscape of rocks and crags, with only the scantiest cover of grass or moss. The brilliant summer sun seared eyes and any exposed skin and reflected back off rocks as heat, making travel at mid-day as impossible as in the desert. Pata Sing enforced strict silence during the journey, and ordered the horses' hoofs to be muffled in those valleys where the echoes were loudest. Once they started the steeper descent into Corninstan, on the windward side of the mountain, the change in vegetation was pronounced. Dark, dry rocks gave way to bright alpine pastures, cut by sparkling mountain streams. In happier times, small flocks of hardy sheep and goats would have been driven up from the valleys to graze until they were forced to retreat down onto the corn stubble by the first winter snow. The lack of any hill shepherds at this time of year gave Pata Sing the first confirmation of the horrific stories which had filtered into Chaw.

Throughout the journey, Xante was troubled by the feeling of a presence in the mountains which she could not explain. She sensed that they were being discreetly followed by a person of some ability in sorcery: neither the powerful magic of the War-chaw nor the subtle influences of her own people, but a tenuous link which tracked their every move without her being able to detect its source. Several times she and Curos purposely lagged behind the main party and concealed themselves to watch for their follower.

'He, or it, stops also, Curos,' whispered Xante. 'I can feel humour as if it toys with us, knowing our intentions.'

'You are sure it is not the enemy?'

'Most certain, the feeling is quite different.'

That night they camped on the very ridge of the path, the only section that was wide enough to allow them to form a reasonably cohesive and defensible grouping. In this exposed position they could light no fires, but despite the clear air, the rocks retained the heat of the autumn sun and there was no wind. She and Curos climbed up a ridge onto a higher plateau and looked down to the East. Most of the land was in deep shadow, but it was not by sight that Xante sought their follower.

'He is there, Curos. I feel him, but as I stretch out my mind he pushes me away as a father would, in play, to stop his baby from touching his face. I can almost hear him breathe but I cannot see him.'

Curos too found himself listening intently. There was strangely no physical noise of wind or cooling rocks or movement of animals – the whole mountain was balanced between autumn and winter. He was standing several paces from Xante but realised he could clearly hear her rhythmic breathing and her pulse, slow as a resting thoroughbred. He remembered the conversation with Tayan of the Night Dragon – life as cold and as slow as a tree in winter but able to burst into fire at the first hint of spring. He moved to stand close behind her until his chest gently touched her back. She did not speak but leaned back until, with her slightly greater height, her head rested on his shoulder, her eyes looking into his. He could smell her hair and her skin and feel her deep contentment – contentment and affection and to one side, as if in a barred prison, watchful and alert, the passion and emotion he had seen at Ki Fru.

'And so at last a Chaw creeps into my mind,' she breathed, her husky voice laden with pleasure. They did not move, so still that nothing moved for eternity. Then the prisoner in Xante's mind gently, so gently, stroked the bars of the cage and Curos exploded in his own wind of passion. The pit of his stomach twisted in agony; molten ice and molten lead flowed in his veins. He flinched away but her arms were clasped backwards around him.

'It cannot be, Curos, we both know it cannot be. But do not go.' They sat down together, quivering with tension which could not be satisfied. In despair, Curos remembered the night when, beside a dying camp fire, two N'gol girls had crept giggling to him to make him a man; his first nights with Hoelun when, after their passion was spent, his attempts at loving her had ended in a frustration of manners; Kataln and others. Never had he been gripped so fiercely or felt so little anger when there was no release. Vaguely, he wondered what memories Xante held in the cage of her mind from when Ki Fru reigned, but there was no resentment or jealousy.

'He is still there, Curos, watching us and smiling.'

'It is a pity that Aalani is not with our company,' he replied.

'Strange you should mention him – if Uncle Aalani were here I could despatch him to seek out our follower. No quarry can hide from him, and he moves much faster than poor Akab.'

Gradually the world turned and cooled, leaving Curos with a dull ache as he dozed into an intermittent but peaceful sleep.

The last stages of the journey were made by night and under

the cover of mature pines which clung to the lower foothills, the residue of a wide forest which had once filled the valleys of the Janix. Splendid as this belt of trees seemed to Curos, it held no message and no solace for Xante-Yani. To her, it was simply the sad memory of greatness which lingered after the destruction of so many forest trees by the Corninstan farmers long ago. Any heart or soul which had existed in the Janix Forest had long departed.

Xante and Curos felt as one, but she was still concerned that they were followed and observed. Near the end of their journey she angrily turned her horse back along the path and standing in her stirrups commanded in a voice of power and authority, 'You who follow us, come forth, show yourself!' There was no answer, no approach. Now it was Pata Sing's turn to be worried both at the volume of Xante's shout and at the implication of her words. As much as was ever possible, Curos calmed the hillman and the advance continued.

From a raised hill, still inside the tree-line, Pata Sing was able to point out the remains of the farming community which the Warchaw had converted into a vast exercise area. Most of the farmers and their families had gone, and the fields which should have been planted with ripening oats were now green with uncut grass. Apple orchards had been cleared to extend the open space, which lay uninterrupted except for a wooden fort and a collection of tents.

'Where were the villagers sent?' asked a Corninstani as his eyes scanned the blackened remains of the once prosperous village.

'They were not sent,' replied their guard angrily. 'They lie under that long mound beside the road. One mass grave for all. The butchers of the West thought them unnecessary. Only those who showed complete subservience were allowed to survive as slaves to farm that small remaining area of agriculture.' His voice broke off into a muffled curse as he remembered the horrors and the carnage which had occurred in this once happy village.

'The Warchaw secure themselves in that palisade fortress,' commented Curos. 'But who occupies the separate camp?'

'Filth, the scum of our nation!' spat the guide, his voice hard with loathing. 'From our western provinces they have been recruited to swell the army that is being prepared to invade Chaw.'

'They assisted in the massacre?' asked Xante.

'No, the Westerners kept that pleasure for themselves. By the time the collaborators arrived, the plain was much as you see it now. Only slowly have the Corninstani realised the truth of what has happened, and many now wish to join with us in revenge.'

'Is all Corninstan so ravaged?' Curos asked.

'Not yet,' replied Pata Sing. 'This area was needed to train horsemen. In other places the Warchaw value the food my people produce too highly to commit such wholesale slaughter, but the rule runs hard on any who oppose them.'

They spent nearly a whole day in hiding and Curos was able to watch the Warchaw unobserved as they trained their reluctant Corninstani allies. Swordsmen hacked relentlessly with blunted swords at wooden posts, and horsemen charged time and time again with levelled lances at a variety of targets: pegs in the ground and poles with padded sacks which would ensnare a lance point. None of the Corninstani rode the mighty war-horses of the West but their mounts were still heavy and stronger than those of Chaw. It was impressively thorough and gave little consolation to a cavalryman like Curos. He realised it was vital to prevent the Warchaw swelling their army in this fashion and was only relieved that there were no Corninstani bowmen being trained to use the heavy longbow of the Western archers.

It was many hours later, deep into the clear but moonless night, when a lone and very drunk Corninstani staggered towards the entrance to the Warchaw fort. He drank deeply from a wineskin slung precariously over one shoulder and exchanged some garbled banter with the two Westerners who guarded the gate. This continued for some short while until one of the huge sentries gave the drunkard a shove which sent him sprawling.

The Westerner's deep, alien laugh sounded through the night as he snatched up the wineskin. After several gulps he passed the container to his companion who then tossed it, almost empty, to a third man who peered down from over the battlement.

'Good,' muttered Pata Sing. 'All three have drunk enough, all we now need to do is wait. First they will sleep and then they will die as the poison bites more deeply.'

'And the man who carried the wineskin, he drank also?'

'He knows the risk if he cannot clear his stomach in time,' replied the Corninstani. 'He was brave indeed for a man of the western provinces.'

'I think Aalani-Galni's soporific spells would have been more sure,' suggested Xante to Curos.

'Possibly, but the Corninstani need their own success and their own martyrs. In a land ruled by the Western sorcerers it may be as well to reserve your power.' He paused for a moment and added, 'Even so, if you could ensure that the man on the inside of the ramparts falls asleep first, it would aid our cause without being noticed!' He felt her half smile, although her face except for those dark eyes was covered.

One of the Warchaw was soon slumping back against the timbered wall while the other paced desperately to and fro in an attempt to clear his misting senses. At last he seemed to realise the danger which was upon him and called out in a voice made frail and indistinct by the rising potency of the poisons which destroyed him. Two dark figures ran silently from the deeper shadows and the long knives of the hillmen did deadly work without a sound or glint of brightness.

This acted as the signal for the start of savage retribution in the Corninstani camp. Those who planned to join Pata Sing killed viciously to show their new loyalty, until the last sobbing groan died away in the tents of death and a grim-faced band emerged with bloodied daggers. They joined Pata Sing's men, who now surrounded the fortress and were piling tar and tallow-coated wood against the dry timber of the walls. Curos held back with his ten mounted bowmen from Topaz Wind and fretted at the delay as the incendiary material was positioned.

Speed was essential if they were to retain the initiative. Only thirty Warchaw occupied the stronghold but even that small number, armed and mounted on their heavy war-horses, would be able to sweep Pata Sing's men aside as they had when they shattered the Chaw T'sands. Curos was about to ask Xante's assistance when a gout of fire sprang up and spread rapidly around the base of the palisade.

'The Warchaw force were too confident and too secure,' he said as the flames rapidly took hold of the dry wood and burned more fiercely as they created their own updraught. 'In this dry season they should have doused their fortress morning and evening to keep the wood damp. It will burn like dried kindling.'

The double reinforced gate was engulfed with flame which was now spreading around the circular wall. Inside, men and horses were screaming in alarm. Ineffective buckets of water were poured down over the parapet and the gate started to move as if to open. Corninstani arrows rushed into the flames, seeking those who attempted to move the blazing timbers.

'Are Sing's men too concentrated by the gate?' asked Xante.

Curos nodded. 'Yes. The Warchaw cannot pass that way, but desperate men will try anything.' He slipped his strung N'gol bow from its horse quiver and nocked an arrow in readiness. His Wind Riders followed his actions without order, although some gestured disappointment as they sheathed their sabres and hooked lances.

The fort was now one blazing inferno from which it appeared no-one could escape. Three Warchaw vaulted over the flaming wall, swords in hands, but were hacked savagely to death by the Corninstani before they could regain their balance. Men cheered as another was shot down to fall into the flames when he rushed through the opening of the sagging gate.

To the side of Curos' vision, a whole section of wooden wall came crashing outwards, sending the Corninstani swordsmen, who had been standing too close, running back from the shower of sparks and falling timbers. Galloping over the flames came a dozen Warchaw heavy cavalry, the counter-attack Curos had feared – iron-clad men made more menacing as the flames reflected off polished hauberks and conical helmets. They rode down the few men who opposed them and wheeled with furious precision in one open line which smashed into the ragged knot of Pata Sing's men.

The Corninstani held together and a desperate mêlée developed as Curos raced his men forward. Eager as they were to join the bloody hand-to-hand combat, Curos used the Topaz archers as he had at the battle of the Corninstan Road. Guiding well-trained war ponies by knees alone, they circled the fight, making well-placed arrows do the work of a dozen sabre cuts. The final Warchaw horseman was dying under a weight of hack-

351

ing swords when two last footmen dashed from the gap in the wall. Four Wind Riders shot them down with ease, closing their ponies up behind the fleeing men as they would do when hunting a swift-footed deer.

Several Corninstani advanced on the wreck of the fortress as if to seek any remaining fugitives. Xante called out to Curos in alarm, but it was too late. The centre of the fire burst up in an intense white explosion which threw the men backwards and scattered those who still surrounded the inferno. Blazing timber whirled through the air, trailing sparks and flames like demented angry dragons. Men leapt and ducked in alarm and then laughed as they realised they were unhurt and that the flames were dying down.

'Curos!' Xante shouted. 'That was one of the Warchaw red stones. Like the one we saw in G'tal.'

'It has destroyed itself,' he called back, not understanding her fear.

'But it will have done its work, Curos. The stones can speak from afar to the sorcerers. Already they will know of this attack and be sending a larger force to cut us off. Surprise is gone. We need to retire quickly if we wish to avoid further combat.'

Pata Sing's reaction to success showed through the smoke stains covering his face. It took some effort to explain the danger to him and he scorned the idea of flight.

'First we will destroy those from the village who assisted the Warchaw and then we will ride to meet this new enemy they send against us.'

Vainly his lieutenant attempted to explain that many of their men were injured and that with six dead and as many unable to ride they were quite unable to withstand another battle.

'There are Zachaw's bowmen to aid us,' Pata Sing replied angrily. 'They are unscathed and lust for combat.'

'Only at my order will they fight,' said Curos harshly. 'We have achieved our aim and cannot reconquer your land with forty men. Let us not throw victory into the jaws of defeat.'

'Do not be too hasty to do the Warchaws' work for them,' argued the lieutenant. 'I did not ride west to murder pathetic survivors from a destroyed village. I rather wish we were able to take them back with us to Chaw and safety.'

Angrily, Pata Sing turned away.

The Corninstani soldiers were no different from the N'gol or the Chaw in their desire for souvenirs of warfare. Valuable time was being lost as weapons and armour were collected and packed into saddle-bags while the ruins of the wooden fortress burned on like the funeral pyre it had become.

Funeral pyre or beacon, thought Curos. He sat his horse, flanked by his stoical Topaz Riders who showed their superiority of race and training by despising any attempt to loot the dead. With growing annoyance, he waited while further time was spent in burying the Corninstani soldiers who had fallen to the desperate Warchaw charge. Curos urged Pata Sing to press on as far as the concealing belt of conifers where they could wait and use the darkness of the night to cross the open ridges into the next valley.

The slow pace dictated by the wounded made rapid progress impossible. They camped before noon and hastily buried one for whom even the slow journey had been too swift. There would be more deaths before they reached Bec Tol, but unlike the Chaw, the Corninstani would not dispatch those of their men who had no chance of survival.

Curos realised that Pata Sing had no intention of haste and was using his declared concern for his wounded men as an excuse to delay and invite further combat with the Warchaw. Already this simple raid had taken Curos away from his main duties too long. After one more attempt to remonstrate with the Corninstani leader, Curos and Xante led their own small group rapidly up into the hills. With them came one of the sekars, while the other stayed with the slow-moving riders.

In five days of hectic riding Curos was back at Bec Tol, to be greeted by an ecstatic Dalgan who had succeeded in his own hit-and-run raid. Moreover he had returned with all of the men he had led up into the mountain passes. In a rare show of feeling, Curos gripped Dalgan's hands. 'More than all else, I am pleased to see you alive. I feared your words of last year that you would never suffer defeat again and live.'

'When one returns victorious there is no need for stupidity, my friend – our enemies die, not us of the Topaz!'

It was a much less happy occasion when three days later Pata

Sing led in the pathetic remnants of his men who had suffered badly at the hands of the Warchaw counter-attack. The Corninstani had tasted their first victory and their first defeat.

44

In the stand of trees closest to the Warchaw's wooden keep Aalani sat, bow in hand, watching the fighting. Primarily, he had followed Xante and Curos to gain access to the land of Corninstan, sure that their raid would cause death and confusion which he would somehow use to his advantage. The image of the Warchaw sorcerer, Valanus, had given new dedication to Aalani's duty to S'lan and his love of Xante had galvanised him into a desperate plan. He was sure now that his niece would never be able to match the direct power of the Western sorcerers but his own cunning and his deadly intent, honed in years of killing for his people, might find an oblique way of defeating or weakening her adversary.

He had allowed himself the indulgence of several weeks in G'tal to recover his composure and to take his leave with May Tang. The precious stones and the coins he had taken from Quinn were hers; he could not give her the child she craved, but it was unjust that her husband had divorced her and cast her off without support. Now she would have money and at least a memory of a brief love which had cut into Aalani more deeply than he would have imagined possible. But that had passed. After that last boyish adventure in G'tal he had buried that frivolous aspect of character; now he was only the deadly assassin who watched over a niece he loved.

A section of the wooden fortress walls was thrown down and the Warchaw cavalry stormed out, crushing those who stood in their path before turning to attack the Corninstani who clustered at the burning gate. Unheeded by the main fighting, several Warchaw scrambled on foot over the fallen timbers and sped away into the night. Aalani raised his bow but then desisted as a plan began to form. Below him, Curos was using the element of Topaz Wind with skill and precision while Xante's bow sang its own song of death. A wounded Warchaw horseman slunk away unnoticed. Aalani felt again the growing power of the Red

Stone and then watched in awe as the remains of the palisade exploded. By that additional light, he saw several small parties of Warchaw horsemen and footmen escaping into the darkness of the plain. They were no threat to his friends, who were still fighting outside the burning castle, and it suited his purpose to let them go. In moments he had scrambled down the tree, unstrung his bow, and run briskly after the fleeing Warchaw.

By dawn seventeen survivors had gathered in a protective group some miles from the smoking evidence of the treacherous attack. Many were wounded, several badly burned. A horseman pointed, then dashed off with a companion. The gaze of the others was directed to a figure stumbling from the trees. Face and head were swathed in makeshift bandages and he limped badly. With great difficulty, he clambered up behind a horseman and was carried away from any danger of pursuit. They could see that his clothes were blackened with fire and that blood trickled from a hastily bandaged cut on his sword arm. As they helped him down, he swore in a voice husky with smoke and fire, 'Murderous Corninstani pigs! Treacherous Corninstani bastards!'

These were the only words of Warchaw that Aalani could utter. He had learned them from the demented ravings of the man whose clothes he now wore – probably the smallest man in the Warchaw army – and who had died as Aalani stripped him and took his identity.

'Keep quiet, Casca,' urged another Warchaw who thought he recognised the pathetic figure. 'Casca Arezo, isn't it?' Aalani nodded and slumped to the ground. They loaded him not unkindly into a cart with several other badly wounded men where he lay in dazed agony.

'It's light now,' said a voice seemingly in authority. 'We cannot wait any longer for stragglers. Riding or walking, we must be clear of this place before they begin to pursue us.'

The cart bumped off and Aalani grimaced and ground his teeth in real pain. He was tall for a Dryad but had been lucky to get the clothes of a small Warchaw which after trimming the trousers were a passable fit in boots. The men helped him to drink, but he feigned total loss of voice as he desperately

356

attempted to pick up the meaning of words he had half learned from Chaw in G'tal, who themselves spoke the language badly.

At midday they stopped, and one passenger who had died on the journey was hastily buried. Men dressed minor wounds themselves or assisted each other. When several attempted to remove Aalani's face-covering he protested violently and screamed hoarsely when the bandages were eased off. His face was a mass of red, eyes puffed and almost totally closed, hair half scorched and matted. One looked at the other and sadly shook his head but they forced Aalani to lie still while a layer of ointment was applied to prevent the infection they thought inevitable.

'No trouble, Casca,' lied the Warchaw. 'It'll begin to heal up in a day or so and then your voice'll come back. It's just the smoke you breathed in.'

In one of a Chaw T'sand Aalani would have been left for dead but the Warchaw kept their people alive and carried them away from the battle at all costs.

Part of Aalani's horrific injury was a genuine, if self-inflicted, burn, but its appearance was made far worse by the application of a fungal irritant, the best means he could devise to conceal his eastern features. His eyes would open in a day or so and there was little which needed true healing. In that time he had to establish the trust of these people or leave them before his appearance and lack of language gave him away. It was one brief chance to learn as much of their ways and speech as possible.

As the cart bumped hurriedly westward, away from any Corninstani pursuit, Aalani reflected on his lack of any firm plan. His one idea was to enter Corninstan, find Valanus and kill him, or distract him from injuring Xante. How it could be done he had no idea. Feigning greater pain than he felt, he sat up and viewed his new companions, attempting to read meaning into their slow, flat speech. He noticed that they had been joined by five other unwounded men who had been travelling to the fortress.

He also began to use his own special skill: the ability to weave an atmosphere of reduced wariness and fear of danger. It worked on forest animals and the Chaw – he hoped it would also reduce the suspicion of these hard, simple soldiers.

Towards early evening they approached two isolated Corninstani homesteads, surrounded by farmland and orchards. Many of those still able to ride were fatigued from the shock and blood-loss of their wounds, and although some would have pressed on, there was no designated commander to make decisions. In disbelief, Aalani saw the Warchaw horsemen encircle the farm buildings as if in attack, driving the occupants before them and dragging them from their houses. A man protested and was cut down, his wife shrieking over his body. A young boy attempted to flee on foot but a Warchaw sped after him, spearing him in the back and leaving him to die. The Warchaw survivors were quite aware that at the camp their Corninstani 'allies' had betrayed them and there was now no mercy for these innocent farmers. They posted a look-out on a small hill where he had a view back down the road and began to loot farms systematically.

A Warchaw with a bandaged sword arm and burned leg discovered a young girl hiding behind a barn and immediately began to rip at her clothes. The others shouted, half laughing for him to stop or make her quiet. With a grin, he knocked her unconscious and despite his limp carried her into the trees. The idea spread and the farm wife was dragged from her husband to suffer the same violation. Aalani shuddered. He collected up some bread, cheese and beer and stumbled off down the road to the look-out. As he went he heard the girl start to scream again. Some of the Warchaw were grinning and evidently would join in later; others looked disconcerted; most were quite indifferent.

Walking down the road, Aalani remembered once seeing a Dryad who had suffered a brain injury after falling from a tree; for days he had been unable to speak and alternated between tenacious attempts to function normally and bouts of frustrated temper when things went wrong. It was a useful model to work on. Aalani placed the food near the guard and handed him the beer. The man drank deeply, using his bandaged hand to steady the stone jug.

'Thanks.'

'Casca,' said Aalani. 'Casca.' He leaned over and shook the Warchaw's hand.

'Thanks, Casca.' The man laughed and began to eat.

'Treacherous Corninstani,' Aalani croaked, trying the words.

358

'Aye, but they've got their reasons.' The guard indicated the farm where the girl had now stopped screaming.

They sat eating, Aalani desperately attempting a few words of conversation now and again until he noticed a small smudge of dust and pointed.

'Thought your eyes were closed up with the burns – not bad sight for a blinded man,' said the Warchaw and leapt to his feet. 'Take your time, Casca, lad. Don't strain that leg. I'll warn t'others.' He ran off, leaving Aalani cursing his own stupidity under his breath.

Pata Sing had seen the rising smoke of burning farm buildings and galloped hard in that direction. The Cornistani came over the brow of the small hill to see their worst fears realised – burning buildings, men hanging from tree branches, women tethered like animals. There were the Warchaw, just a few of them lounging among their infamous deeds, wine and food scattered on the tree-shaded grass – eating in the very shadows of those who had been hanged. Without thought to the exhaustion of the twenty horses and men with him, he charged down on the unsuspecting enemy.

The orchards and hedges erupted: mounted Warchaw, armoured men on powerful horses, lances levelled as they charged. Not the confused, smoke-dazed riders of the night before, but well-prepared, well-trained cavalry on fresh, eager horses. From both sides they bore down on Pata Sing's force with devastation unbelievable to Aalani. As the injured Casca of Arezo, he was sitting alone and vulnerable on the tailboard of his cart, part of the bait of the trap. From behind him he retrieved the flat, rectangular shield and short, rigid sword. There was no danger, so he kept up the pretence of injury and confusion, slipping forward onto his feet, stepping unsteadily towards the fighting.

A Corninstani broke free from the skirmish, galloping his horse towards the women, Aalani a broken reed in his way. Aalani hated horses. The horse reared up when faced with the blank wall of his shield. He cut at its forefeet, blocked the sabre slash and struck upwards with his own sword as generations of the small southern Warchaw, the Italia, had learned to do. It came instinctively with the weapon. He hacked at the horse's

359

hamstring and it crashed over, spilling its dying rider. Aalani checked for danger . . . the other Corninstanis – the ones who had survived – were in a rout, fleeing eastward, followed by the jeers of the Warchaw. He staggered around until someone led him back to the cart – it was beginning to become like his home, he thought.

'Treacherous Corninstani pigs!'

'Aye, Casca, but that'n never ride again. You fair gutted him. A shame about the horse, though.'

'Good?' Aalani croaked.

'Aye, good. One thing, Casca. You've got real grit for an Italia, I'll say that.'

'Frank?' asked Aalani, gripping the man's shoulder.

'What? Oh yes, I'm Frank, Franklinson really, but Frank is my name.' Solemnly Aalani shook the man's hand as he had seen some Warchaw do.

The Warchaw had no idea of the size of Pata Sing's force, whether this was a raid or a counter invasion. After some discussion it was decided that those able to ride well would press on openly across the plain, to warn the provincial garrison. The more seriously wounded, Frank, Casca and four others, would go on along the back road, seeking as much cover as they could and keeping off any likely invasion rout. Roalf Redbeard suggested he could take the girl with him in the cart but the others refused. In a fit of irritation, he cut her throat and left her bleeding on the road. He caught Aalani's eye and lurched towards him, shaking a massive fist.

'Don't look at me like that, Casca, you snivelling southern . . .' He did not finish.

Aalani's dagger darted out, pricking up under Roalf's throat where the big artery ran. Roalf flinched but did not move, did not dare move.

'I'll kill you, Casca.'

The others moved away. It was a private quarrel; Roalf was not liked and Casca had guts.

'You'n dead already, Roalf,' said Frank. 'Put the knife down, Casca. There's a war on, we can't fight each other.'

Aalani backed away warily. He had seen the fear in Roalf's

eyes but he hardly trusted himself. The others evidently did not like Roalf. He was too big and dangerous, but never quite on the front-line when it came to a battle. Aalani might play on that and for the girl, if for no other reason, he would kill Roalf soon.

The next day the small party of wounded travelled through a wooded area and at one of their stops Aalani took the opportunity to walk amongst the trees. It was not forest but it cleared his soul of the blackness of men to hear branches singing. He collected herbs, plants and fungi as he walked. A master of poisons, he also had a working knowledge of remedies and healing.

Over their small camp fire he boiled up a cleansing brew for killing the infection of wounds. Gildas, the man with a stomach wound, was becoming delirious, although the cut had not punctured his gut. Without speaking or asking, Aalani undid the bandages and bathed the suppurating cut. The Warchaw's ideas on basic cleansing of wounds were good but they did little else to aid recovery. He also treated Frank's arm, cutting away an inflamed flap of flesh and bathing the area which had started to heal. One of the others asked him a question but he had no idea of the meaning. He looked blank and shook his head. The man spoke again, looking annoyed. In desperation, Aalani leapt up from tying Frank's bandage and stalked off.

'I only asked if I could use some of his water!'

'I'm sure you can,' replied Frank. 'I think his mind is gone. His head is a mass of burns but he may have had a blow as well. Sometimes he's alright, sometimes he's like a kid. He still can't speak much.' Roalf sneered but said nothing.

Frank Franklinson of Occam followed Aalani into the trees and sat beside him. 'It's OK. We've seen it before when a lad's had a hard knock. Your tongue'll remember a'ter a bit. Your sword arm still works, and you use a dagger fast enough. It'll come back.'

Gradually the words came and the lads seemed really pleased for his recovery. Also, Gildas stopped raving and even Roalf asked Casca to clean his leg wound. For all that, their progress was slow and cut off from the outside world. Frank steered clear of settlements – they had food enough – but whether this was to avoid detection or to prevent any further excesses by Roalf, Aalani was not clear.

On the evening of the third day Aalani took the short, stiff sword he had made his own and began imitating the practice he had seen in the castle's exercise yard. Frank followed with his longer horseman's sabre.

'Cut left head, cut right head, cut right leg,' he called from behind Aalani. Aalani hesitated, desperately having to decode the words before he could act. 'Kill!' Instantly Aalani lunged forward, arm striking upwards, his own body close in behind the shield.

'Its the words that's the trouble,' observed Frank. 'Naught wrong with your swordsmanship!'

They changed roles, with Aalani calling the strikes and Frank exercising until his wound protested. Aalani repeated another gruelling session and they sat down to rest. Beneath the hardly needed face-bandage Aalani's skin seared with salt sweat.

Frank swept an area clear of leaves and drew a map with the point of his sword. Aalani was baffled: was it land and water, or plains and hills? Gildas approached and looked in interest, and with a grin drew a small fish on what must be a central sea. Frank indicated his home, an island to the north.

'Arezo?' Gildas pointed to a spot on the long spit of land, extending into the sea.

'Yes, Arezo,' said Aalani and added, 'Forest village to the north, Caziro, where my mother lives.' An inspired lie, he hoped. Frank nodded.

Gildas pointed to the largest area on the map. 'Rennes, the town of my birth,' he explained. 'A fine city and now I may see it again. I had feared my wound was beginning to rot before your succour.'

Different lands, different people, different languages, thought Aalani, and with sudden fear he realised that any Italia he met would probably use that people's own distinct language.

'You are trained as a healer?' Gildas was asking.

Aalani attempted several answers, thinking he must prepare a better story in advance. 'No, my father, not my mother, gave me my skills,' he tried.

Gildas looked knowingly at Frank who said, 'Look, Casca, me and Gildas here know your secret.'

Aalani forced himself to be calm. The long Warchaw dagger would be used on Frank, a clean swift kill, no need for the poisoned bronze of S'lan.

'We've realised you are half elf,' continued Gildas. 'There's no shame in it to us, these things happen. I've an Imrani wife. You've done right to us and you use skills from both peoples. I suppose your father was from the Forest and taught you some elvish things?'

Aalani nodded dumbly. 'Healing,' he said, to cover his confusion. Inwardly his mind was racing again. There was yet another Warchaw race of people, Elve's People, who lived in forests and had better knowledge of healing. How could he ask about them if his father was supposed to be one?

'There's a High Elf living in the hills above Carish,' continued Frank. 'Did you know?'

'No,' very warily. 'I was not aware of that.'

'Batan, he is called – you have heard of him?' Aalani shook his head.

'We could leave you in Carish if you like,' suggested Frank. 'It will take more than your potions to cure that face of yours, Casca. This Batan is one of your people and has a good reputation as a healer. Give me the name of your Italia Unit and I will pass the word that you are still sick.'

Several days later they camped for the last time in the wooded hills and in the distant evening sun the tall, thin towers of Carish were just visible. Aalani's forays for healing plants had given him an opportunity to hunt small game for fresh meat. His short, powerful, recurved bow was taken as further evidence of his elven origin. Life could be hard, reflected Aalani, as he prepared a stew of rabbit, pigeon and vegetables from the Corninstani farm which had been looted. He had established a genuine friendship with Frank, and the others were no worse than men everywhere. His identity of Casca had been built up steadily and his use of the language was getting effective, but he still had no final plan. The face bandages would have to come off soon, with

363

all the risks of recognition that he was from the Chaw race of people if they did not believe his features Elven.

It was a subtle mix of poisons he added to the stew. They trusted him and watched as he added what appeared to be the usual herbs and flavouring. He would also suggest a few measures of wine because it was the last day they would be travelling together before he turned off to Carish. They would go drowsy sooner than they expected but probably without alarm. Death would be painless and if anyone did find their camp in this isolated spot he would already have led the horses away and left the men's bodies as if robbed: throats cut, clothes stolen or rifled, no possessions or weapons.

45

In Carish, Aalani Galni had made discreet sales of the better Warchaw goods to Corninstani merchants, and with the money he purchased new clothes in the western style before renting a modest house in the name of Casca of Arezo. His strange manner, covered face and claim to be half-elf kept him somewhat distanced from other Warchaw but it did not prevent sufficient contact for him to practice the language and learn a great deal more of their culture. Information on the Elves was more difficult to come by but he had rehearsed a touching story of his poor Arezo mother being deserted by the elvish father.

Aalani still found it difficult to travel on horseback but strode up the hill paths to the cell of Batan the High Elf with all the assurance of his assumed identity. He now posed as Casca, a wealthy half-elf from Arezo, who had been travelling the world in search of knowledge and rare medicinal herbs. While on the high hills he had been caught up in the treacherous Corninstani raid on the training fort – now common knowledge – and had suffered wounds and worse still facial burns when the fort had been destroyed. His pack held gold, seeds and plants. He carried an elven style bow of unusually high quality and a sword and dagger of his mother's Italia people but beneath the still-bandaged face was the Dryad of S'lan with the bronze dagger hidden in his western clothes.

Batan was almost Aalani's age but seemed older. Grief and pain were etched deeply on his eastern-looking face and there was, Aalani realised quickly, an aura of decay clinging to the once great man. It appeared that the stories of dissipation from drink and drugged smoke could well be true. Batan was tall and slightly built, similar to a Dryad, with dark eyes. It would, however, be quite impossible for Aalani to impersonate the Elf if his own Chaw-like face and eyes were visible. The cold austere stone cell Batan had chosen for his retreat had been built for a hermit many years ago, and had done little for his humour. His greeting was curt and he took little interest in the request for assistance in healing the burn scars still visible on Aalani's face.

'The healing will proceed, as you well know', he said, 'but there is a strange distortion and much scarring. The destruction of one of the Red Stones of Gadel releases strange powers, this I can tell you.'

'You are a Master,' pleaded Aalani.

'I was once,' Batan snapped. 'What is needed is regeneration and moulding. It could be done but would take time and cause intense pain!'

'I am not afraid of pain,' said Aalani, 'and I am a healer in some small measure. What was done to me could be learned and used for others. If a sequence could be learned from a Master I would even attempt it on myself.'

'Impossible!' stated Batan. 'I depart tomorrow on an eight day journey to the Capital. There I meet the High Wizard Valanus who has requested my assistance in a Great Venture.' His voice lacked conviction and already Aalani was beginning to suspect that the 'retreat' of Batan was a desperate attempt to prepare himself for this, possibly his last, Great Adventure.

'I am a pilgrim and a healer,' said Aalani, 'my way is free. If it is permitted I would follow and serve the Master Batan and do what service I can. In return I can share the Master's thoughts and learn the little that is in my power.'

'You speak like a fawning Chaw,' said Batan, but Aalani had hit the right note and the next day he left the ancient hermitage, walking at the head of Batan's horse. At first their talk centred on plants and herbs which had some interest for Batan although Aalani believed it to have been many years since he had practiced these skills.

The wayside inn Batan had intended to use was far from clean or friendly and at Aalani's urging they camped in the woods some distance from the village. The routine established was for Aalani to deal with shelter, fire and food while Batan talked. Much of what he said was idle reminiscence but salted within were gems of lore or information which held Aalani's attention deep into the night. The next day passed in similar manner with Aalani again hunting and cooking.

'Do you have family in Arezo?' asked Batan suddenly catching

366

Aalani by surprise – but now he did have an answer at least partially ready.

'Not in Arezo itself, but I do have a daughter. She's twenty eight years old and has talent in the art of magic.'

'She does not travel with you?'

'No, she seeks greater things than plant lore. She will be a true sorcerer of power amongst our people. Her abilities are beyond me.'

'It can be a dangerous path, dangerous indeed. Easily corrupted or destroyed by jealousy.' He looked puzzled and asked, 'Your wife, then, is of the Forest People?'

'Indeed, Master, but she is no more. A bad winter, sickness and . . . I could not face the world or my daughter.' He paused for some time grappling with the need to open some memory or emotion to Batan to prompt a response. He could not compose a lie of sufficient conviction but he had his own memories. Should he reveal them and the secrets of how he loved Yani, in the vain hope of saving her daughter, Xante? The story needed twisting but in essence it was true.

It had been a hard winter and even in S'lan snow lay feet thick and the people starved. At such times the hunters fed the Dryad by culling deer, seeking small animals hibernating underground and trapping rabbits. As a young hunter of twenty-two Aalani could roam the forest with tireless success. The long treks and hard runs merely numbed the sadness he felt as the cold numbed others. He had been warned not to marry Yani, not to attempt to make her love him. Aware that the penalties of S'lan would be imposed on them both if he had disobeyed he had retreated and watched his elder brother take his place in her affection, watched as they loved and cried his own bitter tears. His joy when Xante was born to them was genuine for he loved them both but there remained the hollowness which could never be filled. He had been born a Dryad but could not for some reason be one with them, he loved but could not marry. Now in this winter of despair he and those like him were the people's only hope. As others grew thin and pale Aalani's strength and energy increased as if the very spirit of the forest was in him, strengthening him at every stride.

After two months the winter relented, warm rains fell. Returning from his latest hunting trip Aalani struggled to the long house near the southern meeting place through a sea of mud while already trees were breaking out in bud and birds sang in praise of S'lan. His brother Xatan came to meet him with feeble tread that told of more than famine. Four days previously Yani had become desperately sick, two days later she had died. She had died and Aalani had felt nothing, no warning, no farewell, nothing. He had done everything S'lan had asked, given up all that had been demanded and Yani had died. Now he could not even watch her happiness from afar. Only the need to care for Xante had prevented Xatan from taking his own life. The brothers clung together and wept.

Where Xatan had accepted duty and grief Aalani had cursed S'lan with all his being. At any other time the Dryadin would have killed Aalani before nightfall for his blasphemy but there was another task waiting. Outside the forest the Night Dragon Clan were also starving. The Dryadin had no food but they did have gold and credit in Untin. Aalani knew the city and despite his youth the merchants accepted that he could speak for the forest people. He could not even stay to grieve for Yani but had left immediately for Untin to arrange a caravan of corn and dried meat for the starving Night Dragon Clan.

The story Aalani told to Batan was not this one, he twisted it to make Xante his daughter and moved to a different forest which Aalani would never see, but in his own mind he relived the true events. When he finished he sat in remembered grief sharpened by the shame of speaking as he did. He hoped Yani would look out from the void and understand.

'I fear I bore you with my old sorrows,' he said after a long pause, but Batan had become locked in his own memories.

'No, I should not have pried,' said Batan. 'It is a story similar to my own but yours does you more credit. By the God of Trees I could drink a flask of wine.'

'I have some herbs which if smoked in a Corninstani pipe brings some solace of forgetfulness,' said Aalani. Batan did not answer but instead began to relive his own tragedy.

Nearly ten years previously Batan, then at the height of his power, had travelled into Imran to seek forms of magic long forgotten. With him were his wife and young son for the land was passive under the heel of the Warchaw. In the north of that land they had stayed in a castle of the sorcerer, Neath, who was also interested in ancient magic. It was while Batan and Neath had been exploring the passages under a ruined temple that the last Imrani revolt had swept over the land. The town garrison had been slaughtered and the lightly manned castle besieged. Neath and Batan were desperate for inside the castle were many of their discoveries which could, if captured, rekindle the power of Imrani sorcerers of old. If combined with Neath's Red Stone of Gadel, also in the castle, this ancient knowledge could be used to strike a savage blow at the Order and to the Western Alliance.

The sorcerer and the Elf were too far distant to bring direct aid to the castle and the Imrani were battering the gates and scaling the walls when Batan agreed that the Red Stone should be destroyed. In either haste or error Neath had put forth too much power and the explosion had destroyed the entire central building. Within the fireball had died Batan's wife and child.

'It was my duty,' he sobbed 'but I have regretted it every day since. I would sell the entire collection of Gadel's power to reverse that moment. I now know that a man's first duty should be to his family, they trusted me and I destroyed them.'

'Should I then go to any lengths to protect my daughter?' asked Aalani.

'Without doubt.' Silently Aalani handed Batan the long stemmed Corninstani pipe and lit the packed narcotics in the bowl with a coal from the fire.

They still travelled in the direction which Batan planned but he knew little of reality. Fed a constant stream of drugs and wine by Aalani he rose through fields of memories, happy with illusions of his once-proud knowledge and wisdom which Aalani constantly probed. He spoke of magic and Elven Lore, healing and regeneration; he emptied out at Aalani's feet the storehouse of his mind. He corrected Aalani's speech and errors in the geography of the western lands without comment as one would to a child – possibly he spoke to Aalani as if to his own son passing down the knowledge of his people to a new generation.

After six days Batan's mind was almost broken but his spirit survived and Aalani needed to administer the stronger and stronger doses of drugs. It was at their sparse morning meal that the Elf suddenly threw down his plate and fumbled for a weapon he no longer carried.

'What have you done to me, Casca,' he shouted, his voice a hoarse shadow of itself. 'You have told me nothing, you have destroyed me. In every secret place of my mind I find the smell of your drugged smoke and the footsteps of your presence. What is your purpose?'

'To protect Xante. I will take your place and kill Valanus, or corrupt him with drugs or subvert his soul. I will not make your mistake, Batan, and allow those dear to me to die while I idly seek dreams of old wisdom.' From beneath his tunic he drew the poisoned bronze dagger of S'lan he always carried hidden, but changed his mind. The brilliant steel of Arezo slid easily between Batan's ribs and he died without a struggle.

Aalani was now alone and had as much information on Batan as he could hold but he had to prepare himself in one further way. His features had to be changed to resemble those of a true Elf, an Elf who had been damaged and scarred as he attempted to rescue his family from the blazing ruins in Imran. For some time he shrank from the pain that would follow but at last he began. He set in his mind the sequence of events which he must follow and with a series of exercise, rituals and deep mind control, moved his spirit almost from his body. Almost as another observer, he saw the powerful jitsu-trained hands grasp his skull and begin to move bones, twisting cartilege, cracking joints, moulding and moving muscles and flesh. Desperately he fought the rising surge of pain but the body trembled and harsh whimper sounds uttered from his throat as he rebandaged his head.

His concentration wavered and the pain flooded in sweeping his consciousness away like a slick in a river. He awoke to blinding, excruciating agony; fire of all colours radiated before his eyes, his ears were a turmoil of sound. Dimly he sought through the fog and the flashes for the pipe and the narcotics. A last shred of resolve crushed the pipe and flung the mixture of plant leaves into the fire to pump their sickening fragrance away from him. For two days he alternated between the light and the dark unable to eat, drinking only enough to keep alive.

Gradually the pain eased so that he could move and function. It was enough. He packed his belongings and began to stumble south to the Capital of Corninstan where Valanus was growing concerned over the late arrival of Batan the Elven One.

46

On the plains, as the year wore on into the heat of summer, the mobile N'gol horsemen reigned supreme as they always would unless the enemy could make contact with their herds or their water supply. In the mountains, the constrained spaces with rocks and broken ground prevented the might of the Warchaw cavalry from imparting the crushing blow of its devastating charge. Neither were their archers, for all their range and accuracy, able to keep the larger numbers of the Chaw at a safe distance. At this time, the Warchaw did not have sufficient force spare from subduing Corninstan to attempt a major campaign. Their aim was to crush Corninstani resistance while mapping out the passes and water routes which crossed the O'san to Chaw.

More vital than all else for Curos was to deny the Warchaw any knowledge of this dry, inhospitable land which acted as a buffer between Chaw and invasion. The N'gol tribes which he had moved into O'san had all shared a similar task but tackled it in different ways. The Sand Dragon conducted a campaign of great dash and style, while Pynar of the White Dragon Clan exercised a much more cautious approach which he felt necessary to counter the influence of Turakina.

Further north the Sunrise Horde were faring much worse than the other clans, despite much skill and bravery. The successful hit-and-run tactics of the Dragon and Dog Clans were not easily learned by men who treated warfare as a personal combat and who possessed a fatalistic attitude to the inevitability of death. Time and again they were tempted into making a frontal attack on the Warchaw. In such cases the heavier weapons and horses of the enemy could concentrate on a narrow front to deadly effect which only superior numbers and assistance from the neighbouring clans could contain. Inevitably, the Sunrise Horde losses were high, higher than they could repeatedly sustain. Often the Warchaw could retreat in good order back over the mountains, leaving the tribesmen in defeated disarray.

For Curos to order the eastern tribesman to withdraw would have been quite impossible and none would consent to return without some victory and the promised plunder. The other clans had started to rotate family groups back to their homeland, but this too was impossible for the Sunrise Horde, due to the great distances involved. Recognising the weak area in the Chaw line, the Warchaw began to concentrate their efforts in an attempt to build on past success. Victory here would limit the support Pata Sing's raiders were receiving from the north Corninstan mountain villages. In desperation, Curos was forced to move Khol Dalgan and the men of the Topaz Wind north to show the easterners how the war could be waged.

The Night Dragon Clan had taken naturally to guerilla warfare, but unlike the other peoples, they never left women and children behind. The Clan moved as one and was most adept at making temporary concealed camps in the deep mountain valleys while the dark-clad tribesmen practised their nocturnal skills. Success began to make the small tribe relatively prosperous by their previous standard and they established a profitable trade in captured horses and weapons.

Muekan of the Grey Jackal Clan, a sekar and a warrior, was unaware of the full details of the situation in the O'san as he rode towards the Night Dragon's camping area. Like all N'gol, he believed his people to be truly superior to any other, the natural rulers of all desolate places. The town of Untin, the parched O'san plateau and even the soaring Lune mountains made little impact on Muekan and land was just land, categorised only by quantity of water and grazing. He had completed his training at Te Toldin and had been offered the post of sekar to the Night Dragon, a role few would have been willing to accept, but stories of the evil ways of the dark clan held little credibility for Muekan. In the brief visits he had made to his mother's people, Muekan had seen none of the cannibalism or horrific murders attributed to this poverty-stricken people.

As an elder son, he was expected to make his own way in the world, leaving his mother and father free to rear his brother and two sisters. He was therefore only too pleased to be allocated to his mother's clan, who were reputed to be making great profit by the war. The less successful Sunrise Horde, for all their reputation of bravery, were of little interest to this N'gol fortune-seeker who needed at least a small herd before he could marry.

Ongul, the leader of the Night Dragon, was pleased indeed to have a sekar allocated to his clan, conferring, as he saw it, recognition for his high prestige as the most victorious leader. He was also gratified to learn that the sekar had strong family links with his people and was known by some to have an affinity to their way of life. Any outsider, however skilled, would need to exercise considerable care not to anger those who held life cheaply. To murder a stranger for as little as the clothes off his back and a handful of grain held no disgrace to those who had often faced starvation.

Pleased as he was to welcome the sekar, Ongul had little idea how to use Muekan's impressive skills. The Night Dragon Clan's independent style of warfare was, to Ongul's suspicious mind, best conducted in total secrecy, with only the finest of guidance from the Noyan Zachaw. To call for help or to warn others of danger was exceedingly low on his scale of priorities. The cloaking techniques learned from Chou Suzin were however seen as possibly useful in defeating the enemy and Muekan was dispatched to join one of the small hunting parties which watched a narrow valley pass.

Tayan, who had so surprised Curos and Xante at their first meeting in the D'was, was sixteen years old and the youngest boy among the nearly blind night hunters who operated away from the main clan. With his sighted brother and sister, he was already responsible for the murder of numerous Warchaw Corninstan scouts. Muekan quickly realised that the cloaking which normally deceived so well had no effect at all upon Tayan. Even in quite bright sunlight the boy could detect the sekar when others would have passed him by unnoticed.

On the second night, on the high ridge overlooking the mountain pass, Meukan sat talking with Tayan. Despite his mere sixteen years, Tayan spoke in the matter-of-fact tones of a veteran soldier. The boy explained the achievements of his clan and without any undue pride mentioned his own contribution to his family's impressive tally of kills.

'I have but three to my personal credit,' he explained. 'Such

374

as I can detect quarry from afar in the night, but we lack the precision of sight to use the bow. My brother and sister prevent me from joining close-quarter fighting, where my knife is as deadly as theirs.' He shook his head sadly. 'It is very difficult, Muekan, for a man to live with an over-protective elder sister like Juylan. She truly believes it her duty to the Clan to place her body between me and any enemy. I dream of the day when she will marry.'

'I know you speak so that I will hear you,' said a voice from the darkness. 'I have no need of a husband or children yet, little brother. I have seized wealth of my own and my arm is deadly enough that I need no protection!'

Muekan turned to welcome the young woman Juylan, who with her brother Gei had such a formidable reputation. Before he could speak, Tayan interrupted. 'Call Gei, gentle, gentlest of sisters. There are men moving over the col at the end of the valley.' He pointed to Muekan. 'Watch that open space which they will soon cross. See how they have learned caution,' he added as the figures sprinted across the moonlit patch into the deep shade beyond.

With their detailed knowledge of the ground below, the family were quick to choose a sight for a deadly ambush and were soon ready to move into position. Muekan felt a distinct unease which he sought to hide. Although his habitual calm indifference was unshaken by fear, he felt there was more to be learned before they should attack. To Muekan's surprise, Gei stretched out his arm and gripped his wrist.

'My friend, you are not happy with our plan. You are one of us now and must speak. The Night Dragon only springs when all its people are ready.'

'I cannot explain fully,' Muekan stammered. 'My skills are little practised. I feel there are more of our enemy close by.'

'You sense them too?' asked Juylan, searching the hills. 'I also feel a presence.' Her voice tailed off.

'Then we wait until we are sure,' replied Gei. 'Juylan's instincts have often proved true when I and Tayan have seen nothing.'

'It may not be instinct or luck,' said Tayan after some long time. 'But I now see a dim glow from over the high col to the west, the body-heat of many men who must follow the three we already see. Yes, one of the scouts goes back to them while the other two watch the eastern end of the valley.'

More time still passed before a large Warchaw party came into sight, and began to make a camp hidden among the sparse trees and bushes. By first light they were almost hidden, even from above.

'You have learned one important lesson, Muekan,' said Gei, the elder brother. 'Take note of all your senses. For the hunters of the night, nothing must be ignored. Your clan-blood spoke true to you; in future always heed its warning. All who share the risk have a right to speak. If we had descended to the valley floor our situation would have been perilous.'

The next day was spent in a limbo of unreality as Muekan and the other N'gol looked down upon the Warchaw. Despite the protection of the rocky outcrops, they restricted themselves to the minimum of slow, deliberate movement and avoided any action which would risk exposure.

For some time Muekan sat with Juylan, silently watching the enemy. Eventually the woman said, her voice no more than a breath, 'Truly, you are a Dragon Hunter. You sit still as stone and even your chest is still.'

'No more than yours,' he replied. 'But I have received some training not known to your people.' He took her wrist and murmured, 'Your pulse is too high and your mind too active. Follow my lead, and breathe more deeply, and you could be as unmoving as a lizard who basks in the sun.'

Later while Juylan and Tayan kept watch, Muekan and Gei shared the cool shelter of a deep fissure in the rocks. The elder brother began to question Muekan closely on his lineage and his fortune. Lost in his own thoughts, Muekan did not notice the purpose of the enquiry but later, in the heat of the mid-afternoon, it was Juylan who spoke openly, 'You know of the dwindling numbers of our people, Muekan, and the danger that this may bring?' When he did not answer, she continued softly, 'My brother says you are from a family unrelated to ours and it is my duty to breed with one such as you. I would find such a thing no hardship.'

'You choose me out of duty,' he said with a half-smile. 'The

376

courtship of your clan is strange – more akin to the arranged marriages of the Chaw than the ways of the N'gol.'

'Our women have little chance to learn seduction, life is too hard. My instincts draw me to you, and that is enough.'

'Perhaps I would choose another, out of my duty.'

'The women of the Night Dragon do not compete for men. I claim first and if necessary my knife backs my claim.'

The heat and the lassitude made it difficult to react to the situation, and Muekan always tended to drift with the forces of life. 'I have no objection to an arranged marriage,' he whispered, then added, 'I have no substance to buy a wife and no time to seize a woman as of right.'

'I have herds enough for us to fare well,' replied Juylan. 'Custom means little to us of the Night. We take what we need from the world and give back what we can to our clan. I need a man, the clan needs healthy children.' She sat silent for some time before continuing, 'We do not believe in the right to happiness, but if I were to fill your life with sadness I would understand if you left me. Stay only until the first child is born.'

'I have not known love or hate, Juylan,' Muekan replied. 'My feelings drift as a calm morning mist. I will accept what you offer, but do not ask too much of one such as I, who has little to give.'

Far below the Warchaw stirred restlessly in the burning heat which reflected off the valley walls. In reaction to the forced inactivity, two men began to climb slowly and carefully over the boulders and ridges towards Muekan and Juylan.

'They look directly at us,' breathed the woman in a voice which showed no alarm. 'If we move or they come closer we will be discovered.'

'We will not be seen,' replied Muekan.

'I will attack the bearded one on the left,' said Juylan, ignoring his comment. 'My bow is strung and ready.'

'A wife should at least listen to her husband, although no N'gol would expect her to obey,' whispered Muekan. 'We will not be seen. A Warchaw with sun in his eyes will not see a sekar, even at twenty paces.'

'And if they come closer?'

377

'My knife could outspeed your arrow, but it will not be needed.'

The two Warchaw climbed steadily upwards, stopping often to search the valley with their eyes. At one stage they stood less than thirty paces from Muekan and Juylan and, despite gazing directly at the seated pair, they were unable to penetrate the cloak cast mentally by the sekar. They saw only rocks and stark shadows.

Eventually, the Warchaw retraced their steps back to their camp on the valley floor.

'They are two dead men who have but postponed their evil hour,' said Tayan as he and Gei joined them.

The long day moved on with the infinite slowness that comes from frustration and inactivity. Tayan and Muekan were able to drift into watchful dreams but the woman became increasingly tense, almost to the point of anger, as she waited for the Warchaw to move.

Darkness fell, and the Warchaw scouts departed with swift, fluid movements as they went ahead to seek out any danger. Still the watchers could do little until the main body of men had dismantled the camp and set off to follow their advance party. Juylan was then able to explode into activity as she saddled her pony and secured their small pack of camp goods onto a spare animal. From beside her as he buckled her mount's bridle, Muekan asked, 'There must be a simple answer, but I must ask how you can bypass the Warchaw to warn the clan?'

'The whole mountain range is cut with goat-tracks and paths which we have sought out. Our foe move slowly with caution; I can ride around the route and give Ongul two days' warning.'

'It would be as well for me to follow them with Tayan,' suggested Muekan thoughtfully. 'I can contact a sekar of the Sunrise Horde and ask him to join the clan to act as Ongul's messenger.'

'There is no need for us to ride to warn Ongul, then?'

'Yes, the sekar may fail to arrive; he has a two-day journey at least.' He smiled at Juylan in the darkness and realised that he did not want her to leave. 'Not all sekars are anxious to join your people.'

'It was finally agreed that Gei, and not Juylan, would journey through the hills while the others followed the Warchaw at a

378

distance by higher mountain paths. It was only necessary to keep the enemy in distant sight by day, no more than a glow in Tayan's vision, and to move close once each night to make an approximate check on numbers.

Muekan was able to persuade the sekar of the Sunrise Horde to join the Night Dragon, although he would give no true reason to the man until he was near Ongul's camp. He did not want one thousand blundering eastern tribesmen accompanying the sekar to ruin the ambush that the Night Dragon Clan would prepare.

In the four days of this stealthy pursuit, Muekan became one with Tayan and Juylan, and submerged himself in the ways of the Night Dragon. The Clansmen seemed to move together by instinct, and his two companions knew of their people's preparations before Muekan received messages from the sekar.

On the morning of the fifth day the Warchaw scouts reached a wide open valley with a stream-fed tarn. Skilfully they searched the flat valley floor and the surrounding area, and found no trace of human occupation, save a month-old camp fire. All evidence of the Night Dragon camp which had been there until three days ago had been removed. Several wild sheep drank at the stream and a deer sprinted away from the tarnside and up into the hills. Finding it deserted and possibly unknown to the N'gol, with good pasture, the Warchaw recognised a perfect campsite from which they could plan raids into the O'san. The only routes for attack into the valley were by the narrow entry pass and the wider, but easily viewed, exit. There was little danger of discovery and no danger of surprise attack by large numbers.

The signs that the Warchaw were making a more permanent camp were soon quite obvious to Muekan and Juylan and in the open a more accurate assessment of the enemy could be made. There were seventy or eighty of the Warchaws' light cavalry who were being trained to counter the more mobile N'gol. Also camped with them were twenty Corninstani mounted archers, in their distinctive green uniforms.

Ongul of the Night Dragon allowed the Warchaw to settle into a comfortable camp routine. Particularly at night, the sentries had been carefully observed until their pattern of activity was well known and predictable.

379

After three days, as the long shadows of the mountains deepened, parties of the Night Dragon Clan in their sinister black robes began to move silently along hidden paths towards the plain. The wariness of the enemy had markedly diminished as they relaxed by the deep, peaceful tarn, always cool and fresh from the mountain streams, and they were quite unaware of the dragon which stalked them. Yesugei, Ongul's son, had hastened back from a visit to the Blue Wolves, and all those who guarded herds or watched other paths had gathered into the hills surrounding the enemy.

As he crept towards the Warchaw with Tayan's extended family and associates, about twenty people, Muekan came to understand the dread of the Night Dragon. There was no noise, no speech or stumbling, as they filed expertly through the darkest of shadows. The people moved as if by one accord, as if darkness and danger had fused each individual into a single, many-armed entity. Muekan, for all his kinship with the people, needed almost constant guidance from Juylan. He wondered if each of the silent, wraith-like shapes burned with the same pulse and fire as did his promised bride. Weapons normally hidden under dark cloaks were now openly worn. Each man, woman and child carried their preferred killing implement – straight sword, curved scimitar, long needle-pointed dagger, or crushing maces, axes and iron staves for others.

On the edge of the flat plain they waited for an age as the darkness deepened and the moon set. Juylan lay close to Muekan, her body like a quivering spring charged with deadly energy as she sought to discern any movement in the camp. A second Night Hunter joined Tayan. Near midnight the Warchaw sentries were changed and a new period of waiting began.

Juylan turned to whisper to Muekan that it was time. Led by the two almost blind men who saw so well in darkness, the four of them crawled out across the dry earth towards the two nearest guards. No signal had been given but between the hunters of the night the strange empathy made communication redundant. Seeking the heat of their prey's bodies, Tayan and his companion advanced with a painstaking, silent progress which required little from Muekan's cloaking technique to defeat the keenest eyes and ears. Juylan motioned Muekan to stop. His now night-tuned vision could just distinguish his companions as they reared up from the blackness, bows in hand. Like Juylan, Muekan drew his sword and balanced the heavy throwing dagger – his own very personal weapon. He flinched in surprise as an albino boy, barely thirteen years old with an almost toy-like bow, appeared beside Tayan.

An unexpected, almost electric surge passed through Muekan. In reaction to the subliminal signal the bowmen loosed deadly poison-tipped arrows. Before bowstrings had ceased their vibration, puncturing thuds and hoarse chokings of pain came from less than twenty paces away. Already, Muekan was on his feet and running, Juylan by his side, sword outstretched.

A man sat in agonised shock as his paralysed fingers gripped at the arrow in his upper arm. Wide-eyed, he stared disbelievingly as Muekan's straight sword thrust into his throat. The second sentry's pitiful whimpers of pain ceased as Juylan slashed with practised skill at the side of his neck. Instantly Muekan and Juylan were again lying flat in the darkness, side by side, ears and eyes straining towards the dark-veiled camp. For once, Muekan's pulse was raised with more than exertion. For all his sekar's skill and keen senses, he heard nothing as Tayan joined them and gripped Muekan's arm in a gesture of praise. No noise, no signal, but the rest of the group silently closed up to Tayan.

Another subliminal signal, and they began to crawl forward. Muekan could feel the evil and menace of his Night Dragon kinsmen. Part of his being gladly accepted this strange oneness, but his Blue Dragon Clan instincts recoiled in rejection at the cold-blooded murder which had replaced the honourable warfare of the N'gol.

He could see dimmed cooking fires, and hear the water lapping on the tarn. He picked out the darker shapes of sleeping men. His blood froze as one shape slowly stood upright and walked sleepily towards the nearby rocks. Muekan sensed rather than saw the sudden grasping hands and thrusting daggers which pulled the Corninstani down to a sudden death.

The last twenty paces – still no rush nor sound. These people had done such things many times before, and no-one would ruin this greatest massacre. Gei closed on an outlying sleeper, and swung a short, spike-bladed axe horizontally into the Warchaw's

381

skull. With a sickening crunch and a scurry of twitching arms and legs, the man died.

All over the camp men died, many never fully waking as they were stabbed, slashed or crushed from life. Any man beginning to sit or stand was a focus of instant swamping activity as the Night Dragon Clan now advanced in a crouching run. Too late, warnings were shouted only to be cut short; desperately weapons were drawn by fumbling hands even as children cut throats and women smashed skulls.

A fully awake Warchaw rolled aside from a savage spear-thrust and came up to his feet, sword in hand. The heavy, broad blade glinted in the feeble starlight as it cut down the Night Dragon spearman. With sheer strength, the Warchaw threw aside a second attacker and his dagger ripped into the man's stomach. Juylan dived towards him, arm and sword extended into a single, venomous lunge. The Warchaw parried with his dagger and swung the broadsword as she ducked away to one side.

Following Juylan, Muekan blocked the blow which would have killed her, but his own sword was beaten down across her shoulders and spun from his numbed fingers. He leapt back and away from the Warchaw's backhanded swing and hurled the throwing knife with all his might. The heavy blade and a Night Dragon arrow thudded home, into the Warchaw's chest. Blood oozing from her shoulder, Juylan dashed tigerishly forward and slid her blade into the man's side.

Throughout the camp similar, one-sided fights developed as inevitably some Warchaw or Corninstani gained their feet to fight back with no hope of success or flight.

Muekan gripped Juylan in frenzied relief as the more practical Tayan sought to gauge the depth of the wound.

'It is nothing,' she assured him in a voice almost hysterical with excitement and elation. 'Nothing more than a love-kiss from my husband's sword. Few women can have such a marriage present.'

'A present of life itself for you, sister.' Tayan tried to keep his emotion from his voice. Over Juylan's shoulder, Muekan was watching with unseeing eyes as a party of children stabbed away the last vestige of life from a writhing body.

As the light of morning returned, family groups stripped clothes and belongings from their victims. Each dead Warchaw face was savagely hacked through to the bridge of the nose and the eye-sockets, mutilated to show that it was the Night Dragon which had slain. The whitened skulls would be placed in the mountains as a warning to any who dared enter the land which the Night Dragon Clan now claimed.

Wounds were dressed and the Clan dead mourned – two men, one woman and a ten-year-old girl. Muekan held Juylan's arms against his chest while her brother bandaged the long, but not deep, sword cut across her shoulder. Immodestly she looked into his eyes, ignoring her near nakedness and the pain.

'I have many scars, but I am still beautiful?'

'Most men would find you quite ugly,' he lied. 'You would best be content with the admiration of Muekan.'

'It is as well I am satisfied with Muekan, then,' she replied, her eyes filming with tears.

Later Muekan said to Tayan quietly, 'I know Juylan will recover easily but others of our people will not. Ten or more will die of the hurt they took this night. It is a heavy loss for a small tribe.'

'In last winter's cold, then in the drought of summer, we lost children almost every day and adults every night, Muekan. Ten deaths in one fight may seem a disaster, but our children are fed and healthy.' He indicated the Warchaw horses. 'Those will buy more than enough grain for the winter, and the poorer horses can be eaten. We already have flocks beyond our dreams. Last year we would have risked as much to capture one caravan.' He punched Muekan's arm and laughed. 'You are too serious, my friend. Life is good! I have given you a rich wife who already finds you pleasing. You have achieved prestige in the raid, and the supreme clan welcomes you back as your mother's son.'

'A younger brother cannot give his sister away, even in Chaw, and our women are never given, they go where they will. I have never complained at life, Tayan, and I do not complain now. Before this, I have accepted fate, now I grab it to me.'

'Then grab gently, husband,' said Juylan as she advanced silently into their conversation. 'My back will be sore for many nights!'

'As soon as we are married, my wife,' he smiled at her.

'We are married,' she answered. 'If I call you husband and you call me wife, who will contradict us? You forget our people have no other marriage ceremony.'

'So it is done,' said Tayan. 'First I married off Gei, and now Juylan. Without brother and sister watching, a blind man may seek a sighted wife. I shall lead at night, she by day.' He stopped speaking and smiled as he realised that he was alone, that no-one listened.

47

The heat of summer passed through to autumn and Curos was well pleased with the achievements of his nomadic N'gol army. They had sealed off the O'san to the enemy without undue losses although none had achieved the massive success of the Night Dragon at the 'Valley of Joy'. A rotation of T'sands had been sent into the O'san for experience. More sekars were now trained, and almost fifty T'sands were linked together in Xante's web of sorcery.

Now Curos, Xante and Bhal Morag were all in the capital, where Curos wished to consolidate his political position. He feared that the Council's attention was being diverted from the West by the deepening famine in the southern provinces, centred on Sin Shi where the harvest had failed. Moving the N'gol back to their homelands and allowing the displaced peasants to return to the grain canal appeared a reasonable action now that the Warchaw were being contained. In one respect, Curos' campaign had been too successful; if a few thousand tribesmen could hold back the Warchaw, they could not be as formidable as some claimed.

While Curos argued before the Army Council and Xante planned with Gron Fa how best to organise her growing cult of sekar, the Warchaw activity in the Durin mountains had begun to intensify. One of the first to realise this new development was Muekan, sekar to the Night Dragon Clan. In the freezing early-morning brightness that heralded winter he sat beside a feeble fire in an attempt to relieve an intense chill which had little to do with the temperature or the cold mountain air.

Since joining his mother's people he had seen much to challenge his unemotional acceptance of fate. After the mass murder of the sleeping Warchaw in the 'Valley of Joy', the tribesmen had feasted on horse flesh while the stripped and mutilated bodies of the enemy stiffened. Later, the severed heads had been carried high into the mountains to decorate the main passes as warning to any Warchaw who attempted to come that way. He had taken part in raids through the mountains and into the high hills of Corninstan to leave exterminated Warchaw garrisons with their faces cut through in the mask of the Night Dragon. Muekan accepted that his desperate people showed no mercy, but today he had seen new horrors.

His face was turned defensively away from the body of a Corninstani hill guide who had been leading thirty Warchaw through the hills. The clan leader, Ongul, had wanted information for Noyan Zachaw and so this man and one other had been taken alive. Muekan's wife, Juylan, and another woman had taken turns to submit the two captives to the most appalling tortures. One screamed under the application of hot coals, sharp knives or other devilry while his companion waited in terror, knowing that in a short time he would suffer a similar fate.

The information was scant, confused with sobs of pain and vain pleas for mercy, and Muekan could tell little for certain except that an attack by Warchaw and Corninstani light horses would be made in the far north. This was but a diversion for the main campaign in the south. He tried to shut the screams and the whimpering from his mind and compose himself to contact the Sekar Gron Fa in G'tal.

Juylan's bloodstained hand rested on his shoulder as she leaned down to kiss his neck. Proud of her skill, she expected some sign of appreciation. He could smell the dying man's blood on her face. As darkness fell she would become demented by passion, excited by the joy of killing, and that smell would be with her still. He kissed her wrist and pulled her face down towards his; Muekan had chosen his path and a N'gol did not turn back.

Curos was far from happy as he pointed to the map in Bhal Morag's war room. 'They are throwing good men away, Morag,' he explained. 'Scouting parties here, here and here. Now two hundred men attempt to cut through two thousand of the Sunrise Horde here. We are continually moving men north to counter some new thrust.'

'And in the south we are weak,' added Morag thoughtfully. 'There is only a small force of three hundred at Bec Tol until

386

the 11th T'sand arrives and Dalgan returns. Should I get Pynar to move the White Dragon Clan south?'

'No, I think not. He has some men in the hills and they can fall back on the fort if there is an attempt to cross the passes. It is nearly winter; in forty days the northern passes will be closed with snow, in sixty so will the southern route. If they plan some major attack it must be soon, leaving time to prepare defensive positions on this side of the mountains.'

The next day Konkurate's Blue Wolf Clan fought against Warchaw who had moved through the Lune mountains in small groups before joining up into a heavy combat unit. Konkurate held back this advance but was forced to fight a hard battle and was pleased to accept the help of Turakina's Death Wind. Ongul's Night Dragon Clan, the only group not threatened directly, was too far north to assist. Many of the Warchaw had escaped back into the mountains, and could still pose a threat.

When news of this latest development reached Curos, he summoned Bhal Morag to discuss what they should do next.

'The next attack must be the main one, and it will come at Bec Tol,' said Bhal Morag. 'The Warchaw cannot know we are so well informed and would expect news to take weeks to reach a central commander.'

'For all that, there is little we can do,' replied Curos. 'If the numbers used so far are any indication, Pynar's fifty men in the hills will be crushed. Get them out and back onto the plain where they are mobile. What news of the reinforcements for Bec Tol?'

'The fresh soldiers from the 11th T'sand who will form the new garrison are here, six days away, and Chalak Konn is headed in that direction, escorting supplies of food. We do not have recent news from the fort at Bec Tol, as the sekar there has died from Winter Lung Fever.'

'We must have a sekar in Bec Tol, either Pynar's or Abac's. Any food in the warehouses must be moved inside the fortress, and the buildings outside the wall prepared for burning.'

'Xante believes Bec Tol is impregnable,' stated Bhal Morag. 'She has strengthened the forces in the wall considerably. We could use it to act as bait. If it is besieged we can coordinate

Sand Dragon, White Dragon and Topaz with the 11th T'sand. In less than two weeks the 22nd T'sand and the guards units Abac is training in the O'san could join them to give us six thousand well-trained men on the plain and in the hills. This could be our greatest success.'

'Get the 11th and the guards moving now,' smiled Curos. 'Wan Abac will enjoy a freezing march. Hold the 11th back at the 56th weir on the canal to wait for the others to join them. Our combined force will then be only five days' march from Bec Tol.'

Curos wanted to leave immediately for the battle area in the O'san, but for once Xante was adamant that she must stay in G'tal. Hoelun's children were expected soon but the doctors who attended her were far from happy. Although tall and possessing great inner strength, she was physically thin and frail. The twins had placed an additional strain on her, and a pessimistic doctor explained to Curos, since Chalak Konn was not available, that it was unlikely that both children and the mother would survive.

'Difficult decisions will have to be taken,' he had muttered in a doom-laden voice.

'That will not happen, Curos,' Xante had said with the icy resolve that brooked no argument. 'Of all the Chaw, I owe most to Hoelun and her music. Without her aid I would have fled G'tal. Now she is in need and I will repay that help.'

'You are a midwife too?'

'No, a sorceress and a healer. I believe Hoelun should have two children; I can feel their thoughts as they fight for life.'

Curos knew he should be riding west – he was needed there – but he made excuses to stay: in the capital he could see all events through the sekar, the Warchaw could possibly attack elsewhere. They were all lies to himself. The truth was that he could not bear to leave without Xante.

'Both the King and the Queen are in play,' she had said, 'and one must protect the other.' That was true, but not the only reason he lingered in G'tal.

A week passed and Xante and Hoelun started to battle for three lives. Eventually, a taut and stressful Curos was able to visit his past wife, and present the gifts from himself and Xante.

Later, in their room, Xante challenged Curos with a hint of reproach. 'You do not find this occasion a happy one?' she asked sharply.

'The event in this house is indeed a happy one, Xante, but there are other events we have to talk of. Bec Tol is under attack. The Warchaw have swept Pynar's men from the hill passes and surrounded the castle.'

'I had not heard,' said Xante quietly.

'No, you had other cares. But there is more. Konn is in Bec Tol. He and Abac had arrived only the day before and are trapped inside with only three hundred men.'

'Hoelun must not know, at least not until she is stronger.'

'I should have been there. No other commander of ability could have reached Bec Tol. I might have inspired a better defence, delayed their advance until the snow closed the passes through the mountains; he reproached himself.'

It was on the cold, windy parapet of Bec Tol that Chalak Konn was told that he was a double father. The sekar who gave the news was muffled against the cold but his trembling owed as much to his fear of the enemy. Looking down on the Warchaw camp, Chalak Konn desperately tried to visualise his wife's face in far G'tal, wishing he were away with Hoelun and the two children he would probably never see.

Chalak Konn had little time to think on this, for already the Warchaw were grouping their forces for their first assaults. Trebuchets stood primed between ranks of bowmen, while the massed footmen rested long scaling ladders on the hard earth.

Arrows and stones flew up from the plain toward the walls of Bec Tol. Chaw soldiers ducked low behind the protective embrasures, only to see the missiles spiral away, deflected by the inbuilt force Xante had detected in the walls. The water in the swirling spring rose higher and flowed more turbulently as if angered at this challenge to its power. The Warchaw footmen shouted and ran forward with their ladders, only to find that they too were knocked aside and thrown down by the invisible power. The Chaw soldiers hurled down a rain of spears and arrows into the struggling foe but the spiralling force ruined their aim.

389

'Stop the men shooting,' Chalak Konn shouted to the Ataman. 'Save our arrows.'

'Would you have us stand and do nothing?' asked Wan Abac as he approached from the other side of the wall. 'Should we lie in our beds while our enemy flounder?'

'No, Excellency,' the sekar spoke hesitantly. 'Madam Xante believes the presence of men on the wall will aid the power of the spring.'

'She should know, it is her business,' replied Wan Abac with the respect he always showed for Xante. 'I understand she spent much time improving the effectiveness of this strange defence.'

'Look, there is the Warchaw commander.' Chalak Konn pointed. 'With the tall plume and the standard bearer behind him.'

'Also, there is the sorcerer,' said the sekar in awe. 'I have felt his presence before. From this distance and through the protection of the wall I can sense his might.'

'Greater than Madam Xante?' asked Wan Abac.

'Much greater,' replied the fearful sekar. 'Now he laughs at the commander's fears. No! We are lost.' The sekar ducked down against the thick stone wall. Abac and Konn watched in amazement as a blue light began to develop around the sorcerer. Bright and shimmering like evil fire, it built up and then began to fly forward. Gathering size and speed, it flowed inexorably towards the studded oaken gate set high in the wall of Bec Tol.

Incredibly, this too swirled away, dispersing and flaring harmlessly against the solid stonework. The Chaw soldiers cheered and shouted derision at their foe.

'Fools, they do not understand,' the sekar sobbed, holding his head in clutching hands. 'That was but a fraction of his power.'

'A power we cannot counter,' replied Chalak Konn, helping the sekar to his feet. 'But we will do what we can. You will detect any threat from the enemy. At any change in mood or activity which could herald an assault, tell K'tan Wan to muster the men on the walls. I will arrange some way of pouring water over the gate to keep it sodden in preparation for attack.'

Before he left the wall, Chalak Konn turned to his personal servant. 'Have paper, pen-brush and ink here for when I return.'

'Letters home?' Wan Abac smiled grimly.

'No, not until after dark. I wish to make drawings of the barbarians' trebuchets. Our carpenters are skilled enough to copy the design, I am sure. Such engines could stand us in good stead in an open battle.'

The strength of the fortress, Chalak Konn's organisation and Abac's Iron Guard had allowed the Chaw defenders to forget the Warchaw sorcerers. The battles and skirmishing in Lune and the O'san had gone well, so well that in their confidence the Chaw had started to ignore the greatest threat. Only Xante could attempt to counter that power and she was with Curos in G'tal.

Later in the evening, Chalak Konn called the sekar to his private quarters. He spoke to the man reassuringly, asking him how he was coping with the stress of Bec Tol and the presence of the Warchaw sorcerer. After some talk he pointed to a large paper on the table.

'Would you be able to communicate this to one of your people who had the skill to make an exact copy?' The sekar regarded the carefully drawn characters with a creased brow. It was a fine work of high calligraphy, a letter to Hoelun.

'Lord, I am but an ignorant man, many of the characters I cannot recognise.'

'Ignorance is not equal to stupidity,' said Chalak Konn gently. 'I have had a superior education, but these you could learn in time. I could never master your skills. You need not convey the shapes of the characters; only one who can use the brush well can likewise put them on paper.'

'Gron Fa is very learned and noted for his calligraphy,' suggested the sekar.

'I would prefer another,' replied Chalak Konn. 'It is a letter to my wife on the birth of our children. The calligraphy is as important as the message. I fear the High Sekar Gron Fa would have little sympathy with such feelings.' The sekar smiled with understanding.

'There is one obvious choice, then, Lord. The eminent sekar Lou is most scholarly and has a love of children and of his wife, Lou Suzin. He would represent your style most carefully, down to the choice and quality of paper.'

That night, Curos was shaken awake by Xante. In the dim light, his mind clearing from sleep, the desire for her partially clothed body surfaced from months of stern repression. Usually she treated such weakness with firm amusement, but not tonight.

'Control your thoughts, Noyan,' she said angrily as she stepped back from his bed and sought a robe from beside her sleeping mat. She bit her lip in self-annoyance as she pulled the wide cloth-belt tight and ensured that her neck and chest were fully covered. Any other man shaken awake by a half-naked woman he desired would have reacted more forcefully, but there was not time for apologies.

'There is great danger to Bec Tol,' she said, her voice's husky quality deepened by concern. 'The sekar is desperate with fear. His thoughts are now incomprehensible to Gron Fa and Lou Chi but they believe there is a full sorcerer with the Warchaw.'

Curos was pulling on his shirt, all weariness now forgotten. 'No-one has mentioned a sorcerer! This changes all our plans. Did Gron Fa not think it important? How strong is this sorcerer?'

'Much stronger than I, Curos. Much stronger. I will try to calm our sekar and gauge through him what the danger is.'

'I sleep here while Abac and Konn face death,' growled Curos. 'I should have been on the road with another two thousand men weeks ago!' Despite his anger, he forced himself to sit motionless opposite Xante, as her mind sought that of the sekar in Bec Tol. For Curos' benefit she spoke her thoughts aloud, including the garbled replies from the distant sekar.

Far away across the O'san desert the High Wizard Valanus sat in deep concentration. The stone walls of a hurriedly built chamber shielded him from even the vaguest breeze and shut out all sound. Before him was a sand model of the Chaw fortress and four unflickering candles. Valanus' whole being was tuned to the force emanating from Bec Tol as he gradually built up his own power to a point where he could achieve its destruction.

'You understand what will happen?' Xante was saying to the sekar. 'Explain to the K'tans that they must keep the walls manned for as long as possible. You will know when the moment is near, but will not have time to consult with me. Order the men back off the wall, close to the spring.'

'Can we rely on him?' asked Curos when Xante had completed her instructions to the distant sekar.

'If Chalak Konn can keep our sekar on the wall, we can certainly rely on him to warn when the blow will fall!' Xante replied dryly.

'Saving the men from sorcery is one thing; we now have to plan the next move,' said Curos. 'Dress decently while I rouse Bhal Morag. We will meet in my old study where the maps are kept.'

Throughout the fateful night the High Wizard sat alone, building up his energy for the strike against the enemy castle. The nature and form of the fortress' defences was unknown to him, but by destroying it he would prove his own invincibility to his peers. This was one reason he did not call on assistance from other Warchaw sorcerers, the other being that his main objective had not been the destruction of a Chaw castle but a search for the Amathar. He who controlled that power would rule the Order of Gadel and hence the world. These thoughts caused a brief loss of concentration and his mastery of the immense forces slipped. With a self-deprecating smile, he banished premature ambition and returned his full consciousness to the present task. Twice, he swayed with effort and fatigue as he attempted to increase the circulating field of energy which rotated above Bec Tol. The limit was reached, he must act before dissipation and leakage overcame his efforts. Valanus' spirit soared with elation. In a flourish he cast down each of his four candles and continued the circular movement to scatter the sand image of Bec Tol.

The Chaw sekar who crouched on the parapet, hands pressed to his head, shrieked with relief as much as with fear. Frightened soldiers whose eyes sought to understand the unnatural ring of demonic light followed him in headlong flight. A solid circular ring of dazzling blue fire descended towards the deserted fortress wall. Flowing in counter-direction to the wall's own flux, it sped around the parapet and descended like a destroying wave over the ancient masonry.

In vain, the spring rose and boiled in defiance, but the force in the wall was countered, held still by the hideous bolt unleashed

393

by Valanus. Centuries of stress were relaxed and the very stone-work exploded. With intense, energy-absorbing silence, the forces which had sustained Bec Tol were released and simultaneously each massive stone block dissolved into rubble and fragments. Instead of a high, soaring fortress wall there remained a squalid ring of ravaged stone, sloping evenly down on both sides. Four centuries of suspended erosion had occurred in ten heartbeats.

The power of Valanus was expended. He fell back with self-satisfied exhaustion at the concentrated destruction he had achieved. The spring surged and slowly re-established its circulation but without the amplification of the tuned wall, the effect was a feeble echo of that which had protected the garrison.

48

As the destruction of the walls subsided, the Warchaw engines and bowmen began a hideous volley of death, intended to kill any who might survive the earthquake-like shock and attempt to crawl free. They were unaware of the radial heaps of masonry from the destroyed buildings which now gave shelter to the Chaw.

Well back from the falling missiles, the Chaw garrison waited in battle order for the onslaught which would come. Undaunted, Wan Abac shouted at the guardsmen. 'Now is our hour to repay our debt to the land of Chaw. We have fed well and slept easy while others have starved. We will pay all back to our people with our blood and the blood of our enemies. Our Queen of Sorcery is not here to protect us from the barbarians' Devil Sorcerer, but we will teach the cowards who fight with magic to tremble at the sight of the Guards.'

There was more, much more, and despite their desperate state, Chalak Konn found himself smiling at the words. When addressing soldiers one never mentioned defeat, never spoke of death or wounds. Did Abac intentionally break every accepted rule by intent or just by instinct? It seemed that to him only cowardice was dishonourable.

A trumpet sounded and they heard the drumming hoofs of the Warchaw Heavy Cavalry, iron-clad men with long lances carrying death to all who stood before them. Unlike the mobile N'gol horsemen the garrison of Bec Tol could not flee and returned to fight on their own terms.

Warned by their sekar, the guards wheeled round to face the direction of the attack. Men of iron they were, who scorned armour to wear the rich scarlet of parade-ground soldiers. Abac dressed them in open order, each man a sword's length from his neighbour. Chalak Konn carefully wiped perspiration from his hand on the dusty soil before drawing his sword. It was unnatural for a nobleman to carry a heavy shield on his left arm, but now his only place was in the front rank with his men.

In the first light of dawn, the horsemen breasted the eastern rim of the crumbling mound and began their attack. Over the treacherous rubble the Warchaw reformed their line while at full gallop, and lowered their lances towards the ranks of Chaw who stood blinking against the low sun which shone full in their eyes. Unbelievably, at forty paces the cavalry line was shattered by a volley of javelins hurled with great force and accuracy, the effect being redoubled when the second rank of Chaw guards threw their own spears. As horses reared and plunged in terror and men heaved at reins, the Chaw guardsmen gave a great, unplanned shout of triumph – 'Abac! Abac!' – and charged forward, line straight, short swords stabbing with venomous fury at men or horses. Moments later, Chalak Konn was also running, leading the left wing of the garrison troops to cut into the horsemen's flank. An Ataman led the right wing in a similar fashion. Chalak Konn had forgotten personal safety; his greatest fear was that the Warchaw bowmen would arrive to join the fight.

The mutilated cavalry squadron turned and fled.

'The T'sand of Yec Min could have done no better,' shouted Wan Abac. 'You make me proud to command you.' He only allowed his men time to despatch the Warchaw wounded and collect serviceable javelins before moving off to the west, back into the narrow passes which led from the South road where it entered the Lune mountains. That was the plan suggested by Curos, who hoped that the Warchaw would expect any counter-attack to be directed eastward to Chaw and safety.

Wan Abac formed a rear-guard while Chalak Konn led the regular soldiers to attack the entrance of the pass. It was lightly guarded but they suffered heavily in sweeping aside the mixed swordsmen and archers who attempted to hold them back, surprise and superior numbers combining to push them through.

Now, moving forward at a slow trot, Chalak Konn sought the smaller path off to the south which his men must follow.

'The fools are still surprised at our escape,' laughed a voice by his side as Wan Abac ran up, his even speech an unintended mockery of Konn's gasping breath. 'I'm sure the sorcerer is exhausted by his efforts in destroying Bec Tol's wall. The fire-flash he sent at my men was pathetic. To use horsemen in that rubble when they have such bowmen!' They ran on for half a yetang until Konn's soldiers were forced to slow to a shambling walk. Despite the jeers of the guardsmen, the regular soldiers had no more to give. There was no sign of pursuit and they pressed on in narrow file for some time, hopes and spirits rising with every stride.

'Why are they not following us?' asked Chalak Konn.

'They may not bother,' replied Wan Abac. 'They have achieved their objective, in destroying our fortress and obtaining a centre for attacks into Chaw. A prudent commander would not risk men to chase two hundred fugitives in these hills.'

The survivors from the Chaw garrison toiled on through the hill paths until mid-morning when the chill wind began to blow just a little warmer. The sekar could detect no activity from the Warchaw sorcerer, but they were now being followed at a very careful distance by several horsemen. The path began to descend, leading to a slightly wider valley cut deep into the rock by a fast flowing stream. Some five yetang down towards the south-east, wisps of smoke which rose vertically in the clear winter air could just be detected. Like bars of a cage they stood in the path of the Chaw, proclaiming that the enemy must be occupying the pass ahead of them. After a rapid consultation Chalak Konn and Wan Abac ordered the men forward, aware that the following enemy scouts could be leading more pursuers.

The Warchaw had chosen their position well. The valley closed into a narrow gorge, where centuries of flood water had cut sheer, towering clefts into the hard rock. Any paths bypassing this main route would be steep and difficult to find. Time lost in such a search would allow the pursuing troops to close up and sandwich the Chaw into an even more hopeless position.

'There are but a hundred or so men before us,' suggested Chalak Konn hopefully. 'We should attack them now while we still have the advantage of numbers.'

'Do not be so confident, friend,' cautioned Wan Abac. 'The Warchaw must not be judged by their errors in the ruin of Bec Tol. On this flat, open ground their bowmen can be devastating. At a distance we cannot counter until we close to thirty paces or so.'

397

For all Wan Abac's misgivings, there was no alternative but to attempt to break out through the valley into the plains of the O'san. There, Curos had promised to have horsemen waiting as escort with spare horses to speed up the movement of the garrison. Chalak Konn suspected that far fewer than two hundred horses would be needed.

They separated their force into three groups and started a rapid descent of the hill onto the plain. Already, the Warchaw soldiers had been alerted and were moving into line with a casual purposefulness which told of confidence and professionalism. At various points during Chalak Konn's progress down the undulating pass, he noted the position of enemy's mail-clad foot-soldiers and the archers with their tall bows. He felt a chill, cold sensation developing in his stomach as he lost any hope of seeing his newborn children. If this was to be his life and his fate, he had tasted at least one year of happiness. Some men wasted many years without realising their good fortune, others never rose above levels of indifferent misery.

As the path widened out, the Chaw extended their line to put Wan Abac's guards in the centre with Chalak Konn's regular troops on the two wings. Opposing the Chaw were two lines of Warchaw foot-soldiers with small groups of light cavalry on each wing.

'Are we ready?' asked Chalak Konn, his mouth dry.

'There is little point in waiting for fear to spread,' Wan Abac replied grimly. 'The men are confident; they broke the Warchaw cavalry and charged down the bowmen at the entrance of the pass. At close quarters numbers may sway the fight. We must keep the men moving forward despite the arrows. If our charge falters, the barbarians will shoot us to pieces and just wait for their companions to take us from the rear.'

Cedric of Hereford, Master Bowman and Commander of Archers, looked up the gentle slope to where the yellow-skinned men of Chaw were marshalling their forces to attack. He and the junior knight, Sir Bernard, who had been placed in command 'for experience', had chosen their position to defend the valley against any relief force trying to aid the garrison and Cedric had never expected that he would need to face attack from the mountain pass. What bungling had led to the garrison's escape from the ruined fort he did not know, but it seemed typical of this campaign. The invasion of Corn Land had gone well enough, despite near disaster at the Battle of the Road. But since then the Commanders had lost their grip and too many good men had been killed fighting in the hills and deserts as they skirmished with these savage people.

Why chase after the raiders at all? he thought for the hundredth time. *If they killed a few more Corninstani, so what, we are safe in our castles. We should wait until we are ready to invade and then. cross the mountains in force, not send small groups to be cut to pieces by this barbarous people.* He remembered Wilff of Arren as, from habit, he took command of organising the defence despite the knight's higher rank. The archers were concentrated in the centre to destroy the red-uniformed guards, who would be a real danger if they got close enough to use their throwing spears and short swords. The general foot would have to hold off right and left wings of the Chaw until Cedric could begin shooting into them. The knight and his mounted sergeants would act as a rear-guard, looking down the valley, and could encircle the Chaw if opportunity permitted.

'Always the same in this bloody war,' he muttered as he strung his long war bow. 'There are too many of these little sods. The knights call them "monkey men" and hold them in contempt, but they never run away and the mounted bowmen are too good for our horsemen.' The mass of Chaw footmen was beginning to move forward in that fanatical trotting run, shields held high against arrows, javelins at the ready.

''Ware those in red,' he shouted to his men. 'I want them all skewered afore they reach fifty paces or they'll have our guts out!'

To Cedric's horror, Sir Bernard was leading the right wing horsemen in a charge. From either side the two groups of mounted Warchaw were riding forward, crossing in front of the archers to attack the Chaw Guards who were still out of bow range. Swarming up the valley from behind the Warchaw position were a hundred of the Chaw mounted archers, yellow pendants and sashes flying as they drove their horses forward. It was too late for the Warchaw horsemen to respond and drive them off; already they were committed to their charge on the Red Guards.

The guards' heavy javelins were defeating the Warchaw cavalry. Cedric swore, cursing Bernard, trying to turn his men to face the new threat of the N'gol riders. He loosed two shafts, but then a deadly rain of razor-sharp N'gol arrows fell amongst his unarmoured archers. The nomadic bowmen broke away as Cedric attempted to organise his own men to reply with a concerted volley. Unbidden, the Warchaw foot closed in to protect the archers, only masking their attempt at retaliation. As the Western cavalry retreated, the foot-soldiers closed into a disorganised mass and Cedric shouted orders, trying to open out the line, to organise clear space to shoot.

Now the Chaw foot were closing in unchecked, 'Abac! Abac!' – small, evil-faced men with short swords and large shields who took no heed of death as they pressed on, sensing victory from the Warchaw's confusion. The N'gol archers wheeled in, heedless of the rough, boulder-strewn ground or the few arrows shot against them. Organised defence was crumbling. Another shower of short arrows landed, and Cedric forced his way towards the rock at the edge of the gorge, seeking his own salvation. All around, good men were being hemmed in so that they could not use their heavier weapons, spiked, cut and dragged down by the enemy. Cedric tried to deflect the lazy flight of a heavy spear but it struck deeply into his thigh. Still clutching his bow in his left hand, he hacked at an advancing Chaw with his broadsword and dragged himself to the protective boulders. A sword descended from above. He parried and turned the edge but the flat of the blade crashed onto his skull, sending him reeling.

Moments later, he raised his head from the gravelled earth and looked dazedly across the valley where hundreds of Chaw were pulling down the last of his men. Cedric's stomach twisted in paralysing remembrance of the mutilated and tortured bodies he had seen in the northern hills where the horror of the Night Dragon reigned. He wrenched the spear out of his thigh and fought the faintness from the searing pain. He steadied himself enough to cram a pad of cloth over the wound and waited until his vision cleared and consciousness returned. Further up the slope, he rested again. When he looked back, the fighting had ceased and the Chaw were securing ten or more prisoners. They were not searching outside the area of the battle, and to avoid drawing attention he crawled between rocks and waited.

Less than one hundred paces away, two Chaw commanders were standing together as the leader of the mounted horsemen rode up and dismounted with a flourish only to stagger as his weaker leg twisted.

'Drunk again, Dalgan!' Wan Abac greeted as he grabbed Dalgan's shoulder.

'Drunk on blood and victory. It was worth sparing you to see you fight. I am now man enough and sober enough to accept a joke.'

The Chaw voices with their variation of pitch and tone angered Cedric as much as the defeat itself. They were joking and laughing in the delight of victory, and it burned deep. Despite the danger, he hauled himself up against a boulder and sought in his quiver for a good arrow. At least one of those capering monkeys would die. Slowly, with the infinite care of a professional, he drew back his bow, paused to sight and loosed. The deceptively flat sound of the longbow sent the arrow on its way, its heavy iron pile carrying death. Before the arrow had struck home, Cedric had fallen to the ground and was crawling frantically back between the rocks to safety, unaware that he had killed or that the prisoners the Chaw had taken would pay dearly for his success.

Some time later on the same day Curos and Xante sat grim-faced in the map room of the Zachaw City Mansion. No words were necessary, or would help to relieve their feelings of grief and guilt. The door burst open and the tall, tear-stained form of Hoelun came in, tall and gaunt, her bed-robe hanging off her exhausted body. In the room her momentum sagged as she saw Xante but she gathered her strength and advanced on Curos.

'Treacherous coward,' she hissed. 'Why should you live while the better man is dead? You crept from your battle in Corninstan, dishonoured, and now you leave others to fight and die.'

'Please, Hoelun,' Curos started to say weakly but his head

401

was bowed in defeat. 'He was my friend, too. All soldiers risk death.'

'Friend!' shouted Hoelun in grief-inspired rage. 'You have no friends, just tools who are fooled into following your path and dying for your glory. You wanted him dead, and this was your cunning way of achieving that!'

Xante stiffened at this last remark and protested, 'Hoelun, we all grieve. Why would Curos wish him dead? He was a valued commander and a true companion.'

Hoelun now rounded on Xante with equal venom. 'How would you understand? You are not a true woman. Curos was jealous. Konn gave me children where he had tried and failed. Konn shamed Zachaw's manhood and . . .'

'No!' cut in Curos, 'you have it wrong.'

'I do not, murderer! You have orphaned two newborn children out of pride.'

Xante ran to the distraught woman and grabbed her shoulder. 'Hoelun! Stop this! It is not Chalak Konn who was killed, but Wan Abac.'

Hoelun let out a strangled scream. Her fist flew to her mouth and she slumped into a chair, her face washed over with tears. 'Konn is alive! But they said the commander of the castle had been killed. I knew he was at Bec Tol by his letter.'

'It was the commander of the guards who was killed,' said Curos, his voice stiff with stress. 'He and Chalak Konn led the garrison out from Bec Tol together with much bravery and honour. The loss of either would be hard to me and to Chaw.' He turned to look away before adding, 'They were both friends, Hoelun, for all that you think of me.'

'Oh, Curos, I am so sorry, I was . . .' Her voice tailed off. 'He was so sure he would die, and when I heard I thought it was he. What happened?'

'Wan Abac died instead of Chalak Konn. I wished neither harm but I could say that you rejoiced in the death of Abac,' said Curos spitefully.

Xante looked aghast at Curos. 'Curos, stop this hatefulness.'

'Why? All are free to accuse and denigrate me! I grieve for one as I would have for the other.' He crossed the room to wrap his arms around Hoelun's heaving shoulders and to apologise.

402

'It is the chance of war who dies,' he said. 'I am angry with myself that I was not there. In my guilt I speak stupid words. The garrison had fought clear of Bec Tol and crossed the mountains, until their path was again barred by the enemy. They must have been exhausted, as was Topaz Wind, but Dalgan exceeded his orders to give them aid. In their desperation they were successful. The fighting was finished. Wan Abac, Chalak Konn and Khol Dalgan stood greeting each other as friends, although Abac and Dalgan had been close to fighting each other several times. As they spoke a Warchaw archer shot one arrow at the three of them.'

'From such distance it was not his aim but fate which singled out Wan Abac to die,' Xante said sadly. 'Like many others who died at Bec Tol and in the pass, Abac died without having seen the happiness of a wife and family. His brother in Yec Min will be a rich man.'

49

The walls of Bec Tol crumbled, and a massive cheer rose up from the Warchaw soldiers. Aalani-Galni, Dryad of S'lan and Eternal Forest, cheered with them in the new guise of Batan the elf. He cheered automatically as that part of him which daily lived the deception concealed his true feelings. Deep inside it was the final despair of defeat which cut coldly into his very being.

From their arrival he had realised how much of Xante was in the defence of Bec Tol. The style, subtlety and strength were as clear to him as her footprint would be to a hunter. To take what was there, develop it, augment it into a new, stronger whole, in harmony with its surroundings, was as natural to her as life.

At first he had been confident the walls would hold, and indeed Valanus' fire ball had been deflected. He knew Valanus had more power, but he had thought sheer power would not be enough. Now Bec Tol was in ruins and the cavalry of Sir Sigmund prepared to charge. The mailed fist of the West was smashing through the flowered beauty of the East. Even if the Chaw cavalry repulsed the engines, the Warchaw bowmen and foot-soldiers would be more than enough to destroy the garrison. Curos would be forced to attack – he could not allow the Warchaw to maintain a foothold in the O'san. With Curos would come Xante and there was nothing he could do to protect her.

In two and a half months with Valanus and his companions, he had learned so much – but so little of any value. Valanus seemed impregnable to any physical attack; he regulated his pleasures, had no interest in drugs and little weakness for wine. He had welcomed Batan as a new friend, looking not into the background Aalani had constructed but at the man he had expected. In many ways they had common interests in hunting, healing and plant lore, and their friendship exposed no weaknesses save for the existence of Valanus' companions and his quest for the Amathare.

Hosca the Northman and Bill of Asham, the renowned bowman, fretted angrily that the cavalry were leading the assault but they held no deep grudge against Sir Sigmund. Aalani liked and respected many qualities in Bill and Sigmund but had no point of contact with either the Northman or the fearfully timid man whom Valanus called his seeker.

Aalani's deep thoughts were always hidden, leaving the open face in clear view. His face was scarred, and his head still ached from time to time, so much so that on occasion he could only take to his bed. Sometimes he would lie for several days in an agony of flashing lights and restricted vision, until the attack passed. It fitted with Batan's history – the explosion in Imran and the wounds from the Red Stone which would not heal, the death of his family and the grief. He never smoked or touched wine, although the addiction Batan had once suffered under was well known. The companions respected the inner strength by which he had cured himself.

Aalani sat down, avoiding the Dryad cross-legged position, and clasped his hands to his head. The bronze dagger hidden in his tunic burned with Aalani's need to kill, but there was no opportunity. Valanus habitually wore mail under his long, flowing robe, its well-forged and enchanted rings impervious to Aalani's bronze blade or the stiletto of Arezo. He was sure he could get in one strike if he caught Valanus unaware or fatigued, but there were always servants, companions or guards near him. Aalani cared little for his own life but he had to be sure of the sorcerer's death; always he had hoped for that clear opportunity but now there was no more time.

His mind was blanked with fatigue from months of futile scheming and planning, from the constant wariness to protect his deception. He was so utterly tired. His head rang with echoes of the destruction of Bec Tol, and he heard nothing of the fighting. Where did these echoes come from? Bec Tol was a crumbled heap of rubble, its bell-like symmetry gone for ever. Unbidden, the hunter's searching mind traced the source as he would have attempted to analyse any rustle in the night forest.

Many underground lakes lay beneath the O'san – dark, still water which had seeped down through the rocks. Trickles and small streams flowed with cold, glacial slowness, carrying knots

405

of minerals, gold and iron ore. The spring at Bec Tol drew its heat and its power from deep in the earth where the rocks were hot, and strange, minute creatures combined into a layer of life. It was tenuously linked by resonances from the inching water currents to another place far north in the O'san: a pool, no, an underground lake which echoed to the cataclysm Valanus had caused. The minerals of the earth nearby were giving their own tone to the echo which had confused Aalani.

'Why, friend Batan,' said the deep, sonorous voice of the sorcerer, his hand on Batan's shoulder, 'you look grieved. My greatest triumph – and my friend and companion is sad?' Aalani's flesh cringed at that touch; the bronze dagger burned. 'Is it your head?' asked Valanus in real concern. 'Does the energy bring on your pain?'

Aalani drew himself back from his subterranean passage. Only because his mind had been so slow, so very slow, had he been able to feel his way through the earth's secrets. Valanus' shock wave had acted as an illuminating torch for his probing, that and a deep hidden assistance from the Earth itself. 'Abac! Abac!' Chaw voices were raised in their small triumph, shrieks of men and horses. He, Aalani, the hunter dozed while others still fought on. *One last effort. S'lan give me the strength!*

'No, Valanus, it is not sadness.' The ravaged but open face looked up at Valanus with the restrained smile of true friendship. 'I have felt it, Valanus, the Amathare! Your power and the collapse of the Tower have set the whole earth ringing. It awakens the Amathare; I can feel it.'

Valanus stiffened and then attempted to relax. He was tired, very tired from his exertions but Batan's words had shocked him into wakefulness.

'To the north, slightly west,' Batan was saying. 'Feel the emanation. It contains the elements of power – fire, gold and iron – and the elements of wisdom – water, silver and diamond. Feel it!' He drew on the half-forgotten ravings of the true Batan and his description of the ancient Imrani sources. Valanus was too quick, too dynamic to read all that Aalani had seen, but his perception was almost as keen.

'Yes. I feel its beauty. Its power is low?'

'It has been dead ten thousand years. It needs a hand of power to rekindle its brightness, to give it life that it may augment the power of its master. Even I, Batan, could wield such power.' He felt Valanus stiffen at that, but it added credibility.

'There is this war,' Valanus hesitated, 'our cavalry is repulsed and a Chaw army approaches.'

'Trivial,' stated Batan. 'The foot-soldiers will sweep the area clear by nightfall. The loss of Bec Tol will demoralise the Chaw army. The Amathare calls for a master. We must hasten to it lest another of the Order of Gadel detects it and reaches it first, Lord Neath or the Lady Runanin.' He had hoped only to lead Valanus away, to buy time and wait for the chance he needed.

The Wizard was deep in contemplation and Aalani realised Valanus was stepping through all the events and impressions he had received since releasing the energy. It was a great ability, allowing him to analyse mistakes and strengths, and to recover information others would have lost. Aalani reached for the dagger, the bronze of S'lan. He was standing behind the tall wizard. His arm burned with the fire of death as his hunter's mind, hidden deep under the charade of Batan, chose its spot, the kidney on the right; if only he could penetrate a thumb's width, the poison would achieve his purpose.

'Valanus!' A warning shout. Oblivion engulfed Aalani and Batan died for ever. Jezic the thief stood quivering over Aalani's inert body, attempting to conceal the stone he had used.

'He was going to stab you,' he whined. 'I could not believe it. I saw him draw back the dagger . . .' His voice trailed off. No-one else would have been furtive enough to approach Aalani undetected. Valanus himself was visibly shaken.

'Shall I kill him?' Jezic half whispered.

'No, we must unravel this.' It was the Amathare, Valanus thought, remembering Aalani's words. '*Even I, Batan, could wield such power.*' Had Batan seen a chance of holding the Amathare and been corrupted by its possibilities? There were strange, hidden facets to his character.

The junior sorcerer, Bran, hurried up with two guards. 'Lord, what has happened? Is Batan dead?'

'I do not know, but Valanus lives. You should have been beside me, Bran, it is your duty.' He brushed aside the excuses and stared at Aalani. His whole head had turned reddish-purple as if covered by a massive contusion. Jezic's blow and the disappearance of Aalani's control had allowed his skull to start to return to its natural shape. In places blood smudged through the skin from the ruptures beneath.

'I didn't hit him that hard,' said Jezic in awe at his own apparent strength.

'No, but I have seen nothing like this,' Valanus stated. 'No, Bran, do not touch Batan's dagger! It has malice and evil infused in its making. Get a thick cloth and 'ware the blade.' Hosca the Northman ran up to the perplexed group.

'The garrison have escaped, Valanus. Shall I join the pursuit?' Too much was happening. Too many unexplained events.

'We must hasten,' Valanus said decisively. 'I have detected the Amathare to the north. All else is of trivial importance. I must seize it before it corrupts others or thwarts my power. Bran, take Batan to my tent, bandage him carefully with enough pressure to support . . . As you have been taught. I do not want him harmed. I will speak with him when I return. Hosca, summon Sigmund and organise animals for a long journey.'

'Sigmund's horse was killed in the fighting.'

'He has six others! I want to leave before midday. Time is pressing. Others more skilled in war than I will ensure that no Chaw escape.'

50

Many Noyans had visited the castle of Bec Tol in their army careers, and like Xante had thought the walls inviolable. Its destruction to rubble in less than one day of siege was reason enough to send a spasm of fear through the Army Council of Chaw. Already Po Pi was mustering all T'sands and militia in the west to prepare against a full-scale invasion.

Curos was summoned before the Council, to report in detail as to the events in the O'san. This time he was totally frank as to the nature of the Warchaw sorcery, and its devastating effect on men and fortifications. The use of Xante's sekar in the Chaw T'sands and the menace of the Warchaw threat now gave the Council no choice but to accept the reality of powers they could not understand.

Within a day of the fall of Bec Tol, Curos and Xante were heading west with all the speed they could drive from the Arrow Riders' post horses. Thunder Arrow ran riderless, to conserve his strength. The forces which Curos needed to retake the fortress were already moving into the area in accordance with his original plan, but now he wished to lead them himself and to have Xante available to counter the power of Valanus. Independently, Bhal Morag was also moving westward at a rapid pace with the section of the 22nd T'sand not at Bec Tol. In each town, T'sands or militia were being mustered in fear of an invasion and roads were clogged with marching men and supply trains.

Chalak Konn and Khol Dalgan were moving back to the 35th weir on the grain canal but had already organised a surveillance of the enemy forces. Several sekars who were adept at cloaking had been sent into the foothills in the vicinity of Bec Tol and were giving accurate reports of the numbers and movements of the Warchaw.

It was on the third day of their journey that Xante stopped her horse suddenly which brought Curos back, fearing some injury.

'It is one of the sekars near Bec Tol,' she said, without waiting for his question. 'He has been captured by the Warchaw and has been taken to their camp. He believes they have recognised that he has some ability for sorcery and will torture him.' She looked into Curos' eyes.

'He is very frightened, Curos. He wishes me to kill him.'

'I do not know the man,' said Curos, considering the situation.

'I do, and I do not want to harm him.'

'No, reassure him if you can. If they want to question him there will be time enough before we need to take such drastic action. Another course may occur to us.'

They made camp quickly, leaving Xante free to communicate with the various sekars, but her report to Curos brought no hope of saving their captured sorcerer.

'As we knew, there is a large force of Warchaw at Bec Tol, at least three thousand, and we have no real hope of rescuing him,' Xante explained. 'Our sekar understands this, and accepts he is probably doomed, but he is willing to try and be of some use to us since he can understand Corninstani. From overheard conversation, the Warchaw sorcerer, Valanus, has departed from the main camp. It is believed he has gone into the O'san desert with several companions on some quest or search.'

'What could he search for in the O'san? All that is of value in the desert is water and I doubt it would need a High Sorcerer to find the few waterholes that exist away from the canal!'

While the Chaw commanders pondered the actions of the Warchaw sorcerer, certain Warchaw soldiers had very strong views as to the fate of the captured sekar, in particular Cedric of Hereford, who had survived his wounds and had later returned to the ruin of Bec Tol. He was well used to the carnage of war but not to the despair of defeat and the wholesale slaughter of his men. The Chaw soldiers did not mutilate the bodies of their dead foes in the way of the nomad tribesmen but they had dealt harshly with the few prisoners they had taken. In their anger at the death of K'tan Wan they had killed the Warchaw prisoners while they were still roped together.

Cedric, therefore, had no intention of allowing any delay or mercy to intervene in the fate of any captured Chaw. He was also now convinced that the Chaw were obtaining information of the Western armies' plans – they always seemed one step ahead. The scouts believed that one of the monkey men had some power to make himself almost invisible. Although Sorcerer Valanus would be interested, he was far away and might not be back for weeks, and Cedric was more concerned with stopping spying. On the first night, the camp commander had been persuaded that the sekar's escorts should be executed. Although not practised in the art of torture, Cedric had been quick to learn, remembering the examples left by the Night Dragon Clan.

Now, on this night, half drunk in an attempt to dull the pain from his festering wound, Cedric and two friends dragged the hapless enemy out from the imprisonment cage. The Chaw was obviously too old and untrained to be a soldier, which made Cedric more suspicious. Neither he nor his friends could speak Chaw, but several of the knights agreed to assist.

They hauled the pitiful Chaw across the camp-site to the burning fire where instruments of torture waited. He had ceased his babbling, and now seemed resigned to his fate.

'He'll liven up,' laughed a drunken archer whose only intention was to inflict as much pain as possible on the feeble Chaw. The frail body being dragged between the burly soldiers gave one huge, spasmodic twitch and then seemed afflicted by a rigid seizure, gradually relaxing into the initial limpness of death. Cedric kicked and cuffed the inert corpse, refusing to believe that his prisoner had died.

Many yetang away Xante-Yani stepped tight-lipped from the privacy of the yert tent, and moved to join Curos by the warming glow of the fire.

'It is over?' he asked unnecessarily.

'Yes. It is over. They were about to begin, I could wait no longer. He was so frightened, frightened and sick, Curos. He could not have long endured the pain of torture.'

Curos wrapped an arm around her shoulder and pulled her close to him. 'It is not a task that comes easily. I would have done as much for a wounded companion on the battlefield and for a trusting horse who knew nothing of evil.' He paused for a while and then asked, 'How?'

'He had a weak vein in his head,' whispered Xante, desperately keeping her face hidden from Curos. 'I induced it to rupture and he felt little pain.' She looked straight ahead in the darkness as she continued, 'It was all the help I could give him, Curos, and the Warchaw will suspect nothing unnatural.'

Cedric sat by the fire drunk and angry. His companion looked up evilly. 'There is one other Chaw in this camp!'

'Where, in . . . ?'

'In Valanus' tent. That Elf, Batan, the one you always said was a sham hero. Seems he was a Chaw, 'least he looks like one.'

'Some elves do. Funny eyes, pointing ears, not fit to live with real men.' Cedric eased the bandage on his leg. 'Why's he in Valanus' tent, then?'

'Tried to kill our clever leader with a poisoned dagger. Seems Jezic stopped him.'

'Shame, I don't like Wizards either,' growled Cedric in a foul humour. 'That's it! He's the bloody spy – all along, in our camp, he's been passing our plans to the monkey men and planning to spit that trusting fool Valanus at the right time. With the mountain passes closed with snow we'd have been holed up here, no reinforcements, no way back and no sorcerer or leader. Let's go over to Valanus' tent and have a look at this Batan. If he's a Chaw I'll know it's him, whatever high and mighty Valanus says.' He hauled himself to his feet and shambled off into the darkness, followed by a string of archers.

Inside the tent a lamp burned innocently, but Bran lay collapsed over the camp table, the map on which his head rested a sea of blood.

'Hell's teeth, what's this?' Cedric was instantly sober. He pulled back the boy's head – the throat had been ripped by three savage talons. The straps which had bound the prisoner to the camp-bed were discarded on the floor. Outside, some distance away, a sentry writhed in the agony of silent death from a poisoned knife thrust.

'Guards!' Cedric roared. 'Bring extra torches, search the camp and the plain. I want him caught and I want him killed!'

412

51

Curos and Xante were still two days' ride from their meeting place with Chalak Konn and Khol Dalgan when they met up with a war band from the Sunrise Horde. Twenty warriors were escorting two sekars who had been summoned from the North to aid the attack on the Warchaw raiders.

Xante was preoccupied with the events of the previous few days and spent much time riding in silence, although she kept physically close to Curos as if for comfort. She had hated killing the sekar, and had as yet no plan to counter the awesome power of Valanus. With Xante preoccupied, it was therefore one of the sekars who first detected the nearby presence of a Warchaw sorcerer. Fear and amazement at the power of the Westerner rendered him almost speechless as he stuttered his discovery to Xante. Hastily, she ordered both sekars to restrain themselves from any mental probing which might be detected, and Curos led the group of riders into a sheltered enclave among the rocky hills which would screen them from visual detection by the enemy. The N'gol warriors busied themselves making camp but muttered many angry comments on the delay.

With great care Xante seated herself, to be in a calm, comfortable position, flanked by the two sekars. Using their ability to produce a cloaking concealment, she carefully sought to detect the nature and position of the powerful being who threatened them. This took a long time, and Curos too began to grow impatient. The enemy army were still camped at Bec Tol and were no doubt planning further advances into the O'san to attack the N'gol clansmen.

'It is the Warchaw sorcerer, Valanus,' she announced quietly to Curos much later. 'Valanus and several companions. They are camped in a gully similar to this not ten yetang to the north west.'

'Was it Valanus alone who destroyed Bec Tol?' asked Curos.

'Yes, he came with the barbarian soldiers. His declared purpose was to assist them, but I think even then he sought some object. It is very difficult, Curos, to probe the fringe of his thoughts without being detected. All his mental power is being directed to search the O'san for this Amathare, whatever that is. I believe he is attempting to find it before other Warchaw sorcerers realise he is in Chaw. He is slightly afraid that they will realise he seeks the Amathare for himself.' She shrugged and smiled at Curos and he noticed more than a hint of nervousness in her manner.

'You fear him?' he asked.

'Yes, Curos. I had no idea how powerful the Warchaw sorcerers would be. Even when Valanus destroyed Bec Tol, I did not fully grasp the nature of his strength.'

'When he released the energy at the fortress walls it caused a massive disturbance – I and the sekar felt it clearly back in G'tal. In that instant, Valanus caught a reflection of something. In his fatigue he could not hold the impression long enough to locate it, but now he is scanning northward and eastward across the O'san, into Chaw and beyond to the D'was, possibly as far as the Eternal Forest.'

'What are his plans and who are these companions?' asked Curos, confused.

'I can only discern so much, Curos.' She smiled. 'I can hardly walk up and ask Valanus his purpose! I will rest and then probe again. This time I will attempt to learn more of those who are with him.'

By dawn the next day Xante was able to give much more information to Curos, particularly with respect to those who accompanied Valanus. The first of the companions was a Champion at Arms, Sir Sigmund, a nobleman who had rank and prestige as well as great skill with weapons. With the army in Corninstan he had commanded the heavy cavalry, but he preferred personal combat as the greatest test of his valour. Xante sensed a large, powerful man but was surprised at his level of culture and sophistication – almost reminiscent of Curos or Chalak Konn.

There was little if any pretence of refinement in the second companion: a huge, rustic individual, a true barbarian in every

414

thought or action, who regarded learning or riches with equal contempt. His only thought patterns were of combat, drink and lechery; loyalty and bravery were the only virtues he respected.

The third companion had little, if any, virtue that his friends or enemies would recognise. A smaller individual, he felt true pride in his profession of thief and assassin. Even with such powerful associates he was gripped with fear – a paranoid fear of discovery or detection. His whole nature was furtive and he feared that anyone would glimpse his secret thoughts, in which he deceived even himself. There was in his character just a remnant of boyish innocence. He was not evil or malicious and that alone seemed to link him to his friends.

In contrast, the Bowman with the companions was honest but shrewd. He took obvious pride in his skill but not in killing and had only joined the Warchaw army because there was no other living for him in his own land. In sleep he dreamed of the damp, green, lush countryside which Xante had seen in the mind of the dying Warchaw spy so long ago at the Well of Sorrows in the D'was. The Bowman was more a farmer than a soldier and probably had more in common with Makran than with his Warchaw associates. It was on this last, less wary man that Xante concentrated the longest as she attempted to read the purpose of the strange quest.

It appeared that to Valanus the capture of Bec Tol was only of secondary importance and an excuse to lead a small army into the O'san. There he believed he would find a mystical object which could be used for great evil if discovered by the Chaw. It would give them sufficient power to conquer the western lands. Bowman had little understanding of these deep matters, but he trusted Valanus as a friend and enjoyed the company of the other companions.

'Five men, all with particular skills. Friends?'

'Yes, I think so, and with Valanus.'

'Friends who seek something in Chaw which we ourselves do not understand.' He looked at Xante pointedly. 'Unless what they seek is you?'

'The possibility had occurred to me, and it makes my body tingle with fear. If they detected me I should not be permitted to live or, worse still, perhaps Valanus seeks a concubine. But all the impressions are of an object, a staff or sword. I feel so simple, so stupid, Curos, in that I cannot understand what motivates them.' She rubbed her forehead with fatigue and continued. 'They are not basically evil people and they are certainly not savages, except perhaps one. They talk and jest as a group of Chaw would do, and I can find a parallel for each of them in Chaw. It could be Curos, Dalgan and Makran sitting over there with a rogue from G'tal.'

'But they hate us.'

'More than you or I could believe. They hate, fear and despise the Chaw and the Dryadin. Even the Bowman believes it is essential to at least cripple the Chaw civilisation. Why should an honest, simple man such as he want to kill millions of strangers who have done him no ill?'

They sat in silence for a long time before Xante said desperately, 'I cannot fight him, Curos. I cannot begin to match his ability. It would be like your nephew, little Pa'na taking a sword and bow to fight you.'

'You are tired and think only of direct confrontation, as the Sunrise Horde did when they first attempted to fight the Warchaw cavalry. We must find another way. There is time to think and to plan.'

'We do not have that long, Curos,' she said, shaking her head. 'Our sekar cannot protect me from Valanus' direct gaze if it were turned fully in my direction. We will never remove the Warchaw from Bec Tol if he is with them. By harnessing the power of the Bec Tol spring he could throw back a million Chaw soldiers with ease.'

The next day the sorcerer Valanus and his companions moved slowly north-westward, followed at a discreet distance by one of the Chaw sekar. Only as darkness fell did Curos and Xante come closer to the Warchaw party, as they camped for the night. Xante was visibly shaken by the presence of the enemy sorcerer and her nervousness was beginning to communicate itself to the N'gol horsemen. Her constant covert probing of the Warchaw had yielded few new facts, and nothing that would be of use.

'This is strange, Curos,' she said at one stage during the day. 'I believe the commander of cavalry knows you from the battle

416

of Corninstan Road. He was the horseman who fled when you were protected by your Topaz pendant. He is outlining the new tactics he would use to defeat you in personal combat to the Barbarian.' She smiled briefly. 'It is very important to the Champion, his vanity is wounded.'

'Personal feelings should have no place in war,' replied Curos absently. 'Even pride in skill at arms can be a weakness.'

'Wait, Curos. The sorcerer is joining the conversation to offer advice. He is evidently a horseman and a warrior. I can see him through the eyes of the knight. This is dangerous. I must withdraw.'

'So the mighty Valanus has weaknesses,' mused Curos. 'First, he tries to seek some power in advance of the other sorcerers, and now he shows interest in combat and honour. Is his body mortal, could he be harmed by weapons, perhaps a sudden volley of arrows?'

'Yes. Yes, I am sure he could, but his powers would enable him to deflect any simple attack, however sudden. Great subtlety or some distraction would be needed.'

Their conversation progressed long into the evening, and a plan slowly evolved. At last, Xante said wearily, 'We are decided then, Curos. The hour of death or victory is upon us.'

'Neither of us may survive victory,' replied Curos candidly. 'But to buy the death of Valanus with our lives will give our peoples time to find new leaders.'

'Talk to me not of marriage days or dying days,' Xante mimicked his voice from their conversation in his tent on the first day they had met. 'I am a Hinto, a warrior who takes each day's life gladly and speaks not of death.'

'The D'was and S'lan the Eternal are far distant, and the two people who spoke in that yert just a year ago have changed much,' replied Curos after some time, as he remembered that first meeting.

'Yes, that time is distant in many ways,' she said sadly. 'I am very afraid, Curos. My faith and my affinity with S'lan have weakened during the months. I would that I had never left the forest.'

'My life would have been all the darker if you had not,' he said, fumbling for unaccustomed words.

Xante deliberately misunderstood the meaning and briskly shrugged off any move towards tenderness. 'The great Noyan would have found some way, some alternative plan that did not require Xante-Yani. You must talk to the N'gol. They will not like what they must do and your words need choosing with care.'

The cold, late dawn had only started to break across the eastern desert sky when a war trumpet sounded out a strident challenge. Riding confidently towards the Warchaw came one Chaw horseman, not a N'gol but one of the elite Topaz Wind.

Silhouetted against the bright morning sky, he called out in the Corninstani language, his voice striving to suppress the tone modulation of his own tongue. The Warchaw Champion Sigmund was already buckling on his sword over his steel hauberk when he started at his own name. Curos was challenging the Warchaw Champion to single combat. He recited both his lineage and his rank as commander of Topaz Wind before calling on the Warchaw to fight without the assistance of sorcery. This was the first barrier; Curos was staking all on the pride of the Warchaw and the love of personal combat. If Valanus was a realist he would blast Curos aside with a jet of fire which Xante would be unable to suppress.

The silence at the end of Curos' speech seemed to extend to infinity as his muscles tightened and his heart pounded. 'I am alone and fear no other man,' he lied defiantly. 'Will you not match my courage?'

The reply was courteous and direct and with only the briefest delay to prepare his steed, the mail-clad Warchaw rode from the shadows to salute Curos with his raised sword. In return, Curos bowed in Thunder-Arrow's saddle and the combat started.

Curos had no intention of meeting his enemy head-on, where the stronger Warchaw horse and long broadsword would tell against him. He darted and weaved Thunder-Arrow away, turning and turning again before a blow could be struck. Wiser after his previous encounters, he wasted no effort in slashing at the steel rings of the mail coat but avoided and parried the other's sword as if he strove for a killing thrust.

A hundred paces from the desperately circling horses in a slight fold in the ground, twenty Sunrise Horde N'gol waited, war bows ready. Beside them the two sekars, faces white with fear, strained to conceal the warriors against any glance from the awesomely powerful Warchaw.

Xante watched as several times Curos slipped aside from death but ignored possible opportunities to strike. She grimaced with fear as he struck. He must not lose control. His every instinct would be to kill, but he must hold back. Too quickly for the eye to follow at this distance, the blow opened a gash in the Warchaw's cheek but only caused him to intensify his attack.

The heavy war-stallion crashed into Thunder-Arrow, sending his back legs sprawling. As Curos hauled the horse back to his feet and away, the Warchaw swung the heavy sword in an arc of death which could not be parried. Cheers roared out from the Warchaw's companions as Curos was forced to block the blow and his scimitar flew from numbed fingers. Ducking low, he swung the sword up by its wrist-strap, grasped the hilt and turned back towards the next attack. For all his dragon-like spirit, Thunder-Arrow would be slowed by that collision.

Now was the time. Xante signalled, and twenty N'gol bows sent their deadly shafts speeding towards the two horsemen. At that distance there was as much chance of a hit on Curos as on his foe but that too was part of the gamble. A wash of searing crimson flame scythed across the dim sky, reducing the arrows to harmless, blazing twigs. The Warchaw champion's eyes flickered momentarily from Curos to the fire flash, and the scimitar slashed for his throat.

The N'gol were shooting a second stream of arrows, towards the Warchaw sorcerer. A bolt of energy blasted Curos' scimitar from his hand as it was about to bite into his opponent. The Topaz flashed defiance, brilliant yellow against crimson red, protecting Curos. He saw the second volley of N'gol arrows blaze into nothing before they reached the target, then the air was rent by an explosion more deafening than any thunder-clap and a bolt of pure energy was hurled at Xante. Thunder-Arrow reared up in terror, and only then did Curos register the scream of pain from Valanus as Xante's arrow struck home.

Distracted by the scene of combat and the N'gol arrows, the sorcerer had not realised the danger from one venomous shaft shot amongst so many others. While the N'gol arrows burned,

419

the deadly black poison-wood of S'lan had flown through the fire unscathed. Dark feathers blazing, the arrow had driven its poison-soaked pile deep into the sorcerer's body. As he snatched it clear and launched a wave of flame at Xante, the porous ceramic in the bronze head crumbled, leaving deadly fragments in the wound. He was in agony and enraged beyond thought.

Ignoring any temptation to use his bow and finish his personal combat, Curos drove Thunder-Arrow to where he knew Xante would need his help. The N'gol were stunned by the violence of the sorcery and the Warchaw Champion fled back to his stricken leader. One of the sekars cried desperately, tears pumping from his blinded eyes; the other was reduced to a cindered mound, past all sound or help.

Xante sat cross-legged in Padmasana, the motionless lotus position of contemplation and power. Her eyes closed and her face blank, she prepared herself against the attack which must come from Valanus.

Curos flew from Thunder-Arrow's back, registering that Xante had thrown her treasured bow to one side away from harm; it had done its work and physical weapons would not aid her now. In two strides he reached the sitting girl and took up a similar full lotus pose, knees touching hers. Gently, so as not to break her concentration, he leaned forward to take her hands in a circle of power, like that which she had joined with him so long ago in Te Toldin to share and disperse the grief of his father's death.

He had expected to visualise the same protective ring of fire, but instead it was as if he was deep in the forest of S'lan the Eternal. Around them stood a sentinel grove of dark green trees through which tangled vines and creepers were twisting to form a web which shut out all sun and all power. He felt the thrill of her welcome and the topaz stones came alive, the black and the white joined as one. The yellow disc at Curos' chest flooded with power like an empty cup being refilled.

A distant red glare glowed luridly through the spectral trees and he could smell scorched leaves as their protective barrier shuddered and bowed at the impact. A second hammer blow came, and then a third, but the force could not breach the protective canopy of phantom branches stretched overhead.

420

Beneath the sterile desert, roots radiated the life of S'lan the Eternal.

Curos and Xante were as one, and could feel the agony of Valanus as he battled to penetrate their defence and understand the nature of those who destroyed him. His handsome, bearded face, loved by so many women, was now rigid with pain and the decay which grew within him. Despite this he stood erect and threatening, in the long grey robe of the Order of Gadel, which was drenched with drying blood from the now-staunched stomach wound.

He could not decode the subtle biological secrets of the Dryad poison which corroded his body and weakened his mind with its agony. Curos-Xante felt the horrific shock as Valanus, a High Sorcerer of the Warchaw, realised he was going to die. He called for assistance, but his peers in the Order of Gadel were far away and as helpless as he to undo the deadly hurt of the Dryad arrow.

The tortured spirit achieved a degree of pain-dulling calm and slowly, with infinite care, Valanus started to build a rotating field of energy such as he had used to destroy Bec Tol. He was at the limit of his endurance. Unconquerable suffering washed through him, and his powers began to falter. In one last act of revenge, he unleashed the full might of the accumulated energy. As if in a trance Xante stood up, pulling Curos with her, and turned her face skyward. The illusion of S'lan's protective trees disappeared and hand in hand they stood waiting as the incinerating gout of fire descended.

Xante's arm lifted, open-palmed as if to ward off a blow, and the three Topaz flamed with their own light. They blazed protective yellow, incandescent white and an energy-sapping black which absorbed and destroyed power.

The circling ball of energy descending towards them gathered speed and unstoppable, avalanche-like momentum. Then, under Xante's influence, its path began to curve back towards Valanus. He held up both arms as if for protection and screamed vain, ineffective incantations as his doom rushed upon him. He staggered under the weight of his wounds and the impending defeat. Fire of his own conjuring flooded over the Warchaw sorcerer, and the Champion ran to cover him with a shield. For one horrific instant two already-dead, blazing figures could be seen standing upright as they disintegrated under the intense heat. The bodies fell from sight but the fire burned on, gradually subsiding into extinction.

As if suddenly set free from a petrifying spell, the N'gol of the Sunrise Horde began to move. Their leader screamed a hoarse cheer of salute to Xante and he led his men in ragged charge at the remaining Warchaw. Movement and familiar actions rekindled the N'gol's skill and their pride. The line straightened and their speed increased. Twenty bow arms were raised as one as they closed in to shoot.

Curos turned to Xante, and they smiled in dazed exhaustion at each other.

'A master stroke worthy of a Q'ren, Xante, Jitsu in sorcery. You used the other's strength to defeat him.'

'He half sought death himself, Curos. He could not stand the pain.'

The Warchaw Bowman shot down three N'gol riders before he staggered and fell, hit by several arrows. He could have killed more but he spent too long on each shot – he could not bear to wound a horse unnecessarily. He writhed on the cold, hard ground of the O'san and pulled free a broad-headed arrow from his thigh. Bright blood spurted from the wound, but he gritted his teeth and did not attempt to staunch the flow. He did not want to be alive when the N'gol reached him.

The Warchaw thief was cut down by two N'gol as he fled desperately on an unsaddled horse.

The massive fighter, Hosca, backed into the rocks where the horses could not follow. He sold his life dearly as the men of the Sunrise Horde closed in for the kill on foot. Wounded with swords, lances and arrows, he finally died on his knees, his head pulled back as a N'gol dagger slashed across his throat.

Epilogue

There was little joy among the Chaw and the N'gol as the pale warmth of the winter sun began to flood like a diffused wave over the surrounding hills to dispel the deep shadows of the killing ground.

Six of the Sunrise Horde Ulus had died in the fighting, two more would be dead before nightfall. Always, Curos was shocked by the strength of the Warchaw, whose arrows punched completely through bodies and whose swords disembowelled or severed limbs with a blow. One sekar had burned to death as he threw himself unnecessarily into the path of Valanus' first fire-bolt. He died in a swirling whirlpool of flame which surged towards Xante and then washed back over him. The second sekar was near blinded.

Horses had died – two shot down despite the Warchaw Bowman's care, another grotesquely hacked by the giant Barbarian's two-handed axe. Thunder-Arrow nuzzled Curos and whinnied in pain from the deep bruises in his side caused by the collision with the Champion's heavy charger.

First the horses, then the men, then your friends. Curos walked stiffly to the knot of Eastern N'gol as they inspected their mounts for damage. One sat beside a horse's head as the poor beast struggled to rise, a thick shaft embedded in its chest. The man stroked its head, a hand-axe ready. Tears were in his eyes as he fought for courage to end the agony of a true friend. The horse would be feeling pain as deeply as any man, but the beast had no understanding of war. Close by a man lay propped up against a boulder; he too was transfixed by an arrow which protruded a hand's-length beyond his back. He coughed and shuddered, trying to whisper brave words to send a final greeting to his wife and daughter and a feeble boast of triumph for his family.

Xante stood stroking Thunder-Arrow, her face grey with fatigue. 'Our sekar's eyes will recover,' she said, indicating the man

423

who sat with a light bandage swathing his face. 'He has passed the news to our people that the Warchaw sorcerer is dead. The Tuman rejoices and at Bec Tol our enemy will be trembling in fear.'

'Is Thunder-Arrow badly hurt?' Curos asked as he fondled his horse, one protective arm encircling Xante's sagging shoulders.

'No, only bruised and battered. He needs rest but he feels triumphant, Curos. The other stallion was the first to flee. Thunder-Arrow is not as young as he was, and you use him hard.'

'He is still better than any war-horse in the Chaw or N'gol,' replied Curos proudly. 'He ran circles around his foe and gave me chance after chance to land a killing blow, but I needed to prolong the combat to hold Valanus' attention.'

'Thunder-Arrow may still excel but each battle costs him more, Curos.'

Curos released his hold on the horse's tossing head and turned Xante so that he could see the tear-brimmed eyes which glowed like jewelled black pools from beneath the Dryad head cowl.

'It costs me much too, Curos,' she said in answer to his unspoken question. 'I feel no thrill of victory as you felt when you struck at the Warchaw Champion, and no joy in the success of masterly plans. To me there is only the suffering and the pain and the death. Evil after evil, as we protect our people from the worse evils that the Warchaw would bring.'

Xante's body quivered at the thud of the farrier's axe which carried in the still air and a stricken horse screamed for the last time. She grabbed Curos frantically, and buried her head in his chest.

'This is not my life, Curos. I should be under S'lan's green canopy with a man who loves me.'

He allowed the woman to cry for a time before he said, in a voice made hard to suppress any hint of tenderness. 'You said long ago that your duty would not be easy. There can be no release now. Dry your eyes,' he added more sympathetically 'You must not show weakness before friends or enemies in the hour of victory. It is important that they believe we have yet more to give, that the next victory is assured.'

'The Warchaw Valanus died because he protected his friend

from your sword cut,' she said as she dabbed her eyes with the dark cloth of her veil.

'You did not protect me,' he replied with a smile.

'I did not need to,' she said shortly. 'And you have taught me to be as heartless as you. I am no longer the Dryad, Xante-Yani, but Q'ren Xante the sorceress who has no friends and no people, no lovers and no children. I live only to protect S'lan the Eternal.' Her face was now composed and hard. 'We waste time. There are injured to tend and I would pay respect to the brave men who died.' She did not say which men and Curos did not ask.

They left the battle site at mid-afternoon and continued their journey to the 56th weir of the Grain Canal to join the gathering Chaw forces. After their delays Bhal Morag would be ahead of them, waiting with Khol Dalgan. Xante had drawn more deeply on her strength than she had realised and succumbed quickly to fatigue. Often she finished the day sitting before Curos on the large Warchaw horse he now rode to rest Thunder-Arrow. There was no immediate haste, and he allowed their pace to slow until she slept, leaning back against his chest.

Her recovery seemed rapid and apparently complete. By the morning of the third day she was able to run for miles as the horses picked their way across the bleak O'san desert towards the canal. By afternoon her strength failed again and she was sleeping fretfully in Curos' arms as they halted their progress for the night camp.

Bhal Morag, Chalak Konn and Khol Dalgan paraded their Chaw and N'gol forces to salute Curos and Xante as they arrived. The scarlet guards and the blue soldiers stood stiffly in ranks, the N'gol horsemen in irregular groups. The Great Noyan Zachaw and the Q'ren Xante had removed the threat of the Warchaw Sorcerer, and already each soldier felt he was destined to be part of a great victory.

Bhal Morag and Khol Dalgan were impatient to move the army up to Bec Tol and strike the Warchaw before they recovered from the shock of their sorcerer's defeat. Chalak Konn was, however, much affected by the death of Wan Abac and concentrated on his own particular tasks, saying little as Morag and Dalgan expounded their plans to Curos. In a cramped tent, cluttered with maps and papers, Curos marvelled at the change in Bhal Morag, the once lazy, pleasure-seeking hedonist he had first met in the D'was. Now with methodical and imaginative energy, Morag was planning his first major battle. Despite the small numbers – ten thousand Chaw and three thousand Warchaw – it would be of the greatest significance. If they could prove here that the Westerners could be beaten it would give the Eastern World hope.

With the numerical superiority of Curos' forces a simple, crushing frontal assault would probably have been successful but the Warchaw war engines and heavy cavalry would take a massive toll of Chaw soldiers. As important as victory was the need to test the use of the sekars in controlling the T'sands and the N'gol. If Morag's detailed tactics were effective, there would be few casualties and an outline for the greater battles which would follow. It was also necessary to share the fighting roles between the various forces so that all the men and their commanders gained experience and confidence.

Five days later under cover of darkness the Chaw army moved into position around the ruins of Bec Tol. From the nearby hills Curos looked down at the distant, shrouded battlefield, trying to follow the hidden movements and interpret the report of the sekar. The Warchaw had not had time to rebuild the walls of the fortress and had only succeeded in erecting low barriers behind which they had placed their formidable trebuchets. Scouts had no doubt warned of the Chaw approach, but it was unlikely that the commanders would expect the attack to be launched at night.

Through the ghost-like howling of the winter wind came the War Cries. Triggered by the sekar, each unit raised its voice simultaneously to confuse the enemy.

'Abac, Abac, Abac,' chanted the guards in a long, unending growl in memory of the Iron Man. Curos heard the war scream of Topaz Wind, now led by Foxian, Khol Dalgan's lieutenant, because Dalgan commanded the combined cavalry of the N'gol Dragon Clans. To the far side Konkurate would be leading the Wolf Clans into battle, horses walking carefully behind the 11th

T'sand, ready first to give support with high-flying arrows and then to charge with lance and sabre.

Curos wiped a sweaty palm on his leather trousers although the wind was chill – but he had no bow or sword to grip. Had his father Pa'lin felt so helpless and frustrated as his men moved forward to fight at Corninstan Road? Around Bec Tol battle was joined on all sides as the Chaw pressed in, denying the Warchaw the advantage of their more powerful long-range weapons. The sounds of combat rolled up from below in a roar subdued by distance, thousands of shouting, swearing and dying men rendered anonymous by the numbers. In the darkness the great trebuchets stood unattended as their crews now fought with sword or axe to hold the defensive ring.

From the west a light, as a false dawn, began to grow. The distant Warchaw sorcerers had realised the danger and were lighting the darkness for their beleaguered soldiers. Curos caught the first glimpse of Xante's tense face as she stood beside him, seeking with her mind for information.

'No, I am too weak, Curos,' she answered bleakly before he voiced the question.

'I cannot lose now. Chaw cannot lose.'

'Always, one more effort is needed!' Xante knew her own power was spent and as a passive observer she viewed the growing projection from the West, a sheet of energy concentrating above the battlefield. What plan the western mages had she could not imagine; she detected almost a dozen sorcerers, all as strong as Valanus, but some were far, far away and the spring of Bec Tol seemed to be absorbing energy and feeding it down into the darkness. Unbidden thoughts, new knowledge came to her.

Her mind darted forward to the vortex of the spring and plunged downwards to the deep, where living organisms almost too simple for thought lived off the heat and minerals of the volcanic rocks. Hungrily, they took sustenance from the mind projection from above. Side passages spanned outward under the O'san into endless caverns of prehistoric water. She felt a recent presence – the footsteps of Aalani's mind! Aalani had been this way, and the thread of his thoughts acted as a path marker to the resonating cavern which had so confused Valanus.

427

Further still, she sensed similar caverns connected by almost motionless channels of water. Here was the underground heart of the land, with boundless capacity.

That was it, the Chaw soldiers could not fight the Warchaw man-to-man but Curos had mobilised the whole capacity of the people to absorb the invaders' armies. Now she knew how to absorb the power of the Warchaw sorcerers, any amount of their energy could be sucked down by the spring and dissipated. It was Jitsu in sorcery, and their own might would defeat them if they persisted.

The spring responded to her urging; like an angry being it boiled in rage at its previous defeat by Valanus, but now the Warchaw power was being stored in the limitless lakes. Once the system was established it needed no effort from Xante and slowly she returned, for the spring bore her no malice.

'How is it possible?' asked Curos in awe. 'How can such force be nullified?'

'The Land of Chaw protects its people, Curos. We fight in the one place where I could do this and the great hunter, Aalani, showed me the path.'

'What the Warchaw sorcerers do now is too late and too weak to help their army,' said Curos, studying the scene below. 'It is I who will gain the advantage from their false light; from this height I can see the whole battle.'

Bhal Morag was in the thick of the fighting, his long lance a massive weight in his hand as he lunged and stabbed at the Warchaw. Wide shields blocked his blows, pike thrusts forced him away. Unhurriedly, a Warchaw ground his shield boss against the terrified horse. Bhal Morag attempted to turn away but he was locked in the press of heaving bodies. A glint of steel flashed upwards and the animal pitched forward to its knees, dying. In one, life-preserving motion, he rolled himself backwards out of the saddle, the carcase of his splendid mount between him and the swordsman. As the Warchaw leapt at him, another Chaw horseman hacked downwards. The barbarian's shield flew up, protecting, and the short sword killed again. The lance was still in Morag's hand; he thrust forward and felt the pile sink in deeply before the weapon was twisted away. He drew his own sword and ran back between his own horsemen, seeking a fresh mount. As he hauled himself into an empty saddle, the sekar galloped up, and shouted, 'Lord Zachaw says pull back, the charge has been broken.'

The brightness in the sky grew to form a pale blue disc which circled high above the Warchaw. Its glow was sufficient for accurate shooting with the bow, but the fight was now too close to give space for the archers' skill. From the amorphous, shimmering fire appeared the forms of the remaining High Wizards of the Order of Gadel, and a central vortex spun, descending into the spring. The images swept low over the Chaw like demons, but they now held no power to burn or to terrify. On the battlefield the Chaw sekar shouted derision and defiance, mocking the screaming phantoms of the Warchaw Sorcerers.

'Our people think I hold back the fire,' said Xante. 'They believe the Warchaw are afraid to descend from the sky lest Q'ren Xante should confront them as she destroyed Valanus. If they knew how weak I really am! It is the strength of the land and a trick of this place that saves the people.'

'If enough believe, it is the truth,' said Curos. 'Whatever the reason, our soldiers are heartened while the Warchaw despair.' He gazed at the battlefield below. 'The Warchaw believe Bhal Morag's T'sand is broken. Instead of following his retreat, they move men across to strike at the guards, not realising that Dalgan starts to charge.'

Khol Dalgan had been honoured beyond belief when Curos had allowed him to command Topaz Wind. Now no more than any other true N'gol, he sat at the head of the Tuman of the Dragon Clan's one thousand picked horsemen. His heart would burst; his wife and his father were within the Sand Dragon Clan Ulus and would see him lead. He would conquer or die, as he had told Curos. Before him the battle surged as the Warchaw swordsmen and pikemen savaged the Chaw Cavalry T'sand of Bhal Morag. Warchaw arrows curved high up to fall on the back ranks of the Chaw but they would have no way of knowing that the Dragon waited. He suppressed his excitement and made his scarred face an impassive mask.

The Chaw struggled back and moved to his left, brave men

429

checked and beaten. To his right the scarlet mass of the Guard began chanting 'Abac', 'Abac', beating swords on shields in a crescendo of noise until they charged, shields high, javelins poised. Arrows crossed into them from left and right, rattling off shields, killing men. At thirty paces they threw their deadly spears, drew swords and surged on. All around Dalgan, N'gol quivered with anticipation, but he sat motionless. Before him a clear path opened. The shock of the Guard's volley and charge stunned the Warchaw and beat them back, but after the initial shock they rallied and battled with the smaller men. The Warchaw in front of Dalgan turned and began to charge the Guard T'sand, intent on hemming in the scarlet-clad elite.

The sekar touched Dalgan's arm, it was time. Dalgan roared as loudly as Tinjin of old, and the Dragon hurled forward. One volley of arrows, then bows were discarded onto saddle straps. With sabres and lances they smashed into the unprepared enemy. Dalgan's spear struck home and his horse, Gentle Mare, darted sideways over a fallen body. Pulling his spear clear, Dalgan realised he was in empty space - he had broken through the Warchaw.

Under the impact of a thousand charging N'gol cavalry, the Warchaw ring broke at one point and collapsed inwards with amazing speed. The Chaw streamed forward, the dark blue figures cutting the enemy into several isolated groups which were now fighting hopelessly for survival. Like an irresistible roller, the red of the Guards picked up new momentum and crushed the mail-clad footmen. The Warchaw cavalry attempted to break clear but foundered on the 11th T'sand's spears. Foxian led the streaming yellow banner of the Topaz against them and the solid mass of mail-clad warriors dispersed under a rain of arrows and dissolved into the sea of Chaw uniforms. Above the battle the fire of the Order of Gadel flickered and died. The fight was lost and even the High Wizards could only sustain their effort for so long.

One of the isolated Warchaw groups fought their way clear and fled in the direction of the low foothills, and the safety of the pass which Wan Abac and Chalak Konn had used in their flight from Bec Tol.

'Sechen and some of his Sunrise Horde are guarding that way.

I think they will have some action,' said Curos as he gauged the numbers. A hundred tired Warchaw who had been fighting since before dawn would meet Sechen's three hundred men in the pass, fresh and eager to join the battle.

'Does Sechen have a sekar with him?' he asked.

'Yes, Loze or Ki Dug as we knew him.'

'Tell him I want prisoners if he is able. The Warchaw may surrender.'

Cedric of Hereford ran limpingly, and as fast as his bandaged wound would allow. Behind him came the last of his 'good lads', men who had fought their way with him from the disaster of Bec Tol and the swarming vermin of the Chaw. He cursed the commanders who relied on sorcerers and sent men into such hopeless battles. He stopped suddenly, as he saw the multi-hued Sunrise Horde appear to block his escape route and deploy in a workman-like battle line. He swore violently and began shouting orders. His voice was hoarse and his sword arm was weak and tired, but on this open ground he would show these horseboys who ruled the battlefield.

Amongst the rubble of Bec Tol the fighting had degraded into a massive milling carnage of disorganised combat as the Chaw pulled down the last of the enemy. Curos had no orders to give and none would have listened. He watched as Cedric's distant party of Warchaw formed up into a line two men deep to defy Sechen's charge.

'Stop them, Xante,' he said hastily as he recognised the danger. 'Talk to Loze.' Already it was too late, Sechen's charge was gathering speed. The first rank with short bows ready; the second rank lowered lances as they had learned from Topaz Wind.

As if some hidden hand had stretched forth against the N'gol horsemen, the frontline folded down like toy soldiers in a game. To avoid kicking and dying horses, their companions halted and fell to another volley of arrows. The survivors seemed momentarily immobile with shock, and more fell. Less than half the horsemen turned and fled from the devastation caused by the awesome bowmen.

'Is Ki Dug . . . ?' asked Curos, his voice echoing the disbelief of his thoughts.

'Dead,' said Xante hollowly. 'It's unbelievable, Curos. What sort of men are these Warchaw?'

'The greatest bowmen in the world. Used well they can dominate a whole battle as they did at Corninstan. That is why we risked the night attack.'

Xante and Curos could only watch as the enemy archers escaped, unregarded by the victorious Chaw.

'We have won, Xante,' said Curos bleakly. 'We have won because Valanus was over-confident in the desert and our surprise was complete here. The Warchaw will not make these mistakes again. When next the Warchaw come there will be a full army with many sorcerers; and those archers carry away the secret of our night attack.'

'And you no longer have even one sorcerer,' Xante said sadly, flinching away as he stepped towards her. 'My power is spent and my spirit broken. My soul is burned and the trees of S'lan call to me as never before. I cannot now be of use to the Noyan Zachaw.'